ROARING LIBERTY

THE QUEENSTOWN STORY - BOOK 4

JEAN GRAINGER

To my mother, without whom none of this would have happened.

CHAPTER 1

'What is it?' Matt said as Harp looked up from her book and watched the colour drain from her mother's face and knew instantly something was very wrong. Outside, the bustle of activity as the city came to life on Shore Road, Boston, was loud despite the early hour.

Rose dropped the letter on her plate, right on top of her scrambled eggs and toast. She gazed at Matt and opened her mouth as if to speak, but no words came out.

'Rose, what is it?' he urged.

The bright morning sun shone through the window of their first-floor apartment over O'Malley's Boots and Shoes. They'd moved in the day before St Patrick's Day, finally leaving the hospitality of the Raffertys in favour of a modest yet comfortable home of their own.

It was nothing like the Cliff House, their home in Cobh, County Cork, and it was a far cry from the sumptuous surroundings of the Raffertys, but their two-bedroomed place, with a large kitchen and living room combined, was pleasant and cheerful and served their purposes perfectly.

'Mammy?' Even from across the table, Harp could see the letter was in Liz Devlin's handwriting, a sloping copperplate. But a letter from the Devlin sisters wasn't unusual. 'Mammy, what's the matter?'

Rose swallowed, visibly steadying herself. 'Ralph Devereaux and Marianne's mother have moved into the Cliff House. They're behaving as if they own it. Pamela's redecorating the whole place, and they're hobnobbing with the gentry and the British as if they have every right in the world to be in our home.'

'What?' Harp was shocked. 'Is Liz sure? I thought Ralph and Pamela were in India? That's where Marianne has been sending her letters. No wonder she's heard nothing back. I can't believe this!'

Grimly, Rose passed Liz's missive to her daughter, the pale-blue notepaper now stained with eggs and butter. Harp scanned the neatly written words. Liz was brief and to the point. Ralph had turned up one night, not long after Harp and Rose made a speedy getaway from Ireland in a hail of gunfire, and installed himself in their house. He was telling everyone that it had always been his and that he had only allowed them to stay on out of the goodness of his heart. When he was challenged by Mr Bridges in the hotel, who mentioned that Harp had been bequeathed the house by the late Henry Devereaux when he named her as his daughter and heir, Ralph had scoffed and said in the hotel bar for all to hear, 'If you recall my poor departed brother, he was hardly capable of a coherent sentence, let alone a romantic tryst with the maid. No, he was soft in the heart as well as the head, and his housekeeper clearly tricked him. But it's all been sorted out by the legal chaps now and I'm home in my family's house, so all is as it should be.' The crowd, apart from Bridges, had been receptive to him. They were British officers and Protestant gentry, and it seemed they accepted his version of events.

Matt, who had been sitting in furious silence, pounded his fist on the table. 'The sheer gall of that man! How dare he!'

'And there's nothing we can do.' Rose tried to fight back the tears, but her voice was choked.

'There is,' Matt said darkly. 'I could go back to Ireland to sort him out for once and for all.'

Rose's eyes blazed. 'We've talked about this, Matt. You are *not* going back. You have orders to remain here, you know you have, and surely you're not going to defy Collins himself? You would be a very valuable prize to the British, and they'd take great pleasure in extracting whatever information they could from you under torture before they hang you, so you have to stay. You know too much.'

'Mammy's right, Matt,' Harp said kindly. She was furious herself but was doing her best not to show it, not wanting to make matters worse. 'I know how frustrating it is to have to sit it out here in America when you want to be back there, in the thick of it, but you're doing valuable work, talking to the Irish here, ensuring they know how their dollars are being spent. Pat Rafferty says the take of donations is double what it was before you came, so you're not doing nothing, you know.'

Matt ran his hands through his once sandy now mostly silver hair in frustration. To go from being the commander of a squadron of the IRA, engaging and winning against the Crown forces every day, to making fundraising speeches in Boston was not what he wanted, they all knew that, but lives depended on him staying where he was.

'But to think of him, in your house, Rose and Harp... I... It makes me so angry. He was the one that told Beckett about that night with Pennington, he's the reason I'm exiled, and now he gets to play lord of the manor...'

'I know.' Rose placed her hand on her husband's. 'I can't bear it either, but bear it we must, it seems. And it won't be forever. The war with the British is surely coming to an end, and when we win, Ralph Devereaux and his kind will find life very uncomfortable indeed. People have long memories, and those that made Irish lives hell when they had the British to back them up will suddenly find themselves alone and vulnerable. Ralph is a coward at heart, so he'll leave soon enough. Harp will get her house back. We just have to be patient.'

Harp thought her mother had blossomed in the months they'd been in Boston. She had always been a beautiful woman, there was no doubting that, but her dark-brown hair seemed more luxuriant of late and her skin was glowing. She did have deepening lines on her face – she was thirty-nine years old, and the last few years had taken their toll. Still, her eyes were the same, warm and brown, even if there were signs of crow's feet around them.

'I just want to go back alone, deal with him myself.' Matt spoke quietly.

Rose sighed. 'I can't have this out again. Matt, please. I know you're angry – so am I – but we're under orders to remain here. We have to do as we've been instructed. I want to go home as much as you do, but we have to wait it out.'

'So we just let him grab everything that Henry left to you and Harp, let him walk in and take it over after all your hard work?' A vein in his temple pulsed.

Harp and Rose exchanged a glance that spoke volumes. Matt was upset about the house, but there was more. He hated Devereaux for all he'd done. It was personal.

'What choice have we, Matt?' asked Rose gently. 'He's clearly in with the British, he's well known to all the local gentry families, so they'll welcome him with open arms, and you know the IRA doesn't want to touch Ralph Devereaux for now. He's not a military target, and no one has ever proved he's a spy. He's just an evil, selfish individual. We have to be patient.'

'It's hard to be patient, Rose. I know you're confident of a truce, or some end to hostilities, but what if that's just wishful thinking? They've had us in their grip for eight hundred years – maybe they won't ever give us up.'

'They will, Matt. You know yourself the losses they are suffering aren't sustainable. Public opinion is turning over there and Britain has had enough of war and death and destruction, so it's just a matter of time. But until it happens, you must carry on as you are – and Harp and JohnJoe as well. They've raised so much money for the cause, with their beautiful singing and Harp's playing. The three of you are in more demand than ever. Wait until the truce, and then we can all go home to where we belong.'

Boston was a beautiful city, and it was a joy to live in peace after all they'd endured – and the Raffertys had been so welcoming, nothing was a problem – but Harp knew her mother and Matt were just filling in time. They had physically moved to the United States, but their hearts were still in Ireland and always would be.

Harp didn't say it, but she felt differently. America was rapidly becoming home to her, and she loved the freedom and forward thinking of her new adopted country. Compared with Ireland, she found people were less judgemental, less interested in the doings of their neighbours, and it was a refreshing change. The control of society that was wielded by the Catholic Church in Ireland was something she'd always found suffocating, and there was no space in Irish society for people who were outside of their influence. The Protestants were allowed to live alongside them, but she and Henry Devereaux – one born Catholic, the other Protestant, but neither a believer – were seen as misfits, yet another reason she never felt like she belonged in Cobh. Here, many people were religious, but there was such a broad spectrum of churches and belief systems that none felt as if it had a monopoly. And even the Irish she knew were not as subjugated as Catholics back at home. The Raffertys, for example, went to Mass at Easter and Christmas, and funerals and weddings were held in a church, but the Church didn't seem to impact anyone's daily life. Harp thought back to the days in Cobh, when the priest would rant on a Sunday morning about people being drunk, even going so far as to name names, denouncing anyone who stood outside the church at Mass, or who was not following the 'fish on Fridays' rule. Girls wearing the latest fashions of shorter skirts, common now after the war, were told their mortal souls were in danger, and that they were deliberately tempting men with their harlot-like ways. No blame was laid at the door of men on that subject either – it was always the woman's fault. Every word, thought and action of the people of Ireland were monitored and commented upon by the clergy, and Harp was glad to be out of their oppressive grasp.

She was also enjoying her music. For her, it wasn't only about the fundraising, although she realised how important that was. Playing her harp and singing were also deeply fulfilling on a personal level. She and JohnJoe were so happy when they were performing together. The truth was, she and JohnJoe were blissfully happy when they were doing anything together.

She knew Matt and Rose were anxious to make a home of their own back in Ireland, but she also realised Rose wasn't ready to let her daughter go just yet. Harp had tried a few times to raise the topic, but her mother just assumed Harp would go back with them when the time came.

The horn of the lorry beeped outside. It was JohnJoe, Danny and the others picking Matt up for his new day job. Pat Rafferty had won a contract to restore a beautiful old hotel and had been having trouble finding enough skilled carpenters, so Matt had offered his services. The fundraisers and speeches were usually at night or on the weekends, so working for Pat filled the days. Now Matt stood, gathered his tobacco and matches and took his cap and jacket from the hook by the door. 'This is too much, Rose, too much by far.' He kissed her cheek and left.

Harp waited until he was gone before speaking. For Matt's sake, she had been holding back her anger, but now she felt free to express it. 'Can you stomach the idea of that man in the Cliff House, lording it over everyone, Marianne's stupid mother on his arm?'

She hated Ralph even though he was her biological father, not Henry. Thank goodness the awful man had no idea that his brief dalliance twenty-two years ago with the maid, a very young and impressionable Rose, had resulted in Harp. Only those closest to her knew the truth. And that was exactly how Harp wanted it to stay. Ralph meant nothing to her but trouble. She took a fierce bite of her toast.

Rose shook her head. 'You shouldn't say that about Marianne's mother, Harp. Pamela might not be stupid –'

'She married Ralph – need we have further proof?' Harp replied sardonically. She knew from Marianne that Pamela was mad for Ralph and would do anything to marry him. She'd obviously got her wish, though Harp was sure Ralph just saw a wealthy widow. Taking over the Cliff House was one thing, but a house like that cost money to run and Ralph was totally work-shy, so he'd need to find the funds somewhere. Harp was fairly sure Pamela Pascoe, with her Pascoe family trust fund, was his meal ticket. 'I suppose she's letting him have all Marianne's inheritance. Her father might have been a hopeless gambler, but her grandfather was the one who made that money, and by all accounts he was a shrewd businessman. And Pamela has money of her own as well, according to Marianne, more inheritance. But if Ralph gets his greedy paws on any of it, she can kiss it all goodbye. Thank goodness Marianne and Danny are doing well enough for it not to matter.'

'The whole thing makes my blood boil too,' admitted Rose. 'But you'll get your house back when the war ends. He's made too many enemies to stay in Ireland. I know Matt finds it hard to believe, after all the endless fighting, but I can't help hoping they will come to some arrangement soon. It's hurting everyone too much.'

Harp wasn't sure Ralph would let go of the house so easily, but she thought her mother was right about the end being in sight. King George V had addressed the opening of the Parliament of Northern Ireland in the Belfast City Hall ten days ago. The Unionists were delighted to have him there, but his speech was targeted at those republicans in the audience, men who were in no way loyal to him. It had been a brave move and could have been met with derision and violence – indeed in some quarters it was – but Harp felt it was the beginning of the end of hostilities. She had read the full account of his speech in the newspaper, and now she quoted, "'I appeal to all Irishmen to pause, to stretch out the hand of forbearance and conciliation, to forgive and to forget, and to join in making for the land which they love a new era of peace, contentment and goodwill.'"

Rose smiled at her daughter's ability to recall the king's exact words. Speeches, poems, songs or whole paragraphs from books, many of them obscure, had been quoted verbatim by Harp since childhood. Others found her ability either impressive or odd, but Rose was used to it. The strange thing was that Ralph had the exact same ability. He was extraordinarily clever and had used that intellect to manipulate and cheat his whole life.

Not that Rose had ever mentioned that to Harp. She knew her daughter regarded Henry Devereaux as her real father, not Ralph, and Harp wouldn't want to hear about any likeness between her and the man she thought of as her wicked uncle. And Rose felt the same way. Gentle, kind Henry Devereaux had been the one who raised Harp to be the young woman she was today: beautiful, quirky, talented and amazingly knowledgeable – at least about the things that could be learned from books.

'Do you really think so, Harp? Really?' Despite her earlier optimism, Rose was suddenly doubtful. 'Matt thinks they won't ever let us go, not really. Britain has ruled Ireland since 1169, and look at all the efforts made over the years – rebellions, invasions, wars, negotiations – but nothing ever worked. Maybe some hodgepodge version of home rule will be offered at best, and that will set the whole thing off again.'

'No. This time it's different. We fought for a republic, and we declared a republic in 1916, remember? And then Collins took over, and he knows how to fight them – he gets under their skin in a way nobody else ever did. We had them running wrong, Mam, remember? They were terrified to come out of their barracks in the end, and they know in London that we can keep that up indefinitely. We have the people behind us, we have right on our side, and we have Mick Collins. I believe in him, and if anyone can get us free, it is him. The British are making conciliatory noises for the first time in eight hundred years.'

'I know what they say, but Matt says that saying something and doing it are two different things, and there's been so much loss and destruction, so much hardship and pain... I don't know any more, I really don't. The likes of Ralph Devereaux always get their way in the end. He could never bear the idea that Henry left you the house. It rankled with him so much, not just the house, but the idea that an upstart servant like me would have such notions. That's how Ralph and those like him see us, Harp, as inferior.'

Harp leaned over and took her mother's hand, gazing deeply into her dark-brown eyes. She recited the most wonderful words she knew by heart. "'We declare the right of the people of Ireland to the ownership of Ireland, and to the unfettered control of Irish destinies, to be sovereign and indefeasible. The long usurpation of that right by a foreign people and government has not extinguished the right, nor can it ever be extinguished except by the destruction of the Irish people.'"

The lines of the Proclamation of Independence that was read by Pádraig Pearce outside the GPO on Easter Monday in 1916 hung between her and her mother for a moment.

Then she added, 'They have tried to destroy us, Mam, there's no denying it, but they have not brought about our destruction, and so we fight on and we'll never give up, never. They will be repelled from our country, and Ralph will be repelled from our house. I don't know how or when, but I think what you said to Matt is right. It will happen soon.'

CHAPTER 2

*J*ohnJoe gazed in astonishment at his friend Jerry Gallagher. 'You're not serious?'

'Deadly serious.' Jerry was planing the door they were working on with gusto, feeling the smooth wood with his hand every few strokes to make sure it had the right finish. 'You and Harp are amazing musicians. And when the war is over, there'll be fewer fundraisers to take up your time. You two are getting quite the reputation – it would be a shame to let that all disappear when the cause is no longer the pressing thing it is now. You need to think about going professional.'

JohnJoe went back to sanding. They were preparing the ballroom door together, getting it ready for hanging. The huge restoration project on the Criterion Hotel had everyone on the Rafferty crews working to get it ready in time. Matt was supervising the team fitting the windows, while JohnJoe and his crew were on doors and architraves. Danny was overseeing all the plastering and blockwork, and Pat was working with the architect, who seemed pleased with how everything was going. Between all the teams, they employed fifty men. They'd had to subcontract the painters, and JohnJoe was in charge of keeping them on task as well. Jerry was his very reliable second in command.

The hotel was due to open amid much fanfare the week after next, and the opening night was to be a celebration of Irish culture. Musicians, dancers, a storyteller and the finest of Boston-Irish cuisine would be on offer. The ballroom, one of the largest in the city, was going to be a huge draw, as concerts and performances of all kinds were lining up to book the venue. Pat Rafferty normally didn't bother with restoration – he was more interested in construction – but something about this hotel had taken his fancy and it had become a labour of love. His wife Kathy had teased him that he was having a crisis about getting old and creating his legacy, but behind it all, she was proud of him, and she and Rose had worked very hard at the décor, making sure the whole experience of staying at the Criterion would be one guests would never forget. Rose's considerable experience in the industry had proved invaluable.

'I can't just walk away and let Uncle Pat down, even if I wanted to,' JohnJoe pointed out. 'He's got another contract for building a street of stores and houses, and we'll be starting on that as soon as we've finished here. Pat relies on me. Besides, even if Harp and I wanted to be musicians, we wouldn't know where to start.'

Jerry made one last pass with his plane. 'That's OK, because I'll do all that for you. I've decided I want to be a promoter, someone who books entertainment acts to play at venues like this place when it opens, music, theatre, dancers, all that sort of thing. People love to go out to see a show, and for example, here at the Criterion Hotel, we could do a dinner and a show ticket combined. I'd make the arrangements with the venue, book the acts and take a cut. Simple really.'

JohnJoe was intrigued. 'And that's a real job, like you can make a living at it?'

'Maybe not a proper living at first. I'd have to advertise and hold auditions and build up a portfolio of acts to begin with, but eventually I think I can. A venue owner could ask for a jazz band, or a showtunes singing and dancing act, or a dancing dog, whatever he wanted, and I'd supply it.'

'But you already have a well-paid job. You're a carpenter, and a good one, and you've enough work to keep you going forever. Uncle Pat says you're one of the best he's ever seen, so I don't get it. Why would you leave it for something that might not work out?'

Jerry shrugged and grinned. 'I came over here for adventure, and because the British would have put my neck in a noose if I hadn't, but if I'm going to spend my life laying floors and sanding architraves, then what's the point? I'd have been doing that back in Ballyfermot. I'm only a carpenter because my old man did it before me and his before him – it wasn't my choice.'

Jerry Gallagher was a small dark-haired man in his early thirties. He had sleek hair brushed back from his high forehead and hazel eyes set in a face that was well constructed and symmetrical. Harp had put her finger on it: He wasn't good-looking in any conventional sense, and he was short and slight, but there was something compelling about him, a kind of energy, like he was always thinking ahead to the next thing. He was sociable and friendly, but there was something secretive about him too. You got the impression that what you saw was not really who he was. And you'd be right.

Jerry had been an infamous member of the IRA back in Ireland, mainly for the brazenness of the ambushes and attacks on the British that he led. He orchestrated in particular a very successful attack on a Dublin Metropolitan Police barracks, executing the chief, a known torturer, from four hundred yards away with a single shot to the head. The word was that if Jerry Gallagher chose a mark, he would hit it every single time and the enemy would never know from where the fatal bullet came. That night, with Jerry providing covering fire, the police had been relieved of their weapons and the barracks burned to the ground. The officers were found tied up in their underwear on a nearby bridge in the freezing night air. The photograph of them, half-naked, humiliated and freezing, had circulated widely in republican circles, and the word was that the Royal Irish Constabulary chief had made the arrest of Jerry Gallagher a personal vendetta.

Jerry had to be removed out of the clutches of the British immediately, and like many of his comrades before him, found himself on a boat to Boston, with Pat Rafferty waiting there to give him a job and set him up. Jerry was an unusual character and an unlikely person to have left such a string of audacious attacks in his wake, as he was quietly spoken and gentle and kept himself to himself. He lived in two rooms over a butcher shop on East 4th Street on Telegraph Hill and never went to the bars or out dancing with the other guys who worked for Pat Rafferty. Despite that, he wasn't stand-offish, and JohnJoe liked him.

'So explain to me again what you're thinking?' JohnJoe said.

Jerry nodded. 'I met this guy, Leo Cohen is his name. He's a singer. I heard him at a little bar down in Roxbury, and we got talking. He was telling me how he was signed with some agencies that got him places to perform – gigs, he called them.'

'Wouldn't it be more fun to be on the stage yourself?' JohnJoe helped Jerry right the heavy ballroom door and hang it on the hinges before returning to the second one and placing it on the makeshift bench they'd built for the purpose of preparing the doors, architraves and skirting.

'Couldn't carry a tune in a bucket.' Jerry grinned as JohnJoe screwed the ornate brass handles to the door. 'No, but I'd love to break into that world. It's hard, though. The Irish aren't really big in theatre circles – it's more the Jews run that. Although this Leo says I don't look Irish.' He cast a sidelong grin at big Mick Boyle, who was pushing a heavily loaded wheelbarrow of sand past them. Mick was a block layer from West Kerry who had a florid complexion, wide features and a beer belly.

'Hey, there's more than one kind of Irishman, y'know!' JohnJoe winked.

'And that's another reason for me to sign up you and Harp. You're both gorgeous to look at, and that's a great help.'

JohnJoe laughed uncomfortably. 'Well, Harp is, anyway, that's for sure. And she loves the theatre, and she's a great musician. But going professional? I've never thought about it, and I'm sure she hasn't either. I don't know anyone in the proper music business, but then maybe that's because I don't know any Jews...'

That was the way of it in Boston. The Italians did their thing, restaurants and things like that, the Irish were builders, the Chinese did laundry and had shops – every group of immigrants had their niche and stuck to themselves.

'And so,' continued Jerry, as he stood back and cast a critical eye over the first door to ensure it was perfectly hung, 'if I want to crack that business, I need an act to get started. You just play the music, and I'll be your manager. You'll need a fiddle player as well if we're going to extend your repertoire, but I think I have that sorted.'

'Oh, you do, do you?' JohnJoe thought it was comical how certain Jerry was that he and Harp would go along with his plan.

'Yep, got it all arranged.'

'Hey, do I pay you two old ladies to be gas-baggin' all day?' Pat passed them by with the architect and cuffed JohnJoe playfully on the head. 'This is the future, Eugene. What you think, eh? Is my empire gonna be in safe hands with him and Dannyboy over there?' Pat gestured to Danny, who was smoking a cigarette while plastering a wall expertly.

Eugene Kent had known Pat Rafferty for years and everyone understood that despite his jocular manner, he loved his nephews like his own sons. 'It will go from strength to strength, I'm sure, but we're not ready to be rid of you yet, Pat.'

'Too right, and you won't be. My old lady would throw me out by the weekend if I was under her feet all day, so I'll be brought off a building site feet first,' Pat joked. 'But yeah, we got good boys with these two, and they got themselves two nice ladies too. Behind every successful man is a good woman, and we got the best, right, JJ?'

JohnJoe smiled. He would have loved Harp whatever anyone thought, but it was an added bonus that his uncle did too. Marianne and Danny were married and had a baby girl earlier in the year, a sweet little thing called Katherine after their beloved Aunt Kathy, although to avoid confusion, she was always called Katie. He and Harp enjoyed visiting them, and secretly it was the life he longed for, but convincing his stubborn girlfriend to allow him to propose, get them a nice place, settle down and have some babies was a whole other matter. She loved Katie and was very good friends with Marianne, but she had no desire whatsoever to follow her lead into matrimony. He knew better than to raise the topic, since she shut him down each time he even hinted at it. She was more interested in education and a career than being a wife and mother.

'We sure do have the best,' JohnJoe agreed.

After the two men moved on, he returned to the conversation with Jerry. 'But *why* do you want to do it? Be a promoter, I mean? I understand why people would want to be on stage, but doing all the bookings and making the arrangements... I don't know – it doesn't sound like much fun.'

The other man shrugged. 'When I was a kid, my ma saved up and brought me and my brother to the Gaiety to see the pantomime. My da thought she was cracked as the crows to be wasting money on stuff like that, but Ma loved it too, and so we went. I'll never forget it. The place was magic, you know? All gold balconies and red velvet seats. And when we sat there in the dark with a bag of toffees between us and they were all up on stage, singing and dancing, I don't know, I just... I loved it.' The way he spoke, without shame or embarrassment, made him unusual. He was not like other men, especially those in the building trade, gruff and unemotional.

'And so then I left school, of course, and served my time as an apprentice with my da and my brother in the family business. But every chance I got, I was at a show or a concert or something. My da never understood it, and he was a bit mortified really, I think, but then I joined the Volunteers and he was proud of me.'

The second door was ready for hanging now, and together they lifted it into place beside its partner, screwing and fixing as they went. JohnJoe offered his friend a cigarette as they stood back and admired their handiwork. The doors were six feet wide each and ornately carved; the two of them hung perfectly.

Jerry leaned against the wall as he smoked. 'Being a promoter is a good fit for me, I think. I'm a good talker, and I'm honest and trustworthy. And even if I'm not a singer or a dancer myself, I can tell a good one from a dud every day of the week.' He exhaled a long plume of smoke. 'I used to play a little game with myself, back at home – which acts I saw that would go on to make it, play in the bigger places or go over to England or even over here, and which wouldn't. I had a kind of a knack for picking winners. I'd love you to be my first act, but I guess I'm going ahead with this anyway.'

JohnJoe sighed. 'So you'll be telling my uncle any day that he's losing the best carpenter he's had in years, will you?'

'Well, that's show business, JohnJoe my friend, just show business.' Jerry winked and grinned.

CHAPTER 3

*H*arp sat in Marianne and Danny's new house and admired everything. The house was decorated in an eclectic mix of modern and antique, American and European, and reflected them perfectly. Katie was in her pram, cooing happily at the mobile Matt had made her of brightly painted little fish and birds.

The idea that Marianne wasn't always with Danny, that her bright, free spirit had once been shackled to the peculiar and cold Oliver Beckett, seemed incredible to Harp even though she knew it was true.

Danny and Marianne were perfect for each other. He loved her intelligence and wit, and she basked in the warmth of his love. They'd moved from an apartment to this house with a large yard, and Marianne was dying to get her hands on the bland garden. Harp just knew her friend would transform it to an oasis of colour and fragrance.

Danny, whose early years were spent in an overcrowded tenement in Southie, could hardly believe that a lady as finely bred as Marianne Pascoe was really his. Her childhood might as well have been on another planet, all finishing schools and deportment lessons and life in a fully staffed mansion on a tea plantation in India, but Harp knew Marianne adored Danny Coveney and cared nothing for the trappings of wealth.

She looked as she did that first day Harp met her on the train from Cork to Queenstown. Harp still had to remind herself to call the town she called home, Cobh. The sadness and drama of her life before Danny seemingly having had had no outward toll on her. Back then, making friends with the wife of the commanding officer of the region was dangerous but beneficial to Harp as a member of the Irish women's Army, but to her surprise, the relationship had blossomed into genuine affection.

Marianne was a beauty. Her blond corkscrew curls refused the taming of a brush or comb, and her china-blue eyes and peaches-and-cream skin gave her the look of a Raphael angel, Harp always thought.

'Danny says he draws the line at pink chintz, but he'll love it when he sees it.' Marianne grinned wickedly. She had her husband wrapped around her finger and knew it.

'It's amazing, truly. It's like something from a magazine.' Harp marvelled at the décor.

'Well, they did teach us some useful things in the Swiss finishing schools,' Marianne joked. 'Though more useful might have been how to get away from a horrible husband, or better still, how to avoid marrying him in the first place. Or how to fire a gun and make your escape with your handsome young lover while carrying his child. But strangely they never felt the need to include such topics on the curriculum – it was all interior design and flower arranging.'

Harp laughed. 'You can joke about it now, but it was not one bit funny at the time.'

'Indeed. You and Danny kidnapping me – I still have nightmares about that bumpy old cart.'

'We would never have hurt you.' Harp still felt guilty about it, but kidnapping Beckett's wife was the only way to secure her mother's release from his terrifying custody, so they'd had to do it. Never did they envisage what would happen, that Beckett would go after them all and try to kill Danny, knowing he was the father of Marianne's baby. They'd managed to get Rose out of the barracks, and she and Matt, along with JohnJoe, Danny, Harp and Marianne, had escaped with their lives against all the odds, leaving Beckett dead on the beach where Marianne had shot him.

'I know that, silly, of course I do.'

Harp had called to see her friend but also to deliver the news of Pamela's whereabouts. Marianne was out of her mind with worry about her mother, and with each passing month and no reply to her letters, she feared the worst.

Marianne checked on Katie, giving her sweet-cheeked baby a kiss before turning to make them both a drink. 'I'm making tea, Darjeeling, but would you prefer coffee or black tea?'

'Black tea please.'

'Danny hates tea, and he absolutely loathes Darjeeling, but I grew up drinking it and it reminds me of Shimla. My mother always drank it too.'

'Marianne,' Harp began as her friend busied herself making their drinks, 'we've had a letter from the Devlins, and it seems Ralph and your mother are living in the Cliff House.'

Marianne stopped and whipped around, her face registering amazed delight. 'And she's all right? I mean is she… Oh, Harp, I was so worried! She never answered any of my letters, and I was so afraid…' Fat tears of relief rolled down her cheeks.

'Yes, I think she's fine. The Devlins just said they were living there and –'

'Hold on, they're living in your house?' The reality of what that meant for Harp and Rose suddenly dawned on Marianne. 'But I thought you owned it, that Henry left it to you…'

'He did, but apparently Ralph has told people that it was his all along and he was only letting us stay because he's so good-natured.'

Marianne shuddered. 'Urgh, that slimy toad. What on earth my mother sees in him, I will never know. I'm so sorry, Harp. This must be awful for you, and here I am delighted…'

'You should be. I know how worried you were.'

'Yes, but what are you going to do? I'll write to her there, of course, but it *is* your house. Will you go back and try to get them out? Can you even go back, after everything? Oliver may have told the authorities what he found out about the death of Pennington, and it might be risky for you.' Marianne placed a cup in front of Harp and sat opposite her.

'Well, the whole business of Pennington has very kindly been taken over by the IRA. They claimed his murder, saying he was an informant and was executed. They of course had nothing to do with it, but as a favour to Matt, I think they decided they would accept responsibility. His death will go down as a war casualty, and there won't be any more done about it, so in that regard, we're fine.'

'Oliver is a different story, though. I'd love to see my mother, but honestly, I would be too frightened to ever set foot on Irish soil again. Too much has happened. And what if they arrested Danny or me for his murder? I don't know. Danny says it would be all right, but I don't want to take the chance. But perhaps Mama could come to visit us here. Preferably without *him*.' Marianne paused. 'So will you go back?' she prompted.

Harp thought for a moment. Would she? Should she? 'I don't know. I was thinking of staying on for a while. Maybe continuing my studies or getting a job. Celia, you remember, the Raffertys' maid, has done a bookkeeping course and has left service to work at a wholesaler's. She lived in while she was in service but now has found herself a little apartment in Roxbury. The rent's reasonable and the place is small but suits her needs perfectly. We met for coffee last week and I was saying I was considering staying and she suggested we might move in together.'

Marianne said nothing, but Harp could tell she was shocked. Roxbury was the immigrant neighbourhood, and lots of Black people lived there too, and any time Harp visited her friend, she was stared at. But she didn't care. Celia was a suffragist and had taken Harp to hear the political activist Josephine St Pierre Ruffin speak. There was an educated elite called the Black Brahmins, modelled on the Boston Brahmins – Celia was a member – and they were actively laying the foundations for political and social equality. Harp found the whole topic fascinating and frustrating and had devoured copies of *The Women's Era*, the first newspaper published for and by Black women.

Though the Irish were treated better than most immigrants to the city, given that they held many positions of power, Harp could empathise with people being made to feel inferior in their own place.

Liberal and kind as the Raffertys were, they wouldn't approve of her involvement with the racial question; they believed most firmly that society worked best when the various groups stuck to themselves. They had no real animosity as such towards the Italians or the Jews or the Chinese, but they gave each other a wide berth and it worked well. The idea of her going to live with Celia in that neighbourhood and getting a job would be something they wouldn't understand, so she hadn't mentioned it. Even JohnJoe, who normally supported her in everything, would have reservations, she knew.

'But now I'm not sure,' Harp said. 'Mammy and Matt assume I'll go back, or that JohnJoe and I will, but we've had an offer, actually, of becoming full-time musicians, performing not just for Irish fundraisers but in proper theatres, becoming professionals.'

Marianne was trying but failing to not look horrified.

'And you'd want to do that?'

'Well initially I was a bit taken aback, you know I don't really like being in the spotlight, but then I don't know, it's different, and I've deferred my studies, so I'll have to do something and it feels kind of exciting. JohnJoe loves the idea and Jerry sounds like he knows what he's doing.'

'And where would this happen?' Marianne managed.

'I don't know. Here, New York maybe. I'm not too sure. But it would mean travel, and JohnJoe and I could live on the road, going from place to place...'

To Harp it sounded idyllic, but Marianne was under no such illusion. 'But, Harp, you can't just go off and live with JJ without being married! It's illegal for one thing, and secondly, your reputation! Your mother would have a canary, and to be honest, I wouldn't blame her.'

'Well, I was thinking about that, and I thought I could ask Celia if she could come too? She's a brilliant seamstress, and we'd need costumes. She's also good with figures and that sort of thing, so she could be a sort of chaperone and a helper at the same time. I feel like

I'm letting her down if I don't go ahead with our plan of living together, but this would be a good opportunity for her too so she might agree.'

Marianne placed her cup on the table and fixed Harp with a meaningful stare. 'Harp, I love that you see the world differently from how it really is, I do, but this is not going to be an option. You and JJ are dating but not married, so going to stay in hotels without a chaperone is not –'

'But Celia could come –' Harp interrupted, but Marianne raised her hand.

'Harp, I liked Celia. She seems like a very nice, smart young woman, the little I know of her. But you have eyes and you're not stupid. You can't live with her, or have her supervising you and JJ. She's coloured, and that just won't be acceptable – surely you know that?'

Harp felt the familiar fury rise up within her at this. All her life, people had told her what society expected, what was and wasn't allowed, and she railed against it at every turn. 'Acceptable to whom?' she asked coldly.

'Everyone! Your mother and Matt, Kathy and Pat, JJ even, none of them will accept what you're proposing. Even if you and JJ married, they'd have a hard time with it, but when you're not...'

'So I should get married to please everyone else, is that it? Though I have no interest whatsoever in marriage, I should just do it because it's the "done thing"?' Harp was furious now.

'Would it be so awful?' Marianne asked gently. 'You do love him and he is absolutely besotted with you, so what would be so wrong with settling down, getting a house, having a baby? Why is that such a dreadful prospect?'

'You of all people should hardly be advocating marriage. Look at you and Beckett,' Harp retorted.

'I only married him because my father gambled me away in a game of cards.' The dignity in Marianne's voice caused Harp to pause. 'And I shot him, so I admit that is hardly a great advertisement for the state of matrimony. But Danny and I are so happy, and we love being married to each other, having the whole world know that he's mine and I'm his. JJ and you are not a forced match or anything terrible like that. You love him, so I just don't understand why you won't do it. All around you are happy marriages – your mother and Matt, Kathy and Pat, Kitty and Seamus before he was killed. JJ's a good man, and it's breaking his heart. What are you so afraid of?'

'I'm not afraid,' Harp began, but she struggled to find the words. Anything she said would sound like a condemnation of Marianne's choices, and she didn't feel that way at all. Marriage for Marianne and Rose and Kathy was a wonderful thing. But she feared being subjugated by a system that seemed to be so heavily weighted in favour of men. Whatever bit of autonomy a single woman had, she lost all of it when she married to become essentially her husband's property. Harp's concerns were nothing to do with JohnJoe personally, but an institution that positioned a woman as inferior to her husband was one she recoiled from.

The laws that controlled women in all situations infuriated her. Decrees that justified exploitation of women in the workplace, that proscribed their leisure activities. The New York City Board of Aldermen had enacted a law that forbade women to smoke in public for goodness' sake. She didn't smoke, but she hated that men could smoke wherever they wanted but women couldn't. JohnJoe had laughed at her outrage on that point, although he wholeheartedly agreed on the subject of employment equality or suffrage and fully supported the ratification of the 19th amendment, which guaranteed women the right to vote. But what people failed to appreciate was that each state retained the right to revoke it. Also, while technically all women were entitled to vote, the reality was the system ensured that only certain women actually could cast their vote; coloured women, Indian women – so many were excluded for a variety of made-up reasons. Until all women were free, none were.

Harp knew JohnJoe thought she was a bit silly to be mad about the smoking rule. He, like many good men, missed the point that it was all part of the problem. She tried to explain to him why she felt as she did, how the smoking thing was just another example of how men controlled women. Every aspect of their existence, even their bodies, were at the discretion of men. She cited the case of a pregnant Canadian woman who was sentenced to hang for killing her husband but had the date of her execution delayed in order to deliver her child. There was such public outcry at the judge's decision to execute her, and yet he'd ignored the fact that her husband was a very violent man who had stabbed her nine times the previous year, which meant her sentence should have been commuted to life in prison. The unfairness of it all rankled with Harp. It was the woman's marriage to that man that had sealed her fate; no matter how awful he was, she was his property to do with as he wished, up to and including murder, it would seem. If she'd been a single woman and stabbed by a man, it would have been a criminal offence; but she was married, and that was her problem. It was an institution in which Harp wanted no part. The odds were so heavily stacked in the favour of men.

JohnJoe did understand, and she was in no way suggesting he would ever be violent to her, but the point was that should he choose to, as his wife, there would be nothing she could do about it. And she couldn't even divorce him if she wanted to. Technically, of course, divorce was available, but in reality, judges rarely sided with a woman. If a woman insisted on a divorce, particularly if she was poor, she was effectively giving up her home, her children, everything.

Just four years ago, the women's activist Margaret Sanger was charged with disseminating information about contraception to women. It was an offence to educate women about their own bodies. As a single woman, Harp fell foul of that system too, but at least she was her own person.

Thinking about the man she loved, hearing her dear friend tell her she was breaking his heart, hurt so much, but simultaneously all the reasons not to marry crowded her mind. It wasn't his fault, of course not, but it was the way of the world.

As a single woman, she had her own passport, but if she married, she would have to be a named person on her husband's, thus meaning she could not travel alone. In certain places, even the length of skirts and height of heels were regulated, though nobody ever told men what to wear. Women were not allowed to work in any number of professions, if not decreed by law, then certainly in reality. And married women were subject to even further restrictions. One of Danny's sisters wanted to study law, but the chances were slim to none of her even being accepted to study, let alone actually work as a lawyer. Almost all women who worked filled domestic roles as maids or cooks and came from the lower orders of society, even in Boston. She didn't know one woman with a job except Celia.

A woman couldn't buy a drink at a bar, as Harp learned much to her frustration when she tried in a hotel in Atlantic City last month when they were playing for a fundraiser. She'd gone out shopping and arranged to meet JohnJoe there for a meal. She was a little early so decided to treat herself to a cold drink while she waited. She was told in no uncertain terms that she could not be served until a man was with her and could pay. She'd stormed out in fury, not that it did any good. It probably confirmed what the snooty manager believed about hysterical women.

She could try to explain all of this to Marianne, but Harp knew her friend wouldn't accept it, so she didn't. 'I love JohnJoe. I always have. I doubt I'll ever love anyone else in my life as I do him, but I just don't want to marry.'

Marianne placed her hand on Harp's. 'Well, I tried,' she said with a smile.

CHAPTER 4

$\mathcal{H}$arp sat on the sofa in the drawing room in stunned silence. JohnJoe was also speechless as he stared at his Uncle Pat and Aunt Kathy, who were standing by the mantlepiece at the top of the room.

Danny was walking up and down, trying unsuccessfully to calm a very fractious Katie, while Marianne sat in an armchair with her hands to her mouth. Rose and Matt were looking at each other in amazement.

When Pat Rafferty had summoned his whole family to the Rafferty house, nobody had known the reason. Now everyone was in shock.

Matt was the first to speak. 'You're not serious, Pat? I knew it was what we wanted, but to say they've actually… I mean, how can you be sure…'

'I've had it on good authority, the highest actually, that secret talks between our side and theirs has meant that there's to be a ceasefire next Monday. All active units on both sides are to stand down, and we'll be entering a period of negotiation to bring about the removal of Crown forces from Ireland after almost eight hundred years of occupation. They want peace, and they know they can't beat us now.' Pat's voice was choked with emotion.

'It's really over?' Harp turned to JohnJoe. 'Is it finished? We won?'

'It sure looks that way.' JohnJoe beamed.

'Tell it to us again please, Pat. We can't take it in...' Rose clung to Matt.

'Well, the details are sketchy for now, but it seems a message was sent by Mulcahy to Ernie O'Malley in Tipperary, something to the effect that in light of recent negotiations, active operations were to be stood down.'

Everyone in the room knew the names of the leading figures in the fight for Irish freedom; there was no need for further explanation. Mulcahy was one of Collins's right-hand men, and Ernie O'Malley was a respected IRA commander.

'But that might not mean a negotiated peace? What if it's a surrender?' Matt asked.

Pat Rafferty shook his head. 'No, it's not a surrender. All British units have been confined to barracks, with a view to being shipped home as soon as is practicable. The bones of a peace deal have been on the table for a while now, since we picked you all up in Ireland, as far as I know. They've hammered it out behind the scenes and have come up with a compromise that we can all live with. Of course there's a long road ahead, and I'm not saying it's all going to be rosy in the garden for a time yet, but I do believe we are taking the first steps on the path to peace and independence.'

'Well, considering the death toll is getting higher, not lower, that's surely a good thing,' Rose said quietly, mainly to her husband. Of the entire group, she was the least militant and openly said that while she supported the cause, she was not convinced any piece of land was worth a life.

Matt, on the other hand, was much more of the mind that there was a need for aggressive resistance by whatever means necessary.

They didn't argue as such, but Matt felt that a more draconian approach on the part of the British was always on the cards – full-scale war, martial law everywhere, executions, internment of any suspected IRA personnel – and so nothing short of a very robust response on the part of the Irish would do. 'Is it really happening?' he asked Pat. 'What has been agreed exactly?'

Pat frowned. 'There were a flurry of talks last week, and the result is a truce – that's all I know for now.'

'I thought you'd all be delighted?' Kathy seemed confused.

Harp articulated it for everyone. 'I suppose we should be, and if it's true, then of course it's a good thing. But jubilation isn't really what we feel, inasmuch as we're sort of bewildered. It was going on for so long and now... And the British lie all the time. They crushed the Rising in 1916 with such viciousness, and then they sent the Tans. They refused to ever even contemplate the idea of an Irish republic, so this about-turn seems a little...I don't know...unbelievable? We're all just sceptical, I suppose.'

Pat nodded again. 'I know how you feel, Harp, and there's a lot of bad blood, a lot of pain, and people aren't willing to just say, well, that's that, and walk away. But this next part is going to be so hard. It's what we fought for, it's what we wanted, but you're right – they won't just pack up and go away and leave us alone. It will be hard-won, the peace, every bit as much as the war was. I'm only speculating. I've no idea of the demands, but it's not going to be all we want. We won't get everything. This is a negotiation, and so concessions will have to be made, I suppose, but to what extent and what it will mean – and even if the talks manage to go on – all remains to be seen.'

'Let's hope people don't feel they need to settle old scores before the ceasefire order comes into effect.' Rose sighed. 'Something that would scupper the delicate peace. If the British are genuine, then we must be too. It will require trust, and in Ireland that's a commodity in very short supply between us and them.'

Harp glanced at Matt, aware he would love to settle an old score of his own with Ralph. Matt kept his eyes lowered.

'I'd love to be there, though, in Cobh, to see people's faces when the news gets out,' JohnJoe said with a sigh. Leaving the war they'd all fought in the closing stages had not been easy for any of them. Though he'd grown up in Boston from the age of fourteen, JohnJoe wore his Irish nationality with pride. 'Imagine, the Devlins, and all the people in the shops and pubs, the children in school...'

Rose was smiling now. 'And for Ralph Devereaux, things have a very different complexion now. He won't be protected by his British associations any more. We can go home, Harp, and reclaim our house.'

This time Harp looked at Marianne – after all, Marianne's mother was living in Cliff House. But Marianne was also smiling. Harp knew she was relieved that Ireland and all its problems were in her past, and she had no interest whatsoever in that place of pain and heartbreak. She would also be relieved for her mother to return to India, with or without Ralph.

'So this is it?' Matt was clearly still struggling to take it all in as he turned to his wife. 'We're going home?'

'If it's true and the truce holds, I suppose we can. Provided the chain of command gives you the all-clear. They will, won't they?' Rose replied, her voice suddenly uncertain.

Harp knew her mother was thinking about Captain Robert Pennington. Harp had killed the captain in self-defence when he was trying to rape her, and Rose and Matt had buried his body, only for it to be found later by the British. To say she, Rose and Matt – along with JohnJoe and Danny – had fled Ireland under a cloud of suspicion was to understate the case. But she knew from Matt that the IRA had helped them by taking responsibility for Pennington's death, so hopefully the truce would expunge the captain's death from the record.

Matt met Rose's gaze. 'I would have thought so, but I've heard nothing official yet.'

Harp could hear the edge to his voice, and she understood why he was frustrated. He was the one who'd risked his own life and his men's lives on a daily basis for two long years. Matt didn't resent Pat Rafferty, she knew that – in fact, he was grateful to him – and Pat had done so much, raising money for the cause, that it would have been a very different outcome without that support, but still it must have been hard for the IRA man to hear this momentous news from an Irish American who had never fired a gun in his life.

'And if the ceasefire breaks, at least our lads will have had a chance to regroup, to replenish. We won't be giving up our weapons just yet,' he added darkly.

Harp saw the faint look of disapproval cross Pat Rafferty's face. He'd put so much of his energy and his money into the cause, every ounce of influence he had, every favour pulled in, all to fund and promote the cause of freedom, and Matt casting doubt on the victory clearly didn't please him. But then Pat Rafferty had never lived the reality of war with the British.

Harp shared Matt's reticence. The truce might lead to a peace deal, but the odds were slim. The British were not going to release their stranglehold and just walk away empty-handed; they couldn't countenance that. But the Irishmen and women who sacrificed everything would not settle for anything less. Not now, not after all they'd endured.

'It's over Matt, truly.' Pat hid his annoyance under a smile. 'Let's have a drink.' He nodded at Clayton, the tall, quietly spoken Black butler, who poured each of them a finger of Irish whiskey into Waterford cut-glass tumblers and handed them round. Everyone accepted and rose as Pat proposed a toast.

'For more generations than we can count, our forefathers tried to rid our homeland of the oppressor, but it was our generation that succeeded. To the Republic!' He raised his glass.

Harp caught Matt's eye as JohnJoe's hand squeezed her shoulder. All around the room there were mixed reactions. JohnJoe, Kathy and Pat were overjoyed. Danny was clearly pleased the war was over. He'd played a very important role while he was there, but his life was here in Boston with his new wife and baby; he saw his time in Ireland as a fun skite but nothing more. And Marianne was happy if Danny was happy.

Only Harp, Rose and Matt had misgivings. As the others all chorused 'to the Republic', the three of them shared the solidarity of doubt.

Later, back in their apartment, Harp and Matt sat in silence at the scrubbed pitch pine dining table while Rose made tea, all of them lost in their own thoughts. Rose set the tea tray on the table and sat down with her husband and daughter. 'Well? What do we think?'

Matt had been quiet for most of the evening. Pat looked like he was annoyed he wasn't more jubilant, and she wondered if JohnJoe's uncle possibly thought Matt secretly wanted the conflict to go on because of the position he held within the IRA.

That wasn't it, Harp knew. Nice as Boston was – and their lives here were pleasant – Matt longed to go home. He missed his son, Brian, a doctor in Dublin, and he wanted to be his own boss once more, to live in his own house, to be his own man. He had worked hard at fundraising, and he'd also worked hard for Pat Rafferty, no doubt about it. Pat knew he'd been lucky to have such a gifted trades-man. But Matt Quinn was an Irishman to his bones, and Ireland was where he wanted to be. Harp knew unequivocally that Matt's reti-cence about the ceasefire was based on his deep and insightful knowl-edge of British rule in Ireland rather than any desire on his part for further hostilities.

'I want to go home, Rose,' said Matt softly. 'Is that what you want?'

'It is, Matt. I want to be back in Ireland. Ralph will disappear to India soon, and I don't want the Cliff House to be left empty, getting damp and musty. And Marianne wants me to check on her mother. She wrote to Pamela in Queens –' – she stopped herself – 'Cobh' – she smiled at her use of the new name of the town she'd called Queen-stown all of her life – 'as soon as Harp told her where Pamela was, but she's had no reply. I think as soon as we are sure Pennington's death won't cause us any trouble, we three need to go home.'

Harp sighed. Now was as good a time as any. 'I don't think I want to go back, even if it's peaceful now.'

Up to now, the possibility of return was not there; Matt was ordered to leave and not come back until he was told to. But now that going back was a real option, Harp realised her life had become more and more settled here in America. She didn't want to abandon her musical career just when there was a possibility of it taking off, thanks to Jerry. And there was JohnJoe... How could she leave JohnJoe? She was twenty-one years old now, a grown woman, and she felt it was time for her to live her own life. Yet she and Rose were so much more than a mother and daughter; they were allies and friends, confidantes and kindred spirits.

She looked at her mother, waiting for her reaction. Rose was staring out the window, and her face was a mask. Long seconds ticked by. Then at last she turned her head and looked at her daughter. 'I understand why you want to stay, Harp. But I don't know if I can leave you.'

Matt said nothing, his face impassive. This was between mother and daughter. Harp knew he respected their deep bond, but her heart sank at the idea she might have ruined his plans to return to Cobh.

'I'll be fine, Mammy, I promise, and I'll have the Raffertys to look after me. It won't be forever. I'm just trying to find my place in the world. I thought that was in books and study, and I still love that, but the war taught me that I'm as much a doer as a thinker. Henry instilled a love of books in me, and I'll be forever grateful to him, but he used them to hide from the world. I don't want to hide – I want to see it all, to experience it, to be part of it. Do you understand what I mean?'

'I do, love.' Rose smiled sadly. 'It's perspective, I suppose. The Cliff House and everything that happened there was the centre of our world, but over here, things move so fast that you have to move with them or be lost, and I can see it's a tide you're happy to be carried away on.'

'"Plunge boldly into the thick of life, and seize it where you will, it is always interesting."'

Rose laughed. Harp had a quotation for every occasion ever since she was little.

'Come on, you know this one,' Harp gently admonished. They had always played a game where Rose tried to guess the source of the quotation.

Her mother's brow furrowed. 'Is it the fellow who said "enjoy when you can, endure when you must"? Johann Wolfgang von...von Goethe?'

Harp clapped. 'Yes, and he's right too. We've all endured so much. I feel like I want to do less enduring and more enjoying.'

'And your studies?' Rose asked.

Harp had been the first girl from Cobh to go to the university in Cork, and she and Rose had worked tirelessly, opening their home as a guest house to make the money for the fees. Her studies were interrupted by the war and their flight to Boston, but Harp had written to the dean of studies, a man committed to the Irish cause, and explained the situation and had been allowed to defer her last year.

Harp exhaled. She would need to word this carefully. She didn't want to talk about Jerry's idea, not just yet. Rose would be terrified she was going down a bad road and refuse to go back to Ireland, and then Matt would be heartbroken. 'I loved being at the university. It was so wonderful to be around people like me. It had never happened before. But now that I've lived here for a while and seen that there's more to life than a provincial city in the south of Ireland, I can't just turn my back and go home. I'm not giving up on my education – I'll never do that – but a woman getting to university is such a big thing at home, and then she's expected either to become a teacher and then marry, or if she becomes a member of the intelligentsia, she goes through life being insulted as a "blue stocking". Neither option appeals to me.'

'And what does appeal to you?' Rose smiled indulgently.

Harp shrugged, the lie coming easily to her lips; it was for a good cause. 'I've no idea, but I'd like the chance to find out.' And she wasn't really being dishonest, she told herself, because she still had no idea if Jerry's plan would work.

CHAPTER 5

obh, Ireland

   Ralph Devereaux gazed with extreme distaste out the window of the Cliff House at the harbour stretched before him. He held an Aynsley teacup and saucer, his back to the room and his wife, Pamela.

   'It's intolerable. Simply intolerable that the might of the British, the greatest ruler of colonies the world has ever known, the owners of the Empire on which the sun never sets, should capitulate. No...not just capitulate, *crumble* like terrified schoolgirls in the face of tyranny and terror. How has it come to this?'

   The question was rhetorical, and he knew Pamela wouldn't dare answer for fear of another verbal bashing like the one he'd given her last night. The woman was a moron. He rued the day he married her. He'd needed her money, but he'd swindled more than she had from women over the years, many times over, without putting a ring on their finger. He should never have given in to her wheedling to get him to marry her, and now he was stuck with her.

   The officers with whom he normally socialised were all hiding – yes, there was no other word for it – in their barracks, and it seemed they were all making plans to ship out. It really was inconceivable.

He'd sat in the bar of the Queen's Hotel last night alone, the whole place eerily quiet. The scenes of jubilation that he'd have presumed would have been the obvious reaction of the criminal mindset that had brought this about were notably absent. It was as if those Irish idiots didn't think it was really happening. They'd fought like rats in a barrel, and now that they had what they wanted, the fools didn't know what to do. Typical. Or perhaps they were soon realising that they'd slaughtered the goose that laid the golden egg. Ignorant, layabout drunkards, with not one brain cell to rub off the other, every last one of them.

The British military is the largest employer in this whole town and what have they gone and done? Bitten the hand that feeds them. Serves them right. Let them starve in their tiny houses with their scores of brats they can't seem to help spawning. They deserve no better. But still, he fumed, now what for the likes of him?

He turned and saw Pamela looking like a painting of a medieval martyr, all hurt and miserable. *Honestly, the woman is such a drain.* 'It might not be comfortable for us here, now that the forces of law and order have abandoned us and we are at the mercy of the rebels.'

He saw the fear in her eyes. He liked terrifying her, toying with her like a spider did with a fly. However, he wasn't just teasing her now – he meant it.

'They won't do anything to us, though? I mean, it isn't anything to do with us. We're private citizens?'

He shrugged. 'Who knows? They're lawless at the best of times, and we know they're capable of slaughter. Just look at what they did to Marianne and Oliver.'

The pain crossed her face once more. Pamela was sure Marianne was dead and had never got over the loss of her daughter. Marianne's body had never been found, though her husband's was, reclaimed from the sea, riddled with bullets. The bodies of several of the Cameron Highlanders that were with him on patrol that night, looking for his wife who had been kidnapped by the IRA, were also washed up further down the coast. Marianne's scarf was found on the beach, so they knew Beckett had been with her, but she'd never been

35

found. The gunmen and women – Ralph was sure his niece and her treacherous slut of a mother had something to do with it – had escaped. Matt Quinn, the two Americans and Rose and Harp were never seen again after that day, so two and two clearly made four.

He'd believed that story up to recently as well, until he'd intercepted letters from Marianne to her mother and discovered she was in Boston.

The officer investigating Beckett's death confided in Ralph that they'd done their damnedest to beat the information out of two old people living in a cottage high up in the Knockmealdown Mountains. He'd sought Ralph out as a source of information, something that at one time might have been reassuring but now filled him with dread. If he was known as a British informer, then there was going to be a price to pay if the rebels were in charge.

The officer – Halpin was his name, Ralph recalled – said that they'd provided a safe house for the IRA and Marianne, heavily pregnant at the time too, but that the group left in the early hours of the morning. To the officers' surprise, neither of the old crones cracked and gave them any names, no matter how robust the pressure. They were both dead now. The authorities surmised that Beckett must have caught up to them and got Marianne back, but the IRA would have had people hidden everywhere. That's what made them such a sneaky enemy, but their ungentlemanly behaviour was despicable.

Ralph knew he could go to the authorities with the letters, but he decided against it. He'd use them himself; he'd need all the leverage he could get. The net was closing in, and the sudden reappearance of Pamela's daughter threw a spanner in an already clunky works. She would be Pamela's heir, not him. Old Pascoe, Alfie's much more astute and wily father, had tied the money up in such a way as to make it close to impossible for a subsequent spouse of his daughter-in-law to get at it. She had her own inheritance too, but likewise it was safeguarded against men such as him.

His valet ensured all correspondence was given to him first, regardless of who it was addressed to, so he'd discovered Pamela had put her solicitors in London on alert. She planned to divorce him, and in their letter, they were anxious to assure her that they would protect her interests assiduously. He knew what that meant. She'd get her divorce, and he wouldn't get a brass farthing. He would need to be clever. He could try charming her again, acting contrite and loving, but he hadn't the energy. There had to be another way.

'We don't know for sure she's dead, Ralph. She might have gone with her American chap.' Pamela clung to that belief.

A kinder man might have let her live in that delusion, particularly now that it had turned out to be true, but Ralph was not that man. 'Possibly. She may just be choosing not to contact you and not care that you are out of your mind with worry – of course that could be the case – but I know from living here all my life that bodies are often not returned by the sea around here for many years, if ever. That harbour looks calm and peaceful, but there are so many places a corpse can get caught and lodged. And then there's the strong pull of the tide. Once a body is out into the ocean, well...' He smiled indulgently, enjoying the twisting of the knife. 'Once that happens, you'll never get a body back. Food for the fishes then, I'm afraid.'

Silence hung between them. Ralph relished it.

'I'm going back to Shimla.' Her words cut through the toxic atmosphere.

He turned and gazed at her. Pamela had grown even more dumpy since they left India. She didn't enjoy life in Ireland. She said she felt under surveillance all of the time, terrified of the rebels, and she failed to connect with the wives of the officers and the local Protestant land-owning families. They were tough, resilient people who were usually frugal in their ways and not given to frivolity, and Pamela was frivolous to her bones. There was no substance to her, no hidden depths. She cared nothing for literature or art, music or culture; all she was interested in was fashion and gossip. She bored him senseless. Her dark hair was in need of touching up at the roots, but he would withhold the funds necessary for a while longer, knowing how the half-inch of grey root growing out of her head upset her. True, it was her money, but he was her husband, and for now he controlled the purse strings.

'No, you're not,' he replied, his tone indicating just how tedious he found her.

'I am and you can't stop me. I hate it here and I hate you.'

He could hear the quiver in her voice. She was afraid of him, and rightly so.

'Do shut up, my dear. You really are such a crashing bore.' He turned away again to gaze out the window at the scene below. The naval base on Haulbowline Island, the Army on its neighbour Spike Island, the docks below with boats of every shape and size coming and going – it should have been such a pleasing place to live. It used to be, certainly, but everything was changing.

'Why are you so horrible?' she asked his back.

He turned, placed his cup on the table and smiled, a genuine one this time, and told the truth. 'Because I want to be.'

'But why? What have I ever done to you to deserve this treatment?'

That whining voice grated on him. He sighed and decided he couldn't be bothered engaging with her. He'd go down to the town, see what he could find out.

The staff he'd handpicked were all milling about the house, doing the necessary. The Irish valet he'd engaged at considerable expense to Pamela, who had been trained in Belgravia but was anxious to come back to his home country, ensured everything was shipshape.

Ralph climbed the stairs slowly, as he always did, his wooden leg making his gait awkward. How he longed for the days when he could have bounded up them two at a time. For the millionth time, he cursed JohnJoe O'Dwyer and Danny Coveney. They were the reason he was only half a man. And as for Rose and Harp… He forced their images from his mind. He was in bad enough humour without thinking of that pair of she-devils. When life was right, his parents owned the Cliff House, his peculiar brother was locked in the library, and people knew their place. Rose Delaney was a maid, albeit a pretty one, there for the taking. That was part of the deal: The son of the house – and he was a handsome devil in his youth, he knew – got to have a little practice on the servant girls before trying his hand at women of his own class. It was the done thing. He would not have pressed his advantage there all those years ago had he known what a thorn in his side she would become. *Why can't people not just accept their position in life and be happy about it?* But no, the lower orders wanted independence, and to own property, for goodness' sake. His niece, the daughter of a skivvy, had been studying at a university. Admittedly, it was an Irish one, so not exactly Oxbridge, but still, she had no business getting ideas above her station.

In foul humour he entered his bedroom, where his valet waited. The morning was sunny, so he didn't bother with a coat, choosing instead the cream jacket Maguire held out for him.

'What's the news down the town?' he asked.

Maguire could always be relied upon to inform his master of any goings-on he might have missed. It was one of the reasons Ralph chose an Irishman – he could ingratiate himself into the society of the lower orders more easily.

An obsequious man, slight and short, with waxy skin and thinning hair, Maguire reported the activities of the house faithfully. He told Ralph who was having affairs with who, who owed money, matters of that nature. Information was power, and Ralph stored it all away.

'The Crown forces are all confined to barracks, awaiting orders in the wake of the announcement of the truce. They're being told not to be seen outside for any reason.'

'And what about everyone else?' Ralph knew Maguire got all his information on troop movements from an adjutant on Spike who was some relative of his.

'Life is going on as normal. People are being cautious, not being too overly excited or anything, but they seem happy.' Maguire's thin lips curled in distaste as if the idea of anyone being happy was anathema to him.

He was that most peculiar type of Irishman, Ralph mused. He worked for the British and seemed to despise his own countrymen even more than the enemy. What would have happened to make a man born and raised in Ireland – Ralph had no idea what part; he'd never asked – speak so disparagingly about his own, he had no idea. If it was an attempt to climb a social ladder or to ingratiate himself with his betters, it was foolish, as that would never happen, but still, it suited Ralph's purposes.

Maguire brushed an imaginary fluff or hair from Ralph's shoulder with a brush before bowing slightly and retreating deferentially.

Ralph thought about Pamela. Marianne was her heir, and Pamela wanted a divorce. The Pascoe family machine would spring into action and it would not be good for him, so he simply had to make sure that didn't happen. But how?

CHAPTER 6

'So that's it?' JohnJoe clinked his beer bottle off Jerry's.

It was a warm summer evening, and the boys had knocked off work for the weekend. Harp met them in the park with a picnic, and JohnJoe ran to the corner store for some cold sodas. Of course, the soda was in fact beer, but under Prohibition, the sale and consumption of alcohol was forbidden. People were most ingenius at finding ways around the laws. And the candy store on the corner of the park sold special pop to people in the know. All the Rafferty crew were in the know.

Harp was also having a 'soda'. She didn't like the taste all that much, but it felt illicit and fun and so she joined in. The idea of a young lady sitting in a park drinking beer from the neck of the bottle would have been enough to set tongues wagging in Cobh for a week, and JohnJoe assured her it wasn't what nice young ladies from Boston did either, but Harp wasn't trying to impress anyone and so did as she pleased. Despite the bizarre drinking laws, the liberation of living in America was addictive.

Jerry's friend Elliot had joined them. He worked in a clothes store. Harp had no idea how he and Jerry had met, but they were almost always together, and so the original trio of Harp, JohnJoe and Jerry had become a foursome of late. Harp really enjoyed the new boy's company. While Jerry was resourceful and energetic, Elliot was sweet and shy. They both trod lightly on the earth, and Harp wasn't surprised they were friends. Like Jerry, Elliot was slim and short, no more than five foot one or two, but where Jerry was dark, Elliot, who was of German extraction, was pale with blond hair, cut short on the sides and longer on top. His sea-green eyes were kind, and Harp had taken to him immediately.

'Yep, I'm doing it, I'm leaving the building business and entering show business.' Jerry made a theatrical gesture with his hands, and they all laughed. 'I know a fella, a New Yorker actually but he's here in Boston at the moment, and he's working out of a place they call Tin Pan Alley – loads of music producers up there. He's Jewish. Saul Simon is his name. They run everything to do with theatres and performing, it seems. Bit like the Irish dominating the building trade and the police department.' He grinned. Harp loved his enthusiasm. 'Actually, he told me there's a few acts going on up the West End this evening, a sort of revue, a vaudeville thing...'

'What's vaudeville?' asked Harp.

'It's when a venue puts on a show of all different acts, dancers, singers, comedy sketches, magic, you name it, and they all perform one after the other,' Jerry explained.

'A kind of variety show?' suggested Elliot.

'Exactly.' Jerry smiled. 'And tonight anyone can join in. This lad Saul is going to check them out, and he suggested I should go too and see what they were like. In fact, I think we should all go, just for fun. It's in a speakeasy though, so y'know...'

JohnJoe winked at him. 'I wouldn't have a clue about any such places.' He was joking, of course. The Rafferty boys frequented several illegal drinking establishments around the city. He looked at Harp. 'What do you think? It's Friday night?'

She smiled. 'I'd like to go.'

'Excellent!' Jerry rubbed his hands together. 'Maybe they'll have a harp and you and JohnJoe can give us a tune. And Elliot here can bring his fiddle...'

'Oh, this is the brilliant fiddle player you told me about?' asked JohnJoe in surprise.

'I'm not brilliant at all!' protested Elliot.

'He is,' said Jerry. 'Wait till you hear him.'

'No, no, I've barely touched the violin in years, not since I broke my hand. It was only that Jerry insisted on me playing him "Danny Boy"...'

Harp was still in shock at Jerry assuming she'd agree to get up and play to a strange audience without any warning. 'Wait, I thought we were just going along to listen to the other acts?'

'It does seem a bit sudden.' JohnJoe grinned.

'Fine, fine.' Jerry rolled his eyes. 'If you three are chicken, I won't make you. But I can tell you, as your manager, you're letting a world-class opportunity slip through your fingers...'

Laughing and joking and teasing Jerry about his grand ambitions, they finished their picnic dinner and caught a streetcar to the venue.

Harp had never actually been inside one of the illegal drinking clubs but had heard about them. This one looked like a regular house, a brownstone walk-up, but once inside, the music and the cigarette smoke declared exactly what it was. They paid the entrance fee, Jerry muttered a password he'd been given, and they climbed the stairs, following the sound of people socialising and music playing.

Prohibition seemed ridiculous to Harp, and as far as she could see, it was a totally pointless move as there appeared to be alcohol every-where. Pat bought his whiskey from the local pharmacy, where one was allowed to buy a pint of the stuff every ten days for medicinal use. Written on the label was 'take three ounces of stimulant every hour until stimulated'. Pat showed it to everyone, thinking it was hilarious. The number of pharmacies springing up everywhere was staggering, almost all as a cover business for speakeasies. Canon Brennan, a Catholic clergyman who was very involved in the republican move-ment, ensured their wine needs were met with altar wine, which just happened to be Pat's favourite vintage. Apparently the rabbis kept their congregation equally supplied. For every rule of the 18th amendment, there were five ways around it. The consumption of alcohol wasn't a crime, just the selling or production of it. But it was a law that few took seriously. The ladies of the Anti-Saloon League and the Woman's Christian Temperance Union had their way with Congress, but a law that wasn't enforced wasn't worth the paper it was written on.

Harp clung to JohnJoe's arm as they passed a large middle-aged man with a girl around Harp's age on his knee. She was wearing an almost translucent dress, her hair was an unnatural shade of platinum, and her face was painted with make-up. Everywhere they looked, there were men and women in various stages of intoxication, and between the band and the chatter, they had to raise their voices to speak to each other. They made their way through the crowd to where the bar was set up.

'What will we have?' JohnJoe asked her.

'When in Rome.' Harp winked, and he grinned back and signalled the harassed-looking barman.

'Four Bee's Knees!' he yelled. He passed the drinks to Jerry and Elliot as they were poured. Harp thought hers disgusting and barely sipped at it.

'They add lots of lemon and honey to kill the taste of the bathtub gin,' JohnJoe said into her ear, seeing her grimace.

'It doesn't work. It tastes like cough medicine,' she admitted, and he laughed and hugged her.

They turned their attention to the band, a four piece, and Harp found herself tapping her foot to the infectious rhythm. It was like nothing she'd ever heard before. The singer was a slender Black woman, whose voice was slow and rich and smooth. The rest of the band were Black too, a cellist, trumpeter and guitar player, and the effect was magical. The mixture of races in the audience was a surprise as well. Though there was definite agitation for equality, it was rare to see Whites and coloured people mixing socially. Harp loved the atmosphere, even if the alcohol left her cold.

'They're amazing, aren't they? Saul was right!' Jerry shouted over the sound of the music.

She nodded. The band played their last song and to rapturous applause left the stage. The next act was a solo singer, a tenor, and while Harp thought he was very good, she knew JohnJoe's voice was better. His delivery was saccharin and the songs maudlin, but she smiled and clapped politely when he was finished. Dotted all around were men, none of whom appeared to be joining in the revelry. Jerry whispered to her that they were agents from New York and pointed out Saul in the far corner.

There were three sisters who sang and danced and who were much appreciated by the men for their skimpy costumes, but they were short on musical talent; their voices clashed discordantly. And then there was a magician, who was the only one who managed to get the decibel level down during his illusions. He held the crowd enthralled for the entire act and left the stage having seemingly conjured a white dove out of thin air, to everyone's astonishment.

At the side of the stage were a variety of instruments; clearly all genres of music were played there. Harp was surprised when JohnJoe pointed out an Irish harp in the corner. A violin lay on a nearby side table.

The compère, a White man in his thirties with a well-cut suit and an impressive bow tie, complimented all the acts, gaining a collective round of applause from the appreciative audience once more.

'All right, folks, now we come to the free-for-all, as you know, where any act can step up and show their worth.'

There were whoops of approval from the audience.

'Tonight we are delighted to welcome some friends from New York City who are the movers and shakers in the music industry, so if you feel you've got something special and you want to show us what you got...' A raucous remark from the back, which Harp didn't catch but could guess at by the lewd laughter all around her, caused him to pause. 'Yes, well, maybe later...' He winked and the crowd guffawed. 'But for now we're looking for the next big thing, so here's your chance.'

A queue formed at the front of the stage, and one after the other, a very bad pianist, a passable juggler and a pair of acrobats in sparkling costumes did their thing to lukewarm applause. Last up, a man tried to swallow a burning torch and set his own hair on fire.

During the laughter, Jerry marched to the front of the room.

'All right, who do we have here?' the compère asked. 'Are you planning on playing the spoons or twisting yourself into a pretzel?'

'Neither,' said Jerry, loudly and confidently. 'I'm a manager, and I'm here to introduce a brand-new act. A trio all the way from the Emerald Isle, called...err...Harp and Her Boys.'

The compère beamed. 'Well, ain't that something, folks. There's guys here all the way from Ireland and they call themselves Harp and Her Boys. Let's give them a big welcome now.'

The room burst into applause, and Harp found herself looking around, hoping against hope that Jerry had been talking about someone else or that it was all just a big joke.

To her astonishment, JohnJoe was grinning at her. 'Will we?'

'Will we what?' she asked incredulously.

'Give it a go. There's a harp, and I'll sing – we've done it a thousand times. Elliot, grab a fiddle – there's one on that table.'

'I'm really not...' Elliot said anxiously.

'Elliot, come on, do it for me!' called Jerry from the front, to cheers from the audience.

'Come on, for the laugh.' JohnJoe's eyes were bright with enthusiasm.

Elliot was still pale with fright, but Harp hated to refuse JohnJoe. 'All right, but if that thing' – she gestured at the harp – 'isn't in tune, we can't. It would take too long to tune it up and...' She found herself being led by the hand to the stage.

Jerry dragged the harp to centre stage, then gave Elliot the fiddle that had been resting on the table. Elliot pulled a face at Jerry but stepped up to the stage and quickly tuned the instrument, making some adjustments. Harp and JohnJoe shared a look of impressed surprise when he expertly played a quick scale. If his hand had been broken, it certainly didn't show. Harp sat at the harp and gingerly plucked, fearing the worst. An appreciative whistle and another raucous joker shouted from the back, 'She can pluck my strings any day!' but Harp never looked up from her tuning. To her relief it wasn't too bad, and despite the cacophony of applause and chatter, she was able to adjust the strings that were wildly off-key enough to make it sound passable.

'Is it all right?' JohnJoe asked.

'It'll do.' She grinned. 'So now that you've got us up here, what are we going to play?' She and JohnJoe performed and sang together frequently, and their repertoire was large and eclectic, but they'd never played with Elliot before. Then she remembered how Jerry had got his friend playing the violin again. 'How about "Danny Boy"?'

'Why not?' JohnJoe grinned.

Harp had never heard of "Danny Boy" until she came to Boston four years ago. It was a song the Irish Americans associated with Ireland but not one that was widely known at home. Still, she liked the melody and knew it held a place in the hearts of Boston Irish, so she'd learned it for her American audience.

She plucked the opening notes, and Elliot began to play beautifully. His stance, his composure, all pointed to someone classically trained. Within seconds the crowd had stilled, all eyes on them. JohnJoe began to sing, his gentle melodious tenor filling the small space. Harp harmonised with him on the chorus as she played, and several people were in tears as they sang the last plaintive lines.

'And I am dead, as dead I well may be. You'll come and find the place where I am lying, and kneel and say an Ave there for me. And I shall hear as soft you tread above me, and all my grave will warmer sweeter be. And you will kneel and tell me that you love me, and I shall sleep in peace until you come to me.' Harp and JohnJoe were in perfect harmony.

For a moment, one could hear a pin drop, and then the entire place erupted in tumultuous applause. JohnJoe cast her a delighted grin, and Elliot blushed to the roots of his blond hair.

Jerry clapped enthusiastically as they came off stage. 'That was incredible,' he gushed. 'You three are amazing! It's as if you've been playing together forever. You were the best act tonight by a country mile. And you all look the part too, Harp with your beautiful red-blond hair and your voice of an angel, not to mention the way you make the harp sing. Your name is your destiny…'

'Thank you.' Harp smiled. Playing the harp and being called Harp was something that had embarrassed her for years, but like so many things, she couldn't care less now.

'And, JJ, such depth to your voice! You had them eating out of your hand. And, Elliot, a virtuoso on the violin. The three of you together, well, it's really something special.'

The compère once again took to the stage and finally managed to quiet the crowd once more, though the hollering and applause went on much longer than for any of the other acts.

'Ladies and gentlemen, what a treat we've enjoyed this evening. Our live acts are all here tonight with a view to moving on with their careers to the big time, and I feel like that's a real possibility for so many we've seen tonight…'

As he spoke, Harp saw a very distinguished-looking man tap Jerry on the shoulder, lead him away and hand him a business card. The man was tall and thin and had a thick mass of grey curls, tamed with hair oil. He had intelligent dark-blue eyes and wore an exquisitely cut suit and a gold pocket watch.

Harp and Elliot found a booth in which to sit while JohnJoe went to the bar. Now that the music had stopped, the noise level was much more bearable.

'So where did you learn to play like that?' Harp asked Elliot. 'You're more than just a vamper, that's for sure.'

Elliot smiled. 'My *opa*, my mother's father, was first violin in the Weimar Orchestra in Germany. It was one of the oldest in the world, going all the way back to the 1400s and associated with Bach and Strauss. My mother promised him when she and my father left Germany, before I or my siblings were born, that if she had a child, he or she would play. So my brother and sister and I were sent to lessons from the time we could hold a bow. My brother and sister learned to play well enough, but I was the one – my *mutti* pinned her hopes on me. I remind her of her papa too – she said I looked like him – and she adored him. He died when I was ten. So it's all kind of tied up together, music and memory. Me playing kind of brought him back for her a little, I think.'

'And did you never consider it as a career?' Harp was fascinated.

Elliot dropped his eyes, rubbing his fingers. 'Not since I broke my right hand. My poor *mutti* was devastated.'

Harp was puzzled. She could see nothing much wrong with Elliot's hand, maybe a very slight twist to his middle finger, but she didn't like to say.

He smiled sadly. 'I know it doesn't look bad, but believe me, when you're used to holding a bow in a classical position, even the smallest injury is a disaster.'

'Can anything be done, medically, I mean, to fix it?'

'If I had a few thousand dollars, but that's not going to happen. I would have loved to play with an orchestra. I could listen to them all day and never tire of it, and I longed to have been a part of it all. But some dreams are just not going to happen, so it's best to accept it and move on.'

'But could your parents help out maybe?'

A shadow passed over Elliot's normally sunny face. 'No. My father hasn't spoken to me in two years, and my *mutti* does what my father tells her. My family is what you'd call fractured. Like my hand.'

JohnJoe appeared, and Harp dubiously accepted the drink he offered her. To her relief it was just lemonade without the bathtub gin. The next minute Jerry arrived, his eyes bright with enthusiasm, and Harp and Elliot moved up in the booth to make room for both of them.

'That man that approached us, he was from a place on Broadway, in New York City. He wants to talk to me about you being part of a show there. He's got a vaudeville thing going, he said...'

Jerry was more excited and animated than she'd ever seen him. She could tell he had an enthusiasm for this business that he would never have for carpentry, no matter how good at it he was.

'Look at this fancy business card!' Jerry waved it around the table.

Harp took it from him. *Peregrine J Rothstein III* was emblazoned in gold leaf and beneath it the words, *The Adelphi Theatre, 49th Street,*

Broadway, New York. 'Peregrine J Rothstein the third? My word, what a mouthful.'

'So are we going to head for New York and see what happens?' Jerry sat back, taking a long draught from his bottle of beer. 'If the crowd here are anything to go by, you three have something bright in your futures.'

'I'm game if Harp is.' JohnJoe grinned. 'Uncle Pat won't mind if it's not for too long. The hotel is done, and I'm due a vacation anyway. And sure, it's not likely we'll hit the big time, and if we do, we'll cross that bridge when we come to it.'

Harp chuckled at JohnJoe's use of the Americanism for a holiday. He really was a hybrid of Irish and American, and she found it endearing. She agreed. 'I suppose it couldn't do any harm, and I'd love to see the Statue of Liberty. When I was little, Henry used to read me stories set in different places. The one set in New York was one of my favourites, *Washington Square* by Henry James.'

'What was that about?' JohnJoe asked.

'It was a tragic comedy, I suppose, about a brilliant father and his dull but sweet daughter. Henry used to say it was like us, only in reverse.' She smiled sadly. 'He was very far from dull, of course, but I was such a lost child. If he hadn't nurtured my mind, I don't know what would have become of me. He'd love the idea of me finally getting to New York City.'

'I wish I'd met him,' JohnJoe said quietly, his hand reaching for hers under the table and giving it a squeeze.

'You would have liked him, I think. He was so shy that he rarely spoke to anyone except my mother or me, but he was special.' She turned to Elliot. 'So what do you think about all this? Going to New York and maybe performing in vaudeville?'

Elliot smiled shyly. 'It's not exactly the way I thought my musical career would turn out. But if you want to be a promoter, Jerry, I don't know, I'm happy to give you a chance to follow your own dream, to change your life path.'

Harp noticed a meaningful look pass between the two men, then

Jerry beamed at them all. 'Well, if you three still want me, I do want to be your agent, or manager. I'd love to give it a go.'

'Oh, we'd want you all right,' said JohnJoe. 'We'd need someone to represent us surely. We couldn't just turn up in New York like a bunch of eejits, green as grass! Sure they'd make mincemeat of us. You were only saying on the way over here how it's a cut-throat business.'

'So are we on?'

'We are.'

The four of them clinked glasses.

'I can't believe this is happening,' Elliot said, clearly still trying to process it all. 'I know it might not work out, but it's something, isn't it?'

'It is indeed,' Harp answered. 'We don't have anything to lose, but we should do a bit of practice. And we'll have to figure out how to get my harp to New York.'

When she'd arrived in Boston, the Raffertys very thoughtfully had bought her a harp. She and her mother had had to leave Cobh without any notice, and so everything they owned was still there. She arrived in the clothes she left the house in that final day, and she was so relieved that she'd brought her pen, the one engraved with her initials that Henry had given her on the day he died. It was her most treasured possession. She tried not to visualise Ralph Devereaux in their house, touching her things – or worse, selling or destroying them. It would be typical of his spite to take a hatchet to her beloved harp, once Henry's, though her uncle was so greedy, he'd most likely sold it. At least if he did, there might be some hope of getting it back.

Jerry was still in full flow. 'We need to find a place to live immediately! We'll have to share at first, and I'm sure it will be pretty cramped. Harp, do you mind sharing an apartment with three gorgeous young men?'

Despite Harp's independent views, she hesitated. Marianne was right about one thing: Her mother would be appalled at her living with men on her own.

'I have an idea. My friend Celia –'

'Celia, the maid?' interrupted JohnJoe in surprise.

'She's not a maid any more. She's a bookkeeper. And she's also a brilliant dressmaker. Why don't we ask her to come to New York with us? Then there will be another girl in the flat, which would be better for me, and if things work out, she can do the books for us and manage the wardrobe, which would be good for all of us. Of course she might not want to do it, but I think it would be worth asking her? She's really interested in politics and music, so New York could be an exciting prospect for her too.'

But before any of them could answer, there was a burst of police whistles. Panic immediately ensued. The crowd surged towards the back exit, which all speakeasies had due to raids, and JohnJoe shielded her with his body as the heaving mass of people gathered at the bottleneck beside their booth. There was a backstairs, but the crush of bodies and the confusion made escape impossible.

The federal agents in their suits were followed by uniformed Boston officers, and Harp found herself being shepherded none too gently down the stairs along with her friends and everyone else. On the street outside were several police vehicles, dubbed 'paddy wagons' given the number of Irishmen on the police force.

Harp found herself separated from the men and unceremoniously shoved into a large van with several other women, most of whom were protesting drunkenly. The door closed and she felt the van move off. She should have been terrified but she began to laugh. All around her women in various states of dress and intoxication were singing or complaining, and she cast her eyes upwards.

'You said I'd live an interesting life, Henry. Well, is getting arrested in an illegal bar interesting enough?' she asked, though nobody was listening.

CHAPTER 7

*H*arp had to hide her smile. Matt kept his back to Rose and her as he prepared the meal, but Harp knew he was laughing too; she'd caught his wink over her mother's head.

'I'm mortified, Harp. Truly, I don't know what to say.'

Harp had been bailed out of the police station by a chuckling Pat Rafferty and sent home to her mother, who did not see the funny side of it at all.

'I mean, I know when we were in Ireland, we did some things – I'm not saying we didn't – but that was different, that was to free Ireland and, well, to save you from... Anyway, this is different. A girl, an unmarried girl, in a speakeasy with God knows who, getting drunk and then arrested and having to be bailed out! Harp, I...' Rose's cheeks were bright red, and Harp had never seen her so het up. She knew it was much better when someone was on a rant to let them carry on, to not interrupt, and it would eventually lose momentum.

'You're a good girl from a respectable family, and this kind of behaviour is frankly appalling. I mean, what on earth were you think-ing, going to a place like that? And honestly, Harp, I think it might be best if you came back to Cobh with us, where I can keep an eye on you. A girl can get a reputation, even here in America. It is very hard to shake it off once you do, and I just don't want that for you…'

Harp had no intention of returning to Ireland just yet, but she knew her mother wanted what was best for her and so didn't react. Arguing with Rose when she was angry was a pointless activity. Harp knew her mother still bore the scars of society's reaction when she became pregnant out of wedlock at just seventeen. It mattered not that the father was Ralph Devereaux, the spoiled son of the house who'd taken advantage of a gullible girl; the blame was entirely on Rose. Harp didn't hold with such antiquated ideas – she was a young woman who knew her own mind – but to bring that up at this point would be a terrible idea.

On and on Rose went, 'And as for JohnJoe, well, he'll be getting a piece of my mind, I can assure you. He was supposed to be looking after you, not taking you to a place where you could have been killed.'

Matt was bent over the potatoes he was peeling, but Harp could see his shoulders shaking with hilarity as Rose got more and more outraged.

A speakeasy as a place to get killed indeed? Had her mother forgotten how they all risked life and limb every day back in Ireland?

Rose was really into her stride now, going on about how embarrassed she was that the Raffertys, who had been so kind, had to go and bail her out of the police station.

Harp tuned out. The more she thought about the opportunity to play music and make money from it, the more it appealed to her. When she visited Boston in 1916, she met the famous Chief Francis O'Neill, the most diligent and prolific collector of Irish tunes in the world, and he'd honoured her by naming a tune after her when she helped him transcribe it. He'd mentioned that he thought she had a bright future in music, and perhaps this was how she would access that. She could finish her studies and get her degree any time. But if her mother found out about that plan now, it would send her over the edge entirely, so she thought she'd keep that to herself for the time being.

'And what have you to say for yourself?' Rose was now demanding.

'Mammy, I'm sorry for embarrassing you, and you're right, it is illegal to go to those places, but honestly, even the police were very relaxed about it. We got fined five dollars each and were let go. They're not after the patrons anyway – if they were, the whole city would be in jail. They just want to catch the owners and the drink manufacturers.'

Harp's nonchalance seemed to drive her mother into a further tizzy of frustration. 'That is not the point, Harp, not the point at all. It is illegal to drink here – that's the law. Bad enough you're running around with JohnJoe getting up to God knows what! You seem to have abandoned the idea of studying, and you have no job and no intentions of marrying. How on earth am I expected to leave you like this? I'd be out of my mind with worry. You think you're so worldly-wise, Harp, but you're not. You think you can handle any situation, but you've been very protected and this is a different world. There are different...' – she struggled to find the word – 'different standards of what's acceptable. I can't leave you if you don't understand that.'

Harp didn't ask her mother the question that had dogged her all her life: Acceptable by whom? Who were these faceless people who got to decide what she or anyone else should do? Why should she live her life by some imagined code that meant nothing to her? But she knew such a conversation would not help so didn't respond. Perhaps she was finally growing up, she thought ruefully; the old Harp would have blurted out what she thought.

Matt shot her a warning glance. He wasn't laughing any more now that the future of their return to Ireland seemed to be at stake. He desperately wanted to get back – he'd been itching to go since they set foot in Boston – but he wanted to take Rose with him, and she was getting more and more anxious about leaving her daughter as the day of their departure came nearer.

Harp took his cue. 'Mammy, I'm sorry, and you're right – it was very foolish of me to go there. And I promise I won't do anything so daft as that again. I'll look into resuming my studies here, and Uncle Pat and Aunt Kathy will make sure I'm all right, you know they will.'

Her mother assumed she was moving back with the Raffertys once they left, a notion Harp chose not to correct. There was no way she could breathe a word about the New York thing until Matt and Rose were gone.

'Kathy knows the kind of trouble young innocent girls can get into, and she'll protect her, Rose,' Matt added.

'Matt's right Mam, and I'm sorry for getting in trouble, I'll be much more careful in future I promise.'

She wanted to go forward with her life, not backwards and her mother would never leave her if she thought she was at risk of falling into bad ways. She'd have to convince Rose she was respectable and trustworthy.

She recalled watching the ships sail in and out of the harbour with Mr Devereaux, and he would tell her about India and China and Canada and faraway exotic places, and he said that one day, she would see those magical lands for herself. She believed him then, and now it was happening. It would be hard to be apart from her mother, they were so close, but it was time to live her own life.

Matt could easily provide for Rose and himself, He had a lovely house overlooking the town and was perfectly capable of earning a very comfortable living. If the peace was to hold, Matt would happily go back to undertaking and doing a bit of cabinet making, and they would be contented and safe there.

Maybe leaving the Cliff House forever was the best thing for Rose – no more laundry or cooking for the guests, a break from the constant maintenance of a beautiful but old house.

On Harp's bedside locker was a letter they'd had from Liz and Cissy Devlin. Mammy had read it and given it to her, saying the contents were a worry. Harp picked it up and saw the Queenstown stamp. It felt like a lifetime ago.

She allowed her mind to roam back to Cobh, and the man who thought he was her uncle. He would have happily seen her and her mother hang. He hated her with such passion, it frightened her sometimes. He despised Danny and JohnJoe too, for shooting him and rendering him legless from the knee down. He was so consumed with hate and bile. With anyone else, it might make them half-crazed with a need for revenge, but not Ralph; he was cold and calculating and willing to wait. He would never let it go, she knew.

She extracted the letter and began to read.

Dear Rose, Harp and Matt,

I hope this letter finds you all well. Life here is carrying on, but it's odd since the truce. Hard to say how exactly, but there's an unease here.

You asked us to keep you informed about RD, so here's what we know so far.

The new Mrs D was in the shop a few days ago and looked none too pleased. Apparently she's been seen sending telegrams from the post office in Rushbrooke to a firm of solicitors in London. As you know, nothing happens here that Postmistress O'Boyle doesn't share with anyone who asks so she's going to Deirdre O'Flynn in Rushbrooke but there's not much to choose between her and the local one here. She told Bina O'Flynn that the solicitors replied to Mrs D there too, surely to avoid detection by her husband, and she seemed to be 'stitching him up like a kipper' according to Deirdre.

Things are bad between them, and before the truce, he was seen flirting or maybe more with a string of women. The local staff he employed were full of gossip, though he's let them all go except for this long string of misery Maguire, who is a butler or a valet or something. Before they were all fired, though, there were tales of violence and raised voices.

Harp paused to consider this. A part of her felt sorry for Pamela; she had probably fallen victim to his charm. That was the thing about Ralph – he could be lovely, if it suited him. Harp had never met Pamela Pascoe, now Devereaux, but Marianne spoke so lovingly about her that it was hard to imagine her as an evil accomplice to Ralph. Marianne's mother had a private fortune, so even though Alfie, Marianne's father, had shot himself once he'd lost his daughter's hand in marriage to the oily Oliver Beckett, she was still a wealthy woman. Harp hoped Deirdre was right and that she was successful in protecting her money from him.

Major Jeffers's wife mentioned to Cissy that she was concerned about Mrs D. Mrs D had bruises the last time she met her and seemed very upset. She's tried to call several times but was told by RD that Mrs D wasn't there. He was quite rude and more or less dismissed her from the door.

Apart from that, he doesn't venture out much any more. He's got bills unpaid all over the town, and no sign of payment. It's all very strange.

Anyway, our best regards to you all and we'll remember you in our prayers,

Liz and Cissy

Harp could see why her mother was worried. She would have to tell Marianne. Marianne had written several times to the Cliff House, but no reply ever came. And now with this information, well, something would have to be done.

Harp hated to bring such worrying news to her friend. Marianne had settled so well in Boston and was blissfully happy with Danny and little Katie. But she had spoken to Harp about the pain she felt at becoming a mother without the support of her own mother. Pamela too must be so worried about Marianne.

If Rose and Harp were out of contact, Rose would go out of her mind, Harp knew. At least she could tell Marianne that Rose would go up there and find out what was happening when she and Matt got back. It would gall Rose to see him in their house, but it was surely temporary. How would Ralph take their return? He'd probably sneer and slam the door in her face.

Harp knew she should probably care more, but she didn't. The memories she had, of her and Henry, her childhood with her mother, were all in her mind and in her heart. The house was a lovely place to grow up and she'd been very happy there, but it was her past and this was her future.

The return of Rose and Matt to Cobh would cause a stir, and married into the bargain. Rose had always been careful not to reveal the nature of her relationship with Matt while they were living in Ireland. It wasn't safe considering Matt's role within the IRA. Harp knew her mother would hate the gossip.

That's where she and Harp were different. Harp was an oddball and knew it, and she had long since stopped caring what other people thought of her.

The idea of that town made her weary. She would just stay in Boston and get on with her life here, forgetting about it all. They had achieved what they set out to do, and the British were at the table. They knew the war wasn't sustainable in the long term, and so they were willing to negotiate. Women were front and centre of the process, something that made her so proud, and now it was up to the politicians to hammer out a peace. She'd done her bit, she was proud of her contribution and that of her family, but it was time to live now.

She'd grown up under the shadow of the Great War. Harp was only fourteen when it broke out, while simultaneously the conflict in Ireland raged. She was part of a generation of young people, all over the world, ready and willing for peace and prosperity and a bit of fun. Surely that wasn't too much to ask?

CHAPTER 8

*C*obh, Ireland.

'Really?' Ralph sat back in the leather chair at his desk in the upstairs study of the Cliff House and considered the latest report from Maguire. 'And they are staying at his house?'

'Yes, sir, number six, in the crescent.'

'Interesting.' He dismissed the valet with a wave of his hand. He straightened his jotting pad and fountain pen and processed this latest news.

Maguire hovered at the door, though. He really was a dreary man with a slightly disturbing manner, but he suited Ralph's needs.

'Yes, was there something else?' Ralph asked.

'Well, it's the matter of the wages, sir. The maids you dismissed came up again yesterday looking for the money they're owed, and my own salary is also in arrears.'

Ralph gave him a cutting glare. 'It is in hand, as I already explained. I will have the matter attended to, as I have *already* stated. Please do not be so impertinent as to raise it again.'

Maguire, normally so obsequious, simply nodded and withdrew.

Ralph leaned back in his chair and placed his feet on the hand-carved walnut and mother-of-pearl desk, his fingers tapping his lips in deep contemplation.

When he'd bought it a few months ago, Pamela had the audacity to ask why he needed to spend any money on a desk when he did no work. But he taught her not to question him. She wouldn't be saying anything like that again in a hurry. It was humiliating that the accounts had been frozen, but he could still withdraw small amounts with her signature, so that was something. But still, it was beneath his dignity.

He was glad not to have to listen to her wittering on day and night about her slutty daughter. Marianne had been at it with God knew who, a taunt he liked to use on Pamela when she was eulogising Marianne, and there was no way Oliver Beckett was the father of her brat so she wasn't really deserving of the saintly status her mother had bestowed upon her.

At least according to Maguire, of that she-devil Harp there was no sign, but now it seemed the insipid Rose and her undertaker boyfriend were back and no doubt would have something to say about his installation in the Cliff House.

He sighed and leaned backwards, swivelling around to take in the view of the harbour, resting his head on the headrest of his expensive chair. This had once been his odd brother's library, but he'd removed all of the books – he'd burned most of them and sold any that had value – and redecorated the room so it was unrecognisable.

Trouble was on the horizon.

* * *

ROSE DRESSED CAREFULLY. Matt was waiting downstairs, and they were going to have dinner in the hotel. When she was a maid, it would never have occurred to her to go into the Queen's Hotel, but since she had been the proprietor of the Cliff House for many years, Mr Bridges, the hotel owner, was always courteous and welcoming. He never saw her as competition, but rather another string to the bow of this beautiful seaside town. Matt and she agreed that the best way to announce their return, and the fact that they were now married, was to be seen dining together publicly. Then all they would have to do was sit back and let the very enthusiastic Cobh rumour mill do what it did best.

She'd called to the Devlins earlier in the day, and they'd been delighted to see her and thrilled to hear they'd finally married. Liz needed a stick now to walk – they'd broken her leg when they interrogated her after the incident that had ended with Beckett's death – but she was a tough old bird and wore her injury like a badge of honour. Cissy had been arrested too and seemed less exuberant, less joyful than Rose remembered, and she wondered what they had done to the sweet old lady to quench her light so much.

They asked all about Harp and JohnJoe, Danny and Marianne, and Rose filled them in. They were both still active in Cumann na mBan and were watching the unfolding truce and negotiations with dubious interest.

Rose was surprised that they were not as enthusiastic about the truce as she thought they might be.

'Slippery, that Lloyd George – we know him of old – and Churchill with him. I wouldn't trust either of them as far as I'd throw them,' Liz muttered ominously as she sipped her tea. ''Twas Churchill sent the Tans to us.'

'If he hadn't, though, maybe we'd never have got up the courage to repel them the way we did? 'Twas the atrocities, day in and day out, of the Tans that made people realise that we couldn't take it any more. 'Twas hard, God knows, but I think it had to be that every family in the country was terrorised before we all finally reared up as united.'

'You're probably right, but a truce is a good thing, surely?' Rose asked.

Cissy sighed. 'It might be, but when have we ever known them to keep faith? For all we know, they might be using this time to rearm, to prepare for a desperate onslaught on us altogether. We can't trust them, Rose. We never could and we never will.'

Matt had met his former comrades in the Volunteers, and he was hearing the same thing. She hoped they were wrong. She wanted an end to it all, for once and for all, a negotiated settlement that gave Ireland the republic and the British gone for good. Was she naïve to think it could happen? The Devlins clearly thought so.

She sighed at the deepening lines on her face. She felt older than her thirty-nine years, and she was tired, so tired of war, of worrying, of the never ending nature of the Irish situation, she could weep at times. She'd taken to reading in the small hours of the morning when she couldn't sleep. The crossing had been miserable; she'd hardly kept water down and so was wan and exhausted.

She'd not seen Ralph yet, and it wasn't an encounter she was looking forward to. Matt's house had been well taken care of while they were gone – Rose suspected the hands of the Devlins once more – and it was clean and tidy and the lawns cut. A box of groceries was waiting for them too, so they'd had time to settle back without having to face the inevitable gossip and questions right away. Matt was anxious for her to direct him how to decorate or move whatever she wished. It was their home now, not just his, and she could do with it as she pleased. His house was a large terraced one in the crescent, a half-moon-shaped row of imposing residences so high up over the town of Cobh, they even looked down on the cathedral.

It was a very pleasant house, with large double bay windows to the front offering panoramic views of the harbour. There was a communal garden that was maintained for a fee by a committee, so gardening was optional, and the house was sparsely decorated and needed a woman's touch, she thought. But all in good time.

Once he was back at work and she had the house to herself, she'd get cracking. If she could turn the mausoleum that was the Cliff House into a bright, airy and clean guest house, she could easily make Matt's home more welcoming.

The Cliff House. Now that she was back, it loomed large. She'd arrived there as a skinny little fourteen-year-old kitchen maid, with no family behind her and no future except that of a skivvy. Her parents were poor and had been glad of the placement for one of their children at least. Theirs was a hard house in every way. Survival was all that mattered, and there was no room for kindness or laughter.

'When poverty comes in the door, love flies out the window,' was one of her mother's favourite sayings.

She'd gone back to her parents when she was pregnant, but they would have nothing to do with her then. So old Mrs Devereaux had taken her back, knowing the child to be Ralph's, on the promise that she never reveal the truth to anyone. Harp had been born in that house, with only the old housekeeper to help, and strict instructions she wasn't to make any noise.

In time old Mrs Devereaux died. Her husband had gone before her, leaving only Henry, Ralph's brother. His parents and brother thought him odd. But she thought of him as more unusual than peculiar.

He liked to read and was so knowledgeable and intelligent, but he was very shy and liked to remain separate from others. Also, and this was one of the reasons she liked him so much, he was so kind to Harp. As a little girl, Harp would climb on his lap and he would read to her. She never saw him as aloof or strange; to her, he was Mr Devereaux, and she loved him and he loved her. All through the years, the three of them had muddled along on very little money – there was only a tiny allowance from the elder Devereaux estate – but they managed, and she and Henry and Harp were a little family, untouched by the outside world.

But Henry died, and that all ended.

She pushed thoughts of Ralph Devereaux from her mind; she would need her wits about her tonight. People had been speculating since they disappeared what had become of them, and she and Matt turning up married would have all the tongues wagging. She was dreading the looks of surprise, the whispers, the obsequious enquiries.

Harp would tell her to ignore them, that small towns made small minds in some people and their fascination in the doings of others just highlighted the lack of any stimulation in their own.

Great minds discuss ideas, average minds discuss events, and small minds discuss people. She could hear Harp quoting Socrates and felt such a pang of loneliness for her daughter it was like a physical pain. Sailing away from the dock that day, watching Harp wave and smile up at them, JohnJoe beside her, made Rose wonder if they would ever live together again, ever share their lives the way they had done for so long. Harp was a young woman now with her own life and destiny to fulfil, and Rose was so proud of the person her daughter had become. But letting go was so hard. She also wished she could be sure Harp would not do anything rash, but she had no such certainty. The girl was a firebrand and did nothing that was expected of her.

'Rose!' Matt called up the stairs. 'Are you ready?'

'I'm coming,' she replied, gathering her bag.

It would be nice to have a meal in public with her handsome husband, she thought. He was so proud she was his wife now, and cared not a jot for the whispers and raised eyebrows, if anything it amused him. Matt Quinn was not a conventional man in any way.

He'd raised a child alone, taking care of all of Brian's needs when his wife died. He could cook and launder clothes and saw no reason that he shouldn't. He was quietly a feminist, she thought, and he frequently said that if more women were involved in politics, there would be more negotiation and less bloodshed.

SHE CHECKED her appearance once more in the mirror. Her dark hair had one or two greys now, which Matt said was in her imagination, but they were there. Wrinkles were forming beside her eyes and the lines from her nose to her mouth were deeper than before, but she was ageing and that was all there was to it. She was dressed in a maroon velvet skirt and a pink blouse with a velvet bow at the neck. Her hair was pinned back as always and she feared she looked very matronly, but it was too late to change now.

She came downstairs to see Matt ready and waiting in the hallway. He smiled as she came around the bend of the stairs. He was dressed in a dark suit he'd bought in Boston for Danny and Marianne's wedding, and it was cut in the American style. His hair was completely grey now and thinning a little, but to her he was handsome. His skin had taken the Boston sun well and was tanned, with a sprinkling of freckles across his cheeks. His slim but athletic physique had never changed, and she knew that he loved how he could make her body respond to his. For a deeply private man, he was surprisingly passionate.

'Oh, Rose, you look so beautiful,' he breathed as she descended.

'Indeed and I do not. I'm rapidly becoming an old matron with grey hair and crow's feet, but thank you for saying so anyway.' She laughed and kissed his cheek.

As she moved to the door, he took her hand and brought it to his lips. 'You are nothing of the kind, Mrs Quinn. You're a rare beauty, and everyone in this town knows it. For so long I admired you from afar, afraid to tell you how I felt, and then when I did manage to drum up the courage, and miraculously you let me love you, I was so deep in the Volunteers that I couldn't let your name be up with mine. So tonight, walking into that hotel with you beside me as my wife' – he seemed choked – 'it's something I've waited many years to do, and there isn't a prouder or a happier man on earth.'

Sincerity oozed from every word, and Rose felt fortified by his love. If she had Matt by her side, she could cope with anything.

As they walked down the Smuggler's Stairs from the crescent to the town, they passed the gate to the Cliff House. The garden wasn't as well kept as it was under Rose's tender care, but other than that, nothing appeared to have changed. The Devlins said Ralph had redecorated and had offered for sale some of their possessions. The harp that had been in the Devereaux family for generations and that Henry had so loved to hear her daughter play, the gramophone that was Henry's pride and joy, some of the more valuable books had all been auctioned. The idea of him touching their things, returning the house to the dark dreary place it was before Harp and Rose transformed it to a bright pastel-coloured home, made the bile rise in her throat, but she said nothing.

Matt stopped at the turn of the steps before they opened onto the main street and placed his hands on her shoulders, his eyes locked with hers. 'I know how much that place means to you, and to Harp, and we will find a way to sort this out somehow. I promise.'

Rose nodded. 'I don't suppose we know someone who could deal with him, do we? Or maybe I should go up there myself when I'm in one of my moods – that wouldn't be long putting a finish to him.' She half-smiled.

Matt answered with a grin of his own. 'Believe me, darling, you in full flight of temper is one of the most terrifying things I've ever witnessed, and I've been fighting the Black and Tans for two years. Now if it was simply a matter of arranging a bullet, I would do it in a heart-beat. That fella would be no loss to the world and that's the truth. But the organisation quite rightly doesn't get involved in personal disputes, and besides, things are at a very delicate phase of negotiations – we don't want to give the other side anything to say. The truce has to hold if we're to have any hope of peace, so one of ours bumping off a seem-ingly innocent loyal British subject would never get the green light.'

'Innocent, my eye! But I know what you mean. Not to mention the whole place would know who was behind it.' Rose sighed ruefully. 'Everyone knows the bad blood between us and Ralph.'

'Life will become very unpleasant very quickly for him and his kind. Don't you worry about that.'

'I'm not, it's just that...'

'What?'

They continued walking, Rose speaking quietly. 'But the thing is, now we're back he'd love to drag my name through the mud. Bad enough everyone thinking I was involved with Henry out of wedlock – they must think that, otherwise we would have had no claim to the house – but if it got out that I was also with Ralph...and now you, I couldn't bear it...' Rose's voice broke with the emotion of it all.

'Ah, Rosie.' Matt squeezed her arm to his, his free hand covering hers reassuringly. 'Don't get upset now. It's all in the past. We know the truth, as does Harp, and that's all that matters. You're my wife, and I'm so proud of you, I feel like my heart will burst out of my chest. So let him say what he likes – nobody listens to him anyway. Today's gossip wraps tomorrow's chips. Now put that beautiful smile on your face and let's have a nice dinner in our own town, as free people.'

He nodded at a couple of girls who walked past them wide-eyed. Rose thought one of them was one of the O'Learys; her mother used to do the laundry at the Cliff House. She'd be dying to get home to her mother with the story that they were back.

Mr Bridges was at the door to greet them, and he pumped Matt's hand enthusiastically and kissed Rose's cheek in welcome. 'Mr and Mrs Quinn, can I be one of the first to offer you my most sincere congratulations, and wish you both all the luck in the world. And I insist tonight's dinner is on me. It is wonderful to see you both home and looking so well. We all missed you.'

'Thank you very much, Mr Bridges, that's very kind of you,' Matt replied, making no reference to their disappearance and sudden reappearance.

Rose suppressed a smile. The hotel owner was making out like they had been on a jolly holiday rather than on the run, doing a moonlight flit without a word to anyone. Despite his connections to the British, not least the fact that his wife was the sister-in-law of the second-last brigadier general, Mr Bridges had, throughout the war, tacitly supported the IRA, passing information and allowing Matt to install a waitress in the bar who was his eyes and ears. So much of the intelligence that had the British on the back foot militarily had come from her, when tongues were loosened by alcohol.

'Thank you, Mr Bridges, it's lovely to be home,' Rose replied warmly as they were led to a table.

The dining room was half-full, mostly people Rose recognised, the gentry types, loyal British subjects, some of whom must have felt very vulnerable now that their protectors were absent. Some of the local Protestant families were good to their staff and workers; more weren't. She nodded hello to Major and Mrs Jeffers, who smiled and waved. Major Jeffers was well known for providing alibis for his farmhands who might have been on manoeuvrers with the Volunteers, lying straight into the faces of the officers who came looking for them. He and his wife ensured that no family on their estate ever went hungry either. All the way back to the famine, the Jefferses had seen those who worked for them as their responsibility and were known all over the county as fair and decent people. They had nothing to fear in a new, free Ireland. It was Mrs Jeffers who raised her concerns about Pamela with the Devlins.

On the other hand, the Yorks, who were dining with Mrs York's sister and her husband on the other side of the dining room, should be nervous, Rose thought. Ernest York had been warned, more than once, that if he were to inform on his staff to the Crown authorities, or try to take advantage of the young girls working in the house, the consequences would be dire. He ignored it and still walked with a limp after the beating he got from young Nellie Keane's brothers when she arrived home from work having been sexually assaulted by the master. It had done the trick, though, and when the Royal Irish Constabulary came to investigate, he claimed he remembered nothing of his assailants.

Some of the Anglo-Irish families felt more Irish than English, despite being culturally if not geographically British, and they championed the cause of Irish freedom. Others, like Ralph Devereaux, saw themselves as superior to those they controlled in every way. It was, like everything else on that beautiful green island, very complicated and filled with nuance and subtlety.

'Remember how we had to put the Americans right so often when they assumed that all the gentry were as bad as the British?' Matt murmured as he unfolded his linen napkin.

'I do. They see it as very black and white, but the reality is more shades of grey.' She smiled as she accepted the menu from a waiter.

They perused the offerings. 'I'll have the lamb, please,' Rose said confidently. She'd eaten in restaurants so often in Boston with the Raffertys that it no longer intimidated her.

'And I'll have the salmon, thank you.' Matt returned the menu.

Immediately the sommelier arrived at the waiter's side with a bottle of champagne in a bucket of ice.

'Mr Bridges sent this with his compliments,' the older man intoned, his face a mask of seriousness.

'Oh, thank him, that's very kind, but we couldn't...' Rose began.

Matt placed his hand on hers. 'Thank you, we'd love a glass.'

Rose was surprised. Matt normally would never overrule her like that; he was an egalitarian and didn't see his wife in any way as subservient to him.

He gave her the most imperceptible of winks as both men withdrew from the table. 'Bridges and I had a bet. He told me last year that while he hoped and prayed we could do it, get rid of them, I mean, he didn't think it would happen. So I said it would, and we made a bargain – he would stand me a bottle of his finest champagne if we won, and I'd make him the best gun cabinet in the county if we didn't. So this is an unpaid wager.' He poured her a flute of champagne and handed it to her.

Rose shook her head and smiled, raising the sparkling wine to her lips. 'To the Republic,' she said quietly.

'To the Republic.' He touched his glass to hers.

They enjoyed their meal and were finishing off with coffee when Mr Bridges appeared again. They were the last in the restaurant.

'I'm so sorry, Mr Bridges.' Rose was flustered, realising they were holding up closing time.

'Not at all, Mrs Quinn. I was hoping to speak to you both, actually, but it would be best if we weren't overheard. May I?' He gestured to a chair at a neighbouring table.

'Please, join us,' Matt said. 'And also please share in a glass of champagne. Rose is not a one for hard drink, and I won't finish this alone. It is a shame to waste it.' Matt smiled.

'Well, it is a debt unpaid, and one I am more than happy to pay, so thank you, I will.' He took a glass from another table and allowed Matt to pour him one.

'I'm so happy for you both. Having you back and in such fine form is really wonderful. We had such good days, me in this place, you running the Cliff House, and everything was fine. It feels like a lifetime ago, doesn't it?'

'It does,' Rose agreed.

They chatted for a few minutes about Harp and JohnJoe and their experiences in Boston, but Rose got the impression it was more than just a friendly interaction between friends parted for a time. Bridges had something on his mind, but she could see he was weighing up how to say it.

'Is there something in particular you wanted to talk to us about?' she asked.

He smiled slowly. 'There is, but I don't quite know how to say it.'

'Just spit it out, as the Americans say.' Matt grinned. The two men were unlikely but genuine friends.

'Well, it's just that I have some concerns about what's going on in the Cliff House. Ralph hasn't been out for weeks. He says Mrs Devereaux has returned to India, and she may well have. It was not a happy marriage, and she confided in several people that she was miserable with him and that he was...well...unreasonable. He may have been violent towards her.'

Rose said nothing for a moment, and Matt glanced at her. Then she spoke. 'Mr Bridges, I have no doubt whatsoever that Ralph Devereaux is an unreasonable man and that Pamela was unhappy. Marianne, her daughter, is, as you probably guessed, in America with Danny Coveney. They are married now and have a baby girl.'

She knew the Devlins would not have gossiped, but Bridges had probably put two and two together. Marianne and Danny were not that discreet in their affair, so when they all disappeared in one go, it must have been the conclusion everyone came to.

'I'm happy for her. She needs someone young and decent, and I always liked Danny – he was a breath of fresh air. Please give them my best wishes.'

'I will. But as I was saying, Marianne is very worried. She's written to her mother several times, both here and in India, and has heard nothing.'

'I can't help, I'm afraid. I just have an uneasy feeling about the whole thing, and I felt you should know.'

'I do too,' Rose said. 'I promised Marianne I would try to find out what's going on, but that might be easier said than done.'

Mr Bridges drained his glass and stood. 'Tread very carefully there,

Mrs Quinn. Very carefully indeed. Ralph Devereaux may be Henry's brother, but there the similarity ends. He is, I believe, a very dangerous individual, and as the situation here makes life more and more untenable for people like him, they will become more treacherous. So as I say, be warned.'

'Thank you, Mr Bridges, I will,' Rose answered sincerely.

CHAPTER 9

'So we're really off to New York?' JohnJoe grinned, looking around the table at Harp, Elliot and Jerry. The four friends had arranged to meet in a café downtown on a sunny Saturday afternoon to discuss their plans. 'We're really doing this?'

Jerry nodded, stirring sugar into his coffee. 'I think we should give it our best shot. I've been doing some research, and that Peregrine Rothstein of the Adelphi is the real deal. He's got a revue going there, all sorts of acts, and it's full most nights. He said most of the acts are not exclusive to any one theatre. It's just a case of getting your name out there and then you take whatever bookings you want. He seemed to think we'd be in demand. And he's just one of many who run vaudeville shows. They're very popular with families and so on, and especially at the seaside places in the summer – Coney Island, the Jersey Shore, even Atlantic City.'

'So what do we have to do next?' Harp was excited and fascinated. Her mother and Matt had left for Ireland, and while Rose was nervous and sad at the prospect of leaving Harp behind in America, she had respected her daughter's wish to stay. As much as Harp missed her mother, she liked the feeling of freedom, but leaving Boston and the safety of the Raffertys was a daunting thought.

'You three need to get a repertoire together. I was thinking a kind of a mixture, some Irish, some light classical, some popular tunes from shows maybe? We've got the violin, harp and vocals, but it's a pity we don't have a piano player. Maybe I'll see if I can find someone.' Jerry took a bite out of his chicken sandwich.

'I can manage a few chords,' JohnJoe offered cheerfully. 'Just so long as you're not looking for a maestro.'

'I never knew that!' Harp turned to him.

'Aunt Kathy thought it might culture me when I got here as a kid,' he explained. 'I only wanted to draw and paint and had no interest in school, but I went to Mrs Kawowski three blocks away every Wednesday afternoon for years, and she used to rap my knuckles because I never could learn to read music – I'd just sit there banging out all the popular tunes of the day by ear.'

Jerry was beaming. 'That's fantastic! Perfect! Just swell!'

Harp smiled at Jerry's use of the superlatives commonly used in America. He even had a slight American accent now. 'I suppose the most important thing is to have a show that people will want to hear. How many songs do we need, do you think?'

Jerry considered the question. 'Well, Rothstein said the show lasts for two hours and that there are six acts, so three an hour… So twenty minutes worth of songs?'

Harp nodded. 'Five or six pieces? We can easily do that. And what about somewhere to live while we're in New York?'

'Rothstein says he can help us get a place. Freeport, New York, is a kind of a colony of performers. He says if we want to come, he can get an apartment for us four. I told him we'd be there within the month.'

'Within a month? Hold on, what about Harp? Three guys living together is fine, but how do you feel about it, Harp? Would you be worried about your reputation?' JohnJoe asked, clearly concerned. He'd sworn to Rose he'd take care of Harp and wanted to keep his promise. He and Harp were more intimate than was correct for a young unmarried couple, but that was at her insistence; he'd marry her in the morning if she'd only agree. The other guys on the building site moaned how their girls would barely allow them to hold their hands until they had a ring on their finger, but just like in everything else, his Harp wasn't like other girls.

Harp took his hand. 'You remember what I was saying before our night in the speakeasy ended, well, kind of abruptly?' She chuckled at the memory. 'Well, I was talking to Celia this morning, and if you three are in favour, she'll take a month off from her job at the wholesaler's, so I don't need to ruin my precious reputation by being the only girl in an apartment with three young men. Plus she'll do all our bookkeeping and she's handy with a needle and thread, which is perfect considering we'll need costumes and such.'

She looked around the table for the men's reaction. It would be awful if any of them were against the idea just because Celia had different coloured skin from theirs.

JohnJoe was the first to speak. 'I'm all in favour. Celia's a nice girl and sensible too, and it sounds like she'll be a great help.'

'I'm definitely in favour. I hate selling clothes.' Elliot sighed. 'The old bat who owns the shop I work in treats me like dirt, yelling and complaining all the time, promising the old crones that she can make them look like Gloria Swanson with enough tulle and lace, and then when they end up like a dog's dinner, expecting me to deal with them.'

'And I'm not the best with balance sheets,' admitted Jerry. 'I'm good at making deals, but I hate all that fiddly adding up columns and stuff.'

Harp was relieved and delighted. 'Right! Let's go to New York City and see what the future holds for us. And, Jerry, you tell Rothstein we need an apartment for five. Ask him to arrange a short let in case it all falls flat.'

Jerry shook his head. 'No, no short lets, Harp. Not for me, anyway. This is my new life. I'm taking the risk and giving my notice. I want to give Pat time to find a replacement. He's been good to me, so I'd hate to let him down.'

'I'm all in too,' Elliot said instantly.

Jerry smiled at him warmly. 'Good for you. How much notice do you need to give?'

Elliot made a face. 'Oh, knowing Madame *Bouchet*, as she calls herself – her real name is Aggie Scragg, but I guess that handle wouldn't sell too many frocks –' – he laughed, an infectious giggle that made everyone smile – 'I should probably give her a year's notice, but she is such a pain in the backside that I'm happy to just never show up again. I'm so tired of her. She pretends she's French, but she's from a tenement down the South End and her accent slips more often than her garters, so she's fooling nobody.'

Harp looked nervously at JohnJoe. Her heart was fluttering with excitement and anxiety. 'What about us, JohnJoe? Do you think we should tell Uncle Pat and Aunt Kathy that we're not just going to New York for a while but that we might not be back?'

'What, tell Pat he's losing one of his best carpenters and also me and you in one fell swoop? He's going to love that.' JohnJoe looked sheepish. 'And your mother will go nuts if she thinks you've left Pat and Kathy's house for good, you know she will. She'll have my guts for garters.'

Harp squeezed his hand. She knew he only wanted the best for her. 'It might not be as bad as you think, JohnJoe. Pat is a risk-taker – he wouldn't be where he is today if he wasn't – so he'll understand. His father wanted him to stay and farm the land in West Clare, but he took a chance and came here instead, and look how it all turned out. He might go mad at first, but he'll understand that we need to live our own lives, just like he did. And my mother will know you are taking care of me. She loves you and we'll be careful. I think we should just do it, make the move – go all in. What's the point of living in a free country if you stop yourself from doing things just because other people might not approve? We can do this. We survived the Black and Tans, so surely we're brave enough for anything.'

'I don't think anyone would call you anything but brave, Harp.' Jerry smiled. 'They wouldn't dare. You're wonderful but terrifying. Was she always like this, JJ?'

'She was always unusual, and she always knew her own mind,' JohnJoe said sincerely.

Harp pealed with laughter. 'He has a much more romantic idea of me than the reality. It might seem hard to believe, but I was a real little mouse as a child, no friends, a total oddball. I was a tiny scrap of a thing, with wild hair and strange grey eyes. I was bullied and called all sorts of names, but my father always believed in me. He said I would live an exciting life, far from the confines of Queenstown, County Cork, and it finally feels like he was right.'

JohnJoe smiled adoringly at her. 'You were lovely then and you're beautiful now.'

Harp blushed. She'd always seen herself as the peculiar little child, too thin and small, never saying the right thing.

'He's right,' Elliot said sincerely. 'You're beautiful, Harp, and audiences will love you. All eyes will be on you and not our ugly mugs.'

'You'd better stop now, or I'll get such a swelled head there'll be no dealing with me.' She laughed but enjoyed the warm glow of their affection.

'Are we still going to call ourselves Harp and Her Boys?' Elliot asked. 'I know that was spur-of-the-moment on Jerry's part, but it's kind of nice…'

Without a second's hesitation, Harp replied, 'No, not Harp and Her Boys. That sounds like I'm the ringmaster and you two are the performing seals. I know he was on the spot, but no, that's not the right name for us. We should call ourselves Roaring Liberty.' She'd thought up the name last night.

'I like it. I read something the other day saying this was the Jazz Age, and the author called it the roaring twenties, the Statue of Liberty – it's good.' Jerry nodded.

'And liberty for Ireland,' JohnJoe added quietly.

'Exactly,' Harp said, leaning against him.

'Roaring Liberty it is.' Elliot grinned and raised his coffee cup in a toast. They clinked their cups off his. 'To Roaring Liberty!' they chorused.

Harp drained her coffee and set the cup in her saucer. 'Right. How about we all meet at the house at seven this evening for our first practice? We can use the piano in the music room and my harp is there. Pat and Kathy are out tonight, so we can break the news when they get home, JohnJoe.'

'Talking of your harp, we'll need transport too. The harp alone is going to be an awkward thing to move around. Most places will have a piano, you'd imagine, but not a harp.' Jerry was thinking out loud.

'Maybe Celia can help us with that as well,' suggested Harp. 'She's bought herself a Ford Runabout, would you believe? She loves it, spinning about and causing everyone to look. She drove all the way to Washington to a rally to have coloured women admitted to the organisations that are driving forward with voting rights in the wake of the ratification of the 19th amendment. You'd think that women would stick together, wouldn't you, but she was telling me how some of the suffragists are as bad as the anti-abolitionists were when it comes to coloured women like Celia.'

'Well, we know better than most what people are capable of,' JohnJoe said sadly. 'But it's disappointing in a country so new and full of opportunity that people still cling to old outdated ideas of superiority.'

Jerry nodded. 'Being treated as second-class citizens in your own country is something no Irishman or woman is a stranger to, that's for sure. We live in such a divided world, where people aren't free just to be who they are without someone saying they're wrong. Tell your friend I wish her well in her quest and to never give up. We had all the odds stacked against us in Ireland, the mighty British Empire and all the rest of it, but we stuck to it and didn't back down, and it looks like we finally have the freedom we fought so hard for. Hopefully coloured people will one day enjoy the same.'

'I'll tell her you said that, Jerry.' Harp liked him even more. 'And I'll ask her to join us at the Raffertys' this evening.'

Jerry got to his feet. 'And I told Rothstein I'd speak to you all and call him back to let him know our plans, so I'll do that now – I'll use the telephone in the post office – and let you know what he says when we meet later.'

* * *

PAT AND KATHY were out that night at an Ancient Order of Hibernians function, so the five of them had the house to themselves.

Celia arrived as they were getting started, and she and Jerry formed the audience, sitting on chairs in the music room. Harp saw her friend was nervous at first – she was never sure how she would be received and was once a maid in this house – but the boys instantly put her at ease, and she and Jerry were soon in deep conversation about sets and costumes and various logistics. Harp, JohnJoe and Elliot easily put a set list together, and JohnJoe proved to be a much more proficient pianist than he'd let on, able to pick up a tune with very little effort.

Harp and JohnJoe, accompanied by Elliot on violin, did a romantic duet of 'If You Were the Only Girl in the World', which had Jerry and Celia whooping with delight. And Harp tried the solo of 'A Good Man Is Hard to Find' to the applause of everyone. She really enjoyed it and vamped up the theatrics.

They rehearsed 'The West's Awake', the song Harp and JohnJoe had performed for the famous Chief O'Neill in 1916, and 'I Dreamt I Dwelt in Marble Halls', which was the very first song they'd sung together when they were just twelve and fourteen years old. These were followed by 'The Last Rose of Summer', and as a finale they chose 'My Irish Molly-O', which would hopefully have the audience tapping their feet in time with the rousing chorus. Harp thought for a first rehearsal it wasn't bad at all. She and JohnJoe were very used to performing together, and Elliot played along seamlessly without any need for sheet music. He really was a gifted violinist.

Once they were happy with their set, JohnJoe called Clayton for some drinks. The old butler brought the boys beers and seltzer water with orange slices for Harp and Celia. If he had any objection to serving his former subordinate, he gave no indication of it, and Celia thanked him warmly. The Raffertys knew the girls were friendly, so Harp felt no trepidation at them finding her there, but telling them of their plans filled her with fear.

Despite Prohibition, there was a never-ending flow of alcohol in the Rafferty house. Pat only drank Irish whiskey, but Kathy enjoyed sherry and wine. Harp had an odd glass of alcohol to demonstrate her independence, but she wasn't too enamoured with the taste or the sensation.

The whole Prohibition thing was madness and everyone knew it. Sales of home brew kits were through the roof, with some companies cheekily writing step-by-step instructions on the bag in reverse, saying, 'Do not add grapes. Do not steep for five hours. Do not agitate to release sugars.' And so on. Since transportation and sale of alcohol were forbidden but there was no rule about producing it, every corner store sold gallon stills, malt syrup, corn sugar, hops, yeast and bottle cappers.

'So tell us more about the conversation you had with Mr Rothstein,' Harp said to Jerry as they settled with their drinks in the sitting room. She and JohnJoe had taken one sofa beside the large marble fireplace, and Elliot, Jerry and Celia sat on the other. The fireplace was prettily filled with yellow and orange dried chrysanthemums because the evenings were too warm for a fire; the shockingly harsh Boston winter was still a few months away. Harp had never experienced cold like it the first winter she spent there. Ireland was much more temperate, and while the summers in Ireland didn't get as hot, neither did the winters chill one to the bone.

Harp felt at home in this house now, but she recalled vividly her wide-eyed wonder when she first visited in 1916. This room had seemed beautiful but so austere and nothing like the home she'd grown up in. Kathy had a penchant for modern art and loved clean lines and white open space. The sofas were white and the floor polished oak, covered with a cream and gold rug. The fireplace was also white, and the clock she recalled from her first visit, an awful green thing, was still there. The entire house was decorated starkly, its spare design punctuated here and there with a startling painting or a sculpture that made you stop and look, even if you didn't like it. It had become home to Harp, and it was a house filled with love and laughter, so much so that the atmosphere created by the inhabitants belied the interior decoration.

Jerry swallowed a mouthful of beer. 'Well, he was delighted to hear that we were coming and said he thought he had just the place for us to live in Freeport. Lots of theatre types live there, it seems.'

Harp laughed excitedly. 'So we're theatre types now, are we?'

'Sure feels that way.' Elliot grinned.

Jerry smiled at his friend. 'Rothstein's going to check it out this week and let us know. One of his other acts is touring Europe, so they're moving out. It might be a hovel – who knows. I was thinking I might go there a few days ahead of you to check it out, make sure it's not rat-infested. And if it is, I can set about finding someplace else before you four get there. If I'm to be your manager, I might as well start earning my keep.'

'I'll go with you,' Elliot offered quickly. 'I'm ditching Madame Bouchet and her uppity ways as fast as I can.'

'Great, I'd enjoy the company. So Rothstein and I settled that we'd do our first show on the 19th of September, just four weeks from now. We'll have a five-week run there, one show a day, seven days a week. He runs two vaudeville shows a day, an afternoon matinee and one in the evening, which pays a little more. And he's in partnership with a man called Moses Schultz, so they might arrange for the entire thing to go on tour.'

'And which show will we be doing?' Harp asked. 'The matinee or the evening?'

'The matinee,' said Celia, with a firm look at Jerry.

Harp glanced at her friend in surprise, then back at Jerry. 'What would we earn for the matinee?'

'According to Rothstein, an individual act would get paid around one to two hundred dollars a week. It's the same for a group, so we'd need to ensure we were getting the upper end of it considering there are five of us to be paid.'

'Oh, am I getting paid?' asked Celia. She sounded surprised and pleased. 'I thought I was just along for a little vacation.'

'Of course you are!' said Harp. 'We're not expecting you to do this as a favour, and if all goes well, we're hoping you'll leave the wholesaler's and stay with us permanently. If we make one hundred a week and we split the money five ways, that's twenty dollars each.'

'I get thirty dollars a week in the clothes shop, but I hate that so I'm better off this way.' Elliot smiled. 'And maybe we'll make two hundred, which means forty each.'

Jerry looked worried. 'Well, hold on – that's if I can negotiate the highest price. Rothstein said he'd pay it to us in New York, but in the other places, I'll have to fight for it. And I'll need to take our expenses out of the pot before we divide it up.'

'Well, we haven't a clue about any of that and you're a tough negotiator, I've seen you in the lumber yard,' JohnJoe joked. He turned to Harp. 'Uncle Pat says he's the only one we're to send for supplies – he haggles down to the last cent.'

'I don't know if it's right to divide the money equally. I mean, the musicians are the most important people,' said Celia anxiously.

'And as your agent, I'm supposed to only get ten to fifteen percent of the fee,' Jerry said. 'For that I arrange your performances, accommodations, food, props, costumes and stuff like that and negotiate with the theatres on your behalf. Rothstein and Schultz make the original bookings, but it's up to me to make sure you get paid and get properly advertised and so on. Rothstein was most adamant on that. He seems like a sharp guy but decent, and he warned that there are any number of people on the take in this business and I need to have my eyes wide open.'

'Well, you can't do all that work for only ten or twenty dollars a week, Jerry,' said JohnJoe. 'And you too, Celia – you must be earning more where you are now. I say Harp's right – we split everything equally. I'm sure we'll all be working equally hard.'

'And why don't we do two shows a day, the matinee and the night show, then that would be more than double surely?' Harp suggested.

Again, Celia looked at Jerry. Jerry flushed, and Harp wondered what was making him so uncomfortable. 'Well, the matinee, it's a decent family show. There will be illusionists and acrobats and various performers, singers and dancers and musicians. There's even a performing dog act that's very popular apparently. And Rothstein was so impressed with you three, he said he'd put us as the finale, which is great.'

'And the night show, the one that pays better?'

'Well, it's more of a show for men,' Jerry explained, 'and well, women who don't worry too much about their reputation, if you know what I mean, Harp. I think, you know, dancing girls, the bar is open, and it's... Well, put it this way – your mother would have a stroke if she thought you were performing there. Certain words are used there that are banned in the daytime shows.'

'Like what?' Harp asked.

'Hell, slob, son of a gun, things like that,' JohnJoe muttered.

'Oh, very risqué.' Harp winked then raised an eyebrow. 'And you know this how, Mr O'Dwyer?'

Harp never called him Rafferty as everyone else did, always using his birth name instead. He had been called JJ Rafferty since his first day in Boston. He never explained to anyone that it wasn't in fact his name, and so it just stuck. Rafferty was his mother's name – she was Pat's sister – so he didn't mind. Harp had asked him once if he'd rather change it permanently, but he said no, that he was born JohnJoe O'Dwyer and that was who he was. He liked that Harp remembered and that she was one of the few people in Boston who called him by the name he'd been given.

JohnJoe blushed. ''Cause I went to one in Atlantic City a few years back. Danny and me and a crew were working down there on a job, and they wanted to go so they let me tag along.'

Harp found she was enjoying his discomfort. 'And what did you see there?'

JohnJoe grinned sheepishly. 'Well, I saw more skin and antics than I'd ever seen before, that's for sure. I went in there as an innocent boy and came out, well, if not a man exactly, certainly a boy that had had his eyes opened for him.'

'Oh really? Sounds intriguing.' Harp chuckled. 'All right then, tell me the fee difference? I mean, if we have to keep ourselves in New York City and this Mr Rothstein is willing to pay us to do both, let's do the maths.' She smiled wickedly.

'I don't know, Harp,' JohnJoe said doubtfully. 'It's very racy, to be honest, and the women who perform are expected, I think, to...'

'What?' Harp asked indignantly. She and JohnJoe were equals, always, and she wasn't used to him trying to stop her doing things. She hated the way the other girlfriends of his friends simpered and bowed to their boyfriends' ideas. She wasn't like that and JohnJoe loved her for it.

He blushed. 'Have men look at them…'

'Oh, for goodness' sake, they can look all they like, the stupid eejits. What's that to you or me or any of us here? I know my mother will hate the idea of me being ogled by men, so let's not mention that bit. I'll write every week telling her of the matinee shows and the families coming, and she'll be fine. Please everyone, let's give this our very best effort and take all the shows we can. That way at least, if it fails, we can say we really tried.'

The three boys glanced at each other but said nothing, and Harp felt she had won.

But then Celia stood up, with her hands on her hips. 'Now you listen to me, Harp Devereaux. You may be a genius with the books and able to talk rings around anyone else in this room and silence them all, and God knows you're brave as a lion and stubborn as a mule, but you don't know nothing about real life, so you listen to me. When JohnJoe says "look" he don't mean nothing but "touch", and even if they don't get to do too much touchin', well, they'll tell everyone that they did and more, and once your reputation is gone, Harp, you ain't never getting it back. There's no respectable establishment that will have you once they think you're one of those girls, and there'll be no matinees and no recordings and no fancy career. Right now, I think you three are good enough for the mainstream. But if you take one single step into the gutter, Harp… Well, once a girl's in the gutter, that's where she gets left. The boys here don't know how hard it is out there for a woman, and they might give in to your head-strong ways. But I do know, and I ain't standing by and letting you do this just because you're too naïve to understand how dark and low this world can get.'

After Celia had finished speaking, there was a long silence in the room. The boys sat, looking at the floor, and Harp had tears in her eyes. The Raffertys' former maid glanced from one to the other of them, then dropped her gaze and picked up her bag. 'Maybe it wasn't my place to speak that way to you in this house, Harp. I'm very sorry for it and I'll say goodnight.'

But before she reached the door, Harp ran to put her arms around her and hugged her tight. 'Celia, don't go. This is exactly the reason I need you beside me. You're right, I don't know what I'm doing, but if you keep teaching me, I promise you I'll listen and try my best to learn.'

CHAPTER 10

*L*ater that evening, Kathy's face was hard to read but Pat's wasn't. Elliot and Jerry had left a few minutes before the Raffertys arrived home, and while neither JohnJoe nor Harp was looking forward to it, they decided it was best to have the conversation and get it over with.

Kathy and Pat had been at a formal dinner, and Kathy was dressed beautifully in a silver sheath dress and wearing a diamond necklace and earrings. Her copper hair was cut in her signature bob. She looked like a movie star, Harp always thought. She was fifty-one years old but looked a decade younger. Pat on the other hand could be no other nationality but Irish. He was big and brawny but without an ounce of spare fat on him, with a broad, open face and the pale skin of his country people despite years in the Boston climate. He had dark-red hair that was going a little grey now and amber eyes. Kathy had gentrified him from the rough, tough immigrant he once was, but one knew at a glance that no matter how fine his suit or fancy his hand-made shoes, Pat Rafferty was not a man to be trifled with. He'd dragged himself up by his bootstraps, arriving in Boston thirty years earlier with not a penny to his name, and he'd clawed his way to the top. It wasn't always pretty, as he was fond of saying, but it happened.

'Are you two completely crazy?' he asked.

'No. It's an opportunity we may not get again, and we want to take it,' JohnJoe answered calmly.

Pat Rafferty was quick to anger but also quick to forgive. He'd rant and rave for a bit, but it would be all right, they knew.

'And what are you two lovebirds gonna live on? Have you thought of that?' he asked.

'We'll be paid for performing. We already have one theatre booked, and we have a manager who'll work tirelessly to get us new places to play...' Harp explained.

'And who is this shyster manager? Some New York sleazeball making all the promises, I suppose?' Pat wasn't ready yet to be calm on the subject. 'You two think you're so worldly, but you're green as grass, the pair of you, and if you think for one second I'm gonna let some jerk come in here and take advantage of my –'

'It's not a stranger, it's Jerry Gallagher actually.' Harp was indignant. She liked Pat, but she resented being spoken to like she was a foolish child. 'He's learned a lot about the music industry and –'

'Jerry Gallagher, my carpenter?' Pat was really raging now. He ignored Harp and turned to his nephew. 'You talked him into this stupid scheme too? Oh no, I need him, and he has no business upping and leaving me in the lurch with all the work we've got on! And I need you, JJ. This is a cute idea, and I get it. Girls like that sorta thing, stages and fancy dresses and all, and I'm not saying you two aren't talented – you are, I always said that – but your place, JJ, is here with Danny, as my eyes and ears. You'll inherit it eventually anyway, so you're just taking care of your own business. And Gallagher is as good a woodworker as I've seen, so no. I'm sorry, but no, that's just not gonna fly at all.'

Harp knew she should hold her tongue – after all, the Raffertys had been so good to them – but how dare Pat talk about her like that, as if the lure of a stage and a frilly dress was all it would take to send her off half-cocked. She and JohnJoe had their own lives to live. If she wanted to be dictated to about how she should spend her days, she would have stayed in Ireland, where everyone and their mother felt they had a right to an opinion on how a person lived.

'We're not asking your permission,' she said quietly. Her eyes flashed with rage.

JohnJoe shot her a warning glance. He wasn't afraid of his uncle, but there was a way to handle him and this wasn't it. But she couldn't stop herself.

Pat turned, his face pale with fury now. He'd been a benevolent presence in her life since she was sixteen years old. She trusted him and loved him, but she would not be spoken to like that by anyone. She'd put up with too much as a child and later as a young woman – the bullies, the gossips, the British – and no more would she tolerate it.

'Oh, is that right, Miss Devereaux? You're gonna just take my boy here and my best carpenter and sail off to New York City? You got it all figured out, huh?'

'Yes, we do actually. JohnJoe, Elliot and I are quite good, and we might be able to make it. Jerry will manage us and Celia will –'

'Celia? The maid Celia?' Pat asked incredulously.

'Celia *Williams*, my friend, yes,' Harp said pointedly, giving Celia's last name, something she doubted Pat ever knew.

'Ah well, this just puts the tin hat on this stupid scheme. JJ, come on, you know this is crazy, right? I mean, she's a fine girl and all of that, but are you seriously telling me you are gonna walk off into the sunset to make your fortune on the stage with my best carpenter and a coloured girl in tow?'

'Uncle Pat, that's not fair. Celia and Harp are friends, and she'd be a –'

Pat cut across his nephew. 'Stop this right now. You know as well as I do what way that's gonna go. She's a coloured girl, and nice, as I said, but we know the best way for this country to function is everyone stays in their own lane. You may not like that, Harp, with all your highfalutin ideas – God knows we have to listen often enough to your thoughts on how women are treated and all the rest of it – but take it from someone older and wiser and with a hell of a lot more

88

experience than you, that is how it is and you are not gonna change anyone's mind on that score. No good comes of mixing races, and that's that.'

Harp fumed. How dare he speak to her like that? He was a good, kind man, but he was also sexist and a misogynist and this was born out of ignorance. He wasn't educated; he wasn't widely read. He had experience, of course, in a certain place and of a certain business, but that was not truly experienced. Yet he felt he could dismiss her out of hand. She allowed the words to flow like lava and felt powerless to stop them. "'Prejudices, it is well known, are most difficult to eradicate from the heart whose soil has never been loosened or fertilised by education: they grow there, firm as weeds among stones.'"

Pat stared at her, a pulse throbbing in his temple, but she didn't stop. 'Do you know who said that? No? I didn't think so. A woman, so probably not worth bothering with. It was Charlotte Brontë, in case you're interested. Or what about Marcus Aurelius, have you heard of him? He said, "If someone is able to show me that what I think or do is not right, I will happily change, for I seek the truth, by which no one was ever truly harmed. It is the person who continues in his self-deception and ignorance who is harmed."'

She knew somewhere in her depths she should stop, but she couldn't. 'You think because you have a business and you make a lot of money, that makes you an authority on everything, but it doesn't. Celia is a Black woman, I'm a White Irishwoman, but we are every bit as worthy and valuable as you are, so don't you dare try to diminish us or dismiss us as foolish girls with silly notions. I'm not dragging John-Joe, or Jerry for that matter, anywhere. They want to do this and they will do it, and nothing you can say will stop us. We have our own lives and our own destinies, and just like you defied your father to come here and make a life for yourself, you are trying to do what he did to JohnJoe and me now. You have no right.'

'Harp' – JohnJoe tried to calm her – 'I think it's best if we –'

She rounded on him, her cheeks blazing and the blood thundering in her ears. 'No, JohnJoe, I will not be silenced by ignorance and prejudice! I won't!'

Pat exploded. 'While you're under my roof, young lady, you'll –'

'Pat,' Kathy interjected, her voice low and calm, an unspoken conversation passing in a glance between her and JohnJoe. 'I think the best thing we can all do is leave this for now and come at it again tomorrow when everyone has had time to cool down. Nothing good ever comes from a conversation in the heat of the moment – you know that. Things get said that can never be unsaid, no matter how much we wish that to be the case. So before *anyone*' – she caught Harp's then her husband's eye – 'says or does something they regret, let's all go to bed and talk tomorrow.'

Pat was about to dismiss her suggestion but thought better of it, the indecision evident on his craggy face. His wife had been his stalwart support through thick and thin, and he'd not got to where he was in life by ignoring her advice. Without another word to anyone, he stormed out, his wife behind him.

'Well, that went well.' JohnJoe smiled and Harp felt relieved. JohnJoe loved his aunt and uncle like his parents, and she was afraid he would be upset at her being so outspoken.

She waited for her heart rate to go back to normal, unsure of how to proceed. 'I'm sorry. I shouldn't have been so cheeky...' she began.

JohnJoe shook his head. 'He shouldn't have talked about you like you weren't there, like a dumb schoolgirl with some daft notion.' He crossed the room and put his arms around her waist. 'He's from a different generation, I know, but he should know better. He wouldn't speak about Aunt Kathy like that, and he shouldn't do it to you either. You stood up to him, and I'm proud of you. And you know what? When he calms down, he'll respect you more for it. I've seen it on sites. He goes bullheaded at people – it's how he operates – but he has more respect for people who fight back. I know it's tough being a girl, Harp. I would never have seen it if you didn't point it out. But why shouldn't women have a vote? They live in this world, so of course they should have a say in how it's run. Men paid more, women having to have their husband's permission for things – it's so wrong. And I'm not just saying it to get on your right side. I believe it. So many of the women I know are strong, and they'd buy and sell a lot of the men.

My father was a useless waste of space, but my mam kept us fed and clothed. Your mam raised you all on her own and managed the Cliff House and turned it from a derelict crumbling old house to a thriving business. My sister Kitty is so brave and strong, taking care of Jane and carrying on the fight even after the British killed her husband. And Aunt Kathy, well, without her Pat Rafferty would still be a labourer, drinking and fighting every weekend, and not the owner of the biggest building company in Boston – and he knows it too. See how she talked him down? He knows how she never steers him wrong and how lucky he is to have her. I feel the same way about you, Harp. I'm just so lucky, and I admire you so much. You're the smartest, bravest, most beautiful woman I've ever seen, and I've loved you since I was fourteen, more each day. So never apologise for being you, my love, and I'll never stand by and let someone talk down to you because you're a woman.'

Harp rested her head on his chest and heard his heart beating. She'd never imagined she would fall in love, and certainly not with the very first boy she ever made friends with, but she did. JohnJoe was her first friend, her first love, and she suspected her only one. She could never imagine life without him. 'Will he calm down, do you think?' she asked.

JohnJoe shrugged. 'Eventually he will. I called to Danny and Marianne when you went to meet Celia this afternoon, told them about our plans, and they were delighted for us. Danny said he'd manage Uncle Pat, not to worry. He's all bluster and talk, but he'll accept it in the end. He knows my heart isn't in building, whereas Danny loves it.'

'How are they?' Harp asked. She normally saw Marianne more often, but since Matt and her mother had gone back, she feared she'd neglected her friend. The situation with Pamela and Ralph now living in the Cliff House, though it wasn't Marianne's fault, had made things awkward.

'Good. Katie is growing up so quickly. She was tiny when I last saw her, but she can almost sit up on her own now, and she's so smiley. She looks just like Marianne, all blond and blue eyes, but her smile is Danny's, kind of lopsided, you know? It's amazing really how so many traits get passed on, isn't it? They asked us to come over for supper on Friday night. I said I'd ask you.'

'I'd love to.' Harp sighed. 'It's just hard knowing her mother is living in our house with that slimy snake Ralph. I keep thinking about what will happen when they are finally reunited. I know Marianne is dying to see her, of course she is, but what if she wants to visit the baby, or worse, bring Ralph with her?' The thought of seeing that man again made her cold with anxiety.

'I don't know. Now that Rose and Matt are back and he's there, I suppose he's back in our lives again either way.' JohnJoe squeezed her shoulder and kissed the top of her head. 'If I had my time back, I'd have given him two bullets that morning on the train. I swear, Harp, it's the biggest regret of my life that I didn't finish him off when I had the chance.' He tensed beside her; the subject of Ralph Devereaux always made him angry.

'It wasn't to be,' she said, wishing the same thing. Ralph was rotten to the core. Most villains, even the worst in literature, had some redeeming quality, but in him there was none. He hated her and her mother and saw them as the obstacle to his return to his rightful position as lord and master of the Cliff House. But it ran deeper than that. It was as if he resented them so deeply for having the audacity to try to better themselves. Among his many faults, Ralph was classist, believing firmly that people should stay where they were put, and Rose rising from housemaid to proprietor of the Cliff House galled him in a way that was terrifying to witness.

'If he ever finds out the truth, that he's my father, not my uncle, I don't know what I'd do, JohnJoe,' Harp whispered. Even admitting the truth out loud in the room alone felt frightening.

'How could he ever find out? Who would tell him? You? Rose? Me or Matt?' JohnJoe reassured her.

'I hate that his blood flows in my veins – I feel much more like Henry's daughter than his – but I can bear it so long as he never ever learns the truth.'

'And he never will, darling.'

'So we just need to calm your uncle down, help Marianne reunite with her mother and de facto *him* back into our lives, tell my mother of our New York plans and then stop her swimming across the Atlantic to try to drag me back to Cobh by the hair. And then make a name for ourselves on the stage without losing our reputation or our teeth. Seems simple enough.' She half laughed.

'Not a bother to us.' JohnJoe leaned down and kissed her lips. She responded to him as she always did, enthusiastically and passionately. As she slid her hand inside his shirt, her fingers caressing his chest, he groaned, removing her hand and tucking his shirt back in.

'Oh, Harp, we can't, not here. We're in quite enough trouble as it is. You know they're liberal, but even Aunt Kathy would draw the line with us two making out on her sofa.'

'I know.' She sighed, slipping her hand inside the buttons of his shirt once more. 'I just miss you. At least when I lived with Mammy and Matt, they were out and we had some time to ourselves, but now that we're both back here, it drives me mad that you're only across the hall.'

'I know, I'm the same, but if Kathy thought we were sleeping together, she'd feel she'd have to tell your mother, and well, you know how that would go. We'll go to the shore this weekend, stay over at a hotel – Danny and Marianne will cover for us. We'll have some alone time then, I promise.' He gently removed her hand once more, kissing her palm as he did. 'There is a way we could avoid all this sneaking around and driving each other mad with longing, you know,' he said sadly.

Harp knew what he was going to say, and part of her wanted to just say yes and marry him. 'I know, but I just don't believe in marriage, JohnJoe. You know I don't. It changes everything. In the eyes of the law, I become your property, and I have to take a vow to obey you. I just can't do that, you know I can't.'

'But, Harp, that's the law and I can't change that, but it wouldn't be like that with us. Have I ever treated you like you were subordinate to me? Like your opinion mattered less? I never have, so why would you think I'd start doing it if we were married? Uncle Pat and Aunt Kathy are married, and you think he wears the trousers? You know he doesn't. On the face of it maybe, but nothing happens without her approval. I don't want to own you or boss you around. All I want is to lie with you beside me every single night, to love you without jumping any time someone comes to the door, to call you my wife and to be your husband. I'd be yours as much as you'd be mine. I swear to you.' He wouldn't beg, but the sincerity in his voice tore at her heart.

'I know you would. I…I can't explain it really. I just don't want to be anyone's, not even yours. I love you, I always have, and you love me, but I don't know if I ever want to have children, and I can't ever see myself settling down and wanting to make a home. I'm odd, John-Joe. I always was and I think I always will be. I'm not like other people – I've always known it. Sometimes I think I'm doing you a terrible injustice. You would make a wonderful father, and a husband too, but I'm not sure I'll ever want that, and maybe it's selfish of me keeping you tied to me without ever making a proper commitment.'

The conversation had gone a way that she had never anticipated, and she'd never really voiced her fears out loud to him before, but now that she had, it was as if a weight had been lifted.

'What are you saying, Harp?' JohnJoe's voice was choked, and she felt a physical pain at the hurt she was clearly causing him.

'I don't know exactly, but I have to be honest. I'll probably never marry you, or anyone.' The words came out as a whisper. And though she had never even solidified that thought in her own mind up to now, she knew it to be her undeniable truth.

He released her abruptly and stood up, his dark-green eyes blazing. He was handsome, she knew it even objectively – she saw the way girls admired him – but to her he was her JohnJoe, and she would always love him.

'I will never marry then either,' he announced. 'It's you for me or nobody, do you hear me, Harp Devereaux? I get so mad with you, I could…' He exhaled. 'I have never looked at another girl, not once in the last nine years. And I won't for the next nine, or the nine after that, because there is only one person on this earth that I want to be with and that's you. So if you won't marry me but still want me, then that's what you'll have, because even though it makes me sound pathetic, I'd rather have you in any capacity than not at all. So if this' – he waved his hand around the room – 'is all you can give, then that's what I'll have to take, because life without you, Harp, well, for me it's unimaginable, so that's it. After all we've been through together, I can't be anywhere in this life but by your side.'

'But if we go to New York, we can live there, freely and together, can't we?' Harp asked, only becoming aware of the tears flowing down her face as a fat drop landed on her hand.

'Do you know what that makes you in the eyes of society, though, Harp? And it's not fair, I know it, but nobody will look sideways at me. But an unmarried girl living and sleeping with a man, well, you know what names you will be called and how our families would react. Are you sure that's what you want? It makes me look like a cad, I know that and I don't care, but the rules that you so abhor dictate that a man who sleeps with a woman he's not married to is a bit of a Lothario, publicly tutted about but secretly admired. But a woman is a whole other story – she's a loose woman, a person of low morals. It's not right or fair but it's how it is, and I'd be the reason people said things like that about you.'

Harp stood and walked to where he was by the fireplace. She turned his chin to face her, her eyes raking his face. 'No, you wouldn't. I would be. And I genuinely don't care.'

CHAPTER 11

COBH, IRELAND

*D*ear Rose and Matt,

    I hope this letter finds you both well and enjoying life back in your own place. I miss you both terribly, we all do, but I know it was the right decision for you and we applaud you for it.

Pat is very busy as usual, so he says to give you his love. God forbid he would ever put pen to paper himself. Don't take it personally. I think he signs cheques and writes 'love Pat' on my birthday card and that's where the writing ends!

I wanted to tell you about how things are going here. I don't want to worry you, but you did ask me to take care of Harp, so I feel I have to tell you of their plans. She and JJ, along with Celia, our former maid, and two other men – Jerry, a carpenter from Dublin, and Elliot, a friend of his, I think – have formed a band and intend on moving to New York to perform at theatres there.

I am not at all sure it is a wise move but they are determined, so I've decided to support them since they will do it with or without our help. Unfortunately the night they told us, Harp and Pat got into a blazing row. Things were said by both of them that I'm sure they regret, but it got quite heated. They are both fiery-tempered, so a clash of like minds, I think. They'll patch it up before they go, I can promise you that. JJ and I will see to it.

One of the topics that enraged Pat was the idea that Celia was going too, but rather than a worry, it is a source of relief to me. Harp – and I know you won't take offence at this – is a very idealistic young woman, but her actual knowledge of the real world is lacking and she tends to oversimplify things. Celia, on the other hand, has not had an easy life, and while she didn't have the benefit of a fine education as Harp did, she is much more worldly-wise, and I feel like Celia will be much more aware of potential threats as a result.

So there you have it. They leave on Friday. I'm sure Harp will have written to you by now herself, but please, Rose, try not to worry too much. Jerry has his head screwed on, and Elliot seems like a nice young man, and between JJ and Celia, they will keep her safe.

It's only New York, so not far really. And we'll keep as close an eye on them as we can.

All our love,

Kathy and Pat

Rose heard Matt open the front door downstairs. He had been out late as usual, meeting up with former comrades, trying to calm people down who were upset by the terms of the truce. The curtains were still open, and the yellow harvest moon hung low in the sky. The harbour looked the picture of peace and tranquillity, and as they had done for centuries, the people of Cobh slept with the sea lapping the quayside of their town. It had seen so much, and much of it human suffering. So many people left from there, many never to return. More arrived. The harbour was used by the mighty British Navy, sending and receiving ships to and from their vast Empire all over the globe, from sailing ships to the dreadnoughts, taking their colonies' wealth home to England or fighting the endless wars their next-door neighbour got themselves into. If they weren't fighting with one European country, they were fighting with another, not to mention the Americans and the subjugation of all the colonies. And every one of them was played out here in this place, in one way or another. The Navy, the Army, then the dreaded Black and Tans and the Auxiliaries, the endless coming and going of the Crown forces, felt like the landscape of their lives forever. Could it truly be over? It seemed impossible.

For Rose, to be back here now, after everything, living in Matt's house as his wife, and without her daughter, felt so strange.

She wondered what Harp was doing now. Was she packing for this adventure? The idea that she was so far away gave Rose a pain in her heart. Harp had written to her telling her of the plan and about the argument with Pat, and from Harp's point of view, Pat was being very close-minded, stubborn and judgemental. But Rose knew her daughter well enough to know that she was well able to be pig-headed too.

She found she wasn't as terrified for her as she might have been. Harp was a grown woman and very smart. True, she wasn't worldly-wise, as Kathy put it, but Celia and JohnJoe were, and they would not steer her wrong, so she found she wished them well. She'd written to Harp to that effect. She wished Harp lived here and had continued with her studies in Cork, but life had other plans for her and that was all there was to it.

Rose had explained to Matt that the way she missed her daughter was not like a vague longing but more like a physical ache. She'd always known, even before Henry said it, that Harp was an unusual person and that she would live a remarkable life. Rose didn't want to stand in her way, but leaving her on the quayside in Boston was the hardest thing she'd ever done. She'd kept up a good show – she didn't want to make Harp feel bad about her decision to stay – but once the ship pulled away from the quay, she sobbed in Matt's arms and the sadness she felt was as deep as the ocean on which they sailed.

What if Harp never comes home again? Rose dismissed the thought. It was the path to madness and despair. And if her life had taught her anything, it was that the future was the most fickle of destinations. Planning for it was pointless, and humans were just feathers on the wind, subject to the vagaries of life.

She folded Kathy's letter and placed it in the envelope; she'd show it to Matt later.

She'd gone to bed early, tired after a few days of busy spring cleaning, adding some feminine touches to a house that had only had men living in it for many years. Apart from the night in the hotel when people had been so welcoming and kind, she had not ventured out much. The Devlins had come to tea twice and told her all the news. They were maintaining their sceptical position that the truce wouldn't hold and were very doubtful of the show of good faith from the British side. Of Pamela Devereaux there was still no sign, but Ralph stayed at home as well. Perhaps now that his friends and protectors were confined to barracks, he was scared.

'You're late.' She smiled as her husband climbed the stairs and crossed the room to kiss her.

'Liz and Cissy were plying me with tea and fruit cake.' He grinned as he sat on the side of the bed and removed his boots, socks and shirt. 'How's my girl?'

'I'm fine. Liz and Cissy were trying to bring you around to their way of thinking, I suppose?' She smiled again.

She'd confided to Matt that she suspected a part of the old ladies' reluctance to believe it was over was out of a desire to maintain the fight, that their lives as women freedom fighters were much more interesting than spinster shopkeepers, but he disagreed.

'I don't think so, or at least they're not alone in that way of thinking anyway. It's the general feeling from what I hear. People are wary of trusting the British, and with good reason. They're not above dirty tricks, and this might just be a ruse to buy them some time, but I don't know. I'm on the fence about it all.'

Rose thought about his remarks. 'Well, didn't the British themselves say the only way to rule us was by all-out martial law? And sure that's not sustainable at all. General Macready was most adamant on that and he's commander of the British troops here, so if anyone would know, he would. There's no way the British government would get support for that. The expense of it alone, to keep the whole country under the military cosh indefinitely, would be insane. They have to be feeling the pressure from the American side to leave Ireland too, not to mention the pressure the Tories are under from the Labour side of the house. The pope, George Bernard Shaw, the press over there, the king even, everyone is urging negotiations, so the way I see it, they're being quickly placed in a position where a peace deal is the only way out. So where people are getting the notion that they are rearming from, I honestly don't know.'

Matt sighed. 'You could be right, but then we have been under their boot for eight hundred years. There was plenty of pressure, internally and externally, put on them over that time and they never caved in, but maybe it's just that the people on the ground, the ones who actually fought and died, got no say. They heard about the truce in the papers, and many feel it was done without consulting them.'

'Ah, for goodness' sake, that's nonsense. Of course the negotiations have to have an element of secrecy to them – neither side will want to show their hands. What do they want? The negotiations fought out in every kitchen and pub and field of the country? They'll have to stand back and let the leaders do their best now, and I think they've done a good job this far, getting us to where we are. De Valera got himself declared president of the Irish Republic last week, changed from president of Dáil Éireann, so that's an audacious move.'

Matt snorted. 'Dev will mind himself no matter what, that's sure and certain.' He stood and removed his trousers then got into bed beside her. He lay back, drawing her head onto his chest.

Rose smiled. Despite the widespread love of the American-born Irish leader, Matt was not a supporter of his. He kept that fact to himself usually, and only Harp and Rose knew his true feelings.

'I know you think we can't trust him as far as we'd throw him, but he's served us well so far,' she said, cuddling up to him.

He kissed the top of her head and his arms tightened around her. 'Maybe he has, but he's served himself too, you can be sure.'

'Remember us lying here, the morning they came for us? Beckett and the others?'

'I do.' He sighed. 'I was so scared that day, more than at any other time in the whole thing. I was on the boat out to Spike, and I knew what I was facing, but I'd no idea what was happening with you. I'd tried so hard to keep our names apart, but it was no good. And that

Beckett was such a cold, evil monster, I wouldn't have put anything past him.'

'I was fairly petrified myself, but they just held me, and thank God Liz and the lads were able to get me out. I never again want to think about that walk through the sewers, though.' She shuddered at the memory.

'Ah sure, 'twas only a few furry friends.' He laughed. 'We made it, though. Against all the odds, we survived, and now we can walk our streets without fear or favour. It's wonderful, isn't it?' She felt him smile and the muscles in his body relax.

'It is. And I do think people are looking a gift horse in the mouth. Collins steered us through it. He's happy with the truce, it seems. Harp is very intuitive, as you know, and she knows him and trusts him completely. There's a way to go yet, but we'll get there. We've come too far to give up now.'

They lay in silence for a few minutes, and Rose was dozing off when he spoke again.

'I saw him this evening.'

She knew instantly who he meant and her stomach lurched. It was just a matter of time, of course – Cobh wasn't a big place – but part of her felt foolishly that if she never saw him, she could pretend he didn't exist. She was sure he'd just go, as suddenly as he'd arrived, but she wished he would get on with it.

Ralph Devereaux was mercurial, and she found that without the strength of her brave daughter by her side, the prospect of meeting him was one that daunted her.

As well as a letter from Kathy today, she'd had one from Marianne, saying that she'd written and telegrammed the Cliff House but there was no response from her mother. In it, she begged Rose to go and see what was going on. It wasn't something Rose relished, but she'd do it for Marianne.

At the prospect of being in his company, she reverted to the scared, awestruck maid flattered by the attentions of the son of the house. She knew Matt would do whatever she asked, up to and including murder if she sanctioned it, but she never would, and besides, she didn't need him dead, just gone. Back to whatever hole he'd crawled out of and into their lives nine years ago.

How she'd obsessed about him as a girl, how he'd occupied her every waking moment and much of her dreaming ones, was a source of cheek-burning shame to her now. Ralph was handsome then, twenty-two years ago, and she was foolish enough to think he saw her as something other than a pretty maid and part of the myriad of commodities to which the young heir to the family was entitled. She was nothing to him, she knew that now, and he left her without so much as a backwards glance when his mother had to fund a quick departure from Queenstown for her beloved son. It wasn't a pregnant maid that was the cause of his sudden exodus; she wasn't even worth that. No, it was the disgruntled husband of some woman he'd been carrying on with combined with a lot of gambling debt that made his old witch of a mother bail him out.

Ralph thankfully didn't stick around long enough to know Harp was his child, and Rose had remained deliberately aloof and tight-lipped on the subject. If Henry had not claimed her in his will – dear Henry, kind and loving to the last – Harp's father would have remained a shadowy long-dead never-recalled memory, and no one would have been any the wiser. But through his generosity and love for her and Harp, Henry antagonised his brother, and for the last nine years, Ralph had been an ominous, dark presence in their lives, lurking in the shadows, a malevolent force for evil.

'Where?' Her voice sounded strange even to her own ears.

'On the street. He was coming out of the hotel.'

'Did he see you?'

'He did. He looked straight at me but never spoke, and neither did I.'

She exhaled, a ragged breath.

'Don't worry, Rose, he can't hurt you. Not while I've breath in my body will he harm you or Harp.'

'He can, though, Matt,' Rose replied. 'Not physically, he wouldn't dare, much as he might want to. But he doesn't fight with his fists – he uses information and allegiances and leverage. But he told me once he would destroy me, and my daughter. And I know him. I wish I didn't, but I do. He means it, and he won't rest until he gets what he wants.'

'But what can he do?' Matt asked reasonably. 'If anything, we are the ones with the power. Legally that house is yours and Harp's, so he's trespassing and we can get him out of there if it's what you want. The law is on your side.'

'I know that, but I do think he'll go of his own accord. And we should just let it happen. I've had a letter from Kathy, and it sounds like Harp has no plans to return any time soon, and it's just not worth it to me to take him on now. I love this house, and I'm happy here. Besides, the Cliff House was actually left to Harp, and I as her mother was the guardian of her inheritance until she came of age, so in reality, it's not my house at all. Not to mention the fact that Harp's inheritance is all based on a lie. And if Ralph even suspects... I mean, he might have no idea that he's her father, but what if he does? What if he says that he was with me, and that he knew I became pregnant as a result? His mother might have told him, I don't know, and maybe he's been playing along with the idea that she's Henry's for whatever reason. If we were to challenge him in court and he does know the truth, there's nothing to stop him revealing it. She looks more like Henry, it's true, but what if he can produce evidence? A letter from his mother perhaps? Not only would we lose the house, but my reputation would be in tatters, and you know he'd make sure every newspaper had the story, a salacious tale about a maid who was having sexual relations with both sons of the house she worked in – the press would love it. So I'm not ashamed to say it – I'm afraid of him and what he could do. I've had a letter from Marianne too, asking me to go up there and try to see her mother, and I will, but I dread the thought.'

Matt sighed again, holding her closer. 'I could do it if it would be easier?' he offered. 'I hate the thought of you dealing with him, it feels wrong to let you go up there.'

Rose smiled. 'Easier certainly, but he wouldn't deal with you. I know him, and he'd only let me in out of a macabre sense of curiosity. He'd like to play with me like a spider plays with a fly, but he wouldn't even open the door to you. And we're under instructions not to antagonise them, the gentry, I mean, so an IRA commander turning up at his door would be just what he'd want to go stirring up trouble, saying you were harassing him and all the rest of it. No, best you stay out of it. He won't physically hurt me, I know that, but he'll want to sneer. I do have to try for Marianne, though. If I didn't know what had happened to Harp, I'd go out of my mind.'

'If there was a way I could put a bullet in him, I'd do it.'

'I know, but I –'

'I asked.' The words hung in the warm night air.

She knew what he meant. He had asked the IRA command for permission to assassinate Ralph.

'They said they understood why I wanted to, and that they sympathised, but that the truce was a very delicate balance of trust and suspicion on both sides. The orders direct from Collins himself are that nobody is to do anything that might jeopardise what has been achieved. This is a very precarious house of cards, and any wrong move could cause the entire thing to collapse, plunging the whole country back into a war that neither side can win. He's made it very clear that the harshest of punishments awaits any man who uses this time to settle any old scores, no matter how deserving.'

'I don't want you to do it anyway. There's been enough killing.' She was weary of it all.

'I agree, but he'd be no loss,' Matt replied darkly. 'Nobody's seen Pamela for weeks, and I knew Marianne was worried so I asked around.'

'Who would know?'

'One of our lads is doing a line with the Shand girl, the lieutenant's daughter, and Pamela Pascoe – Pamela Devereaux, I suppose she is now – played bridge with her mother. Pamela said that he was violent and that she was afraid of him. Then she was supposed to turn up to help with the church bazaar and never did, and nobody's seen her since. The mother told the daughter, and she told her secret Catholic Volunteer boyfriend, who told me.'

Rose smiled. The rumour mill of Cobh was as strong as when she left. She could just imagine the whispering behind closed doors when she and Matt turned up out of the blue. For a place that saw so much international traffic through its port, a parochial attitude still prevailed, where everyone had their beak in others' business. 'I'm not surprised. Ralph would only have wanted her for her money. Which of your lads is that?'

'Olan Kennedy. I told him he'd be better off sticking to his own, that mixing up with the daughters of Crown forces will end in tears, but he's mad about her and she about him, it seems. Shand is all right as they go, but that doesn't mean he'll take kindly to his well-bred English rose being seduced by an Irish farm labourer with a rebel past and the arse hanging out of his trousers.'

'Ah sure, love will find a way if it's meant to be.' She kissed his nose, changing the subject from Ralph. 'Look at us.'

'Look at us indeed,' he murmured, then kissed her passionately.

CHAPTER 12

*H*arp held JohnJoe and Elliot's hands as they took another bow. The audience were on their feet, and the applause was almost deafening. The New Amsterdam Theatre on 42nd Street was one of the largest venues in the city with fifteen hundred seats, and it was packed to capacity. Harp beamed and bowed one final time as the red velvet curtain swept across the gleaming mahogany boards.

The five months since they had arrived in New York were a blur of performances and accolades, and Harp had loved every minute of it. Following Celia's wise advice, Jerry had decided to stick firmly to the less salacious end of the market, and it had paid off. He'd been very astute, booking them into respectable venues, ensuring they got wonderful press and building on each performance from the one that went before.

They had started out in the vaudeville matinees and had enjoyed it immensely, making lots of friends in the other acts, but they soon outgrew the variety scene. In the late autumn, or 'fall' as the Americans called it, Jerry felt they were becoming popular enough to try to present a full programme themselves. Harp and JohnJoe were worried they were taking on too much, but Jerry assured them that it would be fine as they were in tremendous demand.

They booked smaller venues to begin with, but those sold out quickly once word got around that Roaring Liberty were due to perform. They'd taken a few side trips to Atlantic City and the Jersey Shore and were due to perform in Boston at the end of the month. It would be their first time back since they left last August, they had planned to go back for Christmas but they were in such demand, time didn't allow it, and so now the whole building crew, including the Raffertys and their friends, had bought tickets. As JohnJoe predicted, Pat had melted, and he and Harp had kissed and made up before they left, the hand of his wife evident in his every move. Harp knew that JohnJoe's uncle had even more respect for her now; it wasn't everyone who had the guts to stand up to big Pat Rafferty. He'd even apologised, an unprecedented development, and she reciprocated, saying she was his guest and he deserved more respect. It had ended with him giving her one of his famous bear hugs, and Harp's heart had gladdened. She would have hated to be at odds with him.

The crowd chanted. 'We want more, we want more!'

As they stood behind the curtains, Harp knew what the audience wanted, and though they played shows almost every night of the week, it never got old for her. It was the same everywhere: They wanted a lively song to sing along to and a sad one to put a tear in their eye and remind them of home. Though most of their audiences were born and raised in America, their hearts and souls had a hankering they couldn't explain for another place, an old country far away. Harp realised very early on in her performing career that it didn't matter whether it was Ireland or Germany, Italy or Russia, the longing was the same. Life in the USA was probably more prosperous for the children and grandchildren of those emigrants, but a part of them, a part they couldn't reach or point to, always longed to go home. Even if that home was somewhere they'd never been. So she and the boys always ended the night by playing to that part of them, that memory of the home country that lived deep in the audience's bones.

She turned to her fellow band members. 'Let's give the nice people what they want, shall we, boys?'

The curtains opened again, and JohnJoe grinned and sat at the grand piano. Gone were the uprights with the dodgy tuning – this one was a Steinway – and Harp's new handmade cherrywood concert harp gleamed beside it. Elliot had enough money for any number of new fiddles, but he'd played the same instrument since he was a boy. It had been his grandfather's, the one thing Werner Krauss had given his daughter when she left for America twenty-eight years previously. He'd had it made for himself by a master violin maker, and Elliot loved it. He'd told her that he had taken his grandfather's last name rather than his father's as a mark of respect to him. Harp didn't pry but got the impression he and his father were not close.

Harp addressed the audience. 'Thank you all, ladies and gentlemen, boys and girls, thank you all so much for the warm welcome. Every day that we get to stand up here and perform for you is a good one. I would like to introduce us, Roaring Liberty' – a huge cheer rent the air – 'before we sing a last song or two. To my right here, on piano and vocals, all the way from the Atlantic coast of County Clare in Ireland is the very talented JohnJoe O'Dwyer!'

The crowd clapped and cheered, and there was a particularly strong contingent of girls in the audience that were cheering and screaming.

'And to my left' – she extended her hand to where Elliot stood shyly – 'a proud grandson of the Schwarzwald, Germany, and a fiddle virtuoso, I think we can all agree, the very talented Mr Elliot Krauss.'

There was another huge round of applause.

JohnJoe then spoke. 'And of course we cannot forget the magic ingredient that makes Roaring Liberty what it is. With the fingers and voice of an angel, ladies and gentlemen, boys and girls, please give a huge round of applause for the star, all the way from Cobh, County Cork, Miss Harp Devereaux!'

There was more thunderous applause.

Harp waited until the crowd had hushed once more in anticipation. For a fleeting second, she saw her reflection in the mirrored glass that made up their set, and somehow she didn't see the young woman that stood before the enormous crowd, each one of them eating out of her hand. For the briefest of seconds, the jaw-length, sleek bobbed hair, the sparkly powder and dark kohl that ringed her dark-grey eyes, the svelte figure in the copper-coloured, dropped-waist dress with the cream fringe were gone, and all she saw was a skinny little girl with a mop of red-gold hair and a pale, pinched face.

She had come a long way, and yet in many ways, she was still just little Harp Devereaux from Queenstown, a peculiar little girl with no friends who lived through books and music.

She returned to her harp, which was on a raised dais where the whole audience could see her, and flexed her fingers. Despite performing every day and some nights, she always felt a frisson of anxiety before she began, terrified she would make a mess of it and the gathering would see her for the awkward girl she felt she truly was.

Heart to fingers, Harp, bypass the head. She heard his voice, as clear as ever, in her mind. She wasn't sure about religion, but she knew on a cellular level that Henry Devereaux had never really left her. And as she plucked the opening strings, she wasn't on a stage in America, fifteen hundred pairs of eyes on her in expectation; she was in the study of the Cliff House, the deep safe harbour of Cork outside the window, her mother in the kitchen downstairs, and she and Henry were together, she playing the harp and he listening contentedly.

She started with the Chauncey Olcott hit 'Too-Ra-Loo-Ra-Loo-Ral (That's an Irish Lullaby)' from the Tin Pan Alley musical *Shameen Dhu*, much to everyone's delight. They always finished with the same two songs, and it worked beautifully every time. Their show was an eclectic mix of all sorts, with Jerry scouring the music shops and vaudeville theatres for new music for them to play. Harp found she enjoyed some of the music the coloured performers were producing, mostly introduced to Harp by Celia in the mixed-race clubs, which Celia was allowed to enter. She loved the sounds of George Johnson, and Williams and Walker; those men seemed to bring an earthiness and authenticity to their music that maybe the more popular show tunes lacked. And the best blues singers were nearly all coloured women – Ma Rainey, Bessie Smith, Mamie Smith, Ethel Waters.

Harp herself had a low, warm voice, a rich alto that seemed to hold audiences enraptured and which naturally projected without effort over the crowd. She knew her voice wasn't to everyone's taste; it wasn't dulcet and sweet as was expected by looking at her. Sopranos dominated the world of mainstream female singers – the higher one could get, the better. But though Harp had no problems reaching the higher octaves, she was much more comfortable in the lower registers.

The final rousing chorus had everyone singing, and the waves of love and appreciation were intoxicating. Increasingly their audiences were becoming more middle class. The vaudeville scene was for the working people, and she feared as they went up in the world, they would lose that grassroots support, but it hadn't happened.

The song finished, and Harp smiled and offered her applause to the audience for their participation. 'I can hear you are all in fine voice this evening,' she said, swinging her knees out to face the audience but remaining on her stool beside the harp. 'You'll put us out of business at this rate.'

There was a ripple of appreciative laughter.

'Now, it's time to go home and let you fine people to your beds. On behalf of myself, JohnJoe and Elliot, I bid you all a good night...'

There was a collective sigh, followed by cries of 'More! More!' from the auditorium.

Harp smiled. This was how it always went. 'Orrr...' – she dragged the word out –'and I'll be murdered for this because we were supposed to be finished twenty minutes ago' – she winked conspiratorially – 'we could do one very last song, but on one condition.'

She glanced unseeing out into the darkness. The stage lights were blinding, but the sense of the collective experience was palpable. She didn't need to see them to know that for that brief time, they were not individuals but a collective, she and JohnJoe and Elliot, the audience, all as one, singing together.

'Cervantes tells us that "he who sings scares away his woes." And I believe that. The power of song is so potent, even when singing alone, but when we sing with others, our voices raised together, a kind of energy is created and it's a force for good in the world. So will you join us one last time before we are all thrown out of here?'

Whoops and hollers of delight were her answer.

She didn't need to consult with the boys. JohnJoe allowed her the opening bars before beginning the piano accompaniment, and then Elliot joined with his soulful, plaintive violin. She began the song most associated with her homeland, and within seconds the audience were in full voice.

'Oh, Danny Boy, the pipes, the pipes are calling, from glen to glen, and down the mountainside. The summer's gone and all the roses dying. 'Tis you, 'tis you must go, and I must bide.'

As her voice soared confidently, JohnJoe joined her, his tenor complementing her.

'But come ye back, when summer's in the meadow. And when the valley's hushed and white with snow, 'tis I'll be there in sunshine or in shadow. Oh, Danny Boy, oh, Danny Boy, I love you so.'

With a wave of her hand, Harp urged the crowd to join in. The song had become very popular in 1915 when Elsie Griffin sang it, and it was now available as a recording.

All fifteen hundred voices sang with such emotion, she was moved.

'And when you come, and all the flowers are dying, and I am dead, as dead I well may be, you'll come and find the place where I am lying, and kneel and say an Ave there for me.'

The volume of voices in the theatre rose to harmonious crescendo as JohnJoe and Elliot accompanied her.

'And I shall hear, though soft you tread above me, and all my grave will warmer, sweeter be, and you will kneel and tell me that you love me, and I shall sleep in peace until you come to me.'

* * *

EARLY THE NEXT MORNING, she and JohnJoe woke to a thunderous banging on their bedroom door. For the sake of decorum, their apartment in Freeport had five bedrooms – all tiny – but she and JohnJoe always shared, and the fifth room was used for their instruments and wardrobe. In his spare time, JohnJoe still loved to sketch and paint, and so rolled-up canvasses were everywhere. When they were living on two different continents, he used to send her drawings he would do of birds or animals, and she still loved his way of capturing them so perfectly with just a few strokes. Her mother would have been appalled at their living arrangement, as would Kathy and Pat, but Harp didn't care.

'What the...?' JohnJoe woke, bleary-eyed, and checked the clock. It was only seven thirty. Because of the hours they kept, they usually slept in until mid-morning. He padded across the room and opened the door a crack. Celia too was on the landing, clearly just woken up.

'Jerry, what's wrong?' he asked, opening the door wider and admitting Jerry and Elliot into the room. The band had been together for so long now, eating together and spending most of every day and night together, they were very familiar with each other. Harp sat up in bed, her woollen pullover covering her modesty – and also keeping her warm, as the New York winter seemed endless.

'Sorry, you two. I know you should be sleeping till ten or eleven, but I need you to hear this.' Jerry had a guitar in his hand, and Elliot stood behind him, looking unusually sheepish.

'Hear what?' Harp yawned.

'Well, go on,' Jerry urged Elliot.

The young man blushed. 'I, well, I was working on a song. I didn't want to say anything, because it might be rubbish, but Jerry saw me working on it and asked me to play it for him and I did, and well, now we're here.'

'It's perfect for you, Harp.' Jerry butted in. 'Elliot doesn't want to sing it himself, but I thought if we could work out an arrangement for it – he already has a basic melody – we could have a serious hit on our hands.'

'Well, let's be having ya, Herr Krauss,' JohnJoe joked, shivering and climbing back into bed beside Harp.

Celia normally slept so soundly and with home made earplugs nothing woke her before she wanted to rise.

Jerry sat in the armchair at the end of the bed, and Elliot took the guitar Jerry proffered. He placed the strap around his neck, which allowed him to stand and play, and picked out a very distinctive melody, the tempo slow and rhythmic. When he began to sing, his voice lacked the resonant timbre of JohnJoe's, but it was sweet and in tune.

'What the tongue can't say, the heart will know. What the hands can't touch, what no one can show, what I daren't speak, for fear you'd go, I'm hoping my love, that your heart will know.

'My thoughts are of you, as you pass your days, when you are near or far away. Oh, how I long for the breeze of love to blow, and that somehow, someday, your heart will know.

'My dreams are vivid, your smile so sure. Is it aimed at me? Whose love is pure? I don't know how I can make it so, but somehow, some-day, your heart will know.

'Until that time, I wait all on my own. No other one can claim your throne. The king of my heart, but I can't let it show, until somehow, someday, your heart will know.'

The last strings of the simple but very catchy melody faded, and Elliot looked uncertain. Harp and JohnJoe applauded spontaneously.

'Elliot! It's wonderful. It's got a wonderful feeling of Irving Berlin or George Gershwin about it. It's so catchy! I love it.'

'Well, aren't you the dark horse, eh?' JohnJoe grinned. 'We've always played other people's music, but think what we could do with a song of our own. How about if we did kind of a riff in the chorus like...'

He jumped from the bed, pulling on his trousers and a warm sweater, and the foursome moved to their small living room, where coffee cups and sheet music were scattered among the furniture and instruments, including a little upright piano with a sweet tone.

The boys were terrible housekeepers, and Harp was worse. Celia did her best to keep some sort of order, but even so the rubbish piled up so fast that the place would give Rose nightmares. They used all of the tableware until there was nothing left and then washed it all in one go. There was no space to wash or dry clothes, but Jerry and Celia brought everything to the Chinese laundry on Doyers Street in Lower Manhattan once a week, while the others were on stage.

Celia had a much firmer grip on the budget, however, and she shopped and made sure everyone ate properly. She also saved them a fortune by making their costumes, so they always looked glamourous and well dressed for a fraction of what it should have cost.

Luckily nobody who visited the apartment cared about the mess. It was a village neighbourhood where all sorts of artists and performers lived, and nobody was interested in housekeeping. Freeport, Long Island, was wonderful, and Harp loved living there. People of all colours and ethnicity coexisted, and she thought it perfect. She had enjoyed life at home and at the Raffertys' with all her needs catered to, but she would happily give it up all over again to live this free and easy life of domestic chaos.

Now she was wrapped in a patched shawl over the brown checked dress she'd hastily pulled over her head as the boys left the room. She'd found the shawl in the dressing room of some place they played on Broadway. It smelled a bit musty and she guessed it had been abandoned, but it was a lovely cerise pink colour and, more importantly, was warm. On her feet she wore the woollen socks her mother had knitted for JohnJoe as a birthday present. She thought she must look a fright, but she had to put so much energy into her stage appearance that when she wasn't working, she didn't bother.

'Something like this.' JohnJoe sat at the upright and used first one hand to pick out the melody, then proceeded to add harmony with the other, filling the melody out beautifully, and then he added some delicate ornamentation to the chorus.

Halfway through, Celia emerged from her bedroom, yawning and stretching, as eccentrically dressed as Harp in not one but two baggy jumpers, a floor-length tartan skirt and a huge pair of sheepskin slippers. 'What's going on out here? Why's everyone awake?'

'Elliot wrote an amazing song, and we're going to perform it on stage.' Harp beamed.

'You really think it might be good enough for us to perform? I'm not too sensitive, so don't say it just so you don't hurt my feelings.' Elliot smiled, and Harp felt a wave of affection for their friend. He was a very sweet and humble boy, and though she'd never seen him with a girlfriend, after the performances, both he and JohnJoe got a lot of female attention.

JohnJoe was more confident, and he flirted a little – nothing that would irritate her but enough to keep the female theatre-goers interested. He and Harp never let on that they were a couple, and so she got her fair share of male attention herself but always politely declined any advances before they turned into anything.

She'd stuck her head into an evening performance one time, out of curiosity, and had to admit to being a bit horrified. It was very seedy. And while she was willing to defy her mother and live her own life on her terms, those terms did not stretch to wearing almost nothing and careering about the stage for men to catcall her. So she was very grateful to Celia for nipping that idea in the bud.

'I think it's a wonderful song, and the arrangement JohnJoe is adding really gives it something unique. It's a great love song, but it's one that will have them tapping their toes and humming it the next day as they go about their business,' Harp said sincerely. 'Well done, Elliot, it's really *swell*.'

When she used the Americanism, the other four chuckled. Harp didn't usually resort to slang words or common parlance when she could use correct English.

'Will you give it a try?' Elliot asked.

'I'd love to.'

They had their old favourites, songs that audiences loved to hear over and over again, and they also added new material occasionally to keep things fresh. But this was the first time they'd had a chance to perform an original song, and Harp was excited. She took the neatly notated sheet of manuscript from Elliot and began to sing, tentatively at first until she became surer of the melody. By the time she came to the second verse, she found she enjoyed singing it. It was a bit rough still, but they could well be on to something.

Celia was looking over her shoulder, and as Harp reached the third verse, she also began to sing, softly at first but then louder, harmonising in a velvety contralto, supporting Harp as if she were a professional backing singer. As the girls reached the end of the song, the boys burst into spontaneous applause.

Harp turned and hugged Celia. 'I didn't know you could sing so well. Why did you never say?'

'You're going to have to join us on stage,' cried Elliot, still clapping.

'No, I think I'll just stick to bookkeeping and wardrobe.' Celia picked up last night's coffee cups and headed for the tiny kitchenette.

'But why? It would be so perfect, having you along...' protested Harp, following her.

Celia shook her head, half smiling, half exasperated, as she filled the sink with water. 'Real world check, honey.' Celia's Southern roots gave her a drawling accent, and Harp loved listening to her. 'White acts like yours don't have coloured performers – you'd never get to play your sort of venues if you did. The likes of Fats Waller might get invited to play a fancy all-White place like the Cotton Club, but that's the exception that proves the rule.'

When Harp looked crestfallen and guilty, Celia dried her hands and gave her a hug. 'Sweetheart, it's not your fault, and you've always treated me right, sharing everything equally. If I had a yen for the music business, then there's a load of ways I could get into it. But no, I'm saving up my money for a proper college education so I can go on fighting for equality in the best way I can.'

'One day soon, Celia, there'll be no more of this stupid colour bar,' said Harp fiercely. 'And you'll have the right to sing where you want.'

'I'm sure you're right, honey,' said Celia lightly. 'One day soon. Sure, we might even have a coloured president one day. Maybe even a coloured woman!'

CHAPTER 13

*R*ose steeled herself to enter the shop. She was probably just imagining it, but had the Devlins seemed less than friendly the last time she visited? She was sure she was imagining it. They'd been firm friends for so long; perhaps they were just busy or worried about something else.

To her relief the shop was empty. Cissy was stocking shelves, and Liz was carving a large joint of home-cooked ham into slices.

They looked up, saw her and then glanced at each other. She wasn't imagining it – something was wrong.

'Good morning, ladies,' she said with a smile.

'Good morning,' Liz replied, but without her usual warmth. 'I thought your delivery went up this morning. Did you forget something?'

Rose paused for a moment. 'No, I got it fine, thank you. I… Well, I just wanted to ask you about something else, actually, the Cliff House delivery? Marianne, you know –'

'The brigadier general's wife, yes, I know,' Liz intoned, her voice cold.

'Well, she's married to Danny now, but anyway, she's worried about her mother. She's written over and over, several times since you wrote to tell us what had happened, and has had no reply. I wondered if they were still getting their groceries delivered, because to be honest, I dread the thought of facing him but promised her I'd try to find out what was happening. I just thought if they were having their normal delivery, then that might be an indication that all was well?' Rose knew she was babbling; something about Liz's demeanour in particular was making her nervous.

'Let me see.' Cissy opened the order book and Liz resumed slicing.

'Well, they are still taking the Darjeeling stuff. Mrs Devereaux came in here a while back asking if we could order it for her. We had to get it sent from Dublin. She said it was an Indian thing, but she'd lived there so long, she'd got a taste for it. Your man the husband hates it, she said, and I can't blame him – it smells awful. So that's going up every week. Let me see the rest of it…tobacco, tea, bread, butter, salt, soap, tinned fruit, rice…' She ran her finger down the list. 'Everything is the same.'

'He changed it to every two weeks from every week,' Liz said, her eyes never leaving the joint of meat.

'Oh, you're right. He did.' Cissy smiled.

'Oh…I see.' Rose thought quickly. Should she confront Liz about why she was so hostile? She really didn't want to. The older woman was austere and not given to emotional outbursts.

'Thank you. I suppose I'd better just go up there and see how she is…' Her voice trailed off.

'You do that,' Liz said coldly.

Rose turned to her old friend, and her rescuer when she was imprisoned by Beckett. 'Liz, are you cross with me? Did I do something to upset you?' she asked directly.

A split second pause as the older woman contemplated her response,

'No, Rose. I just don't see why you should be so concerned about an imperialist woman who has clearly nailed her colours to the mast.' Liz's blue eyes glittered dangerously in her wrinkled face.

'Well, I don't care about that, but she's Marianne's mother and Marianne is really worried…'

'Tis well we know you don't care about that,' Liz replied darkly.

'I'm sorry, but what do you mean?' Rose asked.

Cissy tried to intervene. 'Liz, leave it...' But it was too late.

'What I mean is that neither you nor your husband seem to have any care for the people of this place and what is to become of them now. It seems you are of the opinion that this traitorous truce, a despicable piece of underhanded self-serving politicking that sees us kowtowing to the British forevermore, though we beat them, is something to be welcomed. I'm ashamed of you both, after all we went through together, that you'd support this awful thing and reject the sacrifice of your neighbours and former friends as if it was nothing. But I suppose you always have America to run back to, or your big house where you can be lady of the manor again, and you no better than you should be.' With that final cutting remark, Liz Devlin marched into the back of the shop and slammed the door.

'Cissy, what on earth?' Rose asked, her stomach lurching with the stress of it all.

'Ah, Rose, she's very cut up that the Treaty is going ahead. She feels – well, we all do – that it's wrong. Taking oaths of allegiance to the king of England and giving up the North, it doesn't sit well. She heard Matt trying to talk a group of Volunteers into accepting it, and she asked him what you thought. He said that you thought it was the best chance of peace that we had, and she's been feeling very let down since.'

'And you? What do you think?'

Cissy sighed, and it was as if the weight of the world were on her. 'I think what they did to us was unforgivable, and I can't stomach them here in any way, shape or form. I won't take any oath to the king of that place or any other king either – too much has happened.'

Rose thought back to the news that Cissy and Liz had been arrested for their part in the escape and wondered again what they'd done to two old ladies while in custody.

'I understand your position, Cissy, but I don't think more fighting is the answer, I just don't.'

Cissy just nodded, then gave her a weak smile and retreated into the back to join her sister.

* * *

ROSE SWALLOWED down the lump in her throat as she pushed the garden gate that led from the Smuggler's Stairs to the garden of her former home. She'd hoped Marianne could contact her mother without her help but it would seem she couldn't. Pamela never responded. Matt had orders from the top brass of the IRA to stay well out of Ralph's way and they'd had no option but hope the social pressure of a newly independent country would do it's work in expelling him but he was still here. Eventually, as Marianne's letters were showing more and more desperation, Rose knew she had no choice. She would have to try at least.

She hadn't mentioned anything to Matt of her plan to confront Ralph today, knowing he would at least want to linger outside to protect her, ready to march in if Ralph did or said anything he found offensive, which would be inevitable. If he did that, he could get into a lot of trouble with his superiors.

Ralph had a way of saying just the very thing to cut to the quick, and Matt needed to stay out of it. Things were precarious enough without him being arrested or worse for attacking Ralph. Matt was an even-tempered man and in control of his emotions almost all of the time, but Ralph Devereaux and the way he treated Rose was the exception to that. He made Matt see red, and the risk of an incident was too high if the two men met.

The IRA was in grave danger of a deep and irrevocable split on the subject of the Treaty. Matt and others supported Collins and the Treaty, and while it was far from ideal, the offer that seemed to be on the table was the partition of Ireland into twenty-six counties of a Free State in the south, and six in the North that would remain part of Britain. The concentration of loyal British subjects up there were in the majority, and to force them to join an Irish republic at this stage would surely lead to even more bloodshed. Additionally it would mean the end for Lloyd George, who relied on the support of the Ulster Unionists to maintain his position in Westminster, so giving the entire island back at the moment was just not possible. The Treaty was the best that could be achieved in the interim while the details of a full republic could be worked on further down the line. The oath of allegiance to the king, another term of the Treaty, was clearly a sticking point too, something Matt dismissed as empty words, a meaningless gesture to achieve an objective, but Liz and Cissy and many others disagreed.

Matt tried to bring his former subordinates around to his way of thinking, but tempers were running very high and the anger and feelings of betrayal were palpable. Families and friendships that lasted lifetimes were being torn apart as the two sides turned on each other. The Devlins were a perfect example.

Everyone's tempers were frayed, and the last thing Matt needed was to be involved in an altercation with Ralph right now. She wanted to speak to Ralph herself, find out where Pamela was and report back to Marianne. She would leave it there and never contact him again. Matt had told her of the numbers of Anglo-Irish families who'd cleared out, often in the middle of the night, and gone back to England, a country they had never lived in but which was a more welcoming place than a new and independent Ireland. Hopefully Ralph would follow suit, sooner rather than later.

She'd had another letter from Harp, telling her about her life as a performer, and while Rose was worried for her daughter, a bigger part of her was so proud. Harp was an unusual child, and she found the refusal of her peers to accept her as one of them extremely hard, so the adulation she was now enjoying was long overdue. Rose wished she would marry JohnJoe, but Matt told her to give up on that as an idea, that Harp would probably never marry and they would have to accept it.

Brian was doing a very serious line with a nurse from Dublin called Síle. He'd brought her home last weekend to meet them, and she seemed lovely.

Matt passed on an admonishment from Harp about the lack of

letters, and Síle joked that her beau might not write to his old friend but he talked about her constantly. Rose didn't hear any trace of bitterness or jealousy in Síle's words – she was very sure of Brian and didn't seem at all threatened by his friendship with Harp – and it was wonderful to see; perhaps the two young women could well be friends in the future.

Rose walked across the path where weeds poked up between the flagstones. The grass, overgrown now either side, was badly in need of some care, and the shrubs and trees needed pruning. She would hide her disapproval at how he'd allowed their home to fall into such disrepair and try to keep things cordial, or as cordial as things could ever be with Ralph.

You're a married woman, a former business owner, a person who has travelled, she admonished herself as the familiar feelings of insecurity threatened to engulf her at the prospect of meeting him. Suddenly she wasn't a self-assured woman but that impressionable kitchen maid again, and he was the handsome but feckless son of the house.

She still had her key and toyed for a moment at the thought of just letting herself in as he had done, but she wouldn't do that. The brass door knocker that she'd always kept gleaming was dull and tarnished, and the paint was blistering on the front door. The salty sea air made short work of paint, and it needed to be redone every year. The whole façade was shabby, and the salt from the sea was encrusted on the windows.

She grabbed the knocker with her cream silk–gloved hand and rapped on the heavy teak door. She'd dressed carefully, not in anything that could be described as ostentatious, but not as a maid either. She'd chosen a midnight-blue floor-length velvet skirt and jacket and under the jacket, she wore a pale-blue lace blouse. Her dark silky hair was pinned neatly beneath a cream hat with burgundy silk flowers.

She stood and waited, but no sound or sign of life suggested he was home. Just as she was about to turn and leave, she heard the latch lifted and the door opened. A long-faced man in a black uniform opened the door and arched a hairy eyebrow inquisitively. He was wiry and pale and reminded Rose of a drawing of the famous Ebenezer Scrooge in Harp's copy of *A Christmas Carol*.

'Yes?' he intoned nasally.

'I'd like to speak to Ralph Devereaux, please,' she said in a voice that she hoped betrayed none of her discomfort.

He looked her up and down slowly, assessing who she might be, and clearly decided she was beneath him. '*Mister* Devereaux is currently occupied. Whom shall I say called?'

He made Rose's flesh crawl with his supercilious manner and the proprietary way he guarded her home. But he would not intimidate her; she refused to allow it. Drawing herself up mentally, she replied, 'It is imperative I speak with him *now.*' She hoped the intonation inferred an order rather than a request. 'Tell him Mrs Rose Quinn is here.' She deliberately omitted a 'please'.

'Mister Devereaux is a busy man, and if you do not have an appointment...'

'Who is it, Maguire?' Even without seeing him, his voice made her blood run cold.

The man stood to the side, opening the door wider so the master could see the caller.

'Ah, Rose.' His smile was broad but never reached his unusual grey eyes. His eyes were the exact same colour as Harp's, but hers were warm and full of intelligence and fun, whereas his were dead and inscrutable.

He hadn't changed much since she'd last seen him. His wooden leg was hidden by his trousers, but she knew it was there. He walked with a cane, but if one were to be objective, he was still a very good-looking man. His dark hair was still full and wavy, oiled back from his forehead, and his skin was olive coloured, from so many years beneath the Indian sun, she assumed. He was slighter than she remembered – she thought he'd been much broader than Henry, more of a physical presence than his brother – but either he had slimmed down or she'd imagined it. His charcoal suit was cut beautifully, and his shirt was dazzlingly white.

'Do come in.' He gestured with a wave of his hand that she should bypass the awful Maguire and enter.

She refused to show her horror at his choice of décor. All the lovely bright pastel colours of wallpaper and paint had been obliterated, and the house once again was as she remembered it in his parents' time, dark and forbidding. Where she'd had vases of fresh flowers and cheery prints, he had placed heavy pieces of gloomy sculpture, and the dismal old oil paintings of long-dead Devereauxes that she had dumped in the attic had been reinstated. The painting JohnJoe had done of her and Henry and Harp had been replaced by a horrid portrait of Ralph's father on a horse. JohnJoe's artwork was leaning against the wall, covered in dust and cobwebs. It was the thing she'd found hardest to leave. She longed to ask him for it – he surely wouldn't want it – but she didn't dare give him anything over her. The memory of Henry Devereaux, his golden-blond hair, just like Harp's, his calm intelligent face, gave her courage.

Be beside me Henry, she pleaded with her former employer and dear friend. If only he'd drummed up the courage to propose, and if only her younger self would have had the good sense to accept, she and Harp would have been set up for life, but he never managed to find the words. And if she were honest with herself, she would most likely have refused him even if he had. He died leaving a letter telling her of his love, and how he was claiming Harp as his child in order that she would inherit the Cliff House. He'd never said a word in all the years they'd lived together in this house, but somehow he knew Harp was Ralph's daughter and that his only sibling was a dangerous man.

Ralph led her to the drawing room, and there too he'd managed to turn the clock back. Heavy net curtains, now badly in need of a wash, obliterated the natural light and obscured the view of the harbour. The chintz-covered sofa and the dusty-pink Queen Anne chairs had been reupholstered in bottle green, and the whole place needed dusting and polishing.

'Have a seat, won't you?' he said smoothly. 'Can I offer you a drink? A cup of tea perhaps?' He gazed at her.

Rose could tell he was really enjoying himself. He could see her dismay at the way he'd undone all of her hard work. She steeled herself once more. She would not allow him to talk down to her.

'If you know your enemy and know yourself, you need not fear the result of a hundred battles.' She brought the words of Sun Tzu, the Chinese philosopher, to mind. Harp often quoted him and was an admirer of his way of thinking and his book *The Art of War.* Rose knew Ralph Devereaux to his bones. She was not fooled by any of his antics or duplicity. She could see into the darkness of his soul and wasn't afraid of him.

He took a seat, reclining in one of the fireside chairs, and Rose sat opposite on the sofa, choosing to perch on the edge rather than sit back. She knew that sofa of old; it was comfortable but sagged in the middle, so it was hard to get out of it in a dignified way.

'Tea, please.' She smiled genially. 'How have you been, Ralph? It's been a while.'

He raised an eyebrow quizzically. His look clearly said, *So this is how we're playing it, is it?*

'Very well, thank you, Rose.'

The silence pulsated between them; neither was going to make it easy by blathering on.

'And your wife? How is she settling in to life in Cobh?' Rose knew the use of the new name for the town would rankle with him. He and his type would want the name of the town, like everything else, to remain exactly the same.

'Fine.' He yanked on the ring pull by the fireplace to summon the walking cadaver Maguire. 'Bring tea for our guest and a whiskey for me.' Ralph didn't look in the man's direction when he spoke.

'Very good, sir.' The man backed out obsequiously.

'Is Mrs Devereaux here? I'd like to meet her.'

Ralph smirked. 'Would you really? I wonder why?'

'Well, actually, because her daughter has made an effort to contact her but has not as yet had a reply, and she asked that I investigate.'

'And you're doing Marianne the trollop's bidding now, are you? How quickly you have reverted to type, Rose. I knew the lady of the manor never sat well with you – you are a servant by nature, and you are happiest as such. I've found life is best enjoyed, or at least endured, if one remains where one belongs.'

It hadn't taken long for the veneer of civility to drop. Rose ignored his jibe. 'So is she here?'

'Alas no, she's not.' Ralph spread his hands, a look of contrite apology on his face.

'Has she returned to India? Marianne is most anxious to make contact.'

A flash of what? Indignation? Amusement? Ralph's eyes gave a glimpse of his innermost thoughts, but not enough to be sure. 'Is she? Has she tried writing?'

Rose worked hard not to react. 'Several times.' She forced a smile.

'Oh dear. Well yes, the exact whereabouts of Pamela, oh, it's difficult to know.' He sighed vaguely. 'The way things are here, with international travel problems and so on…hard to tell really. She was intent on visiting India, and I would imagine she's there by now, but you know how difficult communications can be. Now if there is nothing else, perhaps we'll forgo the tea and get on with our days?'

Clearly the audience was over.

'No, I'm afraid that's not enough. Marianne is very worried, and frankly so am I and –'

'You've never even met her, so please don't try the concerned neighbour act on me. You came up here to my home for a nose around, Rose, and we both know it.'

'This is not your house, Ralph, you know that.' The words came unbidden, but she felt relief that they were delivered in measured, calm tones.

He snorted a laugh. 'So this is what this is about? I knew it. Very good, Rose. Poor little Marianne was a mere ruse to get you past the threshold.'

'No, I am concerned for her and her mother as well, but while we're here, this house legally belongs to my daughter, as you well know.'

'You think so?' He smiled and seemed to ponder her assertion.

'I know so, as do you.'

'Well, that's a matter of debate really, isn't it? I am the *legitimate* son of my parents' – his emphasis on the word spoke volumes – 'and my older brother has predeceased me, so by the law of the land, I am next in line.'

'Except that Henry bequeathed it to his daughter, Harp. It is written in black and white, and any court will have to accept that.' Rose never allowed her gaze to fall from his grey eyes.

'Except *is* he her father? That's the thing, isn't it?' He rubbed his chin contemplatively, as if trying to puzzle out a vexing confusion. 'I mean, I know you *claim* he is, and goodness knows what kind of things you got up to in your youth when you were still passably pretty. And since I hear you've recently trapped another man I'll assume your libido has not waned. You must be insatiable, Rose, so it's entirely possible that you seduced my halfwit brother. I've limited knowledge of your skills in that regard, though we both know I do have *some*.' He smiled, and Rose prayed he could not see her squirm. 'But your bastard child's father could be anyone, really. And in court – as you say, that's where any contest would end up – well, it would mean all the details would need to emerge to fully understand any ramifications. I mean, anyone could be her father – your current husband, for example, or the local butcher, or any one of the soldiers who frequented this house over the years. I mean, it could literally be anyone...' He paused. 'It could even have been me.'

Rose used her iron will to stop any reaction on her face, though her guts were churning. She smiled beatifically. 'Ralph, I'm perfectly aware of what you're trying to do, to intimidate me, threatening me and so on. It's your only modus operandi, always has been, but I'm not that impressionable girl any more and you don't frighten me in the slightest. This is Harp's house, and any court will see it as such. Henry was her father, and he loved her very much, as she did him. She *will* return, and she will reclaim her property, and if I were you, I would just leave and spare yourself the expense and humiliation of being evicted and charged with trespassing.'

She leaned forward ever so slightly. She knew Matt couldn't do anything to Ralph, but Ralph didn't know that. He was well aware of her connections now, and she decided to play one of the few cards she had. 'You were very friendly with several British officers, including Oliver Beckett. Your allegiance to the enemy has been noted, Ralph, and as Ireland gains her freedom, life could be extremely uncomfortable for people like you. Another reason, if one were needed, for you to decide to leave here for once and for all and never show your face around here again. Nobody wants you here, Ralph. Nobody.'

If her words pierced him, his face gave no indication of it. He sneered and stood. 'Your rebel thug threats are meaningless, as is your assertion that my brother fathered your brat. If she comes back, tell her from me she'll have a fight on her hands. It's one I will relish and have every intention of winning. Now get out of my house.'

As he spoke, Maguire opened the doors, pushing a tea trolley before him.

'Our guest is leaving, Maguire. Show her out.'

Rose stood, nodded to Ralph and walked past Maguire, her head high.

The hallstand was a mess of coats and umbrellas, but she also spotted a ladies' handbag. Would Pamela have left without her handbag? Perhaps she had many and just left that one behind. But why keep Darjeeling on the order? No Irish or English person drank it to her knowledge, but Pamela did, and she'd told Cissy that Ralph hated it.

She maintained her composure all the way home, and it wasn't until she was inside her own front door that she allowed herself to react. She sat on their bed and the tears flowed. Ralph was a vindictive creature and would take great delight in destroying her. How dare he suggest she was some kind of nymphomaniac? It was so hurtful. How could he and Henry be of the same stock?

She would never forget those weeks after Henry died. Harp was only twelve, and Rose had nowhere to go and no way to support herself or her child. The arrival of the solicitor Algernon Smythe with the news that Henry, dear, loving Henry, had gone to London and signed an affidavit claiming Harp as his child changed their lives forever. The house had been good to them. They'd met Danny and

JohnJoe through that house, not to mention the many other guests and friends they'd made. She met Matt properly when Henry died, since he was the undertaker for the funeral.

Maybe Ralph was right and he would win a court battle. Courts were run by judges, and a judge was far more likely to come from Ralph's class. It might be best to avoid the scandal of her personal life becoming public. She knew she was a respectable woman, but she also knew how he could twist and manipulate; she could emerge as a grubby, gold-digging harlot. Besides, it was Harp's fight, and she seemed to have lots of other things on her mind. From the tone of her letters, coming back to Cobh or even to Ireland was very far down the list of her ambitions.

Rose had gone to the Cliff House to find out about Pamela. She was none the wiser but was suspicious. She hated to worry Marianne further, but she would have to tell her what she found, what Ralph said and about the Darjeeling and the handbag. Wherever Pamela was, there was something strange going on.

CHAPTER 14

*D*ear *Mammy and Matt...*

Harp ran her finger over the ornate initials, HD, on her gold fountain pen, thinking what she should say. Since childhood, she had written every letter with the pen Henry had given her on the day he died. She'd been just a little girl then, eager to go down to the town to see the *Titanic* up close. He'd refused her offer to accompany her and Rose, but before they left, he'd given Harp the pen engraved with her initials.

Up to that moment, she'd been known as Harp Delaney, the daughter of some faceless man never mentioned by her mother except to say he'd died when she was a baby. But Henry told her that day that the 'D' stood for Devereaux. She hadn't understood what he meant at first, but her mother explained it to her.

In the days and weeks after that awful moment when she came bursting in to tell Henry that she thought of him as her real father, and instead found him sitting peacefully in his chair, cold as a stone, that pen had given her comfort. And from that day forward, for better but often for worse too, she was no longer Harp Delaney but Harp Devereaux, known to everyone as Henry's daughter and rightful heir.

'Use this to write your story, Harp,' he'd advised her that day he gave the pen to her, and she was never without it. Even when they had to do the midnight flit out of Ireland after that terrifying night on the beach with Oliver Beckett, she'd had it in her pocket. She was so grateful she'd had the foresight to take it when she'd left the Cliff House for the last time. The idea of Ralph Devereaux in her home was bad enough, but if he ever got his hands on the pen that meant so much to her, well, she didn't know what she would do.

She returned to her letter.

I hope you are both well

Life is very exciting here, and JohnJoe, Elliot and I are 'delighting audiences' according to the New York Times. The vaudeville shows were a lot of fun and we got to meet a lot of people – all perfectly respectable, Mammy, so don't worry – but filling theatres on our own is amazing.

Jerry is such a shrewd negotiator. He makes sure we sell out, and we are becoming quite comfortably off as a result. Celia runs a tight ship too, so it's all being squirrelled away in our respective bank accounts. It's funny – I always imagined myself as a blue stocking, mouldering away happily in some library, living on a pittance, but life takes us on paths we could never envisage.

A wise man – I'll tell you at the end of the letter who, so try to guess (I miss us playing this!) – said, 'Try not to resist the changes that come your way. Instead, let life live through you. And do not worry that your life is turning upside down. How do you know that the side you are used to is better than the one to come?'

So that's what I'm doing, living in the moment and enjoying every second. I know you worry, Mammy, but I promise I'm safe and well. JohnJoe and the boys make sure that nobody untoward gets near me, and I know Kathy has written to you to tell you how sensible Celia is and what a good companion she is to me with all her advice. She thinks I'm for the birds altogether and haven't a clue about the 'real world', and she has to give me what she calls 'a good dose of reality'. So I'm protected very well, I can assure you.

I'll enclose a photograph we had done for some posters that Jerry has made to advertise the shows. Try not to have a heart attack.

Harp smiled as she picked up the picture. Her mother would barely recognise her now.

I met an acrobat – her real name is Ann, but that's not much of a stage name so she is called Gizella – and she advised me on what she called 'my look'. She took me shopping and to a hair salon. It's all the rage over here, sharp haircuts up to the jaw, and then we went to a make-up artist friend of hers who gave me a lesson on how to define my eyes and make my cheekbones appear sharper using rouge and cream. I know you probably think I look very racy, and I do, relatively speaking, but I'm still the same old Harp inside, I promise. I never had much interest in clothes and things when I was young – I remember you trying so hard to get me to look well put together – but according to the people I meet now, I have a very elegant image. I always tell them I get it from my mother, who's much more stylish than me. But I must admit I do enjoy it. I get sent some clothes now, and cosmetics too, because people want me to be associated with their brand. It's a bit mad really, but Jerry says it's good for our image.

JohnJoe too is a bit of a swoon, it seems – girls go crazy when they see him. He thinks it's funny, but he doesn't encourage them. Nobody knows we're a couple, though; we are careful to keep our private life private.

We were in Boston last week and Pat and Kathy came to see the show. They loved it. Uncle Pat has melted completely now. You know he was furious at the start, but he can see how successful we are and how much we love it, so he's accepting it all now. I was worried he might think less of me for fighting with him, but the opposite is true. He pays more attention to me now, and asks me questions about the business. JohnJoe says the only thing his uncle is still miserable about is losing his number one carpenter, Jerry Gallagher. Pat thinks that's a lot worse than losing JohnJoe and me! Not that he's lost us, of course, but you know what I mean.

I miss you and Matt both so much, and I wish you could come and see us and experience it all. Sometimes on stage I don't recognise myself from the small scrap of a child who had not one friend and everyone called a quare hawk.

New York is such a vibrant city, with jazz music really taking off and the vaudeville shows attracting huge crowds. They really are so entertaining, Mammy – I'd love to take you to one. The one we began with at the Adelphi had acrobats who looked like they were made of rubber, and an illusionist called Count Caranzini whose real name was Stan Eggers – he was adorable.

And a comedian called Dino Watts who wasn't one bit funny off stage but hilarious on it. There was a dog called Lucky who could talk and do tricks – honestly, his bark could make words – and his owner was a very fat woman called Louisa who adored Lucky more than anyone on earth, and he her. They were very sweet. Then there was Carla, who was a magician's assistant up until one night on stage when a trick to saw her in half almost went very wrong. Her magician is in jail now, not for almost chopping her legs off but something about a fight with the husband of a bearded lady out on Coney Island – but who knows? It's all very colourful anyway. Carla's trying to get another act going now, looking for another – better! – magician. But everyone is like that here. It's so strange but surprisingly normal for people to be on the lookout for an acrobatic partner or a performing animal or whatever.

I even met Patsy Touhey last week, would you believe it? He was playing at the Lyceum, but he heard about us and came along to the show with his wife. He managed to talk his way in backstage, and after the show, he and the boys and I played a few tunes and sang some songs. His wife is a dancer and performs on stage with him, and he is very funny, telling stories and that sort of thing. But, Mammy, if you heard him play the uilleann pipes... Oh my goodness, it's mesmerising. Honestly.

He knew the tune Chief O'Neill named after me, the one I helped him notate that time back in 1916, and he played it for me. I managed a passable accompaniment on the harp, and Elliot, who'd never heard it in his life before that evening, had it after one or two hearings even though it's a complex tune with a lot of ornamentation. We're going to add it to our set. To hear the great Patsy Touhey say, 'So you're the famous Harp Devereaux,' was something I never imagined in my life. But it happened, and sometimes I need to pinch myself to see if it's all real or not.

Patsy told me Chief O'Neill wasn't well these days, not sick as such, but he's endured a lot of tragedy with the death of several of his children, poor man, and it seems he never goes out now. I wrote to him – Patsy had his address – and he wrote back saying he was delighted to hear from me and was so happy to hear I was making a life in music. He asked that I stop by if I'm ever in Chicago. I'd love to see him again, so JohnJoe said we might make a trip there once this run is over. We're booked to play Reade's State Theatre in New Jersey in July, and Jerry has a whole list of venues all over the place booked between now and the end of the year.

We still live in our five-bedroom apartment in Freeport. Five bedrooms makes it sound enormous, but really they're just two rooms partitioned, and the kitchenette can only take one person standing, and we can hardly turn around in the sitting room now we have the piano in it, but we love it here.

How are things back at home, or dare I ask? I try not to spend any time thinking about anyone unpleasant...

She didn't think her letters were being read by strangers nowadays – it wasn't like the days of the British occupation when it was dangerous to send anything in the post – but she thought she'd better not mention his name just in case.

I know something will have to be done, and now that I'm an adult, it has to be me. And I will. I've been thinking of a solicitor's letter, but just right now, I've other things on my mind. I hope you never see him and that he stays out of your way. You didn't say in your last letter how you feel about the house. Are you contented enough at Matt's place, or does it bother you that man still hanging on? It's hard to tell from all the way over here.

M has written to her mother in Cobh and India again, and to her sister's address in England, and still no answer. Even her solicitors don't seem to know. M made contact with them, and they say they've not heard from her. If she turns up, write straight away. Or better still, telegram.

Pat has some great pictures taken the day Dublin Castle was handed over to Michael Collins and the IRA. I would have loved to have been there. Kitty wrote to JohnJoe, saying how she and Jane were outside on Dame Street while it happened. They went over to Dublin specially from Liverpool. She was thinking about how poor Seamus suffered and died in there at the brutal hands of the G-men, and now that it is ours again, she didn't feel the elation she thought she would. JohnJoe hoped she would meet someone else – he hates the thought of her being lonely, and she's such a lovely young woman – but Seamus is still the love of her life, so I doubt she'd look at anyone else.

It's heartbreaking that some people just can't accept the Treaty. I think Collins is right – it's not perfect, but it's the way to get there – but even over here, there's a lot of rumbling about how the IRA shouldn't accept the authority of the Dáil now. The British have a long history of leaving havoc in their wake, and the idea that all our hard-won gains could be wiped out by internal squabbling is such a horrible prospect. What do you think? Will it be contained? I really hope it will be.

I'm sorry to hear the Devlins are still so vehemently opposed to the Treaty. I even had a long letter from Liz about it, and I'm really at a loss as to how to reply to her. I'm so fond of her and Cissy, and we've been through thick and thin together, but I can't support them in this belief. They say Cumann na mBan is gone mostly to the anti-Treaty side too. To hear them talk about Collins as a traitor, it all just makes me so sad.

The Treaty was ratified and accepted. We all fought so hard for democracy, so surely we must accept the democratic will for peace? Prisoners are all released, and for the first time, we have a chance to go forward as a sovereign country. I personally couldn't care less about taking an oath of allegiance, though I know it sticks in some people's craw. We don't have to be sincere; it's just a means to an end. Why can't those who are opposing the Treaty see that? Pat says everyone is shying away from using the term 'civil war', but it feels like that's what's going on, as the movement is split down the middle.

I'd better sign off now as it's 2 a.m. We were on stage until after eleven and it's the eighth night in a row, so I'm tired. We sleep in late, though, and Jerry makes sure we aren't disturbed.

She felt a pang of guilt. If her mother knew she and JohnJoe essentially lived as man and wife without any such paperwork to legitimise it, she would be so upset. Not to mention living with a man before marriage was illegal, so it was important to keep it a secret. There was a more relaxed attitude to things like that in the theatrical world, but even so, it was a risk.

The Raffertys didn't know, of course, and Jerry and Elliot would never tell anyone. When Celia found out, she had given Harp a *very* long lecture about how careful she had to be and then practically marched her to a birth control clinic in Brooklyn. Harp had been a little embarrassed but glad of the advice. She'd got a diaphragm, which took away the terror of an unwanted pregnancy. She couldn't tell her mother that, not by letter anyway. Maybe one day, when they were face to face... But when would that be? Not for a long time, she was sure.

Freeport was wonderful, the playground of the wealthy as well as a haven for theatre types. Patsy Touhey and his wife lived not too far away, and she and the boys had taken to meeting up with them on occasion for a drink or a chat. It was nice to talk to someone from home. Patsy was a character and always had a multitude of stories; some of them might even have been true. What Harp loved the best about it was how nobody seemed to care what anyone else was doing. Theatre types kept odd hours and lived bohemian lifestyles, and Roaring Liberty blended right in.

She finished the letter.

Write back soon. I love getting letters from you,

Lots of love,

Harp x

P.S. Tell Brian that I never got a reply to my last letter, and that a two-line postcard with a picture of the beach in Bray is not an adequate response to his oldest friend, no matter how busy he is healing the sick!

P.P.S. It was Rumi, by the way. Did you guess? I bet you did.

She sealed the envelope and propped it on her dresser; she'd post it in the morning. JohnJoe was fast asleep. His chest was bare, and there was a slight stubble on his jaw, a golden bristle that she loved the feel of as it caressed her skin when he kissed her. He was broad and muscular, and his chest was covered in golden hair. He was so male, and she adored him in every way. They were best friends and had been since childhood, but they were on the same frequency. He thought as she did on the Irish question, and while they sometimes disagreed, they very rarely argued. She responded to him physically each time he touched her, and when they sang together on stage, a kind of electricity happened. Elliot said once that the intimacy of it felt almost awkward, that an audience shouldn't be privy to such a private sensation. She knew in her heart that he was the only man for her and she the only woman for him.

She sat and watched the rhythmic rise and fall of his chest, one arm behind his head, the other thrown to the side, and she asked herself again why she couldn't marry him. It was a long time since they'd talked about it, but it was obvious he still longed for babies and a home in the suburbs with a white picket fence. She even suspected he was saving his money for a house in case she changed her mind.

There were times when she felt like a dog in the manger, refusing to marry him when there were any number of girls who would be only delighted to be going up the aisle with him. Every show they did, girls filled the front row – Elliot and JohnJoe were both good-looking – but it was JohnJoe they went for. Elliot was slight and blond, but JohnJoe was tall and 'a real dish', as they said. Groups of girls would congregate at the stage door after every performance, waiting for him. They'd pester him for autographs, and he'd have to spend at least half an hour signing them. Sometimes Harp found it hard to take at the end of a long night.

She slipped into bed and felt the familiar comfort of his arms around her. He kissed her sleepily, and she nestled her head on his chest. She loved this man with all of her heart. Then why couldn't she give in to him and marry him? Maybe if she really loved him, she should let him go... The thought made her shiver, and she pressed herself against his sturdy body and closed her eyes.

CHAPTER 15

'What do we think?' Jerry asked, as Harp, JohnJoe and Elliot changed out of their costumes.

'I love the idea,' called JohnJoe from behind the screen where he was undressing. 'What do you say, Harp? After we do the show in Dublin, we can take a side trip to see your mom and Matt? Maybe they might even come to see us! We can get them tickets for the show, put them up in a hotel?'

Harp handed her costume to Celia after climbing into her real clothes. For the stage, she wore sequinned sheer dresses that stopped at the knee in a variety of colours, all painstakingly hand-sewn by Celia, and the new fashion of dropped waists suited her slim figure. She regularly bemoaned the fact that her breasts were tiny, but JohnJoe said she was small but perfectly formed, and that was enough for her. For everyday wear, though, she'd taken to wearing what the Americans called knickers, something that she told JohnJoe would have Rose lying in a darkened room with distress since in Ireland knickers were ladies' underwear; here they were knee-length trousers. She got some odd looks, but she found them so comfortable and she got away with it, being an artistic type.

'I'd love to perform at the Abbey,' she said. 'And of course I'd love to see Mammy and Matt, so it's a yes from me. What do you think, Elliot? Celia? Our first international tour? Mr Yeats and Lady Gregory founded the Abbey Theatre, you know, and Ireland had the first national theatre in the world. It would be such an honour to perform there. It's almost a symbol of Irish culture, and after all we've endured, there's something wonderful about having a theatre where we perform our own songs and music and plays.'

'Sounds good to me,' said Celia through a mouthful of pins, as she sat down to fix Harp's costume. There was a rip in one seam that needed sewing before it got any bigger and the whole thing came apart on stage. 'Though are there many coloured people in Ireland?'

'I've never even seen one, so you'll be very exotic.' Harp grinned. 'You'll be like a glamorous peacock in a flock of boring old pigeons.'

'Well, that'll make a change, I guess,' Celia remarked dryly.

'Sure, if you four are on, then so am I. The idea of sleeping on the ship for a week is the best bit,' Elliot said, yawning.

'Ain't that the truth,' JohnJoe agreed, emerging from behind his screen, shrugging on his jacket.

Harp smiled at him as she removed the sequins from her hair. She was tired, and while the shows were going from strength to strength, especially now that Elliot's song was being played over and over in the music shops by musicians of all kinds and the sheet music was selling like hot cakes, she longed for a break. She'd been to Chicago with one of Rothstein's vaudeville touring entourages, and met up with Chief O'Neill, which was a lovely experience. Patsy Touhey was there too, and the O'Neills came to the show. Afterwards they went to the chief's house for a meal and played music and chatted until the small hours.

As former chief of police, O'Neill knew everything that went on in the city, and he confided to Harp that he was relieved not to have to police Prohibition, as the city was completely in the grip of Italian gangs that ran a very lucrative trade in illegal booze that was being shipped all over the country. Chicago was fashionable and glitzy, but there was an undercurrent of danger there, and the names Johnny Torrio and Big Jim Colosimo seemed to be on everyone's lips. Chief O'Neill said the current crime bosses were almost untouchable, but there was a generation up and coming that would be even worse. He mentioned a New Yorker called Al Capone, who had taken over prostitution and gambling in the city and who was the bane of the police's life, so he was glad to be out of it.

Patsy was right. The chief, to whom the world of Irish music owed so much, had been diminished by the tremendous sadness in his life, that of the loss of his children to disease. He seemed smaller and quieter than when Harp met him in 1916.

As she, JohnJoe and the Tuoheys were leaving the O'Neill house that night to return to the hotel, he'd hugged her warmly and kissed her forehead, and she could feel the genuine affection from this man so many held in awe.

They'd gone back to Boston twice as well, selling out both times, and while it was wonderful to see everyone, the schedule had been exhausting and relentless and they were all in need of a rest.

They had been invited to perform in a studio next month for the inaugural broadcast on New York's first public radio, and it was generating huge excitement. Their performance was going to be recorded. Several of their neighbours in Freeport, vaudeville acts, were getting in on the radio scene, and everyone was saying how it would change the face of the industry forever. The Great Gandolini, the magician who lived downstairs, was terrified and convinced that once radio got a foothold, people would never pay to attend the theatre again, but Harp thought he was wrong.

She was convinced the radio was going to be a wonderful innovation. She remembered discussing the possibility of mass broadcasts with Henry when she was a girl. She had been going through a phase of reading about Heinrich Hertz, the German physicist who discovered radio waves, and Marconi, who made transmitting radio signals something that was accessible by anyone.

She turned her attention back to Jerry, who was explaining how to fit in the Dublin trip around their relentlessly busy schedule. 'We could do the radio interview and record the song on the fourteenth and fifteenth – the studio people are happy with that – and sail the following week. I know we could book in more shows, but we were going to take a break anyway and now is as good a time as any?'

'Whatever you think best, Jerry. Right now, I just want to get out of here without being noticed,' JohnJoe said, raising the curtain on the window. The usual crowd of girls were besieging the stage door below. While they were generally sweet and harmless, tonight he clearly didn't want to spend an hour signing autographs.

'I asked the manager, and there's a delivery door under the stage that leads out to the back alley. So we can get Rudolf Valentino out without being harassed by his adoring fans.' Jerry grinned.

'Hey, lots of them are here for Elliot, you know.' JohnJoe had the grace to look embarrassed.

'Oh yes, about one in a hundred,' the fiddle player said with a smile. 'I promise my feelings aren't hurt, though.'

'And what about my feelings, eh?' Harp tied up her boots and pulled her beloved tweed jacket over her blouse.

Celia rolled her eyes. 'You crazy girl, you know the poor boy has no interest in anyone but you. Although why that is, when he has so many gorgeous girls to choose from who are only longing to marry him and have his babies, goodness only knows.'

'The heart wants what the heart wants.' JohnJoe sighed theatrically. 'And that's all I'm saying on the matter.'

'Will we go to the Cotton Club?' Jerry asked as they ducked out the delivery door into the back alleyway, escaping the gaggle of girls. 'I know you're all tired, but I can't sleep yet – I'm all fired up. And George Johnson is there tonight.' Jerry had taken to bringing them to clubs where the best coloured performers were showcased. The music was new and exciting, and the arrangements inspired them to try new things themselves.

'Do you mind if we don't tonight? I'm starving – can we go for something to eat instead?' Harp asked as JohnJoe slung an arm around her shoulder and kissed her cheek.

'I'm pooped so I'm going straight home. I couldn't sleep this morning with Mrs Lane's arias shaking the foundations,' Elliot moaned. Their neighbour was an enthusiastic but talentless soprano who subjected the entire block to her caterwauling.

'I never hear her,' Jerry remarked.

'That's because you sleep like a stone,' Elliot responded. 'The partition walls are so thin, I can hear you snoring from my room,' he added.

'And I can't come with you if it's the Cotton Club,' Celia said.

Jerry looked confused. 'Why not?'

She sighed. 'In case you haven't noticed, Jerry, it's all White.'

'But Count Basie was playing there last week, and Mamie Smith the week before...'

'I mean the audiences, Jerry. The White folks don't mind listening to our music – they just don't like to sit next to us. You go on to the club. I'll head home with Elliot here.'

Jerry looked mortified. 'No, no, Celia, come back. I'm not going to the Cotton Club if they won't let you in. There's a band I'd like to hear playing at Dino's – come with me to that.'

Celia looked flustered and smiled. 'Well, all right then, so long as you don't make me drink any of those lethal cocktails.'

'Not a bit of it! I'll be sticking to beer myself.' Jerry grinned.

Dino's was a speakeasy where the movers and shakers of the Lower East Side went to hear music, dance and drink. Cocktails were the main drink available, bathtub gin flavoured with fruit juice to kill the horrible taste. Pat had warned them off that before they left Boston, knowing the industrial alcohol that was used to make the gin had wood alcohol, a kind of poison, added by order of the government. The hooch makers thought they could remove it, but in most cases they couldn't and the deaths were mounting. According to Pat, if the taste didn't kill you, then the effects soon would. He had nothing to worry about with Harp; she'd quickly decided she couldn't bear the stuff. Although like the rest of her friends, she still enjoyed Dino's and similar places. One night she'd even seen Texas Guinan, famous in the speakeasy scene, who'd starred in many silent movies as a cowgirl.

The five friends parted at the end of the alleyway, Elliot heading back to Freeport and Celia and Jerry walking off arm in arm towards

Dino's, with Celia calling, 'Night, everyone!' over her shoulder as they left.

'Right-o, my lady,' JohnJoe said, tucking Harp's arm into his as they walked along. 'A hot dog and a milkshake awaits. Or we could go somewhere fancy if you prefer?'

'No, you know I love hot dogs, and a malt milkshake to wash it down would be wonderful. I might even have an ice cream.'

They turned onto a brightly lit street and stood by to allow a bunch of ladies who were clearly having a night out on the town pass by. The women were a bit drunk, and one patted JohnJoe's rear as she passed, to the hilarity of her friends. *So much for Prohibition*, Harp thought.

New York never ceased to astound her. Everywhere was open at all times of the day and night, and it was so vibrant and busy. And though she was constantly warned of the dangers, she never felt threatened. She and JohnJoe went out walking most days, exploring the city. She adored it all, riding the Manhattan elevated railway alongside the Bowery or soaking up the atmosphere in Times Square. They loved the boardwalk on Coney Island and paddling in the sea. And even though she wasn't really a shopper, she did enjoy browsing in the fancy stores on 5th Avenue and buying little gifts for her mother, and occasionally day clothes for herself.

The money was flowing in thanks to Jerry, and Celia took care of their finances with complete transparency. All five of them had a separate bank book, and a lodgement was made each week; Harp would gaze in astonishment as the sum in her book climbed higher and higher. The flat was miniscule but so was the rent, and it still suited their purposes so there wasn't a great deal to spend the money on. All of them had simple tastes in food, and they hardly drank. Elliot was saving for the operation on his hand, Celia planned to use her money to do politics and economics in college, and Jerry was thinking of investing in music venues and maybe even acquiring one of his own.

Only JohnJoe and Harp had no plans, or not ones they talked

about, although Harp suspected JohnJoe was thinking of buying a house as she often saw him looking at property in the newspaper.

'So what's the news?' JohnJoe asked, a joke they regularly shared considering they lived and worked together, although sometimes it felt as if they never had any time just to be a couple. 'You look like there's something on your mind?'

'To be honest, I was wondering if Celia and Jerry might end up as an item,' Harp said. 'I think she really likes him. Did you see the way she lit up when he asked her to Dino's?'

'I did, and I hope they don't get in trouble for it.' JohnJoe sighed. 'People are still very against mixed relationships here. I'd be worried for their safety.'

'I know. It's hard to believe people make such a deal of who is with who when it's nobody's business but their own. I think Jerry and Celia should do whatever makes them happy, and Elliot should stop being so shy and ask one of those stage-door girls out – they'd be only delighted even if you are their first choice. Do you think he ever will?'

'He should, and there's plenty of girls out there for him.' JohnJoe smiled, squeezing Harp's arm. 'I know we joke about it, but not all of them are waiting for me.'

They crossed Times Square, lit up from every storefront, and turned down 45th Street to Joey's, their favourite diner.

'Hey, if it ain't my own sweet Irish colleen!' Joey Sparks, the owner, greeted them from behind the counter as they entered the warm diner. Joey had once confided to them his real name was Iosif Sparshikov and that the moniker Joey Sparks was invented on Ellis Island to replace the Russian that the customs officials found impossible to pronounce or spell. His accent was hybrid St Petersburg and Hell's Kitchen combined, and Harp loved it.

As they entered, he was flipping burgers and pouring drinks for several customers at once, but he kept up the chatter to them as they made their way to their favourite booth at the back. 'My ma and my sister go to the show. Wow, you guys, she don't believe me that I know you two! She say I'm dreaming that the lovely Harp is my real friend, and I tell her no, but she don't believe.'

Harp laughed. She was getting used to being recognised in the street, and now several people in the diner were nudging and looking.

'You're the girl that sings "The Heart Will Know"?' a woman asked as they passed the booth where she and her husband were sitting.

Harp coloured. 'Er…yes, well, with my band, Roaring Liberty, not me on my own…'

'I saw you recently at Coney Island. You were wonderful. I've been trying to get tickets for weeks, but the shows are all sold out,' the woman lamented. 'Could I have your autograph, please?'

Within minutes several people were crowded around, thrusting scraps of paper and pens at her to sign her name. JohnJoe too was being bombarded, and he was answering their questions as best he could: No, Elliot wasn't with them; yes, he was Irish but grew up in Boston; no, he and Harp were not related; no, he had no spare tickets for the shows…

Joey eventually came out from behind the counter and battled his way through the crowd, then ushered them to their booth at the very back, posting the short-order cook, a beefy man called Sergei, to stop anyone else approaching them.

'You are too famous for my diner now, Harp and JJ. Too much people know you and they come to see you. But it is very good for my business, so thank you.' He winked. 'You want the usual?'

'Yes, please,' Harp answered, as she and JohnJoe grinned at each other.

'I think we've made it, Harp,' JohnJoe whispered. 'Not bad for a pair of skinny misfit kids, is it?'

'I wonder what Emmet Kelly would say if he saw us now.'

'He'd think what a damned fool he was to bully such a smart, beautiful and talented girl, but I'm sure glad nobody else caught your eye before I did.' JohnJoe held her hand across the table, not caring who saw. 'I love you, Harp, so much. And you know with whatever you want to do, I'm with you all the way.'

'Thank you, JohnJoe. I know you are and I appreciate it. I don't think I could have done any of this if it weren't for you. You make me braver, and I know you'll always be there for me. Ever since that day when Emmet Kelly threw mud at me, remember? When we went for sweets and I was twelve and you fourteen?'

He smiled at the memory. 'Yeah, I slugged him one, and then his old man came over and was going to give me a hiding, but Danny showed up and busted his face, then you showed him where to bury the knuckleduster. And the cop came to the house to arrest Danny for an affray. You fed him a whole story about Danny being a journalist, and he ended up feeling sorry for us.'

'Ever since that day, you've been my hero.'

'And I'll continue to be, for the rest of my life, Harp.' She could hear the tinge of sadness there.

'JohnJoe, I…' She tried to explain once again.

He raised his hand to stop her, and then Joey arrived with their food and drinks. Sensing it was a difficult moment, he withdrew without interrupting them, nodding to the wall-like Sergei to remain at his post as the diner had suddenly filled up.

'No, it's all right,' JohnJoe said. 'I know why you won't marry me, and I understand it too. I'm not just saying it – I honestly do understand. And if men had to give up what women do every day, none of us would sign up for marriage either. But it just makes me sad, that's all. I want to marry you, Harp. You're the only girl for me, and I'll go to my grave feeling that way, I know I will. But I sometimes think about us having a family, or getting a house together when this is all over and settling down…'

'I'm not saying I will always feel this way, but I think I probably will. You and I have always been honest with each other, so it just feels unfair not to tell you. I don't think I want to be a mother, ever.'

JohnJoe swallowed, and she could see he was trying not to cry. His eyes, suspiciously bright, betrayed him.

'Perhaps it's not fair of me to hold onto you…' she began, barely able to get the words out. The thought of losing him was impossible, but did she have the right to deny her favourite person on earth the joy of a wife and children?

'Don't you ever let me go, Harp Devereaux,' he said quietly, his green eyes blazing with intensity. 'I can cope with not being your husband, nor a father, if that's how it has to be, but I can't live without you. I could never do that.'

To cover his emotion, he took a bite of his hot dog and washed it down with some chocolate milkshake, then changed the conversation. 'So have you heard from your mother? How is it back in Ireland?'

Harp was glad to talk about something different. 'Yes, I got a letter from Mammy this morning, and I've been waiting for a chance to tell you about it. Most people are really welcoming to her and Matt, but the row with the Devlins is still going on, I can't believe, after all we've been through together, it's come to this.'

'Well, the decision about the Treaty has been made now, and Liz and Cissy and everyone else will have to accept it. They can't go throwing away friendships they've had forever just because not every-thing went the way they wanted.'

'I know. I wish I was back there so I could knock all their heads together. But they did tell Mam something interesting about Pamela. Ralph's telling people she's gone back to India, but Mam got the impression something odd was going on.'

'Really?' JohnJoe was clearly taken aback. 'What makes her think she's still in Ireland? Marianne hasn't had any response from Cobh to her letters.'

'The Devlins said when Pamela first came to Ireland, she asked them to order in this special Indian tea called Darjeeling – a kind of red leaf tea – and send it up to the house with the other monthly deliveries. And the order has never been cancelled.'

'Maybe Ralph drinks it.'

'Apparently Pamela told the Devlins that he hated it when she was ordering it before.' Harp grimaced. 'I live here and it doesn't bother me as much as Mam, but I'd still love it if he just left.'

JohnJoe sighed, then finished his hot dog. 'It's hard to know what to believe, and Danny says Marianne is getting more and more worried. Him living there must be really upsetting your mother, and she deserves to live in peace in her own town. Look, let's go over, see the lay of the land and take it from there. I had a thought... You prob-ably won't like it and maybe it's a terrible idea but...'

'Let's hear it.'

'You could pay him off. Ralph is driven by money, we know that. He might take a big payout just to walk away. I know he has the Pascoe money now, though, so...'

'I'm not sure that he does actually. There's another rumour Pamela's cut off his access to her funds. She's independently wealthy, it seems, from the Pascoe fortune and her own parents, but she was in communication with her solicitors and telegrams were sent indicating she was trying at least to cut him off. Nothing happens in Cobh without everyone knowing it. So maybe bribing him will be enough to get rid of him. I'd do it for a peaceful life for Mammy and Matt.'

'Well, if she's cut him off, I suppose that means she's definitely gone back to India. Maybe the letters there just take longer. Danny said Marianne's very upset about not hearing back from either place. She even got little Katie photographed at a proper studio, and her and Danny too, and sent a copy to both addresses, Ireland and India. Danny says she's really hoping her mother would come to Boston for a visit.'

'When did you have this long conversation with Danny?' Harp asked, then sipped her milkshake.

'That's my headline news that I've been waiting to tell you. Uncle Pat has had a telephone installed in the office and another in the house, so Danny called me from there to the post office. It was great to hear from him. He's doing so well. He's got four crews working under him now, and he's keeping on top of them all. He and Marianne are looking to buy a bigger place out at Beacon Hill, where all the toffs live.'

Harp chuckled. 'It will be Danny behind that, not Marianne. She couldn't give a hoot, but he likes the finer things in life, doesn't he? I'll never forget when he came to Ireland to collect you that time when we were children – he looked so glamorous with his beautifully cut suits and handmade Italian shoes. I don't think I've ever seen him not beautifully put together. Even in the height of the war, he always looked smart. No wonder all the girls in Cobh were mad for him.'

'He sure does, but I think he feels a bit that Marianne married beneath her and he wants to give her all she had growing up. He might dress well and have a fancy car and all the rest, but he's still just an Irish Catholic kid from the tenements at the end of it all. If it wasn't for Uncle Pat taking him in from Kathy's sister, he'd be still there. Marianne is a lady, born and raised, and he's just trying to be worthy of her, I suppose. Danny wouldn't want anyone thinking that she was slumming it with him – he's proud that way – and you have to admit they are an odd couple.'

'Well, I don't know, odd matches often work very well. Difference is famously the cause of a solid marriage – look at Anne Elliot and Captain Wentworth in *Persuasion*, or Jane Bennet and Charles Bingley in *Pride and Prejudice*, or Beatrice and Benedict in *Much Ado about Nothing*. Then there's Bathsheba and Gabriel in *Far from the Madding Crowd*, Dorothea and Will in *Middlemarch*. And just in our own lives, Kitty and Seamus, Danny and Marianne, Mammy and Matt, maybe Jerry and Celia… The list is endless.'

JohnJoe hooted with laughter.

'What?' Harp asked.

'You're so lovely but so weird. Fiction and reality blend so seamlessly for you. You spend so much of your life stuck in books, I think sometimes one life seeps into the other.'

'That's true,' she conceded. 'I've lived most of my life through books, but you don't object to all I've learned.' She winked and JohnJoe grinned sheepishly.

She knew most women were prudish about their bodies, physical pleasure seen as the domain of men only, but in that regard, as in everything, Harp was not most women. She read books that were banned because of their racy content, and so she knew a lot more about the intimate side of life than most girls her age, knowledge that JohnJoe frequently saw the benefits of.

'You'll be the death of me, Harp Devereaux, but you're right, I wouldn't have you any other way.' He chuckled. 'So that's what we'll do, go back to Ireland and see if we can't lure that snake out of your house with a big bag of cash. He's shallow enough to take it.'

'He is that, but there's something else. I can't really explain it, but he hates me.'

'He hates everyone. All he has in him is hate...' JohnJoe tried to soothe her, but she shook her head.

'No, I know he does, you're right, but he really despises me. Always has. He sees something in me, something that really riles him up. Since I first met him as a twelve-year-old, he's hated me, and I don't know if money will be enough. He frightens me, JohnJoe. Most people are neither all good nor all bad – we all have bits of both – but Ralph is one of those rare people with no redeeming quality, not one.'

'That just means we need to tread very carefully. But don't worry, I'll be beside you every step of the way.'

CHAPTER 16

*M*arianne and Danny as well as Kathy and Pat came to see them off from Battery Park, and they all stayed at the Plaza on the Central Park side of 5th Avenue the night before they sailed for Ireland. Pat insisted on booking rooms for JohnJoe, Elliot, Jerry, Celia and Harp as well so they could all enjoy a farewell dinner together.

To their surprise, Pat mentioned a big contract he'd just landed to build a new series of lecture halls at Harvard University, and Elliot commented that he knew the campus well.

'How come you're so familiar with the place?' Pat asked conversationally.

Elliot seemed uncomfortable for a split second but went on to explain. 'Oh, I studied there for a while, but I never finished…'

JohnJoe sensed his friend's discomfort and changed the subject rapidly, but it left Harp wondering why Elliot would go to such a prestigious university and drop out and why he'd never mentioned it before now.

They dined on lobster and broiled Spanish mackerel in sauce Colbert, Long Island duckling, celery served au jus and baked sweet potatoes. Just when she was sure she couldn't squeeze in another bite, a tray of desserts arrived. She saw the baked apple dumplings with whipped cream and brandy sauce and had to give in.

Celia hadn't joined them for dinner, choosing to spend the evening with some of her old friends now that she was back in Boston.

After dinner, the men retired to the billiards room, leaving the ladies to take tea in the residents' lounge on the second floor over-looking the park. The beautiful room was decorated in teals and greens and seemed to be inspired by the foliage and trees in the park below. To their relief they had it to themselves, so they relaxed. The room was dotted with easy chairs and sofas, and Kathy sat on a large brocade one, kicking off her shoes and tucking her feet under her. Harp was, as usual, in awe of Kathy's style. She never dressed too young for her age, but there was nothing matronly about her. Tonight she wore a blood-red silk dress cut on the bias that draped over her curves. The shoulder was decorated with tiny seed pearls in the shape of a hummingbird. And in her lustrous copper hair, normally styled straight but currently curly, she wore a mother-of-pearl clip with a dyed feather exactly the colour of her dress. She caused heads to turn wherever she went.

'So how are you feeling about going back?' Kathy asked as the staff withdrew, having left the tea on the sideboard.

'I'm looking forward to it, I think.' Harp poured tea into three Royal Doulton china cups, adding milk to Kathy's and a lump of sugar to Marianne's. She wondered for a moment that she was so familiar with these women that she didn't need to ask how they took their tea. She'd never imagined having women friends – girls had mystified her most of her life – but Marianne and Kathy were as close as sisters to her and she loved them. Harp handed the women their drinks and relaxed on the sofa beside Kathy, her belly fit to bursting after the huge dinner. With them she didn't need to maintain decorum.

As she turned to Kathy, she saw beads of perspiration on the older woman's face, and her cheeks were flushed bright red.

'Kathy, are you all right?' Harp asked, concerned.

Kathy sighed. 'Just a hot flash. God, I'm so sick of this.'

Harp had wondered if that was what was making Kathy irritable.

She'd snapped at Pat several times at dinner, which was most unlike her.

'Is it the menopause?' Harp asked.

Kathy nodded, dabbing her face with some cold water from a jug on the table. 'It's horrible. I suddenly get so hot, I have aches and pains like an old woman, I can't seem to control my emotions, I can't sleep. I can't remember the last time I had a full night's sleep! And it's not Pat's fault, but I just can't bear to have him near me.'

'You poor thing. I remember my Grandmama Pascoe going through it. It wasn't spoken about, of course, but how we women suffer in silence.' Marianne handed Kathy another glass of iced water.

'Aristotle was the first person in literature to identify it,' Harp said, 'the menopause, as the end of a woman's reproductive life. Then in the late eleventh century, a female medic called Trotula de Ruggiero produced a two-part medical report on it. Then in 1821 Dr Charles Negier, a French physician, made the connection between women's age and various complaints. Doctors were quick to diagnose women with "hysteria", coming from the Greek word "hysterus", which literally means womb.'

'Typical man. We're just being hysterical,' Marianne replied.

'I read a book last year, *The Dangerous Age*, by a Danish author called Karin Michaelis,' Kathy said. 'It's about a forty-two-year-old woman who runs away from her husband and everyone she knows to be alone in a villa and to write frankly about her feelings and her longings. It was scandalous at the time. Now that I'm living it, I can't say I blame her.'

She took a long sip of water. 'She said it was as if she were inhabiting the wrong body, like her body and her mind, her emotions, were at war with her and she had no way to fight back.'

'Sounds horrendous,' Harp remarked.

'It's no picnic, that's for sure, but like everything, this too will pass, I suppose. There's a woman on Long Island, she's a kind of herbal doctor, I think – her mother was a Cherokee and she knows a lot about the medicinal qualities of plants – and she made me a tincture that definitely helps alleviate the worst of the symptoms.'

Harp smiled, 'Us women have a lot to put up with, don't we?'

'We certainly do.' Marianne turned from the painting she'd been admiring and grimaced as she sat down opposite the other two women. 'I have the most awful piles since having Katie, but the doctor told me it was normal and they'd settle down, but they don't show any signs of it yet. Honestly, if men had to have the babies, the human race would die out in one generation.'

'You poor thing. My mother suffered terribly with them, but she found vinegar baths helped. Have you tried that?' Kathy suggested.

Harp loved how open Kathy was about bodies and women's matters. She knew her forthrightness on the matter didn't shock either Kathy or Marianne, but most people were mortified to even discuss any aspect of their physical health. Rose was a wonderful mother but a little prudish, and so she could never speak as candidly as she did with Kathy.

'No, the doctor gave me some ointment, worse than useless. Danny threatened to go down to him and, in his words, "shove it where the sun don't shine", but I managed to restrain him.' She giggled, that charming tinkle that Harp had first noticed about her. 'I'll try the vinegar. Failing that, I might try going to your lady. She seems to know more about women's bodies than old Doctor Watson anyway.'

'You should. It can't hurt, and as you say, she at least knows what you're talking about – she has lots of children herself. I don't envy you the piles, but I would have loved a baby.' Kathy sighed wistfully. 'But it wasn't to be. At least we have your two boys. I know they're not mine, but it feels like they are.'

Marianne and Harp shared a glance. It was the great sadness of Kathy Rafferty's life, and while she rarely mentioned it, they knew it hurt her, even still. She and Pat had consulted so many doctors over the years, desperate to conceive, but to no avail.

Harp reached over and placed her hand on Kathy's, and the older woman looked at her and smiled sadly.

'You're such a wonderful grandmama to Katie,' Marianne said. 'And Danny and JJ definitely see you as their mother. Though you didn't give birth to them, you are their mother in every way that matters.'

'I'm so grateful for those boys and for the fine women they chose too.'

Out of nowhere Marianne welled up and wiped a tear.

'What's the matter, dear?' Kathy asked, clearly stricken. 'Have I upset you?'

'Oh no, not you. I just miss my mother, that's all. I don't know where she is, and it seems that Ralph was beastly to her, which I believe utterly but simply can't bear the thought of. My papa was a bit hopeless with money and so on, but he adored her, and she wouldn't know how to deal with a man like Ralph Devereaux. Rose tried her best to find out what's going on, but he sent her away without any answer. He says she's in India but I've written there and nothing.'

Harp had filled Kathy in on the letter from her mother, so she knew of the situation.

'Who have you contacted there?' Kathy asked.

Marianne sighed. 'I think she sold our house in Shimla to pay Papa's debts, so there was probably no point in writing to her there, but I did anyway, hoping the new owners might know where she is. And I sent one to the club – it's a British place and everyone eats and drinks there. I even wrote to the chairwoman of the British Wives Association, Lady Ostenbury – she was always nice when I was a child and very discreet – but I just had a note from a secretary back saying Lord Ostenbury had been recalled to Westminster. Finally, I wrote to my aunt in England, Mama's sister, to see if she'd turned up there, but she has not heard from her. She was going to visit Mama's solicitors in London, though, to see what they know.'

'You could try a telegram, to any of her old friends in India?' Kathy suggested.

'I don't really know who else I could ask, and she might not want people knowing her business. It's a very gossipy place, Shimla, lots of bored Britishers sitting about doing nothing except sticking their noses into other people's business. If I contacted any of them, we'd be the talk of the place, especially after poor old Papa and all of that business. No, they've had quite enough scandal from the Pascoes to date.' Marianne shook her head.

'Hold on, let me think. Pat and I had dinner with a couple a few years ago – they were going out there. I think they're still there to the best of my knowledge. He was some big-shot banker, going out there to run some business enterprise, but she was a farmer's daughter from Wisconsin and suffered no fools, as I recall. She was very nice. Perhaps I could contact her and make discreet enquiries? I feel sure they would know people.'

'Well, if you could, that would be wonderful. And perhaps my aunt will have some news in the meantime,' Marianne said hopefully.

Harp felt a pang of pity for her friend. She and Marianne were a most unlikely pairing, she knew, as different as chalk and cheese really, but they held each other in genuine affection. Marianne Pascoe was the daughter of Alfie Pascoe, the last male heir of the Pascoe Trading Company, an entity that had made several fortunes in the Far East since the mid-1800s under the frugal eye of Marianne's Cornish great-grandfather and grandfather. But as her mother was wont to say, a scatterer follows a gatherer, and Alfie squandered as much of his family's vast wealth as he could get his hands on through a love of whiskey and old nags. Luckily his father saw what kind of man his son had become and tightened up his will to limit Alfie's access to the money.

Though he'd lost her in a poker game to that cold odd fish Oliver Beckett, and couldn't bear to live with the consequences, Marianne forgave him and missed him very much.

Danny was a wonderful husband. His philandering days were well and truly behind him, and he was an ideal husband and a devoted father, but Harp knew Marianne missed her parents. She wished there was something she could do to reunite Marianne with her mother.

'Mammy and I will make more enquiries when I go home. Perhaps your mother confided in someone there of her plans,' Harp said.

Marianne smiled. 'Thank you both. It means so much to me that you want to help me. I long for her to meet Danny and Katie. She'll love them both, I know, and Danny has even said we can offer her a home here with us should she want to come, which is so generous of him considering he's never even met her. He's determined to buy this enormous house with spectacular gardens. I've told him I'm happy where I am, but he says our house is too small. And while I don't want him having to work so hard to pay for it, it is a lovely place and the grounds are really special.'

'I think if you wanted the moon out of the night sky, my boy would try to get it for you,' Kathy said with a smile. 'He's still pinching himself that he's married to someone like you, I think.'

'If anyone should be grateful, it's me,' Marianne protested. 'Danny is the best thing that's ever happened to me, and...well, I shouldn't say really, and promise you won't tell until later, but I'm going to have another baby.'

'Marianne!' Harp hugged her. 'That's wonderful! Congratulations.'

'Oh, another baby in the family! I can't wait!' Kathy clapped her hands.

'I'm excited. I'm not far along yet so Katie will be old enough by the time I'm due to understand the concept at least of a little brother or sister.'

'Oh, that's going to be so wonderful, and how are you feeling? I've heard the first few months are very difficult.' Kathy asked.

'Oh, I'm fine so far, just a little more tired. Danny is so helpful, and he doesn't care that the other men tease him for doing so much with Katie or even in the house – he cooks and even washes up. He's a godsend, truly.'

'And rightly so,' Harp answered with more spirit than she intended. 'Why should we do it all? We conceive and carry children, give birth. The men expect to have a fluffy bundle handed to them and for all of their friends to clap them on the back for a job well done, and then sit at the table to have their meals served and their shirts starched, and for us to be delighted with the opportunity to enslave ourselves to a man...'

'Nobody will accuse you of that anyway, Harp, so you needn't worry.' Kathy smiled.

'I do take care of JohnJoe,' Harp retorted, stung. 'But he takes care of me too. We're equal, nobody better than the other...' she tried to explain, knowing her feminist ways bemused most people.

'And do you think Pat thinks he's better than me? Or Danny thinks he's better than Marianne?' Kathy asked gently.

Harp hated that she'd taken Marianne's good news and turned it into an argument. 'I'm sorry, Marianne,' she apologised instantly. 'It's lovely news about the baby. I didn't mean that...'

'Of course you didn't, Harp. We're all different. I like cooking and cleaning and keeping our home nicely. We had staff when I was young, but I prefer to do it myself. I like Danny being proud of us and how happy he is to come home after a hard day's work to a nice meal and his clothes laundered.'

'I know you do, and there's nothing wrong with it, nothing at all. Ignore me, I'm peculiar.' She gave a rueful smile.

'You're not peculiar, Harp. You're kind and loving and highly intelligent. You're the toast of New York City. But being a wife and mother is not the end of the world either, you know. Who do you think rules the roost in the Rafferty house?' Kathy smiled conspiratorially.

'In public, Pat, but in reality, you,' Harp answered simply. 'I understand that, but men have so much power bestowed upon them because of their gender – I just find it hard to accept.'

'It's true,' Kathy conceded. 'Married women are, in some matters anyway, subservient to their husbands. But, Harp, if you and your husband make decisions together, neither a slave to the other, not through bullying but because he trusts you and you are part of a team, a team of equals, what does it matter? I know you probably think JJ put me up to this, but I swear to you he hasn't. I just can see how much he wants to marry you and how much you are resisting, not because you don't love him – I know you do – but because you are afraid of being tied down and restricted. But just try to see it another way. JJ would never restrict you or have you do anything you didn't want to do. So, the only barrier to married women's freedom is their husbands, and if he's never going to stand in your way, then is it worth the fight?'

'I just don't want to marry anyone,' Harp said, knowing she sounded like a sullen child.

'Or have a family?' Kathy probed.

Harp glanced at Marianne, the perfect mother. She'd lost a little of her slight girlish figure, but her peaches-and-cream complexion and blond corkscrew curls were as endearing as ever. She was blissfully Mrs Danny Coveney, mother to Katie and soon another, and she couldn't be happier darning her husband's socks and making his favourite supper.

'I know you are trying to be helpful, Kathy, and sometimes I envy you both the stability you have, but it's not for me. Not the husband, not the babies, none of it.' She couldn't help but notice the sadness on Kathy's face. Kathy loved Harp, Harp knew she did, but JJ was her boy and her heart ached for him. Harp didn't blame her for trying.

'I offered to let him go, to let him find someone else, but he doesn't want to,' she said quietly.

Kathy patted Harp's leg. 'And he never will, Harp, that's the trouble.'

CHAPTER 17

DUBLIN, IRELAND

*T*he entire audience of the Abbey Theatre rose to their feet, roaring their approval. The theatre had sold out for the entire week of their run. This was their sixth night, and it was as packed as the first. Harp held hands with Elliot on one side and JohnJoe on the other, bowing as the standing ovation went on and on; they'd already done two encores, but the crowd refused to let them go. They had changed their repertoire to include more Irish songs and tunes rather than ones popular in America, but to Harp's astonishment, the entire crowd suddenly began chanting 'The Heart Will Know, The Heart Will Know', over and over again. Clearly Elliot's song had reached Irish ears. She grinned at the blond violinist, who was blushing furiously. 'Come on, boys. They're not going to let us go until we give them what they want to hear.'

JohnJoe sat back at the piano once more and Elliot picked up his fiddle, and soon the entire auditorium was singing along.

It was extraordinary how sales of the sheet music of 'The Heart

Will Know' which had gained popularity already, had exploded worldwide after Roaring Liberty's first radio appearance.

Jerry had approached Thomas B Harms, the famous Tin Pan Alley publisher, bringing the whole band with him to perform the song right in the middle of the shop with the large windows opening onto West 28th Street, where even passers-by gathered to listen. The publisher had immediately offered them $800 for the exclusive rights to the song, and Elliot, Harp and JohnJoe had been all for accepting what seemed like a huge sum. But Jerry had done his research, and instead of jumping at the $800, he went to rival music publishers M Witmark and Sons. Like Thomas B Harms, M Witmark and Sons knew a hit when they heard it, and Jerry had played the two publishers against each other until he walked away with a much better deal, a $5000 up-front fee and fifteen percent of the profit of all sheet music sales worldwide. The song turned out to be hugely popular and had generated over $100,000 since it was released, with the band getting a cut on every single sale. Celia was driven frantic trying to keep track of the royalties pouring in from so many different countries.

Although Elliot was the songwriter, he had insisted on sharing the profits with his four friends. 'I couldn't have sold it without your voice, Harp, and your harmonies, JohnJoe,' he'd said earnestly. 'Celia is the backbone of this band, and Jerry was the one who made the deal. If it wasn't for all of you, this would never have happened.'

After the show, Harp and the others were gathered in her dressing room, reliving the night, when a gentle knock caused a pause in the conversation.

'Come in!' called Harp, and the door opened.

'Well, if it isn't Miss Devereaux, the best code maker and spy I ever had. And now look at her, the darling of the international stage, if you don't mind.'

Harp had never seen Michael Collins in anything but a nondescript suit, his modus operandi during the war being to remain as inconspicuous as possible, but now he was dressed in military uniform and was breathtakingly handsome, tall and broad, with chestnut hair swept back off his forehead. He crossed the room in two strides and placed his hands on her shoulders, just as he'd done the night Seamus was killed.

'I'm as proud as punch of you, Harp. You're a superstar over in America, they tell me, and I'm not one bit surprised at that either. Sure, you're gifted altogether on the harp and you've a voice like a nightingale.'

'Hello, Mick. It's lovely to see you again, and under much nicer circumstances.' She turned to introduce the others. 'You remember JohnJoe O'Dwyer...'

'I do indeed.' Collins extended his hand and shook JohnJoe's warmly. 'How are ya, JohnJoe? Delighted you got out of that scrape below in Cork – he was a right nasty piece of work, that Beckett. And how's your uncle? Well, I hope?'

'He is, Mr Collins...'

'Mick, for God's sake, don't mind that "Mr" thing. Sure, aren't you as old as myself nearly.' He winked at Harp, who couldn't help laughing. 'Tell Pat Rafferty I was asking for him, will you. I must make it over there one of these fine days. We have a lot to thank our American friends for, so we do.' He turned to Elliot. 'And who is this?'

'Elliot Krauss, a Boston boy of German parents,' Harp said.

Collins shook his hand warmly too. 'By God, you're a fine fiddle player. You'd almost swear you'd Irish blood in you, you're so good.' He laughed. 'Is it your first time to Ireland?'

'It sure is, and we're having a great time,' Elliot replied. 'I don't know what I was expecting, but some of the stories Harp and JJ told us about their time here during the war...'

'Would put the hair up on the back of your neck, I know. And they're true too, unfortunately. Still, we're at the tail end of it now, please God. We've all had enough. 'Tis time to put the feet up and enjoy ourselves now.'

'And this is Jerry Gallagher, who –'

Collins's face split into a huge grin, and he embraced Jerry in a huge bear hug. 'I know well who he is. Are you stuck in with these impresarios now? And what are you playing, the spoons, I suppose?' He released Jerry and punched him playfully on the shoulder.

Harp and JohnJoe exchanged a surprised glance; Jerry had never mentioned that he and Collins knew each other.

'Howya, Mick.' Jerry grinned as he lit a cigarette.

'I knew we got you out, but I thought you were building with Pat Rafferty?'

'I was, but well, then this happened...' He shrugged.

'And what do you do, seriously?' Collins asked.

'I do the deals.' He gave a devilish grin and Collins guffawed.

'Oh, lads, I'd have eyes on the back of my head so with this fella, wouldn't trust him as far as I'd throw him.'

'Celia here does the books, so we've nothing to worry about on that score,' Harp teased, going along with the joke as everyone else laughed.

Collins at once shook Celia's hand. 'Welcome to Ireland, Miss Celia. I know your people are fighting hard for equality on your side of the water, and I know you will win. We Irish have only just thrown off the English yoke after centuries of oppression. We understand what it is like to be treated as inferior in our own country, and our hearts are with you in your struggle.'

Celia beamed with tears in her eyes. 'You are very much loved in America, Mr Collins...'

'Mick!'

'Mick. Loved as a brave man and a true leader.'

'Can we take you to dinner, Mick?' Harp asked. They'd been invited to dine at the Shelbourne, where they were staying as guests of the manager.

'Harp, my lovely girl, nothing would give me greater pleasure, but I'm entering the holy state of matrimony soon and Kitty will string me up if I don't get up to Granard first thing in the morning. She's at home at the moment, and there's a number of wedding things she needs my opinion on. I'm on strict instructions to be on the nine o' clock train from Kingsbridge. Now, as we all well know, the lovely Kitty will do exactly as she pleases anyway, but it would seem, for a reason best known to my long-suffering fiancée, we must go through the motions of consultation nonetheless. So I'm off to lay my head down for a few hours before we get on the road.'

'Congratulations. When is the wedding?' Harp asked.

'November, I'm told.' He chuckled. 'I'm a lucky man. 'Tisn't every woman could put up with me, and my Kitty is a rare jewel, so I'll gallop up the aisle like a spring calf, so I will.' He stopped and thought for a moment. 'Sure, maybe ye'd come and sing at the wedding? She loves your music. We were only talking about it the other day.'

Harp beamed. 'It would be an honour.'

'Great stuff.' He winked and gave her a one-armed hug. 'I'll get extra points for that now, so I might get away with less input on the dresses and cakes front.'

'Well, 'twas great to see you again, Mick. Mind yourself now. As you say, 'tisn't over yet, so watch your back,' Jerry warned, referring to the ongoing unrest on the subject of the Treaty.

The anti-Treaty forces had taken the Four Courts in Dublin in late June, and Collins had borrowed two 18-pounder field guns from the British and had blasted the rebels inside. The entire country was in shock that Collins had turned British guns on his own people. Even Harp, a stalwart supporter of the commander in chief, found it hard to accept at the time, but now that she was here, witnessing the reality of civil war, she knew he had to do it.

'Yerra, 'twill all sort itself out, it always does. 'Tis Corkmen and women did the best of the fighting when we were trying to wear the British out, but wouldn't you know it, 'tis the same gang are breaking my heart now over the Treaty. But I'll go down home soon and we'll work it out. They're reasonable men and women and patriots of this country, and sure, they're my own crowd, so we'll come to an under-standing, don't you worry.'

Harp knew he was playing down the depth of resentment and bitterness people felt about the new government and the partition of the country. Matt was horrified at the divisions that had appeared in families and friendships since he'd come back, and she hoped Collins wasn't underestimating the strength of feeling.

'Well, be careful down there. We need you,' she said as she opened the door.

'I'll be grand, Harp. Sure, they'd never shoot me in my own place.' He leaned over and kissed her cheek and was gone.

After they were dressed in their street clothes once more, they strolled over O'Connell Bridge towards the Shelbourne, and Harp and JohnJoe reminisced about the last time they were in Dublin. It was when she was sent to relay a message to Collins from the Queenstown battalion of the IRA, but it was also the night that Kitty O'Dwyer's husband, Seamus, was taken into Dublin Castle for questioning and his tortured and battered body dumped lifeless on Dame Street the next morning. Collins had called to Kitty and begged her to go to America. Seamus was one of his best and most trusted soldiers, and Collins feared that the Crown forces would come after his wife next. That had been the last time Harp had seen him until tonight. Time had taken its toll – he looked a little older, a bit wearier – but he was still the handsome, optimistic joker he always was.

Despite Collins's assertions that it was all but over, the signs of the war were everywhere. There were still armed soldiers on the street, except this time they wore the uniform of the Irish Free State. It should have been a cause for celebration – the old enemy was gone finally – but there was palpable tension in the air.

Harp had hoped her mother and Matt could come to Dublin to see them perform, but Matt had written to say it wouldn't be possible because the journey to Dublin was too hazardous at the moment. Anti-Treaty forces were destroying infrastructure up and down the country, and while Dublin seemed to be firmly under the protection of the Free State army, the same could not be said of the rest of the country. Matt didn't think Rose would be safe enough travelling with him, because he was such a well-known and influential supporter of the Treaty. It would have been nice for them to see her on stage, but it didn't matter. Despite Matt's warnings about the dangers, she was determined to go home in a few days' time and see them then, and JohnJoe was going to come with her.

In the Shelbourne dining room, the manager, Mr Floyd, came to take their order personally. He was a short man and completely bald. He had porcelain-white skin and two different coloured eyes, one blue, one brown. At barely five feet and portly, he was one of the oddest-looking people Harp had ever seen, and she tried her best not to stare as she and Celia ordered roast pheasant with glazed carrots and the boys chose oysters and beef, which came in thick, beautiful pink slices. They didn't ask for any wine, but Mr Floyd insisted on serving them with a bottle of Châteauneuf-du-Pape; he said they couldn't properly enjoy the pheasant or the beef if they didn't match it with a glass of his finest red.

Full of delicious food and wine, Harp retired to her own room and was so tired, she fell into a deep sleep as soon as her head hit the pillow, even though she usually found it hard to sleep without John-Joe. It wouldn't have done to share a hotel room with him in Ireland; the fear of being caught would be too great.

She was woken what felt like shortly afterwards by a persistent knocking. It was almost light outside, and blinking the sleep from her eyes, she threw back the covers and went to open the door. JohnJoe, fully dressed, pushed past her into the room, clearly upset.

'What is it? What's happened?' she asked, still struggling to wake up properly.

'Elliot and Jerry have been arrested. Mr Floyd came to wake me and tell me – thank God you weren't in the room with me. Someone saw them go into the same room, a priest or a monsignor or something, and demanded that the manager investigate. So Mr Floyd felt he had no choice, and he and this cleric walked in on them...'

'What? Walked in on them in the room? JohnJoe, I don't under-stand. What are you talking about?'

He put his hands to his face, and she saw him mentally deliberate before speaking. 'Harp, it seems Elliot and Jerry are... I don't know how to say this... They love each other...'

'Of course they do! They were friends before all of us were friends!'

'I don't mean love each other like that, Harp. I mean love each other like you and me.'

Harp stared at him, reeling. She knew there were men who were attracted to their own sex, of course she did... But Jerry and Elliot? Elliot was quiet and gentle and delicate-featured, but Jerry was a man's man, a soldier, a carpenter. Surely there was some mistake. He wasn't the picture she had in her head at all when she thought about things like this. 'Are you sure that was what was going on?' She kept trying to process it. 'Maybe it was a misunderstanding?'

JohnJoe shook his head. 'No, it's not.' He led her to the bed, and they sat down. 'It's true, and they were found together and have been arrested for it. This busybody cleric couldn't mind his own business. It's a crime, so they'll be charged and sent to prison for years if they're found guilty.'

Harp struggled to take it all in. She knew from the Oscar Wilde trial all the horrible things people said about men like that. She'd discussed it with Henry when she was ten, having read 'The Ballad of Reading Gaol', which Wilde wrote while he was sentenced to prison with hard labour. Rose would not have thought such a subject suitable for a young girl, but she was interested, and Henry explained how homosexuality was part of the natural world and that some people were just born that way. He taught her that the ancient Greeks accepted it as just another facet of life. He told her about the armies of Thebes and how love between soldiers was encouraged, as the generals believed they would more willingly defend or even die for their lover. The Christians, of course, abhorred the notion, citing passages from Genesis about the men of Sodom wanting to sexually assault Lot's guests. But Henry pointed out that it was possibly the violence that those early Christians objected to rather than the act itself. He'd explained gently and without graphic language that people were different and that if humans could accept and even embrace their differences, it would be a much happier world. He made sense as he always did, saying that if people were not hurting anyone, and not forcing anyone to their way of thinking or behaving, and everyone was consenting, then there should be no problem.

It was perfectly logical to Harp, and she had never had reason to revisit the subject again, having never met anyone of that mindset before. But now her dear friends were in real trouble. She knew that what Elliot and Jerry did with each other, even what they were, was illegal, and the court was not kind or understanding on the matter. 'What can we do, JohnJoe? We have to do something.'

'I don't know. Get them a lawyer, I guess?' JohnJoe was as stumped as she was.

'I had no idea… I thought Jerry and Celia… I suppose he was only being friendly to her all along.'

JohnJoe ran his hand through his hair. 'I didn't see it either, although now there's something that makes sense. I walked into the apartment one day just before we left for Ireland. You were out at the diner with Patsy, and I don't know where Jerry was. Elliot was crying. I…I'd never seen him cry before. I got a fright – I thought something terrible had happened. So I asked him what was wrong, and he said that he'd just heard that "The Heart Will Know" was playing on radio stations in California. I said I would have thought he would be delighted, but he said it was a love song and he could never have a love like that, like you and I have.'

Harp listened intently as he explained.

'I thought he was sad because he'd not met a girl he liked, and I said there were loads of girls at the concerts and they were mad about him but he never showed any interest, and then he just said it, that he had no interest in them.' JohnJoe swallowed. 'And then he said that he was in love with someone he couldn't marry. And I asked who, but he just looked at me and didn't say anything for the longest time. Then he wiped his eyes and turned away and wouldn't say anything else.'

'Are you all right about them…you know…being together?' Harp asked suddenly. She'd never had a conversation with JohnJoe on the subject, so she wondered. Lots of men – and women too but more so men, she thought – were appalled at the prospect of two men having a sexual relationship. She was fairly sure JohnJoe wouldn't be like that, but she needed to check.

He gave her a quizzical look. 'Are you asking me do I think it's right? What they're doing?'

'Well, yes, I suppose I am.' She had a cold feeling in the pit of her stomach.

'I'll tell you my feelings about it then. Jerry and Elliot are my friends, and I want them to be safe to live whatever life they want. I've no opinion on what they do in private, as I'm sure they've none on what you and I do when we're alone.'

Relief flooded though Harp. 'So what do we do? Get a lawyer?' she asked.

JohnJoe frowned. 'I suppose so, but I don't know. It would be terrible for this to go to court even. We have to try to keep it out of the newspapers. The more people that know, the worse it's going to be. You saw the big articles about us when we arrived – Dublin was so excited to welcome Roaring Liberty. And so it will be big news if it gets out, and you know how people love a scandal.'

'Let's go and speak to the manager, Mr Floyd, see what he says. Did he sound sympathetic or outraged when he came to tell you?'

'Neither. I think all he was thinking about was avoiding scandal for his hotel. He might not care about Elliot and Jerry, but he cares about the reputation of this place, so he might help us.'

'All right, give me a second to get dressed.' Harp threw on the first item she could find, a grey pinafore dress, and thrust her feet into her shoes without stockings. She ran a comb through her hair and thought she looked at least some kind of respectable.

Together they went in search of the manager. The porter on reception directed them to his office on the first floor, and despite the early hour, they found him in full formal dress, staring out the window onto Stephen's Green.

'Mr Floyd, I'm sorry for disturbing you, but we wanted a word,' JohnJoe began.

The manager turned around, and Harp as always marvelled at his appearance.

'Ah, Mr O'Dwyer, hello. Apologies for waking you earlier on, but I felt you needed to know.' He spoke with a slightly foreign accent and had a pronounced lisp. 'Please have a seat.' He gestured to a tan leather Chesterfield in the wood-panelled room.

The carpet was a deep-pile Axminster of dark red with a gold pattern, and a crystal chandelier hung from the ornate ceiling rose. The couch was perpendicular to a white marble fireplace filled at this time of year with a decorative array of dried flowers and foliage. Harp felt a pang of longing for the peace of Kathy's sitting room, with its same display of dried chrysanthemums, back when she and her four friends had been so excited about forming the band but had no thought of being rich and famous and no idea of the trouble it would bring down on their heads.

'This is a very delicate situation, Mr Floyd,' JohnJoe said as he took a seat. 'And Harp and I were wondering if there was any way we could make sure it doesn't reach any more eyes and ears than it already has?'

'It is in everyone's interests, including this hotel's, that this incident doesn't make the newspapers,' Harp added, trying not to stare at Mr Floyd's peculiar eyes.

Mr Floyd paused, then inhaled quickly and exhaled slowly. Harp wondered if he was going to give them a lecture on morality or go into how sickened he was... Or would he be understanding and kind, or even just pragmatic? He was impossible to read.

When he spoke, it was barely above a whisper. 'I certainly won't say anything. If it was up to me, this unfortunate incident would never have been brought to light. This is not the sort of thing with which I want my hotel associated, but unfortunately Monsignor Lehane is of a different mind. He's a very well-connected cleric, the brother of one of the ministers of the new government. He has the ear of powerful people if he chooses to escalate this, and by the sounds of the fire and brimstone he's been going on with, that is precisely his intention. So I fear things will turn out very badly for your friends and for me.'

Harp turned to JohnJoe. 'What time is it?' she asked.

He checked his pocket watch. 'Quarter past eight. Why?'

'I have to go,' she said, and without a further word to either of them, she jumped up from the Chesterfield and hurried out of the hotel. She hailed a hansom cab on the street outside and climbed aboard.

'Kingsbridge, as fast as you can. There's an extra crown in it if you can do it in twenty minutes.'

'Certainly, madam.' The man clicked the reins, and the horse took off at a fast trot, down the side of the large public park, St Stephen's Green, and then towards the river and onto the quays towards the station. The sweet smell of roasting hops from the Guinness brewery filled the air, fighting for supremacy with the rancid stench of the Liffey on a summer's morning at low tide. Luckily it was still early so the road was clear, and the horse broke into an easy canter.

Harp got out, paid the driver, including the tip, and ran into the huge railway station. The vaulted ceilings echoed with the sounds of commuters, deliveries and trains.

She recognised him easily, deep in convivial conversation with two men as he stood at the gate. He threw his head back and laughed, and Harp saw once again his sheer magnetic power. He was the kind of man who inspired love, trust and enthusiasm for the cause in all he met, and rumour had it that even some of the English grudgingly admired him.

Others, of course, hated him for what he was able to achieve. It was said that the Lord Lieutenant accused Collins of being late for the removing of the Union Jack from Dublin Castle and replacing it with the Irish tricolour, to which the big Cork man replied, 'Ye kept us waiting for eight hundred years, so a few minutes won't kill ye.'

Swallowing her nervousness, she approached. He saw her at once, awkwardly hovering on the edge of the group gathered around him. 'Harp, what has you here?' he asked, glancing at the station clock; his train was due to leave any minute.

'Could I have a word please, Mick? It's very important.' She hoped he could tell from her face it was not something she could discuss in front of others.

He excused himself from his companions and came to where she stood, leading her gently by the elbow into a corner where ancient luggage trolleys were stored. Old habits died hard, she thought; he knew well to make sure nobody could hear or see them talking.

'What's wrong?' he asked.

Quickly she told him the story, and to her relief, he didn't seem appalled or disgusted.

'Monsignor Lehane, that's Cathal Lehane's brother. Right. And you and the hotel manager want the two boys released straight away and the whole thing put to rest?'

Harp nodded, filled with sudden hope.

'Where are they being held?'

'I'm not sure. They were arrested at the Shelbourne so...'

'Probably Store Street, or Kevin Street. But, Harp, this won't be easy, maybe harder even than any military campaign. This is a fledgling state, and I can't be seen to be flouting the law of the land. I have enough people against me without going up against the Church. So you have to help me. You have to be able to look people in the eye and tell them it's definitely not true about the lads, and you have to give me some proof I can take to Cathal Lehane to quieten his brother. Cathal owes me a favour since I got his son out of the clutches of the G-men in Dublin Castle last year, but he still can't act without proof, not if his brother saw the boys in the bed together.'

Harp took a deep breath then blurted out, 'Well, you can tell him Elliot is engaged to me.' She had no idea where the words had come from, but now they were out, and the vital lie was told.

Collins looked thoughtfully at her. He knew it wasn't true, but that wasn't the point; he just needed to be sure she could make it sound true. 'But there's been no announcement of an engagement?'

She held his eyes. 'We were waiting until we were back in America to tell his family, and we are going to meet my mother in the coming days. We're sure everyone will be thrilled.'

'So where is your engagement ring?' He was testing her story, making sure she knew it and could stick by it.

Harp showed him her right hand where she wore a ring her mother and Matt had given her for her twenty-first birthday. It was a garnet, not a diamond, but nonetheless it had a stone, so it would have to do.

'You're not wearing it on your wedding finger.'

'We were waiting to tell our families first, but if you think I should wear it on my wedding finger, I will.'

'I think you should.'

At once she did as he advised.

'So, Harp, how come the two boys were arrested this morning, both in the same bed?'

'I've no idea.' She thought quickly. 'No, I do know. When we left the theatre last night, Jerry was searching for his room key – he'd misplaced it. So he bunked in with Elliot rather than find the porter. It was very late when they got to bed. They were working on a new arrangement – they often work late together – and so that's where the confusion came from. It's all a drama over nothing.'

Collins stood a moment longer, then placed his hand on her shoulder. 'You and JohnJoe were a tremendous help to the cause when we needed you. Jerry Gallagher is a patriot, and he doesn't go on about it, but a braver man you couldn't find. He's the best sniper I've ever seen, and I've seen plenty of them. So if this country owes anyone a turn, it's you lot. So we'll make this go away, Harp, I promise. There'll be reporters at the station, I'm sure, and I'll tell Elliot and Jerry what you told me and make sure they have the story straight for the press.' He glanced towards the platform as the whistle blew for his train, then winked at Harp, turned on his heel and left the station.

Harp felt a pang for Kitty Kiernan, who would be waiting in vain for her fiancée, but she loved Collins for his decisiveness of action and willingness to help. She barely dared to hope that Mick could resolve the situation, but if anyone could, he could.

As she walked back to the hotel, the city was coming to life around her. She loved America, and revelled in her freedom there, but there was something about being home, and especially now, as the republic they'd dreamed of for so long was tantalisingly within their grasp.

The dray horses were lined up outside the Guinness brewery, ready to pull the barrels of Ireland's signature black beer around the city. The street traders, women mostly, were pushing prams in various stages of decrepitude towards the city centre, there to sell their flowers and fruit to those who could afford such luxury. Their raucous laughter combined with carriages, ponies and traps, and the *clackety-clack* of the tram and a few motor cars added to the cacophony of the morning.

A pair of men passed her, ordinary-looking, mid-thirties, she guessed, dressed in dark trousers, jackets, flat caps and once white but now grey shirts, on their way to work in the brewery, and she wondered how they would react if they heard about Jerry and Elliot. Did men know that went on in a way women didn't? Did they see more of it in male environments such as the workplace or the battle-field? It was hard to know; it wasn't something she'd thought much about until now.

She thought back to all the time she'd known Jerry and Elliot. Was there any indication their relationship was anything other than friendship? Maybe. Anyway, what did it matter? They were doing no harm. As far as she was concerned, they were two adults, and while she had to admit the idea of two men being intimate was an odd one, it didn't repulse her. But she knew she did not represent the majority. The fact that neither JohnJoe nor Michael Collins had reacted badly cheered her, but she was in no doubt that if it ever got out, people would not be kind.

Hard labour was generally the sentence for indecent behaviour and seeking to corrupt public morals. She had read about a police raid in New York, back in February 1903, on the Ariston Bathhouse. Twenty-six men were arrested and twelve brought to trial on sodomy charges; seven men received sentences ranging from four to twenty years in prison.

She remembered one week of vaudeville they'd done at a theatre on Coney Island. They'd met the famous Julian Eltinge, a female impersonator of the stage, who had published a magazine on beauty tips. Off stage he was not at all feminine, but JohnJoe told her that there were rumours he was a homosexual. A newspaper article about him had used the phrase 'ambisextrous' to describe him. Things were different in the stage world, she knew – there was a tolerance of things that didn't exist in regular society – but even in that circle, if a man had those kinds of tendencies, he had no choice but hide it until he felt safe. Harp felt a pang of pity for her friends. What a hard way to be, not accepted, judged, incarcerated, humiliated, just for loving someone. It felt very unfair.

She reached the Shelbourne and crossed the lobby towards the sweeping stairs. She was sure JohnJoe would be waiting for her in his room, and she would have to break the news of her 'engagement'. She hoped he wouldn't think she'd gone crazy.

Before she could reach the stairs, a gaggle of men in overcoats surrounded her, calling her name and taking lots of photographs. 'How do you feel about the future of Roaring Liberty, Miss Devereaux?' shouted one of them.

Harp felt very exposed in such a public area, all alone. Normally Jerry kept overzealous fans or members of the press away from the band. She tried to push through the wall of reporters, but they blocked her way, their huge cameras flashing.

'How will you manage without Elliot Krauss?' shouted another. 'Is it true he and your manager, Jerry Gallagher, have been arrested for gross indecency?'

Trapped in their circle, she glared around at the sleazy crew. 'Of course it's not. Nobody's been arrested.'

'So you are confirming they are a pair of homosexuals then?'

'No, of course they're not. Let me pass.'

'Well, none of you seem to have a relationship, Miss Devereaux. Maybe Roaring Liberty is a band for deviant sexual behaviour?'

'I don't have to answer these ridiculous allegations.' She tried to turn in the opposite direction, to get back to the main doors, but they blocked her way there too.

'So how come none of your friends is married or even engaged then?' hissed one of them right in her face, a tall, skinny, ginger-haired man. 'Is JJ O'Dwyer one of them too?'

'Don't you dare print such utter lies,' she snapped furiously. 'Elliot and Jerry and JohnJoe are all perfectly normal men.'

'Yet not one of them has a girl, or even a hint of one,' he countered, goading her. 'And what about you? Do you not have a beau, a pretty girl like you? It is, you must admit, very peculiar.'

She felt herself redden with fury. 'Our private lives are just that – private – so I'll thank you to keep your nose out of our business.'

'Miss Devereaux!' shouted another reporter who was stuck at the back of the crush. 'Is it true a fellow student has come forward saying he saw Elliot Krauss with another boy when they were in school?'

'I really can't comment on tales told by anonymous schoolboys,' she countered. It was the first thing that came into her head.

'Do you know about his Boston landlady who says he regularly had a gentleman caller?' persisted the previous questioner, the ginger man right in her face.

This time Harp knew exactly who he was talking about and laughed, relieved to have a question she could answer. 'The lady in question made a pass at my friend and he rejected her, so make of that what you will.'

'But she says she can identify the gentleman, and the description she gave sounds just like Jerry Gallagher...'

'Whose picture is in all the papers, so of course she knows what he looks like,' scoffed Harp. 'The lady has a grudge, and that's all there is to it.'

'But wasn't Elliot Krauss involved in the Harvard scandal two years ago? There were rumours that he and a bunch of other deviants were caught up to all sorts? He was one of seven expelled from Harvard, including the son of a congressman, and after it, two students committed suicide.'

'That's a terribly sad story and shows the danger of people like you wrongly accusing innocent young men of terrible crimes and ruining their lives forever.'

'If Elliot was wrongly accused, then why did his father disown him?'

'Because he wanted his son to be a doctor, when Elliot only wanted to study music...' Harp said wildly, hoping against hope she wasn't too wide of the mark.

'Really? I think you're covering for him and Jerry Gallagher. I have some friends in the American press who are going to be very interested in this story. You could talk to me, Harp, tell me the whole truth. I'd make sure your friends are seen in the best possible light, considering. But if you have something to hide, then...'

She sighed and forced a fake smile. She'd intended to tell JohnJoe what she'd done before she told anyone else, but now her hand had been forced by this awful slimy man. 'The only thing I have to hide is that I'm engaged to be married to Elliot Krauss. We've been trying to keep it a secret so I could tell my mother in person before telling the world, but I suppose now you'll ruin our lovely surprise by printing it on the front page of your newspapers.'

The crowd of reporters looked blankly at each other, surprised by the twist the story had taken.

'So do you have a ring?' asked the tall skinny man standing in front of her, not as confident now.

Harp showed him her left hand, where Collins had insisted she wear the garnet, as several cameras flashed.

The reporter blinked, clearly disappointed that his line of questioning had hit a wall. 'It's not a diamond,' he accused feebly.

'That's because it's his grandmother's ring' – Harp spoke slowly as if the reporter were hard of hearing or particularly dull – 'and has great sentimental value for my darling Elliot.'

'What's going on here?' Mr Floyd appeared suddenly from the floor above. He saw immediately what was happening and came storming down the stairs to her rescue. 'Leave my hotel this minute, gentlemen! Miss Devereaux, I do hope they've not been bothering you too much...'

The reporters melted away, knowing they were beaten, although the one who had being doing most of the questioning paused to say obsequiously, 'We were merely congratulating Miss Devereaux on her engagement to Elliot Krauss, Mr Floyd. And, Harp, we look forward to seeing you and your fiancée on stage tonight. Thanks for the exclusive.'

'Ah, yes, of course, the engagement... The Shelbourne was very proud to be the scene of the proposal,' said Mr Floyd smoothly. 'Well, I'm sure Miss Devereaux has had enough of your congratulations by now – she has a very busy day ahead of her. Would you like your breakfast served in your room, Miss Devereaux?'

'Yes, please, Mr Floyd,' answered Harp gratefully, then ran as quickly as she dared upstairs.

Closing her bedroom door behind her, she leaned against it, panting, trying to gather her thoughts. What had she done? Everything was spiralling out of control. Now it would definitely be in the newspapers tomorrow that she and Elliot were engaged, and if she said or did anything different from now on, it would look very suspicious. What on earth had she been thinking? It had just come out when she spoke to Mick. It was the perfect proof he'd needed. He'd implied she had to stick to the story for everyone's sake, but she hadn't thought through what that meant. And now it seemed there was no going back.

Poor JohnJoe. How would he react? She'd have to hope he understood. Would she have to go through with it? Marry Elliot? There didn't appear to be any other option. If they pretended they were engaged and then broke it off, it would look very suspicious. But if she married him... The mind boggled. Elliot too might be angry with her for saying they were attached, though he was in such danger, she hoped he'd be more relieved than furious with her for telling such a blatant lie.

First she had to find JohnJoe, confess what she'd done. She swallowed; this was going to be horrible. She wouldn't hurt JohnJoe for all the world, but because of her rash decision, and her telling all those sleazy reporters, his family would read in the newspapers that she had become engaged to someone else and think she'd made a cuckold of their beloved boy. The idea of Danny and Marianne, Pat and Kathy, not to mention her mother and Matt, reading the story over tomorrow's breakfast made her blood run cold. Would her mother notice that the 'grandmother's' engagement ring she flashed at the reporters was the garnet that Rose and Matt had given her? If she did notice, what would she make of it?

Harp slipped out of her room and tiptoed as quickly as she dared to JohnJoe's. She checked the corridor was clear before knocking on the door. He opened it immediately, and once she was inside and the door closed, he embraced her.

'Mr Floyd was just here a short while ago,' he said eagerly. 'They are being released, quietly, out of the back of the station later this evening when there are fewer reporters around, and they'll meet us at the theatre. I don't know how it happened – all he could tell me was pressure was brought to bear from a fairly robust source – but it seems they are going to get away with it. Isn't it great? I don't know what you did when you left the hotel in such a hurry this morning, but clearly it was something pretty smart.'

She smiled weakly. 'I found Collins at the station and asked him to intervene. He told me he'd try, so it must have worked.'

'I knew it, Harp! You're a genius, you know that? A solid-gold genius.' He beamed at her, but his face fell when he saw nothing in her expression but trepidation, and his enthusiasm died on his lips. 'What is it? You don't seem relieved?'

'JohnJoe, sit down. I...I need to tell you something.' Harp's stomach churned and was cold, as if ice were floating in it.

The morning sun shone through the bedroom window as he sat on the edge of the unmade bed. She perched on an ornate fireside chair in the corner of the room, her hands in her lap, a distance away from him. She swallowed. The inside of her mouth felt like the bottom of a bird cage, so dry and scratchy. 'I have to tell you something...' She felt her cheeks blaze. Oh, he would think her so foolish!

'Harp, what is it?'

'JohnJoe, I think I've done something really stupid. It was on the spur of the moment, and it was the best I could come up with at the time, but... You see, what happened was...' She struggled to find the words, and finished lamely. 'I love you, JohnJoe.'

'I love you too, Harp,' he said stoutly. 'And whatever you've done, I'm sure it was the right thing...'

She raised her hand to stop him, shaking her head, and began her story, telling him in as clear a way as she could of the encounter first with Michael Collins and then with the gaggle of journalists.

Long seconds passed after she finished speaking, and he just sat there, his face a mask.

'I'm sorry, JohnJoe. I just wanted to quash the story before it had a chance to begin, and Mick said he had to have proof, because in the present situation, he couldn't be seen to go against the new state and the Church. Elliot being in a relationship with a woman seemed the only way to make things right, and the reporters wouldn't let me alone, and they were threatening to go to the American papers, and so...' She looked down at her hand, adding in a small voice, 'Mick told me to wear my garnet on my wedding finger.'

'And this is going to be in the newspapers?' His voice sounded wooden. 'That you and Elliot are getting married?'

'I suppose so,' Harp replied miserably. 'I could back out of it, I suppose I can, but then... I don't know what would happen if I did that, JohnJoe. I don't know what to do.'

She crossed the room to sit beside him, placing her hand on his shoulder, but he moved along the bed and then stood up. It was as if he couldn't bear to be near her.

'I need to... I just need some time to think, Harp. I'm going out for a few hours to clear my head...' He walked past her without looking at her and went out the door, closing it loudly behind him.

Tears flowed down her cheeks. She'd hurt him, and there was nothing she could do about it. He had looked so crestfallen, so broken; she couldn't bear to see it. What on earth had she got them into? The person she clung to in times of trouble was the person she'd hurt by her actions. She suddenly longed for her mother. Rose would be sensible and would hear her out and hopefully have a solution. But they had another night to do here in Dublin before they could go to Cork.

How was she supposed to perform on stage with him tonight – or maybe without him, if he didn't come back?

The moss-green woollen sweater Kathy had bought him for Christmas was lying on his pillow, and she picked it up. She held it to her face and inhaled the familiar spicy aroma of his cologne. She adored JohnJoe, but now she had to marry someone else or risk prison for Elliot and Jerry, and risk the end of Roaring Liberty for all of them. Her dream life was unravelling at the seams in every direction, and there was nothing she could do about it.

CHAPTER 18

*A*t seven that evening, Harp was in her dressing room alone, waiting and wondering if either the boys or JohnJoe would turn up at all. She'd fobbed the stage manager off with some story about a delay, just in case none of them showed up on time, but as the minutes ticked by, her panic was evergrowing.

Celia was first to arrive; her gentle knock on the door caused Harp to run to it, praying it was JohnJoe. The day had gone on for what seemed like weeks, and she had no idea where he was or what he was doing. She'd gone back to her bedroom and stayed there, waiting for him, until she absolutely had to get ready for the show.

She'd not seen Celia since last night. She'd called her room that morning, but Celia had already gone out for the day, no doubt walking around Dublin by herself just as she'd been doing all week, revelling in the wonderful experience of going into shops and cafés and libraries without being ordered out for being coloured; she could even use the same drinking fountains and toilets. People did stare at her all the time, she told Harp, but out of curiosity rather than disgust, so she made sure she wore the latest fashions and looked her best. It sounded like the stares Harp had to put up with in America, what with her being a celebrity. It had been quite fun at first, although she suspected Celia would find it wearisome after a while.

She hugged her friend; she was so relieved to see her. 'Oh, Celia, you've no idea what's happened...' She sat the other woman down and told her the whole story, and Celia didn't seem as shocked as Harp had expected her to be, only a bit mortified that she'd imagined Jerry was interested in her when he'd only been being nice. Then she got very worried for Jerry and Elliot, and after that she was horrified by what Harp had done to save them. 'Harp, how can you marry Elliot? It's crazy! What does JohnJoe think?'

'Oh, Celia.' Harp was on the verge of tears. 'He's angry, and I haven't seen him all day. I knew he wouldn't be happy, but I didn't think he'd take it this badly – he knows how much I love him.'

She got ready for a Celia-style lecture about her knowing nothing about men, but then Jerry and Elliot arrived in. Both girls could see the fear and shame in their eyes. They knew Harp and Celia were aware of why they were arrested, and they were clearly so worried about how the girls would react. Instinctively, Harp put her arms around both of them, drawing them into a hug, and Celia joined them, sighing as she kissed Jerry's cheek.

'Now I understand why you were always such the gentleman with me, Jerry.' She smiled ruefully. 'But I'll always have a soft spot for you, no matter what.'

'And I'll always have a soft spot for you, Celia.' He sighed, then looked at Elliot with a small smile. 'If things were different...'

'I know, I'd be the one for you. But don't worry, there's plenty more fish in the sea,' Celia joked bravely.

Harp turned to the table and poured them all iced water from the tall crystal jug. 'Was it awful?' she asked, handing the boys two of the glasses.

Jerry shrugged, draining his in one go. 'No worse than being hauled in by the Black and Tans, I suppose.'

'Did Mick speak to you?'

'He did, and he told us what you are doing to save us, Harp, and he told us we had to stick to the story whoever asked. But he also wants us to get out of the country as fast as we can. He doesn't want us to make a liar out of him by accident, and he says reporters will be following us everywhere, waiting for us to slip up. I'm so sorry you had to do what you did. We'll find a way out of it, I promise, once we're back in the States.'

Harp turned to Elliot, wondering if she should tell him what she knew from the reporters about his past. He was slumped in a chair, drinking his water and looking so exhausted and downtrodden, she decided that at this stage, further secrets were meaningless.

'The reporters told me your father disowned you, Elliot. I said it was because he'd made you study medicine at Harvard but you only wanted to play your violin. I hope that wasn't too crazy...'

Elliot laughed bitterly. 'You were spot on, actually, though the degree was engineering, not medicine. He hated me playing the violin – you guessed absolutely right about that. The last time I saw him, after the police raided a party at Harvard, one where we were... Well, there were men like us there. I was expelled, and when he found out, he roared at my mother that it was she who raised me to be a faggot, that she was why his son was a nancy boy, that it was because she had encouraged me with the violin and the music and other unmanly things. He was a brutal man, Harp, and it was he who broke my hand so I would never play the violin again.' His voice cracked. 'He disowned me after Harvard, and he stopped my mother from speaking or even writing to me ever again. That pain was almost worse than my broken hand.'

'Oh, Elliot...' She'd had no idea of the sorrow he carried with him; he was always so cheerful and bright around them all.

'And now look what I've done to you all and Roaring Liberty. I'm surprised you don't disown me as well. You helped me find my music again, all of you, and this is how I've repaid you. I hate you having to lie to save me, Harp...but I'm so grateful. If it wasn't for you, we'd be standing trial here in Ireland and jailed as sodomites, as the officer arresting us so kindly pointed out about eight times.'

'We should never have come here,' Jerry said heavily. He turned to Elliot. 'I should never have brought you.'

'Stop that,' Elliot replied, with more force than Harp had ever heard him use before; he was usually so gentle and quietly spoken, with an easy smile and a placid nature. 'This could just as easily have happened in America, and you know that, Jerry. We'll never be accepted. We just need to...'

'Need to what, Elliot? Be different? Deny who we are? What we feel?' Jerry was agitated now.

Elliot looked sadly at Harp. 'I'm sorry. You took such a huge chance approaching Collins to get us out, and here we are arguing in front of you. Don't worry, Harp. I'll do tonight's show, and then Jerry and I will get out of here and deal with whatever comes. We can sail from Dublin to Liverpool first thing and catch a ship back to the US from there.'

Harp tried to swallow the lump in her throat. Normally when she was anxious, JohnJoe was there, right beside her, but there was still no sign of him and she was increasingly sure he wasn't coming. The show was due to begin in twenty minutes. Should she wait to warn Elliot? She hated having to drop this bombshell, but having her fellow musician find out at the last possible minute would be much worse.

'Elliot, I'm sorry, but...'

'What is it?' He turned to her, and she saw the pain and fear of rejection there in his face. Maybe he thought she was going to ask him to leave the band, or not associate with her any more because of the revelation.

'It's JohnJoe. He's so unhappy. He walked out this morning when I told him, and I haven't seen him since, and now I'm worried he won't turn up at all... I think I've ruined everything. He's wanted to get married before we were even old enough to do so, but I've always refused, and now this. He's so upset...' As she finished, she realised fat tears were rolling down her cheeks. Jerry drew her into a hug and Elliot rubbed her back as she cried. Celia sat, shaking her head, although she was too kind to pass comment.

Harp pulled her face away from the sodden front of Jerry's shirt and turned to Elliot. 'I'm so sorry, Elliot. What are we going to do about the show?'

'Firstly, stop apologising. This situation has arisen because you were trying to help us, and you did. I understand why JJ's upset, but we'll find a way to get through this. None of this is your or his problem, and we're just really grateful that you came to our rescue like you did. Maybe we can just play along with it for a while and hope it dies down? It might once we go back to the States?'

'Let's hope so,' Harp answered miserably. She knew that despite his words, it wouldn't be that easy. The American press would be expecting a massive wedding, especially as Roaring Liberty was always front line news and sold so many papers.

'So if a third of this trio isn't here, what are we going to do?' Jerry asked, switching back into manager mode. They all looked at the clock. It was ten to eight; the curtain would be up in ten minutes. It was a full house, and they'd never performed without JohnJoe. They normally opened with the duet 'Blue Danube Blues', a very popular tune from the musical *Good Morning Dearie*. It set the tone nicely for the show, as the girls got their fill of JohnJoe's charming, slightly flirtatious performance and Harp limbered up her voice on a melody that wasn't too taxing.

'Let's rearrange the playlist and start with 'The Heart Will Know'. You can easily do it as a solo,' Jerry suggested.

'And what do we say to the audience?' Harp asked, stricken.

'That JJ's been taken ill?' Elliot suggested.

'But I don't know what your song will sound like without his voice accompanying mine,' Harp sobbed, fighting back the feelings of panic and despair. 'I've always sung it as a duet, never as a solo...'

'You can, because you have to.' Jerry placed his hands on her shoulders. 'Come on, Harp, you've done things that are much more terrifying – I know you have. You can do this.'

'I don't know if I can...'

'You can,' said Celia. 'Because I'm going to sing it with you.'

The other three turned to her, realising what they'd forgotten – that here in Ireland, where Celia could drink at the same drinking fountains as the White folks, she could also sing on the same stage.

America might be the land of liberty, but for people like Celia at least, Ireland was the freer place.

'That's brilliant!' Jerry said enthusiastically, and embraced her as she blushed, rolling her eyes comically over his shoulder at Harp and Elliot.

Harp found she was actually excited by the idea. Her voice was alto, but Celia's was contralto, and she remembered how well they had sung Elliot's song together that one time.

The stage manager put his head around the door. 'Five minutes to curtain,' he said.

Harp took a deep ragged breath. 'All right, it's decided. It's a pity to do it without JohnJoe on piano, but we'll manage with the harp and the fiddle, like we did at our very first performance.' She fixed her hair in the mirror and used a ball of cotton wool to clean her smudged eye make-up.

'He'll be back. He loves you,' Elliot whispered to her as she stood before him, fixing his tie.

'And I've just told the world I'm going to marry another man, so…'

'He'll calm down and realise you only did it out of loyalty to us. JJ is a good guy. He'll be all right – you both will. We'll sort this out, I promise.'

'But how? I just can't see a way out of this.'

'I haven't thought that part through yet, but let's deal with one thing at a time, shall we?' He smiled. She could see the exhaustion, worry and shame there and wished she could make it better for him.

'"The friend in my adversity I shall always cherish most. I can better trust those who helped to relieve the gloom of my dark hours than those who are so ready to enjoy with me the sunshine of my prosperity,"' she quoted.

'Who said that?' Elliot asked as Jerry opened the dressing room door.

'The eighteenth president of America, Ulysses Grant,' Harp answered, taking Celia's hand to lead her out.

It was fortunate Celia had been dressing in her finest clothes all week thanks to everyone in Dublin staring at her; the red velvet outfit she was wearing was perfect.

They walked purposefully to the stage, the noise of the crowd growing louder with every step. The cheering and clapping took long minutes to abate, and Harp just stood there, a superficial smile on her face, feeling empty and scared without JohnJoe at her side, even though Celia's presence did a lot to help. These were people who had spent their hard-earned money to see Roaring Liberty perform, and she had to put her own feelings aside and give them the show they deserved, no matter what.

As the crowd realised Celia was standing there with Harp instead of JohnJoe, there were rumblings. But the crowd hushed and listened as Harp spoke, praying her voice sounded confident and clear. 'Ladies and gentlemen, girls and boys, thank you all so much for coming to our show. It is our great honour and privilege to perform for you tonight. As you know, two of our three members are in fact Irish. I was born in Cork' – a huge cheer went up – 'and JJ is from County Clare, and of course Elliot here is all the way from Boston, Massachusetts –'

'Get off!' a rough voice from the crowd yelled. 'You and your nancy boys have no business here.'

The scuffle escalated in seconds as the ushers and a few customers tried to silence the man. Harp couldn't see his face, but she could hear him.

'Get off our stage and get out of our country, filthy dirty sinners!' His voice became muffled as he was pushed out of the hall.

Harp continued breathlessly. 'And our guest singer, who has agreed to perform with us tonight, is the very special Miss Celia Harris, also from Boston, Massachusetts.'

The opening bars of 'The Heart Will Know' struck up behind her, not on the fiddle but the piano. She whipped around. It was JohnJoe, and as he played, he fixed his eyes on her, unsmiling. Elliot started playing also, and Celia, realising JohnJoe had joined them, got ready to leave the stage, but Harp grabbed her by the hand and pulled her back to her side. 'You're going to sing with me,' she whispered. 'I've always wanted this, and I'm not letting you get out of it.'

She waited for her cue and began the opening lyrics, and Celia, still holding Harp's hand, performed the duet while JohnJoe played the piano without singing.

Within seconds the crowd was singing along, the earlier kerfuffle forgotten.

'What the tongue can't say, the heart will know. What the hands can't touch, what no one can show, what I daren't speak, for fear you'd go, I'm hoping, my love, that your heart will know.

'My thoughts are of you, as you pass your days, when you are near or far away. Oh, how I long for the breeze of love to blow, and that somehow, someday, your heart will know.

'My dreams are vivid, your smile so sure. Is it aimed at me? Whose love is pure? I don't know how I can make it so, but somehow, some-day, your heart will know.

'Until that time, I wait all on my own. No other one can claim your throne. The king of my heart, but I can't let it show, until somehow, someday, your heart will know.'

As she finished the last line, JohnJoe went right into 'Blue Danube Blues', and this time joined in with Harp and Celia, who, having been at every concert and rehearsal, knew all the words.

Love and admiration poured from the audience, and Harp soaked it all up, forgetting for a while at least the enormous trouble she was in.

CHAPTER 19

*J*erry and Elliot arranged to leave the next morning on the mail boat to Liverpool, and from there to the States. They were relieved to be getting away. Not that England or the United States were any more tolerant, but they had been careless in Ireland and had almost paid a very heavy price. Thanks to Harp they'd escaped prison and worse, but they'd told Michael Collins they'd leave the country and were determined to make good on their promise.

Jerry reached out to touch Elliot's long fingers and delicate hands. 'I'd survive breaking rocks for years,' he said softly, 'but you wouldn't last a week.'

Harp and Celia exchanged a look. It was strange to be around the two boys now, but Harp had told them they didn't need to pretend, if it helped. They didn't kiss or anything, but they were noticeably more tactile. The lyrics of Elliot's hit song seemed even more poignant now, knowing he'd written them for Jerry.

The five friends were dining in a private room at their hotel. For all of them except Celia, it was their last night in Dublin. The manager of the Abbey had approached Celia after the show and offered her a lunchtime concert of her own, and a second one if that was successful. Celia said it was because she was seen as such an exotic creature in

Ireland, but as they all assured her, it certainly wouldn't have happened if she squawked like a crow. Maybe one day her name would be up in lights with Ma Rainey, the famous blues singer. Celia said she'd still rather study politics and economics at college, but she was happy to stay on a while in Dublin and enjoy a little limelight all of her own.

JohnJoe had decided to travel to Liverpool with Jerry and Elliot to see his sisters, leaving Harp to go to Cobh alone. He was making it his business to stay with Jerry and Elliot every moment until they were safely on the boat from Liverpool to the States, just in case of anything else happening. The news of the 'mistaken' arrest and the secret engagement were all over the papers and apparently had been syndicated to Europe and the United States as well.

'Did Harp's Heart Know?'

'Roaring Liberty in Grip of Scandal!'

'Stars of Stage to Wed Amid Rumours!'

The headlines varied, but they all more or less insinuated the same thing, and anything short of a wedding wasn't going to call off the vultures. She and JohnJoe had not yet spoken about the situation at any length, although after the concert, he'd told her that he understood why she had done what she did, that it was to save Elliot and Jerry and also Roaring Liberty. Harp knew he meant it, but nonetheless it was painfully clear his heart was broken. Whatever he said about keeping an eye on Elliot and Jerry, she knew well he was really going to Liverpool because he needed time alone without her, to think.

Sensing her unhappiness, Elliot reached out to pat her hand. 'Maybe we could be engaged for years until everyone forgets about it?'

Celia shook her head firmly. She'd been dead set against the engagement at first, but as time went on, she had seen the sense of it. 'No, anythin' short of a blushin' bride by your side won't do to kill the rumours. Kids and families and all of that, people just wouldn't come to see Roaring Liberty again. Y'all have seen the papers here, and you can be sure they'll be every bit as salacious back home, more so even. You know how people love a bit of scandal.'

They all knew she was right.

'Maybe we could marry but still all live together back in New York? So then it wouldn't matter?' Harp asked, knowing instantly she'd said the wrong thing again.

JohnJoe winced visibly, then stood and went to the window, his hands deep in his pockets. The other four sat in awkward silence. 'It matters,' he said quietly, to nobody in particular.

'Look.' Jerry sighed. 'Elliot and I know what an imposition this is, and we would never have asked you to do it. I hate that we are putting you in this awful situation. If we can come up with a better way...'

JohnJoe spoke without turning around. 'There isn't a better way. You know it and I know it. The police are always cracking down on people like you and Elliot. It's not fair but it's how it is. We can't let them do that to you. Even if Roaring Liberty was no more, we couldn't stand by knowing we could have helped.'

'All right, look, there's nothing more we can say at this stage. I'm so sorry for dragging you into our mess. It's not fair. We'll leave you to it,' Elliot said, getting up from the table.

'I'll come with you,' said Celia, 'to make sure nobody gives you two any trouble.' She, Elliot and Jerry left together, and Harp and JohnJoe were alone.

For the first time since she was twelve years old, she felt nervous around him. His broad back, turned away from her, felt like a wall. The silence hung between them, heavy with all that remained unsaid.

She longed to approach him but couldn't do it. JohnJoe was more than her boyfriend; he was her soulmate, the other half of her. He understood her when nobody except her mother or Henry ever did. They had written every week when he left with Danny for America in 1912 and told each other everything. When she visited Boston in 1916, he'd declared his love for her – she was sixteen and he eighteen then – and while he knew she wasn't ready for an adult relationship, he made it clear he loved her and would wait. She'd never imagined herself being in a relationship, as she'd been a loner since birth, but JohnJoe was different from other people. He knew she was a bit quirky, that she would rather read a book than go to a party, that she got awkward in company, how small talk terrified her. He knew that she'd tried to fit in all of her life and never quite achieved it. He knew how she had had to hit a British officer with a bronze *Venus de Milo* statuette when she was assaulted in her bed, and how Matt and her mother had buried his lifeless body under old Mrs Duggan, who'd gone to her eternal reward due to natural causes that same day, most conveniently.

He knew that Ralph wasn't just the man hell-bent on destroying her but was also her father, something Ralph himself didn't even know. He'd fought beside her in the Irish War of Independence, he'd stayed in Ireland for her, and when they got to America, he'd made it clear that he would love to be her husband. But despite everything, she refused him, time and again. She didn't want to marry anyone, not even her best friend.

But then, in the blink of an eye, she'd told a reporter that she was going to marry Elliot. Just like that, as if it was nothing important, throwing all her principles overboard, even though she'd refused to abandon them for JohnJoe. She had let her best friend and lover suffer and grieve for the home and children he would never have, but when it came to helping someone else, she hadn't hesitated.

'JohnJoe, I'm so sorry...'

'I know why you did it, Harp.' His voice rumbled with that hybrid American-Irish accent, deep and sonorous, that had the girls swooning. He was still standing with his back to her, gazing out the window into the summer night air. 'You did what you thought was right. I just wish it had never happened.'

'So do I, JohnJoe, so much you can't even imagine.'

He turned, and she saw the unshed tears in his eyes.

'I want so badly to marry you, you see, Harp. I never pushed the point because you explained how you felt and I respected it, but I just assumed, foolishly, I suppose, that one day you'd change your mind and we'd get married and maybe even have children of our own, and they'd be healthy and happy and confident, something neither of us were as kids. I've wanted to get down on one knee so often, but I never did, knowing your answer and not wanting to put you in that position. I'm not mad at you, or angry at Elliot or Jerry or anything, but my heart is breaking.'

'Oh, JohnJoe, my darling…'

'I mean it, Harp. It feels like someone is reaching into my chest and squeezing my heart until I can't even breathe…' His voice broke off, and she went to him, wrapping her arms around his waist.

He didn't hug her back at first, but she waited and then relaxed as she felt the familiar sensation of being held in his arms.

'We have to make sure nobody knows about the lie either. We have to let on that you're happy to marry Elliot, or there's no point to any of this,' JohnJoe said, his lips buried in her hair.

Harp groaned. 'I lay awake last night trying not to think about Pat and Kathy and Danny and Marianne and everyone reading about it in the newspaper. Mammy and Matt will have heard now too, and what must they all be thinking?'

'That you dumped me for Elliot.' His voice was choked with emotion. 'And that's what they must think, all of them, Harp, because if it gets out that it's a sham marriage to protect Elliot and his nature, we might as well forget Roaring Liberty ever existed and go back to our lives before any of this happened. And even then it would be with a cloud over us forever more.'

He was right, she knew. But the idea of lying to their families, for them to believe she could hurt JohnJoe in that way, was incomprehensible to her. 'Surely we can tell Mammy and Matt? My mother will get it out of me, I know she will – she has a way. I'm a terrible liar, you know that…'

'You told enough lies to the British over the years, and to your mother about what you and I got up to when we were alone together. You'll be able to do this, Harp. You'll have to pretend to the world that you love Elliot. And I've no choice but endure it. I'll try to pretend I don't care, that we'd already broken up or something…'

'I can't bear it, I can't bear it…' Weeping, she held him close. 'We're in such a mess, JohnJoe.'

'We sure are,' he replied sadly. 'We sure are.'

CHAPTER 20

COBH, COUNTY CORK, IRELAND

She was beneath his usual standard. *But still,* he thought, *she might be useful.* So Ralph turned on the charm to Doris Prince, the youngish, diminutive, bespectacled woman that Bridges had employed at the Queen's Hotel as receptionist. He used to know her older brother Dominic vaguely as a boy growing up in Queenstown; they were on the same cricket team. By all accounts young Doris adored him. *He's rotting like the rest of them now over in Flanders, probably fully decomposed by now,* Ralph thought speculatively.

'I have such happy memories of him, and it is so nice to meet up with one of his friends,' Doris simpered. He'd invited her to the Cliff House once he realised where she worked. Maguire, who used to be his eyes and ears, had become very tiresome, demanding to be paid. Ralph had fobbed him off for months, but eventually the dratted man had issued an ultimatum: Cash there and then or he walked. Ralph told him to get out of his sight.

He was gone a bare fortnight when Ralph had a letter from that wretched trollop's lawyers saying they had sought and won a court injunction to freeze all of Pamela's assets, including the account he'd siphoned her money into, pending an investigation into her whereabouts. Apparently her sister, some dreadful old crone living in rural England, had raised concerns, saying she'd not heard from her sister and all the rest of it. It was most vexing. They knew which bank, the branch even, the account number and everything. It really was a tangle.

His source of income was gone completely, and apparently that dreadful Harp was on her way back. Something would have to happen soon.

So he'd scoured the town for a likely mark. So many of his class were gone back to England, where life was less hazardous, their homes boarded up. And those who remained were either secretly or overtly supporters of the rabble hordes of Irish so saw him as the enemy every bit as much as Rose and that Quinn did. So while she was not his choice, Doris Prince was the best he could do for now. He'd invited her to the Cliff House on the premise that he had an old photograph of her brother that he wanted her to have. It meant nothing to him, a grainy team picture from when they were at school. He'd found it in an old album his mother had kept, full of pictures of him – none of Henry, he was pleased to note. It was as good an excuse as any. He of course inflated the cordiality of their relationship; in truth Ralph barely remembered the insipid Dominic Prince. But when he realised Doris was essentially the personal assistant to that snake Bridges down at the hotel, he figured she might be a handy person to have on his side. Information was power, and he didn't believe for one moment that Rose and her peculiar daughter would just stand by and allow him to keep the house. On top of that, Doris had a house of her own and was single. She was hideously unattractive, but he hadn't't much in the way of options at the moment.

The truth of the matter was that despite his threats to Rose, he knew he hadn't a legal leg to stand on, even if he could afford a solicitor, which he couldn't. He could ruin Rose's reputation, and he'd get some pleasure in that undoubtedly, but it would most likely still go against him and he'd be left high and dry.

If he could just find a way to deal with Harp, Rose would be easy. She still quivered like a leaf in his presence, despite trying to come across as confident. But Harp was different; she wasn't afraid of him, and he knew it.

While she was over in America flaunting her insignificant charms to the masses, she was most likely to leave him alone, but according to the papers, she and her trio of performing monkeys were at the Abbey in Dublin, being fawned over by all and sundry. And apparently she was engaged to some fiddle player, though why the papers thought anyone cared was a mystery. Honestly, it was nothing short of sickening.

Doris Prince was as plain as a dinner plate and had a personality to match. She was quite alarmingly small, being no more than four foot eight or nine, he thought, with the most odd smell – a combination of mothballs and a sickly floral scent. Sometimes those women were so thankful to have a bit of attention, they could be quite interesting and accommodating in the bedroom department. Such devotion and pathetic gratitude could be manipulated, which might make bedding her bearable; he'd have to see.

Dominic was dead and her parents had both succumbed to the Spanish flu, so she lived alone. From the outside, her place wasn't much – a grand farmhouse at best, nothing like the Cliff House – but there could well be cash there. Bridges had employed her to give her something to do, it seemed, besides being stuck all day in that old house on her own, so she wasn't doing the job for the money.

He turned his attention back to what she was saying.

'And my father loved him so. It's just me and Nelson now, rattling about. He's so clever, though. Honestly, I think he can understand every word I say sometimes, and he's ever so protective of me. I never worry when I'm alone because Nelson is very intuitive…'

What was it? A dog, he assumed. She did go on a lot about some creature, but he was usually lost in his own thoughts.

'Oh I agree,' he said expansively, topping up her glass of sherry. 'Animals can be so much more sensitive than humans. I had a monkey when I lived in India, a cheeky little chap he was, but I was very fond of him.'

'Oh, a monkey sounds so exotic! You've lived such an interesting life, Mr Devereaux, serving your country in the Army, and losing your leg, and then living in so many exciting places. I'm rather jealous.'

'Well, losing my leg wasn't a highlight.' He winked and she blushed. 'And please, call me Ralph.'

'Oh, how tactless of me! I'm so sorry, I didn't mean –'

'Please, my dear, don't worry. I was just teasing. I shouldn't, but I feel like I know you already, though we've just met.' He paused and held her gaze. Her pale-blue eyes were enormous through the thick lens of her spectacles. Normally he would spend more time on the seduction, but frankly she wasn't worth his best game, and anyway, time was of the essence.

She blushed a deeper crimson, her moon-shaped face clashing horribly with the pink dress she wore. Her hair was thin and mousy brown, pulled back into a severe bun that did nothing for her.

'I'm sorry,' he said. 'Forgive me please, Miss Prince. I should not have been so forward. I just... Well, it's lonely here since my wife left. She couldn't stand the weather, you see. Pamela is a sun worshipper, and the lure of a sunny villa filled with servants back in India was too much. I can't blame her really. A crippled husband and a dark, cold house were just not enough for her.' He was gauging from her reaction how far to play the sympathy card. *That should do it*, he thought.

'Well, I...I'm sure she made a terrible mistake. You were wounded in battle, defending our country – what could be more gallant? And the weather, well, I love it here. Admittedly I've never been anywhere else, but the seasons here in Ireland, each one brings its own joy. And as for the Cliff House, I've always admired your lovely home, and if your wife didn't appreciate it, well, that is a terrible pity, for I would think most people would be so privileged to call such an iconic house home. I'm quite sure Dominic mentioned you when we would go for walks, and we stopped to admire it, but... Forgive me, Ralph.' She coloured again at the mention of his first name. 'I'm not much used to male company, or any company really. And perhaps a single lady should not be in the company of a married man unchaperoned, or perhaps that's a rather old-fashioned idea now, I don't know – I mix very seldom in society. Mr Bridges knew my father well – they played golf together – and he visits a few times a year to check on me, but when he offered me the position at the hotel, well, I was all aflutter and terrified I wouldn't be equal to the task. But Mr Bridges has been so kind and patient, I feel truly blessed. I thank the Lord every day for his kindness to me.'

'I think Bridges is the one who is blessed.' Ralph smiled. 'But yes, we must give thanks to God for the great fortune He has bestowed upon us.' He bowed his head reverentially.

'Are you a devout Christian, Ralph?'

'Oh yes,' he lied silkily. 'My faith has sustained me throughout my life. My brother, Henry, was an atheist, something that upset my dear mama deeply, as we were raised in such a God-fearing home, but I have never wavered in my devotion to the Creator and I never will.'

'And your wife? Was she a righteous woman?'

'Oh no. I'm afraid I believed, wrongly, I could bring Pamela around, that if she could just see the good God has done in my life, she would grow to love Him as I do. But she wouldn't even countenance a Church wedding – we got married at a registry office in London.'

'Oh dear. So you were never married in the eyes of God?'

'Alas no. I begged and begged, but she was most determined and refused flatly.' He managed to insert such contrition in his voice that she seemed genuinely upset. 'It was a bone of contention between us, because to my mind, a marriage not sanctified before God is not a marriage at all.'

Doris smiled, and he held her gaze once more. He was in his early fifties and she probably barely thirty, but if he could just get her on the hook, he could possibly use her to his advantage. If she hadn't much money – it was difficult to tell as her outfit looked more in vogue thirty years ago – she could still be his eyes and ears in the hotel, which would be something, and if she fell for him, perhaps he could keep her dangling for long enough to get something out of her.

'Where do you go to church?' she asked, and he was stumped. He'd no idea where the Church of Ireland services were held these days, having not darkened the door of any sort of church for decades.

Then he remembered something Beckett had said. 'Oh, I often go to the military chapel on Haulbowline. As an ex-serviceman, I feel the support of my fellow soldiers as we worship together.' Civilians were never allowed out there, so she'd believe it.

'Really? And is there a boat to take you out?' she asked, fascinated.

'Yes, a small launch leaves the quay in time for the service every Sunday morning, but other than that, my daily prayer is private. I often sit outside and contemplate His divine creation. As Cicero said' – he recalled a plaque in his late brother's office that he'd unscrewed when he demolished the room – '"If a man has a garden and a library, he has everything he needs."'

'My sentiments exactly. I adore gardening, and books are my life. I particularly enjoy the lives of the saints, and the Bible too of course. What do you enjoy reading?'

Ralph toyed for a brief second with the idea of showing her the privately published erotic books he'd had sent from Paris, just to get her reaction. The illustrations alone were quite stimulating. But he would probably have to get out the smelling salts if she had any idea about that.

'Oh, the classics. I'm rather boring in my tastes, I'm afraid. But I did read James Boswell's *Life of Samuel Johnson* recently, which mentions the Archbishop of Canterbury's grandfather, which I thought fascinating.' He recalled a particularly tedious conversation between the local vicar and some British officer on the train from Cork yesterday. He'd had a fruitless journey to try to withdraw some money from the bank. He was thankful once again for his total recall ability, even when only half listening. He hadn't the faintest idea what that book was or who the Johnson in the title referred to, but it seemed to impress her.

'Oh, I think you mean Reverend Randall? The last archbishop?'

'Indeed, of course.'

'I'm such an admirer of Reverend Randall Davidson. He's such a peacemaker, trying to heal the acrimonious splits between Anglicans and Anglo-Catholics. He was an adviser to Queen Victoria, you know?'

Ralph neither knew nor cared who she was going on about, but he was a master of seeming to be involved in conversations without actually saying anything. People were morons for the most part, spilling their guts to the first person who showed even a modicum of interest. The duller a person was, the more pathetically grateful they were for his attention, and this plain Jane was Olympic-level dull.

'Indeed.' Ralph gave her one of his rare genuine smiles. 'I couldn't agree more, and if we need anything in this troubled world of ours, it is peacemakers. When I think of the brave souls, such as dear departed Dominic, who gave their lives for us, it behoves us all to find a path to a more peaceful society, does it not? After all, we are all God's children,' he said piously, and she blushed again. Honestly, this was too easy, like taking sweeties from a baby, but he did not want to get ahead of himself. He'd need to do some digging to find out how much use she could actually be before he invested any more time in her.

'So you're enjoying your time at the Queen's?' he asked, topping the sherry up once more. For all her piety, it was like throwing water into a barrel of sawdust, which was interesting because all weaknesses could be exploited.

'Oh yes, it's so nice to work with the public, and people are so kind. Mr Quinn, the undertaker, came in yesterday, as rather embarrassingly, the seat behind the desk wasn't high enough for me. I looked rather ridiculous behind the huge desk, and he adjusted it. His wife and he dined there recently, and he and Mr Bridges are friendly. His wife worked here at one point too, I believe?'

If the mention of Rose gave him any cause for vexation, this young woman would not know it. 'She was the maid here when my brother lived here, yes. I think she went to America or something afterwards. To be honest, I never lived here in those years – I was studying and then in the Army – so I didn't know her.' The fabrication slipped easily off his tongue.

'Oh, she is lovely, and always so elegant. It's as if her clothes come from a fashion magazine, and her hair is simply beautiful, chestnut and so radiant. I must admit to the sin of envy when I see her. But then she is so charming and friendly, she's impossible not to like. Her daughter, Harp, is quite the famous performer, I believe, in New York – lots of people mention her. Imagine, and she grew up here in Queenstown...' – she corrected herself – 'Cobh. And she's world-famous now, and she is visiting this week.'

'I had heard something, I think, but I'm not really up to date with modern things like that, I'm afraid. I'm rather an old fuddy-duddy.' He smiled.

If she knew Harp's surname, she would surely remark upon it. She'd have to have been living under a rock not to have heard of the wonder that was Harp Devereaux; the blasted female was in every newspaper since she got here. Though Doris didn't seem to make the connection, the dozy cow. He made a decision.

'Harp Devereaux is actually my brother's child. Born out of wedlock, obviously, but my brother was a good if feeble-minded chap, and he did the decent thing and provided for his progeny in his will.' He saw her discomfiture and went in for the kill. 'I'm sorry to raise such a distasteful topic, people behaving in such a manner, but I'm afraid that you will hear of it, and since you raised the subject, I want you to hear it from me. If we are to be friends – and I hope we can be, Doris, I hope it very much – then I would not like to start our friendship on a footing of deception. You will find me an honourable man, and I despise lies and underhanded behaviour. Only God can judge, so I will say no more on the behaviour of Mrs Quinn and my brother, but I wanted you to know, as a confidante. Scandal and gossip grow all sorts of legs and arms in a small town, so I just wanted you to hear the truth from me.'

This time she didn't blush, and he knew he had her on the hook. That soft look to the eyes, the gentle smile, the awkward attempt at a coquettish smile – he'd seen it a hundred times before. She was in the palm of his hand now.

'I don't judge you, Ralph, and thank you for telling me. It sounds as if I perhaps misjudged Mrs Quinn. She always seems so nice, but if she took advantage of your brother, a vulnerable person like that... And, well, as you say, only the good Lord can judge.'

'Indeed.' He smiled.

She stood up, perhaps a little unsteadily given that she had the most of a half a bottle of sherry in her.

'I would offer to show you the garden, but unfortunately with my leg, I'm not able for much. Funds don't stretch to a gardener any longer, so the place has become rather overgrown.'

'That's not your fault, and I'm sure what the Lord has taken away with one hand, He giveth with another? You have many other skills, I'm sure. I was, for example, born with very poor eyesight. It comes from my mother's side – she was almost blind, poor dear lady. But like her I have excellent hearing. My papa used to say I could hear more keenly than the dogs, and that's saying something.' She giggled, an irritating titter.

He laughed affectionately. 'That must be a useful skill to have. I don't know if I have any particular skill, Doris, that's the truth. I wish you could have seen it when my parents were still with us – it was really lovely.' He figured he might as well lay his cards on the table. He was banking on the fact that she'd be so excited that any man showed an interest that he wouldn't need to impress her with money he didn't have.

'Oh, I remember it being lovely up to fairly recently, a year or two ago, I would say, because if I passed, I always admired it.'

Rose's handiwork of course, but he'd be damned if he'd give her the credit. 'Oh yes, I did pay for a gardener for as long as my niece lived here. Legitimate or not, my family have a responsibility to her, and I tried my best to honour it. But then she left, and her mother married, I believe. Again, I'm not sure of the timeline, but when I came home, they were both gone, and so here I am, back at the beginning.'

'And not a word of thanks or explanation from either of them, after all your generosity to them? How shocking. You're such a good man, Ralph, and in the face of such adversity to maintain your faith and sense of duty and fairness. Thank you for inviting me here today, and for the photograph of dear Dominic. I shall treasure it.'

'My pleasure, Miss Prince.' He nodded with a smile.

'Doris, please, if we are to be friends.' She extended her hand.

He kissed the proffered tiny gloved hand. She was really abnormally petite, and he wondered if it was a birth defect. 'Doris, I hope we shall meet again.'

She paused. 'Well, and please say if it's presumptuous, but I could help with the garden if you liked? I simply adore gardening and my own house is rather finished, so I long for a project to get stuck into as it were.'

'Would you really?' Ralph made sure he looked absolutely charmed at the suggestion. 'I would be delighted! But perhaps it would not be seemly, an older man, whose wife has absconded, with a...' – he made himself blush – 'very attractive younger lady. I know it would be completely innocent, but you know how tongues wag.'

'"To thine own self be true, then thou not needs be false to any man,"' she quoted pompously.

'You are remarkable, Doris.'

'Not at all.' She looked pleasantly flustered. 'I'm very ordinary. Now, I must get going as I'm due to work at two, and there's a large meeting in the hotel this afternoon – there are plans for a fete or a regatta. It is felt by local businesses that we should try to present the town as open for business despite the disruption caused by the question of the Treaty. So many shops that catered for the international travellers are really on their uppers now as a result of the unrest.'

'And it's not over yet, by all accounts.' He walked her to the front door, his hand protectively on her elbow. 'There's been terrible goings-on all over the place since the truce. It's almost more dangerous now than it was before.'

She sighed. 'I know, attacks and killings every day. When will it end? Sometimes I worry it never will.'

'Well, you take good care of yourself, and if you ever need a man, or even half of one, around the house, you know where to call.' He smiled self-deprecatingly.

'Thank you, Ralph. I shall see you soon.'

CHAPTER 21

$\mathcal{T}$he waitress approached them in the lobby of the hotel that served as a ladies' tea room. They chose the last remaining table, by the reception desk. 'Sit,' Rose instructed her daughter.

Mr Bridges was busy organising a big event involving pleasure boat trips and a fun fair to attract visitors to the town, and the hotel seemed to be bustling. There was an earnest young woman at the main desk, with thick spectacles and a wide face, whom Harp didn't recognise.

Harp knew what was coming. She had arrived the night before without JohnJoe, and Rose and Matt had already heard the story of the engagement and assumed it was a case of crossed wires. They were totally astonished when Harp confirmed it was true. Harp knew they both suspected there was more to the unbelievable story that Harp and JohnJoe had decided they were really just good friends and that she and Elliot were in love and that everyone was very happy with the decision.

Rose had tried to make eye contact with Harp all night, but Harp kept the conversation light and refused to meet her mother's gaze. Matt arrived home late – he'd been at a meeting – and though he greeted her warmly, he seemed distracted. The escalation of violence between the sides who accepted the Treaty and those who didn't was getting out of control, and there was a bitter resentment to it all that had not been there before when all Irishmen and women were on the same side. The Devlins were not speaking to them at all now, and the entire place was a seething hotbed of resentment, bitterness and mistrust.

Harp told them of her encounter with Collins in Dublin and saw the unspoken conversation between her mother and Matt.

'What?' she asked, looking from one to the other.

'He's talking about coming down to Cork,' Matt said tightly. 'He thinks that if he can sit down with them, especially the lads in West Cork, his own place, he can talk some sense into them. I don't know. If anyone can, he can, but they're so angry, and it runs so deep. They feel like he sold them out.'

'Are you worried for his safety?' she asked incredulously. 'Surely not, he's the Big Fella, the one they all looked up to, admired, trusted. They might disagree with him, but they'd never harm him.'

Matt shrugged. 'I hope you're right, Harp.'

The conversation went on, with Rose filling her in on Brian and Síle's recent engagement and plans for a springtime wedding next year. Harp was delighted for her old friend, the only one she had before JohnJoe came along. Though Brian was older than her, he stuck up for her in school against Emmet Kelly and the rest of the bullies, and it had saddened her that he seemed to want more than just friendship as they got older. But they'd managed to get over it and were now good friends. They wrote regularly enough, and she knew he was serious about Síle and was looking forward to meeting her.

Dinner ended and she went to bed, finding it hard to sleep. The night sky over the harbour of her childhood did nothing to soothe her. From the top floor of Matt's house, she could see the dark looming bulk of the Cliff House and wondered if she had been sleeping in that house tonight whether she would feel so restless.

She wondered how JohnJoe was. Had he confided in his sister the whole story, or was he sticking to the lie they'd invented? Part of her wished he'd tell Kitty the truth so Kitty wouldn't hate her, but that was selfish.

She passed a wakeful night, and as soon as she came downstairs, Rose insisted they leave for the hotel. Matt was having some people in that morning to try to call off a revenge attack on Ernest York, a known collaborator with the British during the Tan war.

The new employee of the Queen's Hotel was studiously working on something at the reception desk.

'Good morning, Miss Prince.' Rose smiled. The other woman looked up and seemed startled.

'Good morning, Mrs Quinn.' She returned to her work.

Rose made a face at Harp, indicating that the woman was a little strange. Harp raised an eyebrow; she'd never seen this tiny woman before. Rose whispered, 'I'll tell you later.'

The tea and buns arrived, and Rose waited until the waitress had served. Then she spoke directly to her daughter. 'Now, we can beat about the bush and I'll get the truth out of you eventually, or you can tell me now what on earth is going on and save us both a lot of time and energy.'

'Going on how?' Harp asked, trying to look innocently at the woman who'd given birth to her, raised her alone and been her champion every day of her life.

'Oh, for goodness' sake, Harp.' Rose lowered her voice. 'This JohnJoe and Elliot business. I'm a Chinaman if you have any romantic feelings for that boy Elliot, and you and JohnJoe O'Dwyer are like two peas in a pod, always were and always will be. And no matter what yarn you spin, any fool can see that you're heartbroken, and I'm sure he's not far behind you. So I'll ask again – what is going on?'

Harp hated to see the deep lines of worry etched on her beloved mother's face. 'I can't tell you,' Harp said morosely, the enormity of the situation crashing over her like an icy wave once more.

'Harp Devereaux, there is *nothing* you can't tell me. Are you pregnant?'

Harp was shocked at the straightforward way she asked. Rose was normally much more discreet about such matters. 'No, of course I'm not,' she replied hotly.

'All right then, I'm going to play this as a guessing game – is that your plan? Because believe me, we will not leave this place until I know what has caused you such pain. Harp, if you tell me, it will stay with me. I swear to you. I won't even tell Matt if you don't want me to.'

Resistance was futile, Harp knew. She glanced around. The other tables were all occupied, but everyone was engrossed in their own business. The young woman at the desk was deep in some ledger, and besides, she was too far away to hear anything.

As succinctly as she could, she told her mother everything. Rose listened, not interrupting or showing any emotion whatsoever. When Harp finished, Rose sipped her tea. Neither woman spoke for a moment.

'You cannot do this, Harp. You can't marry this boy, even if it is to save him, and his friend, and the band, because to do so is to sacrifice yourself and JohnJoe. It's not right, and you simply can't do it.'

'I've no choice, Mammy. If I back out, that action, combined with the rumours of what happened in Dublin and Elliot's past, will be enough to draw the authorities on him. They'd be under constant surveillance and if they were caught, Elliot and Jerry could go to jail, and do you know what happens to men like them in prison?'

Rose opened her mouth to speak but closed it again, no sound coming out.

'No. You don't,' Harp answered for her sadly. 'But I would imagine it's not pleasant. Between four and twenty years of hard labour, that's the punishment, not to mention the other inmates. I can't do it to them.'

'But back in America, they won't have committed any crime. Can't they just carry on as before? I mean, I know it will make the papers, you calling off the engagement, but today's news wraps tomorrows chips – you know that, Harp.'

'Not this. If we call it off at this point, then it will cast a pall over the band, and on top of that, it will just add further fuel to the rumours and Elliot and Jerry will be in serious trouble.'

Rose reached over and squeezed her daughter's hand. 'I don't mean to sound harsh, Harp, but isn't that Elliot's problem?'

'Maybe. But we still can't abandon them. And I know you think it's just a band, but JohnJoe and I love Roaring Liberty, so do the boys, and we are living such a wonderful life – I can't think of anything I'd enjoy more than this. If Elliot and I publicly split, then the gossip starts and the story gets out and then the respectable places won't book us any more, families and decent people won't come. All we've worked for, all we've achieved, will be in ashes.'

'So you're going to do it, marry this boy?'

Harp nodded. 'We'll divorce after a reasonable time, but yes, I'm going to do it.'

'I can't believe you're going to sacrifice yourself and JohnJoe for this, Harp. It's very laudable, I know, but it's a lot to ask – a huge thing to ask in actual fact.'

'He didn't ask – I offered. I wish things were different. I can't bear hurting JohnJoe, but I just can't see a way out for any of us.'

'I just don't know, Harp. It's a terrible situation.' Rose was worried, she could tell.

'Any news of the Cliff House?' Harp changed the subject but lowered her voice. The lobby that served as both reception and a tea room was busy.

Rose shook her head. 'Nobody's seen either of them. His creepy butler seems to be gone now too. He was seen getting the train to Cork with his suitcases. Rumour has it that he wasn't paid, so he left.'

'And still nothing from Pamela either?'

Rose shrugged. 'Well, the Darjeeling order from the shop and the handbag left on the hallstand were the only reasons I had to be suspicious, but he was very convincing. He says she's gone, we can only assume to India. There's been no sign of her, and anyway, why would he lie? Maybe Pamela is getting Marianne's letters and not responding for some reason. I don't know her, but as you've often said, she married Ralph, so it doesn't say much for her judgement.'

'But is her solicitor not concerned as well? She wouldn't cut off contact with him surely?'

'I know it's very strange, but to be honest with you, Harp, though I do feel for Marianne, I have enough problems of my own, worrying about Matt and about you. So I'm afraid Pamela Devereaux will have to take a back seat now.'

The table was cleared, and they reverted to conversation about less sensitive topics before climbing back up the hill to Matt's house.

Later that night, having spent most of the day in her room trying to focus on a book and failing, Harp sat at the window gazing out. When the Great War was on and the harbour full of dreadnought and all manner of military vessels, she'd marvelled at how peaceful it was at night there, in spite of the fact that the whole world seemed hell-bent on destruction. It felt a little bit like that now. The country was in the grips of a bitter, bloody civil war, but from up here, it all looked calm.

It had been a free-for-all of attacks and counter-attacks. Bridges blown, roads destroyed, farms and private dwellings set ablaze. It was hard to believe, but it was nearly worse now than under the most merciless days of the British. The fighting was vicious, but the perception was that Collins's Free Staters had the republicans or the irregulars on the run but still held some strongholds, West Cork being one of the main ones, the site of so many decisive battles of the war with England. It was both inevitable and ironic that those most loyal to their own man, a native of the area, would now be the ones to cause him the biggest problems. It was not safe for anyone to be out now; Free State soldiers as well as irregulars were being shot and killed at an alarming rate, often with civilians caught in the crossfire. Any sense of euphoria that was felt at the departure of the British was well and truly dissipated, and everyone was on edge.

The celebrations of the initial weeks after the truce gave way to a renewed effort in training and the procurement of weapons on the part of those who didn't believe a truce would hold. Two new grenade factories were established. And while in the rest of the country the new uneasy peace was welcome, in Cobh it was felt that they, more

211

than anyone else, knew the British of old and they were not to be trusted. Tom Barry, the IRA leader and hero of the Kilmichael Ambush, the most successful strike against Crown forces of the entire Tan war, had been appointed to negotiate with the authorities on behalf of prisoners on Spike Island. The blunt refusal to deal with Barry, or recognise his authority, and the continued maltreatment of Irishmen on the prison island, told them all they needed to know about the true intentions of the British.

To add to that, internal struggles and power plays within the Irish Republican Army meant that the divides between those who supported the Treaty and those who opposed it deepened, and the Cobh battalion had already split from their nearest battalion, Midleton. It was this internal wrangling and jockeying for position that frustrated Matt the most. He was under no illusions as to how duplicitous the English could be, and so a divided Irish Army was ideal from their point of view.

Rose was terrified of anything happening to her husband as he struggled to remain available to both sides. He was walking a dangerous path, with neither faction of his former comrades trusting him because of his unwillingness to be drawn.

Harp stood at the window of the Quinn house and looked down and to the right. There it was, the Cliff House, her house, standing dark and lonely against the headland, watching over the harbour as it had done since it was built almost two hundred years ago. She didn't undress but sat in the rocking chair, her eyes fixed on the inky horizon, lit by the full moon. Why could life never be simple? It felt like there was always some obstacle to overcome, some crisis to weather. Suddenly she felt very young and scared. Perhaps her mother was right; maybe she should just call off the engagement and let the boys to their fate, give up Roaring Liberty, come back here and fight for her house and get it back from the slimy Ralph. She could likely return to her studies at university and continue her original path of academia. Or she could just marry JohnJoe and live in Boston, give up the music and live as a wife of the heir to a large business – she would want for nothing.

She caught her reflection in the mirror over the dressing table. She looked nothing like the studious girl she was. But for all the magazine covers and hairdressers and fancy clothes, was she the same girl inside? She considered it and knew instinctively the answer: She wasn't. And there was no going back. That girl was gone.

"'It is hard to contend against one's heart's desire; for whatever it wishes to have, it buys at the cost of soul.'" The words of Heraclitus escaped her lips, and she smiled.

She'd had a habit as a child of quoting famous people. Some adults thought it precocious, and perhaps they were right, but to her it was a way of solidifying her perception of the world. It helped her make sense of things. She did it less frequently now – well, not aloud at any rate – so reverting to her childhood habit made her feel a nostalgia for her younger self.

She knew she would never sleep; she had too much on her mind. She slipped on a coat of her mother's that was hanging in the wardrobe – it was a still night and not really cold, but she might be glad of it – and crept downstairs, hoping not to wake anyone. If her mother thought she was going out at night alone in normal times, she'd have vetoed it, but now with everything going on, she would have had a heart attack. But Harp had heard Matt come back, so her mother would sleep soundly, knowing he was safe.

The back door scraped across the flags, and she winced at the noise it made. Pressing on, though, she slipped out into the moonlit night. The crescent of houses curved elegantly around the hill overlooking the harbour, and the familiar *tink, tink* of metal on metal from the moored fleet of sailing vessels below could be heard in the night air. The salty tang too was instantly familiar. She thought that perhaps she should be frightened, but she wasn't. This was her place, her home, and she could never feel nervous here.

She walked to the end of the terrace and turned up the hill, her breath labouring slightly as she climbed. The stone wall of the cemetery had not changed even a little, and she knew to lift and push the little gate at the same time to get it open. The heady scent of woodbine and sweet william that grew in profusion around the final resting places of the gentry and the aristocracy of the locality gently scented the warm night air. She picked her way across the churchyard, through the gravestones, many of which dated back to the 1600s; several were lopsided or had even fallen over. This higgledy-piggledy place felt so different to the Catholic graveyard, where all the headstones were neatly arranged in rows.

She saw the one she came to visit as she rounded the corner of the old church, and it gave her comfort. The large grave was one of the most imposing in the entire churchyard. The black marble recumbent slab sealed the dead below ground and bore the names of all of her dead Devereaux ancestors. The carved white marble angel was still there too, standing at the head of the Devereaux plot, a tall and forbidding creature, standing well over six feet tall, one winged arm outstretched and pointing out to sea, the other bent with a celestial finger to its lips, urging silence.

In the moonlight she approached it, then sat on the black marble and rested her back against the angel's plinth, as she'd done so many times throughout her childhood after he died, and she felt the welcome familiar calmness come over her.

'Henry Devereaux.' She traced his name with her finger. 'I'm in trouble, Henry, and I don't know what to do,' she whispered in the night air. 'I'm in this awful mess with Elliot and Jerry, and I think I've broken JohnJoe's heart. My mother is sure I'm making a mistake, and she would fight me more vigorously if she wasn't out of her mind with worry over Matt and the situation here. Everyone back in Boston will be perplexed about the Elliot thing, and they'll see what it's done to JohnJoe, so I'm unlikely to be welcome there. I can't stay here unless I want to lose him and expose Elliot and Jerry to what might be a terrible fate, and I don't think we can just carry on as normal after this. I honestly don't know what to do.'

She sat in silent contemplation, willing him to speak to her, to give her some guidance, but none came. Still, she enjoyed the peace just being beside his grave brought her; it was the first time she'd felt calm since this whole thing happened. She had no idea of the time, but she could see the beginnings of dawn begin to break in the east.

CHAPTER 22

'*M*y goodness, poor Harp! That sounds like a dreadful pickle to be in.' Ralph feigned sympathy as he pruned the roses beside Doris. The girl was recounting the conversation she'd overheard between Rose and Harp.

'I would dearly like to help the girl, and her mother as well, but her husband has warned me off. He's one of the rebels, you know? Did terrible things to soldiers going about their lawful business here, boys most of them, just as dear departed Dominic was, and who knows what else he's capable of? I've no desire to rock the boat, as it were, but I do feel some sense of responsibility towards them, even if they shun me. I wish they wouldn't, of course – Harp is family. But her mother was determined to make a match for herself with the Quinn fellow, and any association with the Devereaux name just recalled her disgrace, I suppose, so she wanted to close that chapter of her life and play the respectable married woman. But for Harp to be forced into something as deceitful as a marriage to, well, someone like that...' He forced a slight blush, and she too looked scandalised at such immorality. 'Well, I would like to intervene, offer her some better advice.'

'From what I heard, Mrs Quinn was trying to talk her out of it. She seemed to think Harp should marry someone called JohnJoe, but perhaps that was not for her daughter's good either. But as you say, I was taken in by her too, seemingly so nice and friendly. But since knowing you and realising what sort of person she is, I worry for Harp's morals too.'

Ralph fought the urge to snort in derision. Worrying for the morals of a girl she didn't even know? The 'Delusions of Doris', as he'd come to label her opinions on almost everything, were the sign not just of a feeble mind and a malleable character but also that most unattractive of traits, the thinly veiled ambitions of a single woman with no prospects when an even vaguely eligible man was around. Much as he despised his niece, and God knows he couldn't bear her, she at least wasn't a sanctimonious nobody like Doris. He fought feelings of despair. Had it come to this? Paying court to the dowdy Doris in order to fund his next meal? How had he sunk so low? He had always survived on his wits, living in London, in Shimla. He'd had lean times, undoubtedly, but never like this. Rose and Harp were nothing if not smart, so they wouldn't take long to figure it all out.

He'd been most frustrated in the Bank of Ireland when he discovered that Pamela's lawyers had frozen his assets, assisted by that snake in the grass Maguire, and he'd let the teller have it both barrels. It wasn't until he stormed out in a fit of temper did he see Maisie O'Neill, the coal merchant's wife. He owed money to him too, so undoubtedly the scene in the bank found its way back here. No, this was an all-time low. Could he marry Doris? The prospect made him shudder.

He'd at least managed to plant the seeds of judgement and disapproval for the Quinns in her fertile mind, and his work was paying off. True, he'd had to endure hours of tedious gardening with dozy Doris, but at last she'd provided him with something useful. Immediately he'd thought of blackmailing Harp, threatening to expose her plans to marry a sodomite.

He needed cash, and she was absolutely filthy rich due to flaunting her angular body and warbling on stage – people's tastes never ceased to astound him – so he could simply threaten to expose her and demand she pay for his silence. It was one option. But she was not stupid and so might outwit him.

But perhaps there were other things he could do, other avenues to explore. He wished Doris would stop wittering on and let him think.

The idea of entangling himself once more repulsed him, but Doris mentioned that she had to go to Cork next week to see her father's stockbroker, so there was probably something there. He'd been to her house, and it was modest by the Cliff House standards of course, but there were some nice pieces of furniture and artwork, and the house and grounds were immaculately kept.

'I've brought some veal chops and some potatoes and green beans from my garden. I could cook us some supper if you'd like?'

'Oh, Doris, my dear, you spoil me. I feel so unworthy of the care you've bestowed upon me, really I do. You're as lovely as this dahlia.' He picked a flower and handed it to her.

'That's a peony, you silly.' She giggled and he smiled. 'And I'm not spoiling you... I like having a...friend.'

'I like having a friend too,' he said, mock-shyly. 'You know, an old man such as I, and a soldier, I'm not very adept at emotions. My mama was a wonderful woman, but she was not one for feelings and such, and my father, well, he gave my mother a peck on the cheek once a year on her birthday and I believe that's where any intimacy began and ended.' He chuckled slightly, causing her to redden. 'And I know I have nothing to offer you, but I want you to know that you are very special to me and I value your friendship enormously. Even if I can't tell a dahlia from a peony.'

'I don't care about what you have or don't have,' she said quietly, laying down the secateurs and removing her gardening gloves. She was wearing her thin mousy hair differently, though no less unflatter-ingly. She looked nothing short of ridiculous with it hanging from her temples in ringlets more befitting a child.

He sighed inwardly. She was angling for the kiss; he knew it. The thought wasn't one he relished, but perhaps he should, to draw her in a bit closer. Funds were running precariously low, and he needed to get some cash from somewhere. If he could wrangle another invitation to her house, he could perhaps have a nose around to see if there was anything there he could pilfer to turn into ready money. In order to do that, though, he'd need opportunity, ideally an overnight visit. The prospect repulsed him. And she was such a goody two shoes that she'd hardly let him in her bed without a ring on her finger. He tried not to think about it. For a brief moment, an image of Sarita, his Indian lover, flashed before his eyes. She was a beauty, with her caramel-coloured skin, jewelled navel, brown eyes ringed seductively with kohl and a cascade of sleek dark hair. She was an heiress to a fortune – her father was an astute Indian, a rare enough creature – and she longed to be accepted by her White masters. Of course she never would be, but he'd held that like a carrot before her for years. He could never go native publicly of course, he would be ruined, but she never understood that, and having her in his bed was a delight. But this Doris creature on the other hand definitely would test him. Still, desperate times called for desperate measures. He would try to extort it from Harp, and failing that, he'd have to go the Doris route.

He'd had so few invitations of late. The women of the locality of their class who remained in Ireland had stopped asking him to dine because he'd turned up once or twice without Pamela and they were all concerned enquiries– females always did that, clucking about each other like old brood hens – so opportunities to dine at someone else's expense were non-existent. He had debts everywhere so didn't dare show his face downtown. Bridges had even called to the house looking for the hotel bill to be paid; how pathetically middle class of him. The man was a joke. Working every day at his little seaside hotel, when he'd married well and had family money as well. But no, he could be found washing dishes apparently if the need arose. And Ralph had it on Beckett's authority that the British were watching Bridges; he was altogether too friendly with the rebel side of things, despite the fact that he was of their stock, educated at Harrow, and his sister-in-law was married to the brigadier general before Beckett. Odious man.

'Well, in that case I would love to have dinner with you.' He smiled.

'I would offer to open a bottle of wine, but to be honest, I try to steer clear of alcohol.'

'Oh, I am an abstemious person by nature, so please don't worry on that account.'

He thought of the bottle of sherry that first day. She was abstemious? He begged to differ. She was insufferable, so sanctimonious and pious.

'Well then, we shall have a delicious dinner and fine Irish water to wash it down.' He chuckled and she tittered. At least he'd eat this evening; the cupboards were literally bare. Once she got into the kitchen and saw that, she would surely want to help him out; that would tide things over for a while anyway.

Ralph thought back to the many ups and downs of his life. He'd usually managed to turn his fortunes around with a bit of card sharking or becoming involved with a sometimes unsavoury deal, but in order to do that, one needed to be involved in society. Which he wasn't.

Over dinner he gently and expertly grilled her once again on the conversation between Harp and Rose. So the peculiar little witch was going to marry a nancy boy, was she? Well, wouldn't the newspapers love to hear the sordid details of that? As Doris droned on and on about begonias or azaleas or something equally mind-numbing, he was deep in thought about how best to proceed.

If he could wrangle an invitation to dinner at her place, that would be the best thing. He'd surely pocket something of value without her realising. She wouldn't expect him to make a move on her, though he'd have to up the flirting a bit to make sure she was well and truly hooked, and he'd play the 'how I'd love to ravish you now but I have too much respect for you' card, which he figured should be enough for the meantime at least. He could promise marriage in the future once he and Pamela divorced. She'd wait until he was free, which would be approximately never.

He extracted the cigarette case that he'd stolen from a man on the train. There were a few Woodbines left, and he'd been rationing them. The gallant young man had got up to help a woman with several children get off at Rushbrooke, leaving his ivory and brass cigarette case on the seat, opposite where Ralph sat, so he pocketed it and got off at Rushbrooke as well; he then just caught the next train to Queenstown. He would never call it Cobh no matter what the bloody rebels said.

She gazed at him and then at the case, a quizzical look on her face. 'To Anthony with love from B xx,' she read slowly.

Ralph smiled. 'Anthony was a comrade of mine. His girl gave him that for his twenty-first birthday. He died in my arms, a shell, and he asked me to have it, to remember him by.'

'Would you not have returned it to her?' He heard the slight disapproval in her tone.

'By the time I found her, Spanish flu had taken poor old Beatrice, I'm afraid,' Ralph responded instantly, 'like so many other good souls. Your lovely parents among them.' He patted her hand gently.

She nodded but removed her hand demurely.

He inhaled the smoke deep into his lungs, exhaling a long, thin blue plume. The harbour, normally a hive of activity, largely attributable to the Crown forces, was eerily calm. The vast majority of men in uniform were confined to barracks because of the truce, and there was a sense of a pregnant pause in the air. He would have enjoyed going down to the hotel to see if he could get someone to stand him a drink and find out what was happening, but he didn't dare. Still, at least he now had this mini troll opposite him to be his eyes and ears and she would report faithfully, so that was something.

'Mrs Quinn and her daughter also discussed Mrs Devereaux,' Doris said slowly. Clearly she had been weighing up whether or not to say anything.

'Oh yes?' Ralph remained nonchalant. 'What about her?'

'Oh, they were speculating about her whereabouts.'

Ralph's brow furrowed in confusion. 'Why would they wonder that? Rose came up here and asked me outright, and I told her that Pamela was gone back to India. Pamela's daughter, Marianne, is friendly with Harp – she was married to one of our chaps here, and they lived here for a time. Apparently Pamela has not contacted her daughter, though to be frank, I think it is more to do with the fact of

Marianne's promiscuity than any great mysterious disappearing act on the part of my wife.'

'Whatever do you mean?' Doris asked.

'Oh dear Doris, you will think my family very immoral, and I hasten to tell you Marianne is no relation of mine, but I'm afraid there's another rather sordid tale to tell. Marianne was married to Brigadier Oliver Beckett – he was the officer in command here in the barracks – but she was involved with another man, an American, and bore his child. Her husband was killed by rebels, and so she absconded with her lover to America. Pamela may be a bit too highly bred for this place and she may have abandoned me, but she *is* a moral woman and was appalled at her daughter's behaviour. She was mortified, to be honest, and didn't feel comfortable in society really after that. I think Marianne's antics were some of the reason she left. So if Marianne is not getting replies to her letters, the answer is more likely staring at her in the mirror.'

Doris nodded. 'It's been a lot for you to have to deal with, and none of it your fault. My heart goes out to you, Ralph.'

CHAPTER 23

*H*arp sat in the public garden, across the road from the Devlins' shop, her heart heavy. It felt like just when she should be so happy, everything was turning to ashes before her eyes, personally and for her beloved country.

She heard the faint *ding* of the Devlins' shop door being opened. It would normally have been the first place she visited after seeing her mother, but Rose had told her about the scene between her and Liz and how they'd not spoken since.

Liz and Cissy had been such close friends, such allies during the Tan war, and now that closeness was another in a long list of casualties of this bitter civil war.

She and JohnJoe had licked ice cream here so often. It was here he'd first defended her when Emmet threw mud at her dress in 1912. It was here years later that they'd often stolen a kiss behind the bandstand. If her mother knew she was kissing a boy in public, she would have had a stroke, but Harp never cared about things like that. Her JohnJoe, the only boy she'd ever loved or ever would love, was probably just as miserable in Liverpool.

Matt had warned her to be extra vigilant, as despite not publicly taking sides, he was seen as a supporter of the Free State, and that made him and his family a target from the anti-Treaty people. Harp could not believe her country had come to this. It was all so horrible.

Sitting here now, looking at the islands of Spike and Haulbowline, the entire scene of her childhood laid out before her, she felt so bereft. Henry was gone, her home was in Ralph's hands, and her mother lived in terror of something happening to Matt, a very real fear considering the number of assassinations that had happened of late. There were people on the anti-Treaty side who believed that the agreement was a bad one, and felt they had no other option but to take arms against it, but there were also rogue elements who were using this new phase as an excuse to settle old scores, or taking the opportunity to behave unscrupulously. She'd heard of looting, theft, sexual assault of women, and there appeared to be no consequences. Matt warned her about the maverick bands of men, free from the strict chain of command they had been trained under, roaming the place looking for trouble. One family, the six Mulcair brothers, had squared up to Matt last week and refused a direct order from their former OC to hand in their weapons. They were apparently armed to the teeth and entirely lawless.

She would leave for America as soon as she could, she decided. Staying here wasn't the balm to her soul she'd hoped it would be. Nobody was happy. It would be best just to go back and try to forget about this poor battered place. She would love to take Rose with her, but Rose would never leave Matt, and Matt was determined, more so now than ever before, to help bring an end to the civil war.

However, going back to America came with its own issues. She'd had a telegram from Kathy asking if the reports in the newspaper were true that she and Elliot were to be married. Harp assumed the Raffertys had contacted JohnJoe as well, demanding an explanation for the same question. She didn't know what, if anything, he'd said.

She had gone to Henry's grave every day and sat there, talking to him and wishing he had some wisdom to impart, but she didn't get any sense of him. She used to go there so often as a girl and felt close to him there, but even that had disappeared. She'd never felt so lost.

'Harp!'

She heard her mother's voice and spun around. Rose was walking towards her, a basket on her arm.

'I didn't know where you'd gone. You never came down for breakfast, and when I checked, you were up and gone already,' Rose said, smiling. Harp thought her mother looked older for the first time in her life. The stress of the political tension taking its toll.

'I couldn't sleep, so I got up and went for a walk.' Harp moved along on the bench and her mother sat beside her, placing her basket of groceries on the ground. She had, for as long as Harp could remember, shopped at the Devlins' and hated going to O'Connell's, an inferior establishment in every way.

'How are you feeling?' Rose asked gently.

Harp shrugged and sighed. She kicked at a pebble with her toe; she scuffed her new boots but didn't care. 'Where would I begin? Terrible. Heartbroken, confused, torn, tired... The list is endless and it's all bad,' she answered honestly.

'Oh, Harp. I don't know what to say to you, except nothing is worth this. I really think you should call off the engagement to Elliot. You can't let this mess destroy your life.'

'I think it already has.'

'Oh, my love.' Rose took Harp's hand, and together they stared at the sea. 'What a mess,

I wish I could do something to help.'

'You can.'

'What?'

'Come across the road with me now. I'm worried for you too. My situation, well, I don't know what will happen, but you are not sleeping, worrying about Matt and this whole civil war mess, and you haven't seen anyone since we've been back. So how about we visit Liz and Cissy, see if we can't fix that? I'd feel better going back if that was at least sorted out.'

Rose shook her head. 'You didn't see the way Liz spoke to me, and the way she spoke about Matt...'

'Mammy, I know, and maybe it will be the same again this time, but if we go in together, and Cissy is there too, then at least we can say that we tried. You know Liz, her bark is worse than her bite, and she did risk her life to get you out of the clutches of Beckett. So surely it's worth one last try?'

'I don't know, Harp. I swore I'd never darken their door again.'

'"Anger is an acid that can do more harm to the vessel in which it is held than on anything it can be poured."'

'Mark Twain.' Rose smiled.

'Too easy.' Harp stood and offered her mother her hand. 'So will we try, just once, together?'

Rose exhaled and took the proffered hand, standing with a sigh. 'I'll try, for you, but if they, or more likely Liz, say anything rude, then I'm leaving.'

'As the Americans say, it's a deal.'

It was after lunchtime, and the streets were quiet. People were anxious, venturing out only when absolutely necessary.

The shop was empty when they pushed the large glass door in, the *ding* of the bell loud in the quiet interior. It looked exactly as Harp recalled it: the U-shaped counter running along the three internal walls and the large plate-glass window facing onto the street. Behind the counter were neatly arranged jars and tins, and everything had its place. It smelled of cooked ham and sugar, laundry soap and tobacco, as it always had. She inhaled appreciatively.

Cissy was wiping the shelves and spun around. 'Harp!' she cried. 'And Rose! Come in, come in. Oh, 'tis wonderful to see you, lovie, and looking so sophisticated. I can hardly believe it when I see your name in the papers. And Julia O'Sullivan the other day was telling me that her sister Eileen sent her a *Billboard* magazine from America with you on the cover.'

Cissy bustled out from behind the counter, her face a beam of pleasure. She embraced Harp, and Harp reciprocated. The jollier of the two sisters had barely changed, just a little older, small and wiry, with bright twinkling eyes and her clothes covered in a pastel-pink housecoat as she always wore. Harp noticed she walked with a limp now that wasn't there before. Rose had told her the British had roughed her up when they questioned her.

Harp relaxed; this was a good start. She willed Liz, her old mentor and friend, not to be sharp when she came out.

'Liz,' Cissy called in the direction of the back of the shop, where a door linked their dwelling to the business. 'Come out and see who's here. You won't believe it.'

Rose stood stock-still, her face a mask. Harp could feel her mother's trepidation, but also her longing to repair the ruptured friendship. Seconds later, the door opened and Liz appeared. Harp watched her and willed her to be kind.

She saw an instant of reluctance, a flash of something in the older woman's eyes. Liz never spoke but walked out, lifted the hatch in the counter, crossed into the shop, then went straight to the door. For an instant, Harp thought she was going to leave, but she simply turned the sign from 'open' to 'closed' and flicked the latch upwards, ensuring nobody would push the door in. Then she turned and faced them both. Like Rose, her face was inscrutable, and Harp feared she'd made a terrible mistake. Her mother shouldn't have to face another rejection.

'I'm very glad to see you both,' Liz said, standing square before them. As she spoke, Harp could hear in the delivery that it was a rehearsed speech. Liz was brusque by nature and not given to overly flowery language. 'And I owe you an apology, Rose, for the way I behaved the last time you were in here. I'm very sorry, and I wish I hadn't said it. I should have come up to you and apologised, I know, but I... Well, I didn't, and I should have. You and Matt are our closest friends, and more decent, honest and brave people you'd not find, and I was wrong to say what I said. I was, and still am, very disappointed about the Treaty, and I lashed out at you and that wasn't fair at all.'

'Apology accepted,' Rose replied with the dignity she was synonymous with. 'We go back a very long way, Liz, and I hated us being at loggerheads. Let's just forget it.'

Neither Rose nor Liz were the hugging type, but a smile of genuine affection and friendship was shared. It was enough.

'I made a porter cake last night. Will we go in the back and have a cup of tea and a slice?' Cissy suggested.

'I'd love that,' Harp said, feeling something approximating happiness for the first time in weeks.

'So, Harp, I read in the paper that you're to be married,' Cissy said as she made tea. 'Some chap called Elliot Krauss? I must admit we were astounded because we were sure yourself and JohnJoe were an item, but sure, you were only children and maybe you've moved on?'

Harp glanced at her mother and forced a smile; this was the beginning of the biggest lie she'd ever told. 'Yes, Elliot and I are together for a while now. He's lovely. I would have brought him home with me to meet everyone, but he had an urgent matter to attend to in New York and had to get back. But I'll bring him next time.'

'And JohnJoe, how is he?' Liz asked.

'Oh, he's fine, he sends his love. He's in great demand from the girls, I can assure you. The stage door is thronged each night with ladies wanting his autograph.'

'And does he have anyone special?' Cissy asked. 'We were always mad about him, such a lovely lad.'

Harp thought her face would crack with the fake smile, but she kept it going. 'I'm not that sure. He has lots of girlfriends, but we travel so much and we perform in the evenings…'

'I know,' Cissy said. 'Seeing you become so famous is just wonderful, Harp. We can't believe it sometimes that it's our little Harp up there. Henry Devereaux would be so proud of you, love.'

The four women sat at the kitchen table, the site of so many meetings, social and military, over the years, and chatted easily. It was as if nothing had happened, though they steered clear of matters political.

It wasn't until they got up to leave that Liz said, 'I know we see things differently on the subject of the Treaty and everything, but I am truly sorry for what I said, and I will never say or think anything of the kind again. So no matter what happens, your family can rely on our friendship.'

Harp didn't trust herself to reply so just nodded, a tear rolling down her cheek, and Rose took Liz's hand.

Finally, Cissy spoke, unusually solemn and earnest. 'Liz and I decided last night that it's over. We all fought for democracy, for the right to determine our own fate as a sovereign nation, and even though the will of the people is not what we want, we cannot call ourselves democrats if we refuse to accept it.'

Liz nodded.

'So we're not fighting any more. Not with guns and bombs anyway. We'll participate in the democratic process and we'll argue our case, but we'll use a ballot box, not a bullet.'

'Good for you.' Harp squeezed their hands. 'Now, will you two take care of my mam for me?' She then turned to Rose. 'And you'll look after these two ladies?'

Rose smiled and nodded.

'You three are very important to me, and at least there is one good thing to come out of this visit – it's that we are all friends again.'

'That we are,' Liz agreed, and went to the door, turning the sign back to 'open' once more.

'Thank goodness. O'Connell's is not the standard we're used to,' Rose murmured, and the ensuing laughter released any remaining tension. 'The ham is too fatty, and Matt says he's doing something odd to the tobacco.'

'We'll send up your usual list in the morning with Jimmy.' Cissy chuckled.

Rose linked her daughter's arm as they strolled home. It was an overcast day, and the mist rolled in from the bay as they turned up the Smuggler's Stairs. The path took them past the gate of the Cliff House, but neither woman looked in. To see the overgrown garden and the general unkempt look of the place made them sad.

'Thank you,' Rose said, and Harp knew what she meant.

'You'd have sorted it out yourself in the end either way, or they would.'

'Maybe, but you made it easier. We're a bunch of stubborn old women.'

'And you wonder where I get it from?' Harp laughed. She too was relieved. The odd domestic arrangement between Rose and Henry and the secret of her conception had made Rose appear stand-offish, and she had very few friends. She didn't let people in – it was safer that way, she'd always thought – so the Devlins were a rare find.

'It's good to hear you laugh,' Rose said. 'I'm so worried about you.'

'I'll be grand, Mammy. Try not to worry. When this is all over, will you consider coming back to America?' Harp asked as they came to the top of the steps and took a breather, turning to take in the panorama of the harbour. The sky was a dark greeny-grey, reflecting a sky that was threatening rain. Ireland was lush and green, and despite the rain they'd been having, the plants and flowers grew in vibrant profusion. It struck Harp how nature just carried on; it took no notice whatsoever of the messes humans got themselves into.

'For a visit?'

'No, to live. We could be a complete family again.' Harp took a sidelong glance at her mother and could see she was deliberating.

'Matt wouldn't want to, but if I insisted, he probably would for me.'

'And would you want to?'

'I loved it there, I really did. But I think not. My instinct is to go to be close to you. That would be the main draw for me, to keep an eye on you, to keep you safe. But as Plato reminds us, "Don't force your children into your ways. They are created for a time different to yours."'

Harp laughed. 'You never told me how odd I was when I was a child, spouting quotations all the time.'

'You weren't odd, you were interesting. You still are.'

'I *was* odd. A child who constantly quoted philosophers and poets, kings and presidents, who had no idea what to say or how to be around another child. I was too precocious for my own good.'

'A little precocious perhaps,' Rose conceded with a smile, 'but I prefer quirky and endearing. Henry was so proud of you, and so am I. You've taught me so much more than I could ever teach you. I'm a lucky woman to have been given such a special child.'

'Emmet Kelly used to call us the quare hawks, Henry and me, did you know that?'

'Well, Emmet Kelly is as thick as a brick, always was, and so are every seed, breed and generation of the Kellys. If any one of them had a brain cell, it would be lonely, so I'd take that as a compliment.'

Harp smiled at her mother's fierce defence of her. 'Remember the day we went to see *Titanic* and they were making fun of me, so you knocked him and his henchmen off the blacksmith's gate?'

Rose laughed. 'I do well. Little brats, upsetting you.'

'So you're sure you wouldn't come, to America, I mean?' Harp tried to keep the sadness from her voice. She and her mother would always be close, always be there for each other no matter where they lived, but it would be nice to have her physically closer.

'No, my love. You have your own path to follow, and your own life to live. So far, it's already proving to be exactly as Henry predicted. He said you would have a fascinating life, and it's certainly that. So no, I'll let you live it and wait here for you to visit and keep your old mammy updated.'

Harp would have loved Rose to come back to America, but she was probably right; it was time to fly the nest for good.

'A little less fascinating would be better.' She sighed ruefully as they began walking once more.

CHAPTER 24

*D*oris was busy in the kitchen, and she'd put Ralph in the sitting room to wait. It would be a frugal offering as usual: boiled potatoes without butter, whatever vegetables she had growing in the garden, cabbage by the smell, and a lump of tough meat. She was a parsimonious cook with no effort made at indulgence, but any port in a storm, he supposed. He knew he was hedonistic by nature, and so Doris's thrift made him cringe.

He'd have murdered for a glass of whiskey as an aperitif, followed by a nice bottle of Burgundy to wash down the awful stodgy food, but this was not such a house. He took in his surroundings. It wasn't a fine house by any standard, but it was comfortable enough, he supposed. The dog, Nelson, was a gentle old thing and he quite liked dogs anyway. It reminded him of a vicarage or something of that nature. The grounds were immaculate; an errant daisy would not dare show its head to Doris Prince. The sitting room was small and had too much furniture for its size. The armchair he sat on was overstuffed and lumpy, and the antimacassars had been embroidered inexpertly by the hand of his hostess, no doubt. A wobbly hand had threaded 'The Lord is my shepherd' on each one. He rolled his eyes.

The smell, competing with cabbage for supremacy, was a combination of must, mothballs and lavender wax polish. The house smelled like an old woman, and it repulsed him. He tried to summon up the scent of Sarita, a wonderfully exotic combination of sandalwood and jasmine. And her hair…oh, how the fragrance of her dark silky hair drove him wild. She was a real woman, Sarita. He found himself thinking of her often these days, and wondering how she was. He'd sent a telegram to her, testing the waters. A letter would have been more intimate, but he had no time for that. He thought that if she was still besotted with him, perhaps he could get her to send him the fare and he could go back to Shimla. It would cause a bit of a stir, but at least she had a fortune to inherit and a very nice villa on her father's plantation. But he'd received a curt reply saying that she was married, that she knew he'd stolen from her and that if he ever contacted her again, she'd call the police. So that was probably that. Pity, though. She might have been beneath him socially, being native, but she was a lioness in the bedroom, and he'd enjoyed her while he had her.

He caught a glimpse of himself in the oval gilt-framed mirror over the fireplace. He was still a good-looking man, he thought dispassionately. Of all of his faults, he knew he wasn't vain; it was simply a statement of fact. His father had been good-looking, and so was he. Henry looked like their mother. Not awful, he supposed, but delicate and fine featured, whereas he and his father were more robust and striking. His dark hair, which was inclined to curl anyway, was becoming unruly for the want of a cut, but he owed his barber for three already so didn't dare appear again. His black hair was curling over his collar now, and only hair oil was keeping it in check. He'd run out of his own so had gone rooting about in Rose's things and found some kind of oil, so was using that instead.

The olive complexion he achieved after so many years in India had faded, but he was still darker than most people around here, and his grey eyes were interesting. More than one woman had told him over the years how she felt she could get lost in his eyes. Romantic old claptrap, but they were an asset.

So in terms of resources he possessed, he was good-looking and well bred, had a glorious if entirely fabricated past, was well travelled and was extremely intelligent and astute. He could make women fall for him relatively easily and had the ability to subtly flatter powerful men and gain their trust.

On the deficit side, things looked rather more bleak. He was living in a house not legally his and without the means to argue the point, he had no money whatsoever and no real way of acquiring any, and he had no friends.

However, he had one other asset: the information that Harp was in trouble. He'd thought of little else but how to monetise it to his own advantage.

She was still in Queenstown. Doris had seen her several times around the town and reported it faithfully. But Harp had made no approach to him regarding the house. He didn't know what to make of that, whether it was a good thing or not. Would she just send the bailiff? Or have her solicitor write to him? Or turn up demanding his departure? If he was evicted, what then? He would be homeless. He'd been on his uppers before, but he'd never panicked. He'd ensured he was always in the company of monied people even if he had none of his own, so all he had to do was apply a bit of charm or pressure and it generally came good. Had he really come to the end of the road?

He could hear Doris singing a tuneless hymn from the kitchen. Could he bear it? A lifetime of her? He might have to. This house was all right, he supposed, but she would drive him around the bend with the holiness and the endless manual labour. The woman seemed to think he should spend his days in productive activity, gardening or preserving food in cans and jars for the winter. She was so wretchedly middle class, with her stinginess and industry. He was a gentleman, a different class of person entirely, and she hadn't a clue.

'Ralph, tea is ready,' Doris called.

He cringed. People of his class ate dinner at night. The notion of 'having one's tea' at 6 p.m. was strictly a lower-order class construct and one he'd never experienced nor had any desire to.

Was he imagining it, or was she a little off with him this evening? Surely not. But she did simper a little less when he arrived and seemed to be quite matter-of-fact or something.

He stood, feeling for the Webley he had tucked into his trousers. He didn't dare go anywhere unarmed these days. The rebels were running amok now in ways they had never had the audacity to do before, and all his predictions were proven correct. The Irish were an uneducated, uncultured, unruly lot who needed a firm hand. The moment they drove their betters away was the beginning of the end for them. They were like cornered rats; they'd savage each other in the end. He couldn't care less, but he would not risk being caught in the crossfire, or be used to settle an old score about the presence of the Protestant ascendancy. So he made sure he was always ready.

'Oh my goodness, my dear, that smells simply divine,' he gushed as he entered the tiny drab dining room. The walls were littered with hunting prints and embroidered pieces with Bible quotations, and the small polished mahogany table and brocade-covered hard-backed seats were well worn. A sideboard groaned under the weight of knick-knacks, tiny figurines of ladies in crinoline and scampering woodland animals.

'Oh, it's nothing, just some bacon and cabbage with potatoes, all grown here in the garden. Well, the pig wasn't.' She gave him a tight little smile. 'That poor fellow was once the bane of Ernie Hargreaves's life. The creature had become most territorial and aggressive in the end. Poor Hyacinth told me at church last Sunday she was very fearful of it and had to have Ernie throw the food from a distance, so the slaughter and conversion of the old chap to chops and rashers was more an occasion of relief than upset.'

'Indeed. How grateful we are to Percy and of course Ernie and Hyacinth for this fine feast.'

Doris looked blankly at him. Normally he could make her laugh, a sound just like a rose-ringed parakeet that used to nest outside his bedroom window in Shimla. The thing drove him mad, chirping early each morning, so he shot it in the end.

She dished up the feast, and he found it tasted quite nice. He was, as usual, ravenous.

They chatted amicably enough over the meal, but he could tell there was something on her mind. He was extra charming and flattering in case she was thinking about giving him the old heave-ho. He might find her insufferable, but she was his last card now.

They finished, placed their knife and fork together and bowed their heads. She thanked the Lord for the bounty they'd received, and he tried to look suitably devout.

'Let me make you a cup of tea?' he offered. 'You've been working so hard, making this delicious meal.'

He fully expected her to decline, to say that she would do it, of course, but he was stopped in his tracks when she replied. 'Thank you, Ralph, that would be lovely. I normally wash up while I'm waiting for the kettle to boil, so if you could see to that as well? I'll go into the sitting room – I need to sort out a few bills – so if you could make a pot and bring it in there, we could enjoy a cup together. Also there is some shortbread in the blue tin.'

She swept out, Nelson at her heels, leaving him nonplussed. While he tried to figure it out, she popped her head back in. 'Milk and half a teaspoon of sugar,' she instructed. 'I know I'm sweet enough, but the Lord allows a little indulgence on the part of the labourer, I think.'

Ralph had never to his recollection made a cup of tea in his life before. He drank coffee at home and had figured out how to use a percolator recently after Maguire left, so he assumed tea was the same. As for washing dishes, well, he'd have to do it for now, but if he was left with no choice but to shackle himself to Dreary Doris, she could think again if she thought he was going to become a skivvy for her. Now was not the time to show his hand, though, so he rinsed the plates and cutlery in the large Belfast sink and put them to drain on the wooden board beside it.

He added the tea leaves to the teapot and filled it with hot water from the kettle on the black range that sat squat in the kitchen. Though the Prince farmhouse lacked any elegance, it was pleasant to be somewhere warm and tidy on such a dreary evening.

He laid some cups, a jug of milk, the teapot and the tin of short-bread on a tray and carried it to the sitting room. Doris had put a match to the already-set fire, and the room had a cheery glow as she pulled the curtains. It was a dark evening as it had been cloudy and overcast all day.

'Ah, the cup that cheers but never inebriates,' she said, pouring a cup.

'So how was your shift at the hotel today? Interesting?' he asked, sipping the tea, which wasn't great, if he was honest.

'Did you boil the water for the tea, Ralph?' Doris asked, wincing as she sipped.

'Well, I used it from the kettle?' he replied, hiding his irritation at being spoken to as if he were a schoolboy.

'But I banked down the stove for the night, so it wouldn't have been boiling. You would have had to boil it on the gas.'

'Oh, I wasn't aware.' He dismissed her accusatory tone, struggling to remain charming.

'But how could you not know that water needs to be boiling in order to make tea? I don't understand?' She peered at him through the ridiculously thick spectacles, clearly expecting an answer.

'I suppose I never really made tea before – I've always had staff and so on – so I apologise.' He knew he sounded snippy, but honestly, she was the last word.

'Well, you don't have staff now, my dear, so I should have thought learning the basic life skills would be useful.'

She was so condescending and smug. He would have loved to dump the tepid tea over her stupid ugly head but restrained himself. 'Indeed it would.'

'I would make another pot but one hates waste, so perhaps tonight we'll do without, offer it up as a sacrifice.'

Ralph had to concentrate on not reacting. Was she serious? She wasn't going to waste another spoon of tea leaves? Surely not. And was she actually taking it all back, including the tin of shortbread? She really was extraordinarily awful.

Doris left for the kitchen with the tray, and Ralph took the opportunity to have a good look around to see if there was anything worth pilfering. But something about her gimlet eyes behind the glasses made him realise she wasn't as dozy as he first thought. Some of her remarks too of late had been quite sharp.

She might be on the lookout for a man, and while she did want him, he suspected that she was all too aware not just of his impoverished situation but of his reluctance to become a working man, so she wasn't going to be taken for a mug either. He decided the best line of attack was contrite honesty, appeal to her Christian values of charity.

He stood as she came back in. 'I'm sorry, Doris, I should have known. The truth is that I'm a bit hopeless in the kitchen. Mama didn't believe it was any place for a boy, and well, my fortunes throughout my life were such that I didn't need to know anything about such matters. But as you quite rightly point out, I do now need to know if I'm to survive at all. Would you help me?' He tilted his head slightly to one side and softened his gaze with a hint of a smile. It usually did the trick.

She gazed at him in that disconcerting way that made her eyes seem enormous because of her glasses. 'Hmm,' she said non-committally.

There was a long silence.

'Is that a hmm, yes, or a hmm, no?' he quipped.

'It's a no, I think,' she said slowly, almost to herself.

He was taken aback. 'I...I don't understand? I thought we –'

'Yes, I know you did. I thought you were nice, and being honest, I've not had much male attention in my life – none, to be truthful. So I was flattered and foolish, I suppose. But a friend took me aside today and warned me about you. And I realised that perhaps the perception I have may not be completely accurate. Would you mind if I asked you some questions?' She peered at him, her gaze disconcertingly piercing.

'Well, of course, if that's what you –'

'Where *exactly* is your wife?'

'I told you, she left me and is in India, Shimla, where we met and where she spent most of her life.'

'Really? And you're sure of that?'

'Well, it was a rather acrimonious departure, so she hasn't

contacted me, but I –' Ralph was trying to think quickly; this had suddenly taken a turn for the worst.

'Do you owe a lot of money?'

He felt like a rabbit in the headlights. 'Well, I do have some debts. All gentlemen carry a degree of debt. It's –'

'Did you hit your wife?' Again she cut through his answer, like a knife through butter.

'What? Of course not!' He was outraged. 'Who on earth is saying such scurrilous things?'

'It doesn't matter. Someone I trust. I thought – well, I hoped, I suppose – that it wasn't true, but I can see now that it is.'

'Doris, how could you think such a thing? I swear to you… Well, at least give me his name! I cannot have people slandering me –'

The conversation was interrupted by sounds outside. Nelson growled and bounded from his resting place before the fire to the window. The Prince farmhouse was at the end of a long well-tended lane, and callers were few.

'Who's there?' Doris asked, stricken.

They heard the sound of glass being smashed out in the hall. Ralph drew his gun from the waistband of his trousers and gestured with a finger to his lips that she should remain quiet. He went to the window, flattening himself against the adjacent wall, and moved the heavy damask an inch, dropping it again. Doris held the dog's collar, the animal growling ominously all the time.

'There are three or four of them at least,' he whispered.

'Who?' she demanded.

'How the hell should I know?'

'Please do not use such foul language in my home,' she replied coldly, all pretence at cordiality gone now.

Suddenly, the front door was kicked in, the wood splintering. Ralph went to the hallway, his weapon cocked and ready. 'Get out of this house immediately!' he said in his most authoritative British accent.

'Oho, 'tis lover boy, Hopalong Cassidy! We wondered if you'd be here.' The one in front spoke. There were five of them, all dressed in overcoats, with handkerchiefs around their necks and faces.

'Who are you? Leave this house immediately! You're trespassing.'

They laughed and responded by firing a shot into the floor just inches from Ralph's foot.

'Now, we know old Doris has a few guns here – her old man was a great one for the grouse, don't y'know – so we'll be taking them if you don't mind.' The one who did all the talking was putting on an affected accent, and the others laughed. There was the smell of whiskey from them, and Ralph realised they were all drunk.

'Miss Prince isn't here and –'

The man pushed past Ralph, knocking him over. He lay sprawled on his back for an instant before scrambling to right himself. He'd managed to get used to the wooden leg, but getting up from the floor was still a challenge.

The men barged upstairs and came back down just as he was vertical once more, bearing two rifles, a shotgun and several cartridges of ammunition.

'Not much of a haul, but it will do.' The one who spoke earlier chuckled. 'Off we go, lads!'

As he left, he shoved Ralph hard in the chest again, sending him flying backwards once more. As he fell, he hit his head, and he heard their raucous drunken laughter filling the night air as they strolled out. The swagger of them, the sheer audacity and disrespect with which they'd abused him, rose up inside him. How dare these guttersnipes treat him so? And Doris wasn't much better, letting him face them all alone. He dragged himself up and got to the door just as they were approaching the bend of the lane. He took aim, and using all of his well-honed skills, he exhaled slowly as he squeezed the trigger. And with a single shot to the head, he killed the one who'd pushed him.

The ensuing yelling and screaming gave him pause to smile. The others didn't come back to seek revenge, choosing instead to get their fallen comrade to a doctor or a hospital. He could have told them not to waste their time; it had been a direct hit with a highly disapproved-of dumdum, or expanding bullet. He'd bought some in India on the black market. They were banned from most theatres of war because of the inhumane death they caused, but he wanted them for precisely that reason. *Let him suffer*, he thought; Ralph had suffered enough.

He turned to find Doris, ashen, standing in the hallway, her hand on the dog's collar still. Nelson was barking loudly now.

'Did you…did you shoot that man?' She could barely get the words out.

'To protect *you*, yes, I did. He's dead and he can't hurt you,' he answered indignantly.

'But they just wanted the guns! I would have given them to them. There was no need for… He was leaving, Ralph. You shot him in the back' – her voice dropped to a whisper – 'in cold blood.'

'To protect you…' he said again, moving towards her. Nelson snarled and Ralph stepped back.

'Get away from me! You're the devil incarnate – evil follows you. I knew it. I didn't want to believe it. I tried to tell myself he wasn't being truthful, but on some level, I knew it. But what Mr Bridges told me, and now this, I'm in no doubt – you're a monster. All that stuff about being friends with Dominic – it was just to worm your way into my affections. I'm a fool, a stupid fool, to think someone like you would like me for me. You're on your uppers and you need a meal ticket. I might have been a fool, but I'm not entirely without intelligence. Get out of my home!'

'Doris, calm down, you're hysterical.' He tried to approach her again, but this time she backed away, crashing into the hallstand. She was definitely unhinged.

'Get out of my house, you…' – she paused, barely able to formulate the words – 'murderer.'

'Oh, for God's sake, Doris…'

'Get out!' she screamed, tears flowing down her cheeks.

CHAPTER 25

*H*arp and Rose were sitting in the kitchen, discussing the wondrous effects of the herbal concoction the woman in Boston had given Kathy to treat her menopause symptoms. She was doing so well that when Rose told old Doctor Lane about it, he stunned her by asking if he could order some for his patients.

'He was so interested, Harp. I was astounded,' Rose said. 'I knew he was nice – he was always very approachable when you were little and was very good to Henry. But he explained how it was hard on women, that from the age of thirteen or fourteen until well into their fifties, they had to manage menstruation, and then just when it should be getting easier, it gets so much harder. He didn't name anyone obviously, but he described women enduring awful things altogether and all in silence, and he said how he wished there was something he could do to alleviate the suffering. He spoke about ways of avoiding pregnancy too, that would have Father Doyle denouncing him from the pulpit. You could have knocked me down with a feather.'

'It's nice to hear of a man who takes women's health seriously. I always liked Dr Lane. Remember how good he was the night poor old Molly's father stabbed Danny? He drove him to the hospital in his own car and everything.'

'God rest Molly. She had her whole life ahead of her,' Rose said sadly. Molly had stayed at the Cliff House the night before she fled to America to join an order of nuns there. 'God had other plans for her. I forgot to tell you, Eleanor Kind died in Sligo too, peacefully in her own bed, surrounded by her animals. The community gave her a great send-off – she was well loved up there. The parish priest wrote to tell me. He said Eleanor asked him to let us know.'

Harp never forgot the kind old lady who was being dragged kicking and screaming to San Francisco by her well-meaning but forceful brother. She desperately wanted to stay in Sligo and look after her animals, but the brother had convinced her that she shouldn't. In the end she slipped Molly her ticket on the quayside, changing the course of both of their lives.

'I'm sorry to hear that. She was a gentle soul,' Harp said.

'She died as she lived, in her own place, on her own terms, at a good age – no need to be sad. After all the death we've endured, it's nice to hear of such a passing.' Rose paused for a moment. 'So do you think Kathy could arrange to send some of that tincture for Dr Lane?'

'I'm sure she would. If she ever speaks to me again.'

'She will, but either you or JohnJoe will have to tell them the truth.'

'I know.' Harp sighed. 'But how?'

The women sat in companionable silence, each lost in their own thoughts, and for a moment, it felt like the old days.

Just as they were going to bed, a boy arrived to the front door with a message. Rose took the note and closed the door, her hands trembling. She opened it and scanned the contents. Harp's mouth was dry – had something happened to Matt?

'It's from Mr Bridges. There was an attack up at the Princes'. You remember Doris Prince – you met her at the hotel? Her brother Dominic died on the front and her parents were lost to the Spanish flu?'

'I do. What about her?' Harp was confused.

'She just turned up there, to Bridges. Apparently the Mulcair brothers went up there tonight, looking for guns or trouble or both. Anyway, Ralph Devereaux was there, and there was some kind of incident. Apparently Ralph shot Cormac, the second eldest brother, killed him instantly. As they were leaving, so not in self-defence.'

'They're the ones Matt warned us about, the Mulcairs?'

Rose nodded. 'Gone to the other side, but more than that. They were always hard to manage, but now they're totally out of control and answer to nobody. Mr Bridges says that he's heard that they're saying they're going to get Ralph tonight and burn the house, and if they say they will, then you can be sure they'll do it. They went into Dathai Flannery's and attacked his daughter because she was walking out with a Tommy last year. They cut her hair and tarred and feathered her and probably worse, but Dathai couldn't bring himself to say the words. The poor girl is in a bad way, and Dathai and Hannah are beside themselves. Then the gang went to old Major Williams – sure he's ninety if he's a day, and he was always very good to our side during the war – and they shot his old dog and took his guns.'

'But they can't just burn the Cliff House?' Harp was aghast. 'They can't. It's not even Ralph's, it's mine. I have to do something! I have to warn Ralph, I just have to. I know he's...well, whatever he is, but I can't just stand by and do nothing!'

Rose took her coat from the hook. 'Well, you're not going down there on your own.'

'No, Mammy. Anything could happen, and Matt would never forgive me.'

'Harp Devereaux, I am coming. Let me leave a note for Matt.' She scribbled a note and left it on the hallstand.

The women crept out, walking quietly across the gravel to the front of the houses on Matt's terrace and staying in the shadows until they reached the top of the Smuggler's Stairs. They quickly went down the steps, wincing as the garden gate screeched on its hinges. In their day it had always been well oiled.

There was one light on in the downstairs drawing room and no sign of anyone. Harp exhaled; at least they weren't too late.

Rose went to the front door and this time did use her key to gain entry. It turned quietly, and they were greeted to the sound of music. Rose looked perplexed.

Harp whispered, 'It's our old Edison phonograph. He's playing Bach.'

They entered the drawing room and saw the meagre fire smouldering in the grate; the Queen Anne chair hid him as he faced the hearth.

'Ralph, it's me and Harp. We need to talk to you.' Rose spoke gently.

He never looked around but they heard his voice. 'Of course you do.' He sighed, sounding weary.

Harp walked around to the front of the chair, standing between him and the fire. The room had changed a lot since she last saw it. The horrid old oils they had jettisoned to the attic were restored, and the lovely lilacs and pink touches they'd added were all gone. It was dark outside now, the moon obscured by clouds, and the fire the only light, but the décor, even in the gloom, was awful.

'What do you want?'

'You're in trouble, and we wanted to warn you,' Harp said clearly.

'You two want to save me, is that it?' He seemed to find the idea funny. He was dressed neatly as always, in a three-piece suit, and his hair was longer than she'd ever seen it.

'The Mulcair brothers are on their way. They want revenge for their brother, and they want to kill you and burn this house.'

'And so you've come here like a pair of angels of mercy, is that it?' He snorted. 'Because I'd rather face those neanderthal thugs than be indebted to you two, I can assure you of that.'

'No, I want to save my house actually,' she whipped back. 'They can do what they please with you.'

'Ah, come now, Harp, that's not very nice, is it, considering we're family?' He smiled sweetly. There was a shadow of stubble on his jaw, and a dark curl escaped from his oiled hair, falling onto his face.

'If you go now, Ralph, just get away from here, then we can try to convince them not to destroy the house. It's you they're after...' Rose said.

'And why would I do that?' Ralph asked, clearly bored, as he examined his fingernails.

'Because you'd stand a better chance of surviving, and your home, *our* home, would still be here...' Rose finished feebly.

'*Our* home – is that what we're calling it now, Rose?' He sneered. 'As I recall, the last conversation we had on the subject, you were issuing my marching orders, so it's a little late for us to play happy families and pretend we all care about this old pile, don't you think? This is a miserable house, and all who live in it are cursed. My parents hated it and each other, their parents before them the same. Henry was a pitiable creature, scared out of his wits to live, staying up in his room reading about places he'd never go and experiences he'd never have. And as for you two, a servant and her bastard brat, your greed only got you so far, Rose, didn't it? It didn't bring you happiness. And you murdered a man in this house, Harp. And your mother and her creepy undertaker lover dragged him out and buried him. No, better it burns actually, and all the memories in it. Good riddance.'

'Henry was not a pitiable creature, as you call him,' Harp spat, stung at his vitriol. 'He was a wonderfully kind and loving man, and he was happy here. We were happy here with him. So don't think I'll let you poison this place for me, because I won't. We were happy here. We loved and were loved, something you have never nor will ever experience, Ralph. You are the one to be pitied, not Henry.'

The voices outside were soft, but the boots on the gravel were not. They were here.

The ferocious banging on the door seemed even more shocking in the silence after Ralph's last remark.

'Devereaux!' they called. 'Open up!'

More banging.

One of them shouted through the letterbox. 'We'll torch the place either way, so you can die roaring or come out and face us – the choice is yours.'

Something splashed against the window of the dining room, and they saw movement. They were dousing the house in petrol. One match and all the old wood would go up like a tinderbox.

'I'm going out to them.' Rose was gone before Harp could react.

Harp stood stock-still as Rose opened the front door. There were raised voices, indeterminate words, Rose's higher-pitched voice conversing with rougher male tones. Then boots on the carpet, thundering across the hall, first towards the kitchen.

Harp's nose was assailed with the fumes of petrol; they were inside now, pouring it everywhere.

'Stop, please stop!' she screamed, racing up the stairs after two of them, choking on the fumes as she tried to catch up to them. Rose followed two others making for the back of the house, pleading too, explaining who she was, who Matt was, but to no avail. One match and the whole place would be ablaze in seconds.

Harp reached the second floor moments after them and saw they were making for the attic rooms, where she'd slept for most of her childhood. She couldn't bear for it all to burn, not now, not after everything.

She ran up after them, taking the narrower stairs two at a time, begging them to stop, but they were throwing petrol indiscriminately from the jerrycans they carried, totally ignoring her pleas. The small top landing was even smaller than she remembered. One of the men kicked in the door of her old bedroom, then they stopped. Harp appeared at their shoulders and, like the men, gazed.

Harp knew immediately who the bound and gagged woman was, despite having never met her. She ran to the bed, ignoring the men, and removed the gag and the ropes that bound the woman to the iron bedstead.

'Pamela, oh my God! I… We had no idea! Let me get you up and… Marianne has been out of her mind with worry…'

Pamela spoke, her voice hoarse and raspy. 'Marianne is alive?'

'Yes, she's alive and well and living in Boston. Here, let me help you.' Pamela was very unsteady on her feet and needed assistance.

'Get out of my way,' Harp demanded of the two Mulcairs, who she saw now were no more than fourteen or fifteen years of age. 'Now!' she shouted, and they did as she commanded.

She led Pamela down, half carrying her down the stairs, until eventually they reached the ground floor. Rose was there and so was Matt, who seemed to have somehow managed to convince the two men Rose had followed not to torch the house. The place reeked of fumes, and Matt was trying to usher them out. One spark and the whole place would go.

The gathered crowd looked up as Harp and Pamela, followed by the two young Mulcairs, came downstairs. Once down, Harp was able to properly assess Pamela. She looked emaciated. Her hair was matted, her skin was filthy, and she smelled awful.

'Pamela?' Matt approached her, and she just nodded. 'You're safe now, don't worry. You're among friends and you're safe.'

Pamela's knees seemed to give way, and Matt scooped her up in his arms and carried her out, Rose, Harp and the Mulcairs following.

They gathered on the lawn. As Matt sent one of the boys for Doctor Lane and his car, the first windows of the dining room cracked. To their horror they saw orange flames licking the glass inside the house.

'Ralph is still in there, Mam! I have to...' Harp ran towards the French doors at the side of the house.

'Harp, no!' Rose cried, but Harp was gone.

The side garden was overgrown, but she was able to get through the shrubs and grass and climb up the steep grassy bank to the glass doors. She wrenched the French doors open, and then she saw him, still sitting in the chair, facing the fireplace. The hallway and the dining room were in flames, and the fire was rapidly spreading, licking under the door of the drawing room.

She didn't dare enter but called from the doors. 'Ralph, please, come out! Please! Nobody wants you to die in here.'

'I'm sure that's quite untrue, Harp,' he said wearily.

The door leading to the hallway, the source of the flames, had now caught fire. Through the French doors was the only way to escape, but he just sat there, unmoving. The floorboards and wallpaper were in flames. And the old wicker chair she used to use when she played the harp had gone up like tinder.

'I don't want you to die!' she screamed.

'Why not?' he asked, calm as if they'd met on the promenade and stopped for a chat.

'I just don't.' She pleaded, 'Please, get out, come over here to me. The whole house will be engulfed in minutes. Please.' She could feel the heat on her face now.

To her relief he stood and approached the doors. She stretched her arms out to him. 'Hurry, Ralph, please...'

He walked towards her, stopping en route to pick up a painting, which he threw out the door and down the slope. She didn't see which one it was. Then he took her hands in his, standing in the threshold of the only escape route. For a horrible second she wondered if he would drag her into the flames with him. But he didn't. He just stood there, holding her hands and gazing at her face, his grey eyes a perfect reflection of her own.

'We have to go, Ralph.' She tried to drag him, but it was as if he were rooted to the spot. The rose velvet curtains on one side of the French doors were now engulfed in orange and yellow flame. Her face was burning from the intense heat, but he wouldn't budge.

Rose and Matt were below, screaming for her to retreat, but she couldn't let go of his hands.

'You're the only good thing I ever did,' Ralph said sadly. 'Perhaps I couldn't bear that thought. That might be why I hated you so much. But it's true. Henry loved you and was proud of you, but I should have been too and I wasn't. He was a better man than me and deserved to be your father. Go and live your life, Harp, and make a better job of it than I did.'

His hands released hers, and with one hard shove, he pushed her back and sent her rolling down the grassy bank away from the house. Harp watched in horror as the large pelmet over the doors fell and a blaze of flame engulfed the room, the curtains and Ralph Devereaux.

CHAPTER 26

*M*att Quinn placed the bridle with its gleaming brasses and black feathers on the head of one of the black mares as JohnJoe tacked up the other. The hearse was polished and gleaming.

'Rose and Harp are above at the Cliff House, seeing if anything is to be salvaged.' Matt said as they climbed up onto the front seat. Both men were dressed in dark suits with black top hats, as befitting undertakers. Motorised hearses were common nowadays and Matt had considered investing in one, but people here seemed to prefer the traditional one. He had a car for the mourners, but the coffins were carried in the glass-sided hearse, pulled by two black horses.

'Of all the funerals I've done in this town, and God knows there have been plenty, this is the strangest.'

Once JohnJoe had heard from Matt about the fire and the danger Harp had been in, he rushed over from Liverpool. No matter what happened now, he would never leave her again. The idea that she might have died was one he couldn't bear. 'And to think I was trying to dispatch him years ago, and now I'm at his funeral,' he said.

'We'd best make sure he's actually dead this time.' Matt smiled grimly, clicking the reins for the horse to move off. 'If I hadn't prepared his body myself, or what was left of it, I'd still be doubting it.'

'I can't even think about that night, how it could have gone.'

'I know, but Rose and Harp are strong-minded women. At least Rose had the good sense to leave me a note – I nearly collapsed when I read it. But they came out without a scratch, and that's all that matters. Luckily I was able to get there to talk the Mulcairs down, as they normally don't listen to a word anyone says. They were drunk and in a state after their brother being killed.'

'They were hell-bent on revenge, so it was incredible that they backed down. What did you say to them?'

'Ah, without Cormac and the older brother Peter, they were just kids, barely out of short pants. Peter was at a meeting of the anti-Treaty side and probably wouldn't have given the go-ahead for the attack on the Cliff House, knowing our connection to it. So I just said he'd be furious with them when he got back and found out what they did, and they seemed to accept it.'

'Still, we were so lucky, considering all that's going on,' JohnJoe said.

'I know. The whole place is descending into chaos. Every day there's something, an atrocity, a reprisal.' Matt nodded a greeting at a couple who were walking up the hill.

The sight of Mr Quinn doing a funeral wasn't an unusual one, but everyone was talking about the death of Ralph Devereaux and the burning of the Cliff House.

'I think it's almost over, Matt,' JohnJoe said. 'People haven't the appetite for it. I know the attacks are horrendous, but they are becoming fewer and the Free Staters are getting a handle on it all. They are the democratically elected government and have the support of the people. It was that very support that won the Tan war for us, so it will be the same this time. People have had enough.'

'I hope you're right, JohnJoe, because I'm an old man, and I can tell you now, I've had more than enough. I want to live a peaceful life with Rose by my side, I want that more than anything else. I'd be happy now to spend my days burying the dead of the town, who all die as old men and women in their beds. These last few years have seen too much bloodshed, too many young lives lost. We just want to live in peace – is it too much to ask?'

'No, and I think it will happen' – JohnJoe paused – 'for you anyway.'

'And what about you?'

'I've no idea. We're in a real mess and maybe I shouldn't have come back, but I got such a fright thinking something might have happened to her. And I thought Harp might want me around for the funeral...'

'She does of course want you around. And not just for the funeral either.' Matt cast JohnJoe a sidelong glance as the mares pulled up the hill to the Cliff House. 'Look, I know you had some story about her and this Elliot fella, and it being all over with you two, but Rose wasn't believing it and I don't think I do either. Tell me to mind my own business if you like, but neither of you are happy.'

JohnJoe sighed. 'It's complicated, but yes, I'm miserable, and I think Harp is too. We want to be together, but...'

'Well, if anyone understands that, it's me. I loved Rose Delaney from the day we buried this fella's brother in 1912. But I could never say it. I was too shy for years. I never thought a lady like her would have any interest in me, and then once I got up the guts, and I found out she felt the same as me, I was stuck in the Volunteers and it would have been too dangerous for her to have her name linked to mine. We had to pretend like there was nothing between us, and it used to nearly kill me.'

'I remember.' JohnJoe smiled. 'Did you know him well, Henry?'

'I did, as much as anyone knew him, I suppose. Like chalk and cheese, they were, Henry and Ralph. Henry was a gentleman, a bit of an oddball for sure but a decent man who loved Rose in his own way too. And he adored Harp. She's the amazing girl she is today because of both of them. What poor old Reverend Wilkes will find to say about the other brother, well, that's to be seen. He was a nasty piece of work, and they'll be hard-pushed to find a person to say otherwise. Bridges in the hotel was telling me he set his sights on a youngish woman out Rushbrooke way, but she witnessed him shooting the

Mulcair lad and so that put paid to any romance there. He was only gold-digging as usual anyhow.'

'I can't believe he didn't save himself,' JohnJoe said as they turned in the avenue of the Cliff House.

'First decent thing he ever did,' Matt replied grimly.

The funeral service was short and to the letter of the law in terms of how it was conducted. God was beseeched to take His son Ralph into the bosom of his arms in heaven, and Reverend Wilkes wisely didn't say anything about the deceased at the homily. A smattering of people were in the small Protestant church, but the only mourners were Rose and Harp, with Matt and JohnJoe as support, Mr Bridges as a gesture to the family and beside him a woman in her thirties, dressed all in black, a single peony in her hand. The Devlins too had come, to mark their respect to the family, if not Ralph.

Pamela was in hospital in Cork, recuperating after her ordeal. She'd been kept a prisoner for months, hardly fed. Ralph had made her sign cheques, but once the solicitors and bankers got suspicious about her whereabouts, they froze those accounts too. Just what Ralph planned to do with her long term was unclear, but thankfully the Mulcair attack on the house had freed her. Marianne had been informed, and she and Danny were awaiting the day that she could leave hospital and come to Boston.

They walked behind the coffin as Matt and JohnJoe, along with two gravediggers, shouldered the coffin to the Devereaux grave. It was a place of such familiarity to Harp that she never could feel sadness there. Matt had arranged for Ralph's name to be carved on the family stone, directly beneath Henry's.

The vicar intoned the prayers as the coffin was lowered, and Harp and her mother stood by, dry-eyed. The prayers over, the tiny group just stood there.

Harp met JohnJoe's eye and nodded. She walked to the open graveside. 'Ladies and gentlemen,' she said to the astonished gathering. Speeches at a graveside were most unusual, and unheard of from a girl. 'Today we bury Ralph Devereaux, the last of his generation. He had a complicated life, and an interesting one. He travelled the world, but Cobh, or Queenstown as he insisted on calling it' – there was a ripple of laughter from the gathered crowd – 'was where his heart was. So as the last remaining Devereaux, I want to say, goodbye, Ralph. Rest in peace.'

She began to sing, and her voice rang out over the harbour in the still air.

'Amazing grace, how sweet the sound, that saved a wretch like me. I once was lost, but now I'm found, was blind but now I see.'

The crowd joined in, and soon Rose, Matt, Mr Bridges, Cissy and Liz, Doris Prince and JohnJoe were all singing with her.

''Twas grace that taught my heart to fear, and grace my fears relieved. How precious did that grace appear, the hour I first believed.

'Through many dangers, toils and snares, we have already come.'

Rose and Harp shared a smile.

''Twas grace that brought us safe thus far, and grace will lead us home.'

The vicar joined in now too, glad to have some participation in what could have been a very peculiar funeral indeed. JohnJoe stood beside Harp, and as they sang the last verse, she felt his hand take hers, squeezing it gently.

'Amazing grace, how sweet the sound, that saved a wretch like me. I once was lost, but now I'm found, was blind but now I see.'

* * *

THAT EVENING HARP and JohnJoe went for a walk, and without deciding where, they ended up at the charred site of her home.

'I'm so sorry, Harp. I know what this place meant to you,' JohnJoe said as they stood in the garden. The windows were all smashed, the roof gone, a few blackened rafters all that remained. The façade was smoke coloured now, and the acrid smell still hung in the air.

She couldn't speak; words just wouldn't come. Hand in hand they walked around the house. There was no question of salvaging it. The petrol the Mulcairs had poured meant the fire blazed intensely for hours. Apart from the four walls – and they were blackened – there was nothing left.

The drawing room, where Ralph had died, was the only room that still looked like a room, and as Harp walked around the corner towards the grassy bank she'd clambered up to try to get Ralph out, she saw in the bushes the frame. She had a vague memory of Ralph throwing something out before taking her hands, but she didn't know what it was. She lifted it up. The glass was smashed and the frame damaged, but the painting inside was still intact.

'JohnJoe, look.' She called him over and showed him.

It was the painting he had done inspired by an old portrait of Henry Devereaux. He'd reproduced it and added Rose and Harp to create a family portrait, and Harp had loved it.

'Ralph threw this out?' JohnJoe was confused.

'Yes. I couldn't see what it was, but just a few minutes before the whole place went up in flames, he threw it out. He must have wanted to save it.' Harp was astonished.

'He was a deeply peculiar man, Harp, that's all I'll say.' JohnJoe carefully removed the canvas from the broken frame and rolled it up.

'He was that.'

She had not told anyone of their last exchange. But as they walked towards the Smuggler's Stairs, she said, 'He knew he was my father.'

'Did he? How?'

'I don't know, maybe he always knew. But that night, he said that Henry loved me and that he was proud of me. That Henry was a better man. That Ralph should have been proud of me too but wasn't. And then he said to live my life and do a better job of it than he had, and then he shoved me back down the grassy bank.'

They walked along in silence, neither knowing what to say.

'I suppose we should just let him rest in peace now,' Harp said eventually. 'It's over. We never knew who he really was, and now we never will.'

EPILOGUE

*J*erry and Elliot were out when they returned to Freeport mid-morning.

The crossing had been a sad one. The news of Collins's assassination in West Cork had shaken Harp to her core. It still hadn't sunk in that big, handsome, funny Mick Collins was dead, but he was. Killed in his own place by his own people, something he never thought could happen. Kitty Kiernan would never walk down the aisle to marry one of the most loved Irishmen who ever lived. Harp cried every time she thought of it.

Once they were safely inside, with no risk of anyone seeing them, JohnJoe's arms went around her waist and he kissed her deeply. She responded as she always did to him, with passion and hunger. He moved towards the bedroom, barely stopping the kiss as he led her. Once inside his room, the door locked and the key turned, they wasted no time. They made love silently and urgently, the intensity of the emotion too tender for words.

Afterwards, as she lay in his arms, she finally spoke. 'Imagine – we're back here and Celia is still in Dublin.' Harp missed her friend but was delighted at her opportunities.

'She's selling out, last I heard. They are loving her over there, and it must be nice not to be treated as less than your White counterparts for a change.'

Harp agreed. 'And if things work out with this new man of hers, she might stay.'

'Is he Irish?' JohnJoe asked.

'No, he's from Edinburgh, would you believe. He's in a band. They were playing the same venue as she was, and they got to talking. He lives in London. She told me she might go there with him, but she's not giving up her education either. If anyone can break the mould and have it her way, it's Celia. I worry for her with a White boyfriend, but while people would stare and have something to say, I'm sure they'd stand a better chance of acceptance on that side of the Atlantic.'

'That's true. I hope it works out for her, but we'll really miss her.'

'We will. I could use her steady advice, especially now. Even if Roaring Liberty can't survive me calling it off with Elliot, I have to do it, I know that. But what if it draws all holy hell down on their heads? Celia is so level-headed – she takes the emotion out of situations or something. The boys never even answered our telegram asking them not to say anything about it to anyone just yet. They must know I'm going to call it off and are trying to ignore it.'

'We'll talk to them and come up with a plan. I don't know what yet, but we'll figure something out. I love you more than I love the band, or the money or the fame. You might never marry me, and I have to accept it, but I'd give up everything I have for you, Harp.'

She sighed, the weight of the world on her once more now that she was back. After the fire, when JohnJoe turned up, she had collapsed in his arms and knew there was nowhere else on earth for her. She could not marry another man, she just couldn't, no matter what.

He went on. 'The Great War taking so many young people…well, it's changed how we see ourselves. We only get one life, and we shouldn't sacrifice our happiness for anyone or anything else.'

'All right, I'll tell them tonight, or whenever they get back. I'm dreading it, but you're right – we can't sacrifice ourselves.'

'Good. Now I wonder if that pair thought to get any food in? I'm starving.' JohnJoe climbed out of bed.

'Me too.' Harp giggled, wrapping herself in a sheet. They wandered to the kitchen, and as JohnJoe scrambled some eggs, Harp flicked through the mail that had arrived in their absence. 'I hope Mammy and Matt will be all right. She looked so sad as we –'

'And what's this?' JohnJoe picked up a cream embossed envelope, with *Harp and JJ* written in neat handwriting they didn't recognise. He handed it to her as he went to fetch their breakfast. He placed a plate of eggs and toast before her and looked over her shoulder as she extracted the card inside.

Harp read aloud. 'You are cordially invited to the New York Philharmonic's performance of a selection of works by Beethoven, Bach, Strauss and Handel, with a special performance of Paganini's Caprices at Carnegie Hall on September 2nd at 7 p.m.'

'That's tonight,' JohnJoe said, perplexed. 'Who sent it?'

'No idea. There's no name on the card or anything.' Harp turned the cream card over, but there was nothing to indicate the sender.

'Will we go?' he asked.

'I'm exhausted but I'm intrigued too, so I think we should.'

He didn't answer but smiled.

They slept all afternoon and woke refreshed and ready for the mysterious concert.

Once they were ready, they admired each other as they left for downtown. Harp was wearing a midnight-blue sequinned dress that Celia had made for the stage that hung from her slim figure. She liked it so much, she wore it off duty too. The fringe was silk, and it shimmered against her bare legs as she walked. She'd done her strawberry-blond hair as a stylist had advised her, straightening the waves with a hot iron, and wore more dramatic make-up than she would have in Ireland for fear of scandalising her mother; she had to admit the overall effect was pleasing. JohnJoe looked very dashing in his tails.

'It might be one of the theatre owners, sending us free tickets, or maybe even Carnegie Hall, wanting the press to see the lovely Harp

Devereaux gracing their theatre,' JohnJoe suggested as they sped in the cab.

'Or we could be swamped by press wanting to know about Elliot's and my wedding,' Harp said ruefully.

'We'll brazen it out if we have to.' JohnJoe reached over and took her hand.

The theatre was a wonderland of lights and music, with everyone dressed in their finery. There was a reception in the lobby, and a champagne fountain overflowed. An usher took their invitation and immediately greeted them. 'Miss Devereaux, Mr O'Dwyer, we've been expecting you. Welcome. Please come with me.' He indicated they should climb the stairs ahead of him.

Harp glanced at JohnJoe and suppressed a smile. Being treated like VIPs still felt odd. If only people knew their origins as two scraps of kids who didn't fit anywhere.

The usher led them to the entrance of a private box and nodded his respectful departure. To their astonishment, the box had only one inhabitant – Jerry.

He stood and embraced them both, grinning from ear to ear. 'Champagne?' he asked, offering them some from a bottle of Bollinger on a side table.

'Yes, please. But, Jerry, what's happening? We –'

'Hush. All will be revealed. You just need to have a little patience.' His eyes twinkled with mischief.

'Where's Elliot?' JohnJoe asked, accepting a glass.

Before Jerry could answer, the crowd burst into applause as the conductor approached the podium. Harp and JohnJoe took their seats. The conductor, a tall thin man with long white hair tied up in a black ribbon, tapped his baton, and the music filled the cavernous theatre. Harp recognised it as 'Bagatelle No. 25 in A Minor' by Beethoven.

'I know that one. Mrs Kawowski used to batter my fingers for that. It's called "Für Elise".'

Harp just nodded and smiled.

Pieces from Handel's 'Messiah' and some Strauss waltzes all

followed without a break, until the conductor finally turned to the audience and spoke.

'Ladies and gentlemen, it is a tremendous pleasure to conduct this fine orchestra this evening, and I sincerely hope you are enjoying our programme so far. This next segment will showcase one of the most exciting young talents to emerge in the music world for many years, performing what has been described as the most difficult piece for violin ever composed, Paganini's Caprices. These twenty-four pieces are demanding and complex, loaded with double stops, left-handed pizzicato and endless spiccato bowing. Tonight you shall hear a selection. Prepare to be impressed! I give you...Elliot Krauss!'

Jerry was beaming now, ear to ear, as Elliot, dressed in white tails, appeared on the podium.

What followed had the entire theatre in stunned appreciative silence. The music, which served alternatively as a virtuoso showpiece and a profoundly expressive example of technical mastery, showed Elliot's musical skill in a way performing with Roaring Liberty never could.

He played with such ease, and such dexterity, it brought tears to Harp's eyes. Jerry reached over and grasped her hand, and when she turned, she realised he too was weeping.

Finally Elliot finished, and the ovation was deafening. The orchestra stood to applaud him too, and Elliot shyly took a bow and left the stage.

The interval followed, and people began to move excitedly towards the bar for refreshments.

'I...I'm speechless. Did you know?' Harp asked Jerry.

'I knew he was good, but that good? Not really. His broken hand had stopped his career in its tracks, but he had enough money saved up for the operation to fix it, and here we are. Since we came back, he's done nothing but physical therapy and practice, and one night I convinced him to take a night off and come to a party, one of *ours*' – he winked and smiled – 'and that conductor was there.' He pointed to the stage. 'Someone asked him what was the most difficult piece ever to play, and he said Paganini's Caprices. And Elliot just said, "I can play it."'

Harp and JohnJoe hung on his every word.

'Most people there had no idea what it even was, but a violin was found and he just played it, like that, in the living room of a theatre chap in the Bronx. You could hear a pin drop. Then the conductor offered him a place in the orchestra there and then.'

Before he could go on, Elliot appeared, his face glistening with perspiration, and Harp threw herself on him, enveloping him in a hug. 'Elliot, we had no idea, none. You were amazing,' she gushed.

'We're mortified now, making you play the old dirge we do.' JohnJoe chuckled.

'Not at all, I loved every second,' Elliot replied, grinning.

Jerry poured them all a glass of champagne and raised a toast. 'To Elliot.'

'To Elliot,' they all chorused.

Elliot took a sip but then put his glass down. 'And now that we four are here, I have something to say. I was going to write, but, well, this has to be done in person.'

For a horrible moment, Harp feared he was going to officially propose, and she cast JohnJoe a panicked glance. But Elliot remained on two feet.

'Harp and JohnJoe, we are so sorry for all you were put through in Dublin. We're not sorry for what we are, and we never will be, but we are both so sorry that you two were drawn into it. We owe you our lives, literally, Harp, because if you'd not gone to Collins that day, well, we'd be in prison now.'

Jerry gave him a nod of encouragement.

'And I know you were being kind, so incredibly kind and protective, when you told that journalist we were engaged, but...' Elliot swallowed and Jerry gazed nonchalantly towards the stage. 'Harp, please don't take this the wrong way.' He grinned. 'But you're not my type, and so I can't marry you. I'll leave the band. My heart is more with the classical music anyway, and now that my hand is better, thanks to an operation funded by Roaring Liberty, I can get back to it.'

Relief flooded through Harp and she exhaled.

'I've been offered this position with the orchestra, and there's a way for people like us to live in this world, which just doesn't exist outside of it. We still have to be careful, of course, but not everyone is hostile to our ways. Jerry and I are going to be very vigilant, but we'll live our lives together. We'll live near Freeport – a friend has a place we can rent, and lots of other people live there too, so it won't look suspicious – so we can see lots of each other if that's what you'd want?'

'Of course it is,' Harp and JohnJoe said in unison.

Elliot's eyes shone with unshed tears. 'We've loved being part of Roaring Liberty, but any association with us could tarnish you even more than we have already. And again, we are so sorry. A new fiddle player, as you insisted on calling me' – he grinned – 'won't be hard to find, and a new manager too...'

'And from the bottom of our hearts, thank you,' Jerry finished.

'Hold on.' JohnJoe held his hands up. 'I get why this guy is moving on – he's not bad on the *fiddle*.' He winked and nudged his friend. 'But why are you jumping ship?' he asked Jerry.

'Well, we just thought that after everything, the best thing would be...' Jerry coloured with embarrassment.

'Do you want to leave Roaring Liberty?' Harp asked.

'Well, of course I don't, but...'

'Then you're not. We're losing Elliot, and Celia is on to pastures new as well, so we're a band of three for now, but we'll find replacements. Not as good of course.' She smiled at Elliot. 'But then it's business as usual.'

'And the newspapers, once the word gets out that the engagement is off?'

Harp laughed. 'I shall be poor old Harp Devereaux, jilted but remaining strong. It will be a five-day wonder. We'll tell our families the truth, of course, but I'm happy to play the sad and lonely miss, abandoned by her chap. Anyway, as my very wise mother says, today's gossip wraps tomorrows chips.' She laughed again. 'It's a new generation, a new era. It's 1922 and anything is possible.'

They enjoyed the rest of the concert as four friends. Jerry and Elliot were invited to an after-party at the conductor's home. They invited Harp and JohnJoe along, but the pair politely declined.

'I'm so tired after the crossing and all of the excitement, I think I'll have to go to bed. But it was a wonderful night – thank you both. We'll see lots of each other, Elliot, and, Jerry, it's back to work for you first thing Monday morning, so don't be late.' She kissed them each on the cheek. 'See you later.'

They left and JohnJoe linked her arm.

'Will I hail a cab?' He asked.

'No, let's walk towards Central Park,' she said. 'I've missed it. It's funny, isn't it, how New Yorkers love this patch of green so much, and we have nothing but green in Ireland and people take no notice of it at all. Maybe people don't always appreciate what's right under their noses.'

'Maybe they don't, but I always appreciate you,' he said sincerely.

'I love you, JohnJoe O'Dwyer.' She kissed his nose. 'Let's walk all night.'

'I thought you were tired?' he asked, smiling.

'I'm tired of people, but not of you, never of you.' She cuddled up to him as they walked.

'In those shoes?' he glanced doubtfully at her silver high-heeled sandals.

'I'm used to them now – I can walk for miles. Women are made of tough stuff, all we endure for fashion.'

'Are you saying us men are soft?' he teased.

'Some are, but no, not you. You're the exact right mix of hard and gentle.'

'I was reared tough, but this place has knocked the edges off me. I couldn't believe the luxury when I came here first – soft beds, as much food as you wanted, heat in the winter, indoor privies. It was like another world to me.' He winked and tucked her arm into his. He almost never mentioned his life in the industrial school before Kathy and Pat rescued him and brought him to America, but Harp knew it was a place no child should ever be sent.

They walked and chatted amiably, reliving the last few weeks and all that had happened. Through the city streets, lit up like it was midday, they felt each other relax, the tension of all they'd endured gradually seeping away.

Half an hour into their walk, a horse-drawn carriage trotted past, and Harp hailed the driver, leaving JohnJoe briefly to go and speak to him.

'Very extravagant.' JohnJoe laughed as she beckoned him to the kerb.

'We can afford it.' She winked at him.

He helped her aboard, they drew a rug over their knees and cuddled up as the carriage made its way up the street and entered Central Park.

The driver stopped at the Gapstow Bridge, beside the pond.

'What's happening?' JohnJoe asked.

'Out you get.' Harp smiled.

'But I'm all comfortable now,' JohnJoe complained.

'Do what the lady says.' The driver commanded.

'What?' JohnJoe looked quizzically from one to the other but climbed out of the carriage.

Harp exhaled and gazed at the boy she'd known since she was twelve years old. Her only friend for many years, her protector, her lover, her champion. And for the first time in a long time, she heard Henry's voice again. It was the advice he gave her when it came to playing the harp, but it seemed even more poignant now. *Heart to fingers, Harp. Feel it straight from the heart to the fingers, bypass the head.*

She led him to a part of the pond obscured from the public path. Being recognised in public was becoming something they were used to now. As he opened his mouth to speak, she put her finger to his lips.

'Sssh.' She said quietly.

All of her reservations, doubts and fears didn't disappear, but they were overridden by the words of Plato, a man she'd been quoting since she was a child and whose wisdom had been an anchor to her at times when she was pitched about on the ocean of life.

'Every heart sings a song, incomplete until another heart whispers back. Those who wish to sing always find a song.'

'Harp? What's going on? He asked, bewildered.

Harp leaned over and took his hand.

'JohnJoe O'Dwyer, from County Clare, you are the other half of me. You have been since I was twelve and you were fourteen. My life without you makes no sense. Will you marry me?'

THE END

ACKNOWLEDGMENTS

I have loved writing this series so much and it's with much sadness that I say goodbye to Harp and her friends and family.

Cobh, where the story is set, is across the river Lee from where I grew up and so was part of the daily landscape of my childhood. It struck me even as a child, how historic and intrinsic to the Irish story that place is.

As a tour guide, I had the great privilege to take many descendants of those who departed this country to see where their people came from and it was an experience that never failed to move them and me.

If any place holds memory, the quayside in Queenstown/Cobh does that. If you ever get the chance to go, you should.

I've had so much help in my career to date, I've been so very fortunate. I'd especially like to thank my editors Helen, Susan and Abby, you are invaluable. I love the covers of these books and that's down to the talent and skill of my cover designer Elena.

I must also thank my team, Carol, Barbara and Diarmuid who do all of the donkey work for none of the glory. Having these magnificent people in my corner has made this job I do not just more successful, but also so much more fun. Thank you all from the bottom of my heart.

To my advance readers, who between them have such a mind-boggling skill set, from life in India to motor mechanics of days gone by, thank you. I would be lost without you.

And finally, to you, the readers. You make me an author and for that I can never thank you enough.

ABOUT THE AUTHOR

Jean Grainger is a USA Today bestselling Irish author. She writes historical and contemporary Irish fiction and her work has very flatteringly been compared to the late great Maeve Binchy.

She lives in a stone cottage in Cork, Ireland with her husband Diarmuid and the youngest two of her four children. The older two show up occasionally with laundry and to raid the fridge. There are a variety of animals there too, all led by two cute but clueless micro-dogs called Scrappy and Scoobi.

ALSO BY JEAN GRAINGER

To get a free novel and to join my readers club (100% free and always will be)

Go to www.jeangrainger.com

The Tour Series

The Tour

Safe at the Edge of the World

The Story of Grenville King

The Homecoming of Bubbles O'Leary

Finding Billie Romano

Kayla's Trick

The Carmel Sheehan Story

Letters of Freedom

The Future's Not Ours To See

What Will Be

The Robinswood Story

What Once Was True

Return To Robinswood

Trials and Tribulations

The Star and the Shamrock Series

The Star and the Shamrock

The Emerald Horizon

The Hard Way Home

The World Starts Anew

The Queenstown Series

Last Port of Call

The West's Awake

The Harp and the Rose

Roaring Liberty

Standalone Books

So Much Owed

Shadow of a Century

Under Heaven's Shining Stars

Catriona's War

Sisters of the Southern Cross

If you would like to read another of my series. Here is the first few chapters of The Star and the Shamrock, a series set in Ireland during WW2 for you to enjoy.

The Star and the Shamrock

Belfast, 1938

The gloomy interior of the bar, with its dark wood booths and frosted glass, suited the meeting perfectly. Though there were a handful of other customers, it was impossible to see them clearly. Outside on Donegal Square, people went about their business, oblivious to the tall man who entered the pub just after lunchtime. Luckily, the barman was distracted with a drunk female customer and served him absentmindedly. He got a drink, sat at the back in a booth as arranged and waited. His contact was late. He checked his watch once more, deciding to give the person ten more minutes. After that, he'd have to assume something had gone wrong.

He had no idea who he was meeting; it was safer that way, everything on a need-to-know basis. He felt a frisson of excitement – it felt good to actually be doing something, and he was ideally placed to make this work. The idea was his and he was proud of it. That should make those in control sit up and take notice.

War was surely now inevitable, no matter what bit of paper old Chamberlain brought back from Munich. If the Brits believed that the peace in our time that he promised was on the cards, they'd believe anything. He smiled.

He tried to focus on the newspaper he'd carried in with him, but his mind wandered into the realm of conjecture once more, as it had ever since he'd gotten the call. If Germany could be given whatever assistance they needed to subjugate Great Britain – and his position meant they could offer that and more – then the Germans would have to make good on their promise. A United Ireland at last. It was all he wanted.

He checked his watch again. Five minutes more, that was all he would stay. It was too dangerous otherwise.

His eyes scanned the racing pages, unseeing. Then a ping as the pub door opened. Someone entered, got a drink and approached his seat. He didn't look up until he heard the agreed-upon code phrase. He raised his eyes, and their gazes met.

He did a double take. Whatever or whomever he was expecting, it wasn't this.

CHAPTER 1

Liverpool, England, 1939

Elizabeth put the envelope down and took off her glasses. The thin paper and the Irish stamps irritated her. Probably that estate agent wanting to sell her mother's house again. She'd told him twice she wasn't selling, though she had no idea why. It wasn't as if she were ever going back to Ireland, her father long dead, her mother gone last year – she was probably up in heaven tormenting the poor saints with her extensive religious knowledge. The letter drew her back to the little Northern Irish village she'd called home...that big old lonely house...her mother.

Margaret Bannon was a pillar of the community back in Bally-creggggan, County Down, a devout Catholic in a deeply divided place, but she had a heart of stone.

Elizabeth sighed. She tried not to think about her mother, as it only upset her. Not a word had passed between them in twenty-one years, and then Margaret died alone. She popped the letter behind the clock; she needed to get to school. She'd open it later, or next week... or never.

Rudi smiled down at her from the dresser. 'Don't get bitter, don't be like her.' She imagined she heard him admonish her, his boyish face frozen in an old sepia photograph, in his King's Regiment uniform, so proud, so full of excitement, so bloody young. What did he know of the horrors that awaited him out there in Flanders? What did any of them know?

She mentally shook herself. This line of thought wasn't helping. Rudi was dead, and she wasn't her mother. She was her own person.

Hadn't she proved that by defying her mother and marrying Rudi? It all seemed so long ago now, but the intensity of the emotions lingered. She'd met, loved and married young Rudi Klein as a girl of eighteen. Margaret Bannon was horrified at the thought of her Catholic daughter marrying a Jew, but Elizabeth could still remember that heady feeling of being young and in love. Rudi could have been a Martian for all she cared. He was young and handsome and funny, and he made her feel loved.

She wondered, if he were to somehow come back from the dead and just walk up the street and into the kitchen of their little terraced house, would he recognise the woman who stood there? Her chestnut hair that used to fall over her shoulders was always now pulled back in a bun, and the girl who loved dresses was now a woman whose clothes were functional and modest. She was thirty-nine, but she knew she could pass for older. She had been pretty once, or at least not too horrifically ugly anyway. Rudi had said he loved her; he'd told her she was beautiful.

She snapped on the wireless, but the talk was of the goings-on in Europe again. She unplugged it; it was too hard to hear first thing in the morning. Surely they wouldn't let it all happen again, not after the last time?

All anyone talked about was the threat of war, what Hitler was going to do. Would there really be peace as Mr Chamberlain promised? It was going to get worse before it got better if the papers were to be believed.

Though she was almost late, she took the photo from the shelf. A smudge of soot obscured his smooth forehead, and she wiped it with the sleeve of her cardigan. She looked into his eyes.

'Goodbye, Rudi darling. See you later.' She kissed the glass, as she did every day.

How different her life could have been...a husband, a family. Instead, she had received a generic telegram just like so many others in that war that was supposed to end all wars. She carried in her heart for twenty years that feeling of despair. She'd taken the telegram from the boy who refused to meet her eyes. He was only a few years younger than she. She opened it there, on the doorstep of that very house, the words expressing regret swimming before her eyes. She remembered the lurch in her abdomen, the baby's reaction mirroring her own. 'My daddy is dead.'

She must have been led inside, comforted – the neighbours were good that way. They knew when the telegram lad turned his bike down their street that someone would need holding up. That day it was her...tomorrow, someone else. She remembered the blood, the sense of dragging downwards, that ended up in a miscarriage at five months. All these years later, the pain had dulled to an ever-present ache.

She placed the photo lovingly on the shelf once more. It was the only one she had. In lots of ways, it wasn't really representative of Rudi; he was not that sleek and well presented. 'The British Army smartened me up,' he used to say. But out of uniform is how she remembered him. Her most powerful memory was of them sitting in that very kitchen the day they got the key. His uncle Saul had lent them the money to buy the house, and they were going to pay him back.

They'd gotten married in the registry office in the summer of 1918, when he was home on brief leave because of a broken arm. She could almost hear her mother's wails all the way across the Irish Sea, but she didn't care. It didn't matter that her mother was horrified at her marrying a *Jewman*, as she insisted on calling him, or that she was cut off from all she ever knew – none of it mattered. She loved Rudi and he loved her. That was all there was to it.

She'd worn her only good dress and cardigan – the miniscule pay of a teaching assistant didn't allow for new clothes, but she didn't care. Rudi had picked a bunch of flowers on the way to the registry office, and his cousin Benjamin and Benjamin's wife, Nina, were the witnesses. Ben was killed at the Somme, and Nina went to London, back to her family. They'd lost touch.

Elizabeth swallowed. The lump of grief never left her throat. It was a part of her now. A lump of loss and pain and anger. The grief had given way to fury, if she were honest. Rudi was killed on the morning of the 11th of November, 1918, in Belgium. The armistice had been signed, but the order to end hostilities would not come into effect until eleven p.m. The eleventh hour of the eleventh month. She imagined the generals saw some glorious symmetry in that. But there wasn't. Just more people left in mourning than there had to be. She lost him, her Rudi, because someone wanted the culmination of four long years of slaughter to look nice on a piece of paper.

She shivered. It was cold these mornings, though spring was supposed to be in the air. The children in her class were constantly sniffling and coughing. She remembered the big old fireplace in the national school in Ballycreggan, where each child was expected to bring a sod of turf or a block of timber as fuel for the fire. Master O'Reilly's wife would put the big jug of milk beside the hearth in the mornings so the children could have a warm drink by lunchtime. Elizabeth would have loved to have a fire in her classroom, but the British education system would never countenance such luxuries.

She glanced at the clock. Seven thirty. She should go. Fetching her coat and hat, and her heavy bag of exercise books that she'd marked last night, she let herself out.

The street was quiet. Apart from the postman, doing deliveries on the other side of the street, she was the only person out. She liked it, the sense of solitude, the calm before the storm.

The mile-long walk to Bridge End Primary was her exercise and thinking time. Usually, she mulled over what she would teach that day or how to deal with a problem child – or more frequently, a problem parent. She had been a primary schoolteacher for so long, there was little she had not seen. Coming over to England as a bright sixteen-year-old to a position as a teacher's assistant in a Catholic school was the beginning of a trajectory that had taken her far from Ballycreggan, from her mother, from everything she knew.

She had very little recollection of the studies that transformed her from a lowly teaching assistant to a fully qualified teacher. After Rudi was killed and she'd lost the baby, a kind nun at her school suggested she do the exams to become a teacher, not just an assistant, and because it gave her something to do with her troubled mind, she agreed. She got top marks, so she must have thrown herself into her studies, but she couldn't remember much about those years. They were shrouded in a fog of grief and pain.

CHAPTER 2

Berlin, Germany, 1939

Ariella Bannon waited behind the door, her heart thumping. She'd covered her hair with a headscarf and wore her only remaining coat, a grey one that had been smart once. Though she didn't look at all Jewish with her green eyes and curly red hair – and being married to Peter Bannon, a Catholic, meant she was in a slightly more privileged position than other Jews – people knew what she was. She took her children to temple, kept a kosher house. She never in her wildest nightmares imagined that the quiet following of her faith would have led to this.

One of the postmen, Herr Krupp, had joined the Brownshirts. She didn't trust him to deliver the post properly, so she had to hope it was Frau Braun that day. She wasn't friendly exactly, but at least she gave you your letters. She was surprised at Krupp; he'd been nice before, but since Kristallnacht, it seemed that everyone was different. She even remembered Peter talking to him a few times about the weather or fishing or something. It was hard to believe that underneath all that, there was such hatred. Neighbours, people on the street, children even, seemed to have turned against all Jews. Liesl and Erich were scared all the time. Liesl tried to put a brave face on it – she was such a wonderful child – but she was only ten. Erich looked up to her so much. At seven, he thought his big sister could fix everything.

It was her daughter's birthday next month but there was no way to celebrate. Ariella thought back to birthdays of the past, cakes and friends and presents, but that was all gone. Everything was gone.

She tried to swallow the by-now-familiar lump of panic. Peter had been picked up because he and his colleague, a Christian, tried to defend an old Jewish lady the Nazi thugs were abusing in the street. Ariella had been told that the uniformed guards beat up the two men and threw them in a truck. That was five months ago. She hoped every day her husband would turn up, but so far, nothing. She considered going to visit his colleague's wife to see if she had heard anything, but nowadays, it was not a good idea for a Jew to approach an Aryan for any reason.

At least she'd spoken to the children in English since they were born. At least that. She did it because she could; she'd had an English governess as a child, a terrifying woman called Mrs Beech who insisted Ariella speak not only German but English, French and Italian as well. Peter smiled to hear his children jabbering away in other languages, and he always said they got that flair for languages from her. He spoke German only, even though his father was Irish. She remembered fondly her father-in-law, Paddy. He'd died when Erich was a baby. Though he spoke fluent German, it was always with a lovely lilting accent. He would tell her tales of growing up in Ireland. He came to Germany to study when he was a young man, and saw and fell instantly in love with Christiana Berger, a beauty from Bavaria. And so in Germany he remained. Peter was their only child because Christiana was killed in a horse-riding accident when Peter was only five years old. How simple those days were, seven short years ago, when she had her daughter toddling about, her newborn son in her arms, a loving husband and a doting father-in-law. Now, she felt so alone.

Relief. It was Frau Braun. But she walked past the building.

Ariella fought the wave of despair. She should have gotten the letter Ariella had posted by now, surely. It was sent three weeks ago. Ariella tried not to dwell on the many possibilities. What if she wasn't at the address? Maybe the family had moved on. Peter had no contact with his only first cousin as far as she knew.

Nathaniel, Peter's best friend, told her he might be able to get Liesl and Erich on the Kindertransport out of Berlin – he had some connections apparently – but she couldn't bear the idea of them going to strangers. If only Elizabeth would say yes. It was the only way she could put her babies on that train. And even then… She dismissed that

277

thought and refused to let her mind go there. She had to get them away until all this madness died down.

She'd tried everything to get them all out. But there was no way. She'd contacted every single embassy – the United States, Venezuela, Paraguay, places she'd barely heard of – but there was no hope. The lines outside the embassies grew longer every day, and without someone to vouch for you, it was impossible. Ireland was her only chance. Peter's father, the children's grandfather, was an Irish citizen. If she could only get Elizabeth Bannon to agree to take the children, then at least they would be safe.

Sometimes she woke in the night, thinking this must all be a nightmare. Surely this wasn't happening in Germany, a country known for learning and literature, music and art? And yet it was.

Peter and Ariella would have said they were German, their children were German, just the same as everyone else, but not so. Because of her, her darling children were considered *Untermensch*, subhuman, because of the Jewish blood in their veins.

To continue this novel click this link
https://geni.us/TheStarandtheShamrocAL

Made in the USA
Columbia, SC
09 July 2022

63176167R00169